Sister, Sister

Donna Hill

Carmen Green

Janice Sims

St. Martin's Paperbacks

SISTER, SISTER

ISBN: 0-7394-2067-4

Printed in the United States of America

St. Martin's Paperbacks edition / October 2001

St. Martin's Paperbacks are published by St. Martin's Press, 175 Fifth Avenue, New York, NY 10010.

Contents

Thicker than Water

Donna Hill

One

Angela Richards put her glass down on the smoked-glass top of the kitchen table, barely able to meet her husband's incredulous stare. Mark's question bounced back and forth in her head until it throbbed. She knew he was right. Every fiber in her body screamed at the absurdity of her decision. But it was family—a totally dysfunctional family—but a family nonetheless.

When she'd walked away from her mother, her sister, her niece, ten years earlier, she swore all the way from D.C. to New York that she would never go back. That she would never allow them to inflict that kind of pain on her again. She'd broken her self-imposed promise once when she'd returned to put her grandmother to rest and stand stoically at her grave site. Now it was to keep vigil over her ailing sister, Gayla.

Mark pushed away from the table and paced the black-and-white tiled floor while stroking his goatee. This was the room where decisions were made, Mark mused, not in the bedroom, where passion could be confused with reason. It was here in the kitchen where he and his wife cooked, cleaned, shared meals and their dreams, where they planned their lives.

Until now they'd always found a means to meet halfway, no matter what their issues may have been. But today, there was no compromise, and the table that separated them barely represented the rift that had sprung up between them like a leak in a sinking boat.

"Answer me, Angie," Mark suddenly shouted, halting his pacing.

The boom of his voice snapped her to attention. Her reluctant gaze found his stony one.

"Make me understand why you would go back there. After everything they've done to you."

"My sister is sick, Mark," she mumbled. Even to her own ears she didn't sound convincing.

"When was the last time Gayla did anything for you, Angie? Where was she when you had pneumonia? . . . Busy," he answered for her. "And when you had the operation for that fibroid a few years back, where was your family then? Occasionally on the other end of the phone."

She sat there, staring at her hands as he continued his verbal assault.

"And how many times have you lain in my arms crying about how it had been growing up in that house, how you felt like a servant instead of a member of the family? Angie, how many school functions did your mother miss? How many birthday parties? You had to practically drag yourself out of your own sickbed to make arrangements for your grandmother because Gayla 'just couldn't handle all the pressure.' "

He stared at her for a long, hard moment, his sandy brown face flushed with his ire. Angie watched the pulse pound dangerously in his temple.

Mark pulled in a deep breath and stepped to the table. Bracing his palms on the smooth wood top, he leaned toward his wife.

"I love you, Angie." He reached out and covered one of her clenched fists with his open hand. "More than life itself. I've seen how broken you were inside and the time and strength it took to get you where you are." Slowly he shook his head. "Going back there . . . will negate everything you've worked for—we've worked for."

She fought back tears, shielding her face with her free hand.

"Baby," he whispered. "You've got to know that."

Angie finally looked into her husband's loving gaze, saw

the depth of the concern and sincerity there. She also felt his pain.

"Mark, I don't think I'll ever be able to explain it, explain why I believe in my soul that going back to D.C. to take care of my sister is something I must do. And not for Gayla or my globe-hopping niece, Tiffany—not even for my mother, but for me."

"I'm coming with you," Mark said adamantly. "I ca—"

"No." Gayla squeezed his hand and looked unflinchingly into his eyes. "I've got to do this on my own. And we both know that."

Knowing from the determined look in Angie's eyes that this was a battle he couldn't win, Mark resignedly lowered himself into a chair opposite her. Silently holding her hands, he prayed that this wouldn't be the trip that crushed her spirit for good.

Two

Angela stared out of the train window as it sped out of Manhattan, hurtling toward New Jersey, Philly, Delaware, Maryland, and finally Washington, D.C.

Her stomach suddenly clenched. All during the night she'd debated about her decision. Each time she was on the brink of changing her mind, she'd hear the panic in Tiffany's voice: "Auntie, please—you've got to come. Mom can't do this alone. She's too proud to ask you herself."

Angie squeezed her eyes shut, feeling all her old buttons being pushed. The need to be needed—wanted.

"Why can't she get a nurse?" she'd tossed out like bait.

"Auntie, you know how Mommy is about strangers. The only one who can do this is you. Besides, she'll be happy to see you. It's been a while. And you'll only have to stay for a couple of weeks. Just until I get back from this photo shoot. I promise."

"Tiffany, your mother and I haven't spoken since your grandmother's funeral. I just don't—"

"Please, Auntie."

Angela pushed out a breath, envisioning her haughty, self-centered sister wrinkled in discomfort and helpless. The angst that she would endure just to see that would almost be worth the trip, she thought, and hated herself for feeling that way. "Two weeks, Tiff. That's it."

"Thank you, thank you," she'd gushed. "Can you be here by Friday? My flight to the coast takes off at eight A.M. on Saturday morning."

Angela pursed her lips and rolled her eyes. It never even occurred to Tiffany to change or cancel *her* plans. But Angela couldn't fault her, not really. That was the way Gayla had raised Tiffany—to be an exact replica of herself.

"I'll see you Friday, Tiffany."

"Thanks, Auntie," she sighed in relief. "You won't regret this."

Angela thought about that conversation now as she sat on the hard plastic chair in the Union Station waiting room, waiting for the arrival of her niece. She tried to peer around the nonstop press of flesh in the massive station with the hopes of spotting her.

Her train had arrived nearly forty minutes earlier and Tiffany had sworn she'd be there to meet her. People continued to flow around her. The waiting arca patrons had changed faces three different times since she'd arrived.

Typical, she mused, scanning the crowd once again. Of course her time wasn't important. And the longer she sat there, the more she began to feel that this was a big mistake.

Finally Tiffany arrived, turning every head, male and female, as she strutted confidently toward her aunt. Tiffany carried herself like someone important, someone you needed to know, and the questioning whispers, wide-eyed looks, and less than subtle gawking was just the effect that Tiffany Lawrence lived for.

She was breathtaking, Angela admitted. The young woman had the face of an angel and the body to go with it. The combination of her picture-perfect looks and get-ahead personality would take her far in the demanding life of high fashion.

"Auntie," she beamed, sweeping her glasses from her nose with a practiced flourish. She leaned down and planted an air kiss in the vicinity of Angela's cheek.

Angela was certain that the onlookers were bewildered as to how these two unlikely souls could in any way be related.

"I'm so sorry to have you waiting like this. Traffic was horrible. Ready?" Tiffany turned on her heels without a backward glance and headed toward the exit.

Angela shook her head, picked up her two suitcases, and followed in Tiffany's wake.

The first ten minutes of the twenty-minute drive were spent with Tiffany telling her aunt all about the exciting places she'd been, the gorgeous men she'd met, and the scads of money she was earning. "My next goal is television," she said with determination. "Then it's on to the movies. I'm going to be a star."

There wasn't room in Tiffany's rapid-fire dissertation to get a word in edgewise, so Angela just nodded in all the right places. Finally Tiffany took a breath and Angela leapt at the chance.

"How is your mother?"

For the first time since Tiffany confidently strutted into the waiting area of Union Station, Angela caught a hint of pain, perhaps glimpsed vulnerability casting a shadow across her niece's perfect features. But like the practiced performer she was, in a breath that hint of uncertainty was replaced with a smile.

"Oh, you know Mom. Never one to complain. She's a real trooper." She sighed. "I don't know how she does it."

Angela frowned. They couldn't be talking about the same woman. Gayla's middle name was "complain." "Really?" she muttered. "I guess I *have* been away for a long time."

Tiffany snatched a quick glance at her aunt. "What happened between you and my mom?" she asked, her voice suddenly reed thin and childlike.

What happened? Angela wished she could pin it on one incident, one moment in time, but she couldn't.

Angela cleared her throat. "A lot of things, Tiff. For a very long time," she answered in a hollow tone.

"Mom never talks about it." She twisted slightly in her seat. "She doesn't talk to me about much of anything," she ended on a weak chuckle.

Angela reached over and patted her niece's thigh. "You

know how your mom is. She's very much into herself. But that doesn't mean she doesn't care. Gayla . . . well, Gayla . . . is Gayla."

Tiffany's smile wobbled at the edges. "Sometimes I wish things could have been different, you know."

"Different, how?"

"That I would have a real family like all my friends. That holidays would be happy occasions and not snide-fests. Most of the time I feel like I'm all by myself . . . an orphan. Dad's been gone for forever. If he calls once a year it's a lot. The most I've seen of him was his signature on the child support checks. And those stopped years ago."

"Have you tried to talk to your mother about how you feel?"

"Sure. Mom simply tells me how hard she works to give me a life my friends are jealous of, and all I can do is complain."

Angela was quiet for a moment, more from the surprise of the revelations than her inability to comment on her sister's behavior. She struggled for something to say, something to ease the hurt that underlined Tiffany's poignant words. But the truth was, she had no comment. Over the years the wall that had been erected between herself and Gayla had become a hurdle she was no long able to clear. And unfortunately, Tiffany sat on the top unable to be reached by either side.

Angela stole a glance at Tiffany's profile, perfect in every way, except for the emptiness that hung like weights beneath her eyes. She reached across the short distance that separated them and clasped Tiffany's hand that held the gearshift in a death grip and gently squeezed it.

"Don't give up on your mom," Angela offered as her only bit of counsel. "She loves you . . . and so do I."

Tiffany offered a tight smile as they pulled into the driveway of the two-story town house.

Angela tugged in a breath, not knowing what to expect in the days ahead. One thing she was certain of: it wouldn't be easy. "Let the games begin," she muttered.

Three

When Angela stepped inside Gayla's four-bedroom home, she was immediately thrown back to the last time she stood in this very same foyer, the night that had marked the final break between the two sisters.

Angela shivered slightly as the rush of the ugly words hurled that night rode through her in waves. Briefly she shut her eyes and pulled in a steadying breath.

"You ok, Auntie?" Tiffany asked, placing a light hand on Angela's shoulder.

Angela pushed a smile across her mouth. "Yes, fine," she lied smoothly. "Is your mom in her room?"

Tiffany's countenance darkened. "She rarely comes out." Her eyes darted away. "Let me take your bags upstairs. I'll put them in the guest room at the end of the hall while you visit Mom." Her closing comment was more like a plea than a statement.

Angela stood there for a moment, watching Tiffany trot up the stairs. She shifted her shoulder bag from the right to the left, patted her hair, and wondered if she should freshen her lipstick. She dug in her purse, then stopped, realizing that she didn't need to freshen her lipstick any more than she needed a toothache. She was stalling for time, delaying the inevitable—seeing her sister for the first time in five years. What she wanted was five more years. Maybe Mark was right. She should have stayed in New York where she belonged, or at the very least accepted his offer to come along.

Tiffany appeared at the top of the stairs. "Auntie?"

Angela's gaze snapped upward as she smiled weakly and headed for the stairs.

Gayla's bedroom, like every other room in the house, was perfect, from the sleek wood furnishings, hand-sewn throw pillows, silk drapes, and overstuffed down comforters to the gleaming hardwood floors and the queen resting on her four-poster throne.

Slowly Gayla turned her head toward the door, her gray-green eyes instantly appraising her sister. "You've gained weight again," Gayla greeted.

Angela clenched her teeth and crossed the threshold. "How are you feeling, Gayla?" she asked, determined not to step onto any of the land mines.

"How would you be feeling if they had to . . ." She covered her mouth to muffle a feigned sob.

Angela wanted to roll her eyes or at least smack Gayla, just once, but held herself in check. "Gayla, women have hysterectomies more often than you think and come out of it just fine. Be thankful that it wasn't something more serious."

"The doctor said I need rest," she whined. "That I shouldn't try to do much of anything for at least two weeks."

Two weeks, fourteen days . . . an eternity, Angela mused. "You'll be fine before you know it," Angela assured her sister, praying that it was true. "I'm going to get myself settled; then I'll come back and check on you."

"Can't you bring me something to eat first? I'm starved, and Tiffany was in such a hurry to pick *you* up," she pointedly indicated, "that she didn't have time."

Angela could feel the old resentment stir inside her, slowly rise, and settle like a lead ball in her throat. "Sure," she murmured from between her teeth, then turned on her heels and headed downstairs.

"The menu is on the fridge," Gayla called out feebly. Angela cringed.

* * *

Angela familiarized herself with Gayla's kitchen as she prepared a bowl of chicken broth and a sandwich. Posted on the refrigerator door was a list of Gayla's dietary requirement during the recovery process—outlined by the hour, day, and quantity. Angela was hard-pressed to believe that Gayla's doctor had been this specific in his or her instructions. It read more like Gayla's penchant for exactness. Angela was surprised that there wasn't a team of specialists hovering around waiting to be pressed into duty.

She placed the light meal, along with a cup of herbal tea, onto the silver serving tray and marched back upstairs. This was going to be the longest two weeks of her natural-born life.

Gayla made three additional requests: more tea, her pills with water, and a tedious adjustment of her pillows—all before Angela had the opportunity to set foot in her own room.

By the time she sat down on the side of her temporary bed, she felt like screaming—or crying. She was no longer Angela Richards, high school guidance counselor, wife of Mark Richards, and friend to many. She'd been recast in her childhood role of Cinderella.

Angela covered her face with her hands. Why had she come back? What masochistic bent did she have that would compel her to hurt herself this way? She removed her hands and gazed around the pristine room.

In her heart of hearts she knew why. She knew the real reason.

Four

Angela found Tiffany in the living room sifting through a stack of CDs. She turned at the sound of her aunt's footsteps and put her smile in place.

"Hey, Auntie. Get settled?"

"Yes, after several delays," Angela answered drolly.

The corner of Tiffany's mouth flickered. "Mom." The one word said a mouthful.

Angela crossed the parquet floor and took a seat in the corner of the mauve leather sectional couch, curling her bare feet beneath her.

"So," Angela exhaled, "catch me up on your career. What's this latest shoot about?"

Tiffany turned from her sorting and faced her aunt. "She's jealous of you, you know."

The statement was so out of the blue, delivered so matter-of-factly, it left Angela momentarily stunned. She could imagine damn near anything about her sister, but jealousy wasn't one of them. She chuckled nervously. "Gayla isn't jealous of anyone. Especially me."

"Then you don't know your sister very well," Tiffany returned as she crossed the room to sit opposite her aunt. She pushed aside a loose spiral curl. Her gold bracelet twinkled in the waning afternoon light.

Angela sat up straighter. "What do you mean?"

"She's always believed you were the one who succeeded at everything—your marriage, your education, your career." Tiffany slowly shook her head and reached for the pack of cigarettes on the coffee table. She tapped one out, brought it to her lips, and lit it, all before asking, "Mind if I smoke?"

Angela's right brow rose an inch, then lowered. "It's your house."

Tiffany blew a puff of smoke into the air, then stared hard at Angela. "I know Mom is hard to take. She acts like she has it together, but she doesn't. She's scared of you, of who she is, what she isn't, and now she's scared of me and the life I'm making for myself. Why do you think she surrounds herself with all . . . this?" she asked with an expansive wave of her hand. "Do you really think it's an accident that she's had three husbands and a career that could fill the *New York Times* want ads?"

"Your mother's choices, the decisions she's made in her life, have nothing to do with me," Angela insisted. "Gayla has always had a mind of her own."

Tiffany crushed out her cigarette and stood. "As long as you keep believing that, things will never change between you." She headed toward the stairs, stopped, then turned. "And I really wish they would. I've got to finish packing."

Angela sat there for several moments trying to make sense of all that Tiffany had said. For years she'd lived in Gayla's immeasurable shadow, absorbed her insults and slights, all quietly condoned by their mother. Over the years Angela had begun to believe the things her sister said about her and in turn believed that how she was treated was somehow deserved.

In time she'd grown accustomed to being the outcast of the female trio and accepted her role, blooming like a starved plant for water at any little compliment, any show of kindness. Never did she understand why she didn't fit in, wasn't deserving of the same love her mother rained down on Gayla. And those feelings of inadequacies filtered into every crevice of her life. So much that she'd denied herself and her husband the joy of having a child of their own, thus unable to toss her unworthiness onto her child and her into the role of mother. Instead she nurtured and guided her students, gave what she could of herself to Mark. But always, always looking through the window into Gayla's perfect world, and hoping to one day find herself included there.

Jealous! Tiffany was obviously confused. But the thought stayed with her even as she mounted the stairs in response to Gayla's beck and call.

Five

Gayla was sitting upright on her throne when Angela appeared in the doorway.

"Need something?"

"I heard voices downstairs," Gayla snapped as if conversation were an unheard-of activity in the castle.

Angela fought to keep from rolling her eyes. "Tiffany and I were talking."

Gayla's eyes widened, then narrowed suspiciously. "About what? That modeling foolishness of hers?" she huffed. "Traveling all over the world, leaving me here alone all the time, after all the sacrifices I've made for her," she rambled on, her voice becoming more strident with every utterance. Gayla snapped her glance in Angela's direction. "Be thankful you don't have children. They just grow up to be ungrateful."

Angela's stomach knotted over the children she didn't have and the lonely one—Tiffany—who wanted to have a family. "Did you ever consider yourself lucky to have children, Gayla? Maybe instead of viewing motherhood as a some sort of burden, you could put that energy toward being a mother to your daughter instead of trying to be a Santa Claus who thinks the answer to everything is to shove a gift certificate down her throat!"

Blood infused Gayla's pale features. Her gray-green eyes darkened like storm clouds sweeping in over the ocean. "How dare you!" she hissed. "You—of all people. What do you have? A little piece of a job working with a bunch of riffraff New York thugs that call themselves students, a husband who . . . who only stays with you because it's easy—"

"Enough, Gayla!" Angela's chest heaved and her body trembled with rage.

Gayla laughed viciously. "Mama never wanted you. You were the mistake—not me." Her eyes suddenly filled with tears. "Not me."

Angela stood there for a split second, then spun away knowing that if she stayed a hot minute longer she would slap the taste out of Gayla's lying mouth.

Shutting her bedroom door, Angela braced her back against it for support and let the tears finally flow.

When she looked up, her reflection stared back at her in the oval mirror above the dresser. What she saw was hurt, etched into a deep chocolate brown face, with short, always-in-need-of-a-perm hair, and a size 14 body. The years of emotional deprivation hung on the fringes of her long curly lashes, outlining the startling honey-tinted eyes. She pressed her full lips together and moved out of view.

Gayla's verbal lashing reverberated in her head. *"Mama never wanted you . . . who only stays with you because it's easy . . . you were the mistake . . ."*

Angela covered her face with her hands. It had been like this for almost as long as she could remember. She and Gayla had always been at odds: over toys, clothes, hair, friends, and mostly their mother's affection. And in all the years that they'd been sisters, Angela never fully understood Gayla's underlying resentment of her—especially when it was always Gayla who walked away with the spoils. Except when it came to Mark . . .

She'd met Mark Richards in one of romance's greatest cliché locations—the supermarket. They were both standing near the fresh fruit, testing cantaloupes.

"I never could tell when one of these things was ripe," Mark said.

Angela grinned and turned in the direction of the thoroughly male voice but was momentarily taken aback by the rugged good looks of the man. Most of all she was captivated by the lush fullness of his mouth. In that moment she felt as if she'd been struck by an electric current that shot straight to her heart. That was the only explanation she could offer to explain knocking over the eight-deep stack of cantaloupes all over the supermarket floor. The melons rolled like bowling balls down the aisle, causing havoc among their fellow shoppers.

Mark and Angela ran behind the runaway fruit, dumping them in abandoned shopping carts, alternately giggling hysterically and feeling utterly ridiculous.

Mark snatched up the last one in a smooth bowling move and dumped it into the cart. He turned triumphantly toward Angela, who had tears of laugher streaming down her cheeks. She was holding the stitch in her side with one hand and her mouth with the other.

"I'm sorry," she sputtered, fighting down the last bouts of giggles.

Mark's eyes twinkled with delight, his large frame still shuddering with laughter.

"I gotta give it to you. This was one of the most original introductions I've ever experienced." He pushed the cantaloupe-laden shopping cart to the side, out of the aisle. "Mark Richards." He stuck out his hand.

"Angela Fleming," she returned, accepting the firm handshake and wishing she'd worn her contact lenses instead of the heavy-framed glasses.

"I'm new to the neighborhood. Just moved in up the block about a week ago."

He has a great voice, Angela thought. "Really. Welcome to the neighborhood. This is a great area to raise a family, wonderful school system, community activities, churches, low crime. . . ." Her voice drifted off when she realized she was rambling.

Mark was staring and smiling at her, and her hands fluttered to her multicolored-scarf-covered rollers. Her face heated with embarrassment.

"It's just me," he said in a tone laden with possibility.

"Oh," she responded, immensely relieved. "Me, too."

"Are you finished with your shopping?"

She laughed lightly. "Yes. I really only came in for some bread and juice."

"Uh, if you're not in a rush, I'll walk out with you."

"Sure. I'll wait up front."

And that's how it began. Mark was a master at making her feel wonderful about being Angela Fleming. She finally began to appreciate the dark skin that he loved to stroke, the full figure that he stared at shamelessly. It was Mark who encouraged her to return to school and finish her degree in social work. Through his unabashed love she could almost forget the hurts and loneliness of her childhood and accept the notion that she was *worthy* of being loved. Almost.

She needed her husband now, needed to hear his reassuring voice. Angela reached for the phone.

". . . Baby, you know your sister," Mark was saying. "You know she has a tongue like a saber. If you intend to stay there, you're going to have to keep out of her way." Inwardly he'd fumed, having listened to Angela repeat the ugly things her sister had said. But he wouldn't tell her "I told you so" and make her feel worse.

Angela sighed. "I don't know why I thought this time would be different. But Tiffany said something really strange today."

"What?"

"She said Gayla was jealous of me and always had been." She relayed the conversation.

"Hmmm. That would explain a lot. But from everything you've ever told me, it was Gayla who was your mother's favorite."

The truth stung for a moment. "Exactly. But the things she said today . . . it was as if she truly resented the life I've made for myself."

"She's an unhappy woman, babe. Even with all the 'things' she has." He paused a moment, thoughtful. "I know I tried to convince you not to go back there, but . . . maybe this is the time to find out what's really behind Gayla's animosity toward you and your mother's indifference. Use the same skills on them that you do at work to turn those kids around."

"Whatever ails Gayla and me will take more than a college application and an after-school job with a mentor to make things better," she said with resignation.

"You know what I mean, Angie. And don't ever underestimate what you do, how important what you do is to all those kids. My question is: Do you think it's worth it—for you and Gayla, but mostly for you?"

"I don't know, Mark. I really don't."

"Well, you have fourteen days—three hundred and thirty-six hours and counting. You went back there for a reason. And when you're ready to admit to yourself what that reason is, you'll know what it is you have to do."

Angela thought about her conversation with Mark as she prepared Gayla's "prescribed" supper. He was right. Deep down she hadn't come simply to take care of her sister. She'd come seeking the truth, seeking some healing to finally close up the hole in her heart and possibly bridge the gap between her and her sister.

Where to begin? she mused, sliding the salmon steaks into the broiler. She honestly couldn't remember the last time she and Gayla had a conversation that didn't turn ugly. Maybe she'd wake up in the morning, curled up next to Mark, and this would all have been a bad dream. Yeah, right.

Six

It was six o'clock in the morning when Angela heard a light knock on her bedroom door. It took her several moments to orient herself to her surroundings.

Pulling herself up from beneath the tangle of sheets, she sat up and turned on the bedside lamp. She blinked several times bringing the room into focus. *It wasn't all a bad dream.*

"Come in," she mumbled, rubbing her eyes.

"Hi, Auntie," Tiffany whispered, peeking her head inside. "Sorry to wake you, but I wanted to say good-bye. My cab should be here any minute."

"Oh. Right." Her thoughts began to clear. "Come in," she repeated.

Tiffany stepped inside and closed the door behind her. "Mom's still asleep," she said almost apologetically.

Angela yawned. "What time does she usually get up?"

"Around nine. Sometimes later. She never was an early riser." Tiffany smiled weakly and stepped closer. "I really appreciate this, Auntie. I mean I know it was asking a lot for you to leave Mark and your job . . . but . . ."

"It's okay, Tiff."

Tiffany blew out a breath and took a seat on the side of Angela's bed. She lowered her head as she spoke. "Auntie . . . I know you may not believe this, but . . . Mom is a very unhappy woman. She's lonely. She's bitter and she resents you, all for reasons I don't know, but it's colored every aspect of her life. And underneath it all I think she wants to be your friend." She paused. "Mom needs a friend, Aunt Angie."

"Well, I really—"

"I didn't ask you to come just to look after her. I could have gotten a nurse, or whatever. I was just hoping that this time together would help you two figure out what was wrong between you. Why we can't be a family. Why Grandma is . . . Grandma."

"Tiffany." Angela reached out and clasped her niece's hand seeing the girl-woman with new eyes. "There's been thirty-plus years of bad blood between your mom, grandma, and me. I've tried; believe me I have. But I can't see how two weeks will fix all that's wrong between us. I really don't."

Slowly Tiffany stood. "I just want her to be happy—for once," she said sadly. "And she never will until whatever is poisoning her is finally flushed out." She headed toward the door, stopped, and turned. "And you're the only one who can do that. If you want to."

Angela sat in bed staring at the closed door, listening to the cab pull away. She sat there thinking about what Tiffany had said, Gayla, Mark, what she in her heart knew. She didn't want to be the answer, the savior, the redeemer. She simply wanted to get through these two weeks as quickly, as painlessly, and with as little bloodshed as possible. But she also knew that was merely a fantasy. If she didn't try to break down the wall between her and Gayla there may never be another time.

Angela showered and dressed, added a layer of resolve, and headed toward her sister's closed bedroom door. She knocked lightly and waited.

"Come in," came a response that sounded almost weak and feeble. Angela rolled her eyes and stepped in.

"Morning," Angela greeted, pumping cheer into her voice. She forced a smile to go along with it.

"Oh, you're finally up." Gayla cast her catlike eyes in Angela's direction. "Thought you were going to sleep the morning away like you did when we were kids."

Angela felt the slow burn in her chest, that old sensation of thinking she needed to get ready to defend herself, explain her behavior. Not today.

"That was a long time ago, Gayla," she said in a flat monotone. "I would think we've both changed since we were kids."

"Some things never change," Gayla returned. She snapped open the magazine she was reading and summarily dismissed Angela's presence.

Suddenly, like an unexpected gust of wind, Angela was on Gayla in a flash. She snatched the magazine from Gayla's hands and threw it halfway across the room. Gayla's mouth dropped open and her eyes widened in alarm.

"Have you—"

"Shut up! Just shut the hell up. I've put up with your crap for too damned long, and I'm not gonna do it anymore, Gayla! If you want me to stay here one minute longer you'll shut your mouth, start acting like a human being instead of a bitch, and treat me with some respect."

Gayla's high-yellow complexion turned a dangerous shade of red, and for an instant Angela thought that maybe she'd gone too far. But in the next breath, she really didn't care. Gayla deserved that and more.

"I'll be back with your breakfast shortly."

With that Angela spun away and shut the door solidly behind her, rattling the original John Biggers painting that hung on the wall.

Gayla sat in stunned silence. Her body shuddered with outrage but mostly surprise. She'd never seen Angela so angry—and at her. Gayla almost saw hate in her sister's eyes. *She* was the one who should be angry, resentful—even hateful. It was all Angela's fault that things were the way they were between them and with their mother. *Her* fault. Hot, bitter tears ran in a steady stream down her cheeks.

Seven

Gayla was red-eyed and flushed when Angela returned. Angela tried to keep the surprise from her expression, as Gayla had never been one to show emotions—other than demanding or hysterical ones.

"Enjoy your breakfast," Angela said, placing the tray on the bedside table.

Gayla wanted to tell her sister how she felt, the hurt she'd lived with, the resentment. But she didn't know how. For years they'd lived as sparring partners on either side of the ring—always waiting for the bell, ready to throw a knockout blow.

Angela looked at her for a brief moment and in that instant Gayla saw the pain in her sister's eyes, the uncertainty, the questions. And then it was gone. The moment had passed.

"Thank you," Gayla mumbled to Angela's receding back, snapping open her white linen napkin and plucking out a slice of grapefruit.

Angela returned to the kitchen and was sipping a cup of chamomile tea in the hope that it would calm her frazzled nerves when the phone rang. It rang three times and wasn't picked up. Frowning, Angela reached for the white wall phone and instantly regretted it the moment she heard the voice on the other end.

"Hello?"

"Angela? Is that you?"

She should have known it wouldn't be long before her

mother called. She was surprised that the call hadn't happened before now.

"Yes, Mom, it's Angela." She briefly shut her eyes.

"So, you made it," Marlene said. "You could have called me."

"I've been busy."

"Too busy to call your own mother, obviously. How's Gayla?" she added quickly before giving Angela a chance to respond to her remark.

"Coming along." Their latest altercation flashed through her thoughts. "She's having breakfast."

"Please make sure that she gets whatever she needs. She has to keep up her strength. This is just awful for her—she's so young. I know she must be in so much pain and . . ."

Angela had already turned her brain to "off" as her mother rattled on about Gayla, Gayla, Gayla. Not once did her mother ask how she was doing, indicate that she appreciated the fact that Angela had left her home, her job, her husband to take care of a sister who by all accounts couldn't stand her. But it was okay, Angela reconciled. She was used to it.

"Were you planning to call me at all?" Marlene suddenly segued, snapping Angela out of her dormant state.

"Sure . . . as soon as I got a minute."

"You've been there since yesterday," she accused. I would think—"

"Mom, I really have to go. I'll call you later. Want to speak to Gayla?"

Marlene sniffed in offense. "I'll call her later. She needs her rest. I—"

"Fine. I'll let her know you called. Bye, Mom." She quickly hung up before her mother could slip in another dig.

Being in the company of Gayla and her mother had the same effect as being in a minor car wreck. There were no visible signs of injury, but after careful examination you could see the damage inside.

Angela returned to the table and sat down, took a thoughtful sip of her tea, and tried to really think when it all started—why it all started.

She gazed up, staring out of the kitchen window. Two little girls were in the yard next door playing a rough-and-tumble game of tag. Their giggles and squeals of delight danced in the spring air. Angela smiled as the long-buried memories of her and Gayla's once-joyful youth slowly struggled to the surface. There was a time when they were happy together, laughed and played together. She remembered Gayla's ingenuity at finding the most incredible hiding places when they played hide-and-seek, and her own ability to weave the most wondrous stories, which would fascinate Gayla for hours. Once upon a time they were friends. When did it change? At what moment had things gone so terribly wrong? Her gaze settled again on the frolicking children and images of her and Gayla playing on the small patch of grass at the front of the three-bedroom Savannah, Georgia, home loomed before her. She was about eleven, Gayla eight. Gayla was jumping rope, practicing some new moves, crossing her feet and jumping on one foot. Angela was reading a book about Zeus and wondering what life would be like if real gods and goddesses walked the earth, causing havoc with the humans.

Both of them were totally absorbed in their worlds, trying not to hear the shouting that spilled out from the partially opened windows and around the seams of the door. The shouting and slamming of doors that had gone on for hours.

Angela tried to shut out the words by reading faster, trying to escape. But the shouting wrapped around her and squeezed, sped up the beat of her heart. Sweat slid down her back, even though the spring afternoon was cool.

Then suddenly the front door swung open and their father, Glen, came storming out.

Gayla stopped jumping. Angela lowered the book to her lap and watched him walk to the car. He turned once, flashed a parting smile at Gayla, then Angela, before getting into his car and pulling away.

Marlene stood in the open doorway, eyes swollen and red from crying. She held her arms tightly across her waist.

Gayla, with panic etched onto her face, dropped her rope and ran to her mother. Angela couldn't seem to move.

Marlene embraced Gayla, planting kisses on her head and making soft, soothing noises. She looked across at Angela for a long moment, appearing to see something in her that she'd never before noticed until then, and the realization, the acceptance, was so painful that Marlene couldn't bear the sight of her any longer. She turned away, taking the clinging Gayla with her into the house.

Angela never understood the look in her mother's eyes, but she'd never forgotten it. Whatever her mother had seen somehow changed the fabric of their relationship as mother and daughter and ultimately Gayla and Angela's relationships as sisters.

Angela wiped away the tears that had formed in the corners of her eyes. Didn't they realize that she'd lost him, too, that day, that she hurt, too? Instead her mother and Gayla seemed to form an alliance of comfort that only included the two of them, leaving her out. And the harder she tried to win back their favor: excelling in school, doing everyone's chores, looking after her sister, the further they withdrew.

Slowly Angela pulled herself up, understanding gradually filling her. Was Gayla aware that the day their father left was the day everything changed? But why between them? Why?

Eight

Gayla inched out of her bed, holding her stomach and biting her bottom lip to keep from crying out.

"Damn it," she muttered, shuffling toward the bathroom. All she wanted to do was wash her face, and it seemed like an insurmountable task, the frustration of it making her feel sorrier than usual for herself. She hated the sensation of helplessness, neediness. Sure, she put on a good show, as if she had it all together. But the reality was she was scared as hell all the time. Scared that her facade would crumble, scared that everything that she loved would be taken away. So she shielded herself from hurt, disappointment, and loss by keeping everyone at bay, keeping the wall in place. If she couldn't be touched, be reached, she couldn't feel and couldn't hurt ever again.

Angela stood at the threshold preparing her hand to knock when she heard the sounds of muffled moaning and the uneven shuffle of slippered feet. She hesitated, then pushed the partially opened door and stepped inside.

Her stomach momentarily tightened and a long-forgotten warmth and sense of protectiveness that she'd once felt for her sister pushed its way to her heart. She hurried across the room and gently braced the stooped form of her sister, sliding her arm around Gayla's waist for support.

"Let me help you," Angela said softly.

The words, spoken so tenderly, rushed straight to Gayla's heart. She glanced at her sister and for an instant remembered the little girls they once were, with Angela tending to Gayla's scraped knee or bumped elbow or helping her find her misplaced toy with a tender patience born only of love. The collective memories of their childhood. The private, personal recollections of two lives joined at the heart. How did they get to this rocky, bitter place? Where had their love gone? She no longer knew. But at that moment, in this one instance, unselfish sisterhood felt so right—the thing she'd been missing. It was a golden opportunity, an emotional vantage point from which reconciliation and healing was clearly in sight.

"You should have called me," Angela continued, pushing open the bathroom door while helping Gayla clear the lip of the entrance.

"I didn't want to bother you . . . not after—"

"That's why I'm here, hon," Angela said, surprising herself with the endearment.

The shadow of a smile tinted Gayla's mouth. "Thanks."

Angela gingerly released Gayla once she'd braced her palms against the sink for support.

"You gonna be okay?" Angela asked. "I can stay if you need help."

"I'll manage."

"It's no big deal. I used to change your diapers, you know—or I tried to." She put one hand on her hip. "And Mom loved to put us in the tub together to save hot water."

For the first time since Angela's arrival Gayla actually laughed. Her eyes sparkled and a healthy glow flushed her face, the memory temporarily warming her.

"Remember that Barbie doll I had to take in the tub with me?" Gayla asked over her giggles, holding her stomach.

"Oh, you mean the one that never had on any clothes and only had one leg?" Angela's eyes danced with mischief as she recalled the battered doll that her little sister couldn't live without.

"Just 'cause she was a little handicapped didn't mean I couldn't love her," Gayla said, feigning hurt feelings. "So what about you and that damned itchy mohair sweater that you wore everyplace you went?"

Angela burst out laughing and began scratching her arms in memory of the tattered garment. "Girl, please don't remind me. But you got to admit I was flyy."

"Yeah, right. Like Mama used to say, your taste is all in your mouth."

Their gazes caught and held for a moment and bit by bit they began to sober, looking around the small space for somewhere to escape. Once more, the wall of distance threatened to rise up between them.

"Yep, Mom always had a line for everything," Angela said on a long breath of air, knowing that the "magic" had just left the building.

Gayla cleared her throat. "Yeah . . ."

"Well, I'd better let you get yourself together. I'll . . . be . . . around if you need anything." She closed the door behind her and stood there for a moment until the sound of rushing water in the sink snapped her into action.

What did her sister see when she looked at her? Gayla wondered, appraising herself in the mirror. Did Angela, like others, see a very attractive woman in her late thirties with shoulder-length auburn hair that still held its luster and fullness, a firm body kept in shape by diet and exercise, fair skin kept soft and supple from daily moisturizing? Did she see the college graduate, relatively well read, who owned her home, maintained a sizable bank account, held a decent job as a marketing manager at the *Washington Post,* and had a beautiful daughter?

In total, Gayla Fleming-Holder-Morris-Davis appeared to have it all—a wonderful life, one that others would envy. But beneath the surface was a different story. And for all of Angela's plainness, her ordinary life, *she* seemed to be the happy one, the one who had truly succeeded, the one who enjoyed who she was. She always did.

"Are you all right in there, Gayla?" Angela asked from the other side of the door.

A flash of distant memory seized Gayla. "Just fixing my

face," she replied, remembering the old line she'd handed her sister more times than she could count.

How many mornings had Angela asked the very same question when they were teens sharing the same bathroom?

". . . are you all right in there, Gayla, or did you fall in?"

"I'm fixing my face. You could use a little work yourself."

"That's hard to do when you never come out," Angela tossed back.

"Don't hate me because I'm beautiful," Gayla said, applying another coat of mascara. "Maybe if you paid more attention to how you looked, you'd have a date on a Saturday night with a guy instead of a book." She opened the bathroom door and stepped out, knowing she looked good.

"Maybe dating isn't that important to me."

Gayla laughed. "That's what all the wallflowers say." She sashayed across the room and grabbed her sweater. "Mom says the same thing about you," Gayla added, going for another dig. "She just won't say it to your face."

Angela looked away, the momentary sting of her sister's caustic words pinching her features. For an instant, Gayla felt a wave of guilt. But the reality was, Angela made it all so easy. She was the perfect scapegoat. And as irrational as it was, when Gayla made Angela feel bad, feel less important, she felt better, stronger, as if her belligerence toward Angela somehow leveled the playing field between them . . .

Angela had never seemed to need much. She was content with few friends, her books, and being alone. Gayla, however, craved attention, affection—in any form—and she would do whatever was needed to get it, even if it meant sacrificing her sister in the process. Did that make her a bad person? She never knew, never really wanted to think about it, until now.

She gazed at her reflection. What did she really see? An

unhappy, lonely woman who'd done all the right things that turned out so terribly wrong.

Gingerly she made her way out of the bathroom and was surprised to see Angela sitting on the side of her bed. Angela quickly came to her side.

"Don't want you tripping or anything." She slid her arm around Gayla's waist.

Gayla had to admit it felt good to lean on her sister and not pretend that she, too, didn't need anyone.

"Thanks, again," Gayla murmured as she eased onto the bed.

"Can I get you anything?"

"No. Not right now."

"Okay . . . well, I'll be downstairs." She turned to leave, then stopped. "Oh, Mom called. Said she'd call later."

"Did you two . . . talk?"

"Not really. No more than necessary," Angela answered drolly. "Why?"

"Just wondering."

Angela stood there a moment, as if mentally debating something. "Gayla, what happened to us?" she asked before she lost her nerve.

If this had been another time when Gayla wasn't feeling so vulnerable, she probably would have tossed the question off with one of her snide remarks. But she wanted to know, too. She wanted the answers she'd been searching the better part of her life to find.

"I . . . I don't know, Angie."

Slowly Angela recrossed the room and sat beside Gayla on the bed.

"I've asked myself that question a million times over the years," Angela confessed. She looked into her sister's questioning eyes. "We used to be friends once." Her voice hitched a notch. "You were my best friend."

"So were you," Gayla admitted, and the admission felt good, deep-down-in-her-soul good.

"Remember the day . . . Dad left?" Angela asked.

Gayla nodded.

"It hurt so bad," Angela said softly. "I loved him so much."

Gayla looked at her sister as if seeing her for the first time. "You did?"

Angela frowned. "Of course I did. How could you think I didn't?"

"Because . . ." She hesitated, trying to pull her words and thoughts together. She looked hard at her sister, seeing that fateful afternoon spring up between them. "Because you acted like . . . like his leaving didn't matter. Like you didn't give a damn."

"Didn't give a damn?" Angela asked incredulously. "I felt as if my whole world was coming apart. Like I'd been set out on a boat in the middle of the ocean with no direction."

"You didn't act like it. All you seemed to care about was your stupid books and sitting in your room. When I crawled in your bed that night wanting to talk to you, you wouldn't answer me, wouldn't answer my questions, tell me why Daddy was gone," she said, her voice wobbling. "Mom cried almost every night for weeks, but you never came to her, tried to make her feel better. It was me. You weren't there for her. You weren't there for me."

Angela tried to make sense of what Gayla was saying, trying to relate her experiences, her feelings, to her sister's. How terribly far apart they were, how different.

The phone rang, cutting off any further conversation.

Gayla tugged in a breath and picked up the bedside phone.

"Hello . . . Hi, Mom. . . ."

Angela waited a moment, hoping Gayla would tell her mother to call back some other time, that they were talking. When she realized Gayla had no intention of hanging up she rose from the bed and left the room, shutting the door quietly behind her.

Nine

Angela returned to her room and stretched out across her bed. What had just happened was about as close as she and Gayla had ever come to getting to the root of what stood between them. She saw a side of her sister she'd forgotten—a kinder gentler Gayla.

Being in her presence again resurrected so many old feelings and, to Angela's surprise not all of them bad. But what was most disconcerting was that her and Gayla's recollections and resulting feelings from past events were completely different. She closed her eyes.

The night her father left, that first night when she didn't hear his laughter, smell his scent when he peeked his head in to say good night, was the worst night in her life. She'd felt so confused and frightened, yet she couldn't react. It was as if everything inside her had frozen. She tried to remember Gayla crawling into her bed with her that night, the questions that Gayla asked. But she couldn't. She'd been too numb with her own grief.

Had Gayla held that against her all these years? Was that what had caused the uncrossable chasm between them?

Their mother didn't help. If anything, she contributed to the chaos by what appeared to be intentionally pitting sister against sister. Why? was the million-dollar question.

Angela pulled herself to a sitting position. She had two choices: leave things the way they were, do her bit and go home or confront her sister and her mother and hopefully put it all to rest.

She tugged in a breath and headed back to Gayla's room. If there was one thing Angela had learned in counseling her teens, it was that once an opportunity presented itself for open discussion, don't let time or circumstances interfere. The chance may never come again.

Determined, she knocked on Gayla's door.

"I'm resting," Gayla said.

"I need to talk to you, Gayla. We need to talk."

"Not now. I'm tired."

Angela opened the door anyway and stepped inside. "Yes, now."

Gayla's gaze flashed in Angela's direction, pure disdain simmering in her eyes. "I said I was tired," she ground out and shut her eyes.

"You weren't tired a little while ago."

"Well, it's obvious that you have no understanding of what I'm going through, or else you would have more consideration for my health. How do you expect—"

"Then why don't you tell me, Gayla. Tell me how you feel, what you think. Talk to me—for once, just talk to me."

"Talk to you! Humph. How would you ever understand? Your whole life is one neat little package. You have everything in order. No missteps for you."

Angela squeezed her eyes shut for a moment, trying to make sense of what her sister was saying. "What makes you think I have it all together? Did it ever occur to you that I have feelings, too, doubts, too? That I hurt—that I get confused and uncertain?"

"No." She folded her arms like a petulant child.

"Why, Gayla?" Angela pleaded. "Tell me why? I need to understand."

Gayla pressed her lips together as if defying the words to spill out of her mouth. Suddenly she snapped her head in Angela's direction. "You were the only one who went on as if nothing happened. You shut me out; you shut everyone out."

"That's not true. I—"

"Isn't it?" Gayla challenged. "Did you ever ask me how I felt? How Ma felt? No. You didn't care."

Angela swallowed hard and tentatively stepped closer. "I did care, Gayla, more than you know." She shook her head slowly. "I . . . I didn't know what to do. I guess I couldn't really grasp what was going on, and to keep from hurting I shut down." She looked across at her sister, hoping to see understanding dawning in her eyes.

"I can't count the number of times I came to you and you turned me away."

"Gayla, I was eleven years old; I didn't know how to help you. I didn't know how to help myself. And then you and Mama turned on me as if I'd done something wrong when I needed comfort just as much as you both did."

"Mama never turned on you," she spat. "She loved you. More than me."

"What?"

"You heard me. She always did and you know it."

"How can you say that?"

"Because it's true!"

"Gayla, you—"

Her eyes narrowed. "I saw my chance and I took it," she said defiantly. "For once *I* could be important."

Was this at the root of it all—Gayla's insecurities, about what? And still after all these years, the bad blood lingered between them for a misunderstanding that had grown to monumental proportions. Angela was stunned by the sheer simplicity of it all and how insidiously it had destroyed what could have been.

"Gayla, it wasn't what you thought. You were important," Angela said, fumbling to regain her footing and the unwieldy thread of conversation.

"You have no idea what I thought, Angela, what I felt. You never did."

"Once upon a time I did. You were my sister once, not my adversary, my competitor. We were friends, and then one day we weren't. All these years I felt so totally alone,

Gayla, and I could never understand what I'd done. I needed Mama back then. I needed her to help me through it. But the both of you shut *me* out. I needed you to be my sister, too."

For a moment, Gayla's expression appeared to Angela to soften as a flash of what once was moved across her face. And then it was gone.

"You don't know what it feels like to lose over and over again. You don't know anything about me, Angela. And it's too damned late to try to figure it out now. Just leave, okay. Just leave me alone—like you've always done."

Angela's eyes filled with bitter tears and slid slowly down her cheeks. She wiped them away with a swift swipe of her hand, turned, and walked out.

Gayla hadn't thought about the day her father left in years. She hadn't wanted to. In one fell swoop she'd lost her best friend and her dad. And it seemed as if she'd been losing ever since. The only source of comfort she could find at the time was her mother, who for the first time seemed to pay her attention. And she fed on it. As she bloomed into her teens she sought solace elsewhere, first with Tiffany's father Brian . . . and then the others, looking for what she didn't know—still didn't know.

She sighed deeply and shut her eyes, the old waves of anger, regret and betrayal rising within.

Angela went downstairs and out the back door. She needed some air to clear her head. She sat down on the wooden bench beneath the partially enclosed porch and watched the gray storm clouds move swiftly across the horizon. She smelled rain. How *apropos,* she though wearily. *Just like in the old horror movies; thunder and lightning clap and flash outside of the mansion while the inhabitants warily wait for something awful to happen.*

She crossed her arms for warmth as a chilling gust of wind stirred the leaves and blew her hair into disarray. Angela shivered, but she'd rather sit through a snowstorm butt-naked than go back inside at the moment. She closed her eyes and suddenly wished she had a vice like cigarette smoking or drinking. That's what characters in crisis always did. They either lit a cigarette or poured a drink. And if this wasn't a crisis she didn't know what one was, and she felt totally ill-equipped to handle it.

How could Gayla think those things about her, believe them? Was she really that cold, that indifferent? That was never how she saw herself.

It was all so unclear now. For so long they'd lived with their own versions of thc truth that no matter what the reality was, it wouldn't change anything. The wounds were too deep.

For a moment, standing in Gayla's room, looking into her eyes, Angela saw the flash of hurt, of vulnerability. She couldn't remember ever seeing that look in her self-assured younger sister's eyes before. Well, maybe once a very long time ago. Funny, it was an afternoon pretty much like this one. There was a distinct chill in the air, and you could hear the thunder in the distance. Both she and Gayla were home. She was washing dishes and preparing dinner, while Gayla sat on the kitchen chair, twisting and untwisting her long auburn hair.

By the age of sixteen Gayla Fleming was fully aware of her budding womanly charms, her unique beauty, and her ability to manipulate a situation. Angela remembered how everyone Gayla met always told her how pretty she was, that she would probably be one of those "lucky" women who would get a man to take care of them and she'd never have to work hard or struggle for anything. And Gayla believed it, every word of it—from family and friends—she needed to. "You got it made, Gayla," was her mantra. It never occurred to her that it would ever be any different.

Brian Lawrence was proof that all of the accolades were true. He was captain of the basketball team, a senior with scholarships being tossed at him like loose change. The young women hovered around him like swarming bees, smiling, cooing, and praising everything he said or did. And not only was he a vision to look at; he was also smart, not just some good-looking jock who only made it through school because of how many points he scored on the court. He could have had any young woman he wanted—and he chose Gayla. The way it began was so casual—so Brian.

To this day, Angela wasn't sure why Gayla told her about Brian; they'd stopped sharing stories long before that afternoon. The only conclusion she could come to was that Gayla wanted to push it in her face that she had someone and Angela did not.

". . . I was just coming out of my math class—definitely not my favorite—and he was standing outside of the classroom door, leaning against the wall," Gayla was saying. . . .

"Hey," Brian said in greeting.

Gayla turned in the direction of the inviting voice, and her heart turned over in her chest. She'd never been one of the many who flocked around Brian, as much as she may have wanted to, she confessed, surprising Angela with her frankness. She felt it was so classless and common—two things she would never be. She'd also heard all the rumors about Brian Lawrence—his relationships never lasted more than a few weeks. But the young women seemed to be so thrilled that they'd been "chosen," if only for the moment, that it didn't matter. They could always brag about how they "had been with Brian" and compare notes on his prowess. "I'm smarter than that," Gayla said. "After I'm done with Brian Lawrence he'll never want anyone else."

"What are you going to do that everybody and their mama hasn't already done to keep Brian?"

Gayla stared boldly at her sister, raising her chin in challenge. "I'm going to make him love me," she declared.

Angela slowly shook her head. Gayla always thought everything was so easy, that all she had to do was wish it and it would be true. She never had to work for anything, earn anything. And as much as Angela would never admit it out loud, she resented Gayla for it. And she resented her mother for allowing it.

Just like the prior weekend. Her mother had given Gayla money to replenish her wardrobe, which she insisted was completely outdated.

"Gayla, you just bought new pants, skirts, and tops two months ago," Marlene complained as Gayla posed sullenly in front of her.

Gayla turned on the charm. "Aw, Ma, come on. Just a few things. Nothing much. I saw this flyy sweater that would really bring out my eyes. Lisa said it was made for me."

"Lisa's your best friend," Marlene said in a monotone. "I wouldn't expect her to say anything else."

Angela watched the entire exchange from her seat in the corner of the couch, heard the way her sister's voice went from a soft cajole to a tender plea, how she convinced their mother how nice she would look in the sweater, and how desperately she needed something new.

Angela was in her first year of college, still living at home because they couldn't afford for her to go away, nor could they afford to pay for her to stay even if she lived at home. So she held down a part-time job during the week as a waitress, a movie attendant on the weekends, and had a full class load. Every other cent she made went to pay for tuition and books; the balance went to her mother, "to help out—earn her keep," as Marlene would put it. Not to mention the housework she did or the innumerable errands she had to take her mother on because she'd purchased a little piece of a car to help her get from job to job and to her classes.

If she had two nickels to rub together she would move out, but she didn't. Most times she was too tired to really give a damn what went on in her household anyway, but that afternoon was different. Her sister was making her stomach turn, and she snapped.

"Why do you let her do that to you, Ma? Why?" Angela jumped up and shouted in frustration.

Gayla and Marlene turned to look at Angela as if she'd lost her mind.

"What is your problem, Angela?" Marlene responded. "Every time I get ready to do something for your sister you have a problem with it."

"Problem?" she challenged.

"Yeah, either you got your mouth screwed up or you're rolling your eyes. Why can't she have anything without you getting some kind of attitude? You have a job. Your sister doesn't. If I can't do for her, who will?"

Angela was so angry she was shaking. She wanted to scream, knock some sense into her mother and the smug look off her sister's face. But she couldn't. And until she could get out and away, she was stuck. There was no knight on a white horse in her fairy tale, she thought drifting back to her sister's monologue.

". . . and after we get together and he gets his basketball scholarship we'll get married and . . ."

Angela had stopped listening. Gayla had no clue about the real world. She was so accustomed to everything being handed to her it never occurred to her that life wasn't that easy. But as always, for Gayla it was.

She'd landed Brian Lawrence all right. And for a while, Gayla actually seemed like a changed person. She was pleasant, laughed a lot, seemed to have traded in her barbs for kinder words. Those few months that she was Brian Lawrence's girl Gayla bloomed. She was even prettier, if that were possible. She was in love. Then as swiftly as it all began it came to a grinding halt.

Angela would hear Gayla in her mother's room late at night, the sobs drifting from beneath the door and her mother's comforting noises. Gone was the sparkle from Gayla's gray-green eyes, the lightness from her voice. She walked around the house like a ghost, only coming to life if she could find something nasty to say to her sister.

But Gayla's attitude wasn't the only thing that changed. Her body slowly began to change as well. And that's when Angela knew—her seventeen-year-old sister was pregnant.

Upon first realization Angela's reaction was "Serves her right." But in the next breath, she felt sorry for Gayla. It was bad enough that she wasn't prepared for the real world; she certainly wasn't prepared for a child. Brian hung around for a while and folks thought that maybe things would actually work out for him and Gayla, that they wouldn't contribute to the statistics of being black, teenage single parents. They were both beautiful to look at, and Angela had to admit that Tiffany was truly an exquisite-looking child. But having a beautiful, healthy child and a cover girl for a girlfriend wasn't enough for Brian. He had a career to think about, and baby and girlfriend didn't work on his résumé. Sure he sent money for Tiffany and dropped in from time to time over the years, but that was the extent of his involvement.

Angela sighed deeply. She hadn't thought about that episode in Gayla's life in years. Tiffany was her niece, a bit spoiled and self-absorbed at times, but she loved her and couldn't imagine life without her in it. She'd never really thought about how having a child so young and being abandoned by the first man you ever loved had affected her sister. They were so estranged by that time, it was almost as Gayla had said—Angela didn't care. The truth was she'd long forgotten how.

But she should have been there for her sister—some kind of way. She should have found a means to get through to her, give her some support. No, she shook her head. She wasn't going to put that weight on her shoulders. Neither Gayla nor her mother made it easy or possible for her to be supportive or a part of the family circle. Once Tiffany was born the bond between Gayla and her mother seemed to strengthen even more. They had each other. All Angela could do was try to get out as fast as she could, leave them to their own devices, and, she hoped, build a life and find someone in it who didn't treat her as an afterthought.

And when she finally did, she saw a side of her mother and sister that closed the last door to her heart.

Ten

After more than a month of prodding and cajoling by Mark she'd totally run out of excuses for why she didn't want him to meet her family: from not having the time to take off from work, to her sister being out of town or in between husbands, to her mother being ill.

"I want to marry you, Angela. I want to love and be with you for the rest of your life. I want your family to know that," he'd said as they lay in bed together.

The mere idea of bringing Mark to meet her mother and sister made Angela's heart race and all the old insecurities, the hurts, would resurface in such a rush she had to catch them in her mouth and swallow the bitter bile back down. Mark thought she was wonderful, bright, fun to be with, attractive. For the first time in her life, since her childhood relationship with her dad, she felt special again. She didn't want to risk losing that wonderful feeling at the hands of her family—if you could call them that.

But here she and Mark were, sitting outside her mother's home, and she was shaking like a leaf.

"Are we going to sit in the car for the rest of the afternoon or are we getting out, babe?" Mark gently asked, cupping her clenched fist with his hand.

Angela knew she had that deer-trapped-in-the headlights look in her eyes, but she couldn't help it.

"It's gonna be all right, baby." He clasped her hand tighter. "I love you, and I'm not going to let anybody or anything hurt you." He looked deep into her eyes. "Do you believe that?"

Angela swallowed and nodded numbly.

"I'm here, on your side," Mark tenderly assured her, before leaning over and kissing her long and deep. Slowly he eased back and gave her a gentle smile. "Let's do this."

"So, Angela hasn't told us too much about you, Mark," Marlene commented as they sat in the living room of the three-bedroom house her children had grown up in. She looked hard at her prospective son-in-law as if searching for the flaws. "But she never did seem to take us into consideration when it came to her decisions." She took a sip from her cup of tea and waited.

Mark casually crossed his right ankle over his left knee. "I'm pretty sure I was sitting right next to Angie the night she was telling you about me—about us. About a month ago, right, baby?" He turned to Angela and gave her a warm smile.

Marlene's expression pinched for a moment.

"I'm sure what my mother means is that Angela is usually so close mouthed about things. I'm sure there's more to you than the few comments she shared over the phone," Gayla chimed in. "Mama's always met my boyfriends." She laughed. "Prospective husbands." She arched a brow before lifting the glass of rum and Coke to her polished lips and looking Mark over as if he were dessert.

Mark didn't flinch. "I'm proud to say that there is more to me than meets the average eye." He chuckled. "Not like so many people . . . all surface and no substance." He looked from one woman to the other. Casually, and not with any bravado, Mark told them about his childhood, his large, loving family that he couldn't wait to make Angela a part of, his education at M.I.T., and his degree in engineering. "As for my goals, right now I'm working for a great computer installation company—wonderful perks, solid salary, and loads of potential. In another five years I intend to have my own. For me and Angie. This is fine for now, but a man has to have something he can call his, and you'll never get rich working for someone else." He appraised the two inspectors thoroughly, assuring himself that he'd solidly put them in check and let them understand he was no pushover and neither would he sit by and let them maliciously attack Angela.

"How did you two meet?" Gayla quizzed him, both baffled and annoyed that her plain-Jane sister had landed someone like Mark.

Mark and Angela looked at each other and laughed, recalling the grocery store mishap that changed their lives.

"That's our little secret," Mark answered for them both, already knowing that little sis would find some way to demean that special moment for them. Angela smiled at him and squeezed his hand in gratitude.

The remainder of the visit seemed to drag by for Angela, but Mark handled her mother and sister as deftly as a card shark running the table; he was so swift with the one-on-one deal, they couldn't keep up with his hands or his feet. Little by little the knot that had sat in the center of Angela's chest began to ease, and before she knew it, Mark was taking her hand and leading her to the door. It was almost over. She'd gotten away unscathed. Almost.

They were standing at the door and Mark had said his good-byes and was heading to the car, parked at the curb, to give the women a few minutes to themselves.

"Seems like you might have gotten lucky," Marlene said to her daughter.

"I think I'm very lucky," Angela replied.

Gayla looked her up and down. "It's gonna take more than luck to hold a man like Mark." She turned her glance toward him. "What Mark needs is a real woman, one who can keep up with him. That he would be proud to have on his arm when he's making it big in corporate America." She looked at her sister. "How long do you really think you could hold his interest? Be honest, Angela. You're about as exciting as a wet dishrag, and you look like one, too. When are you ever going to do something with yourself?"

"Oh, Gayla, stop teasing your sister," Marlene said without much conviction. "But I got to admit Gayla does have a point, Angela. Men like Mark will lose their interest fast if you can't keep 'em entertained. I know his type."

"I'd like to know his type," Gayla said, running her tongue across her lips.

"Leave us alone, Gayla," Angela said through her teeth, knowing the kinds of games her sister played and that the old saying "blood is thicker than water" had no meaning for Gayla. If she saw something she wanted, she went after it and didn't give a damn who got hurt in the process. She wouldn't get her claws on Mark.

Gayla gave her a long look, seeing her short hair, plump body, and simple attire, Angela believed. And suddenly Angela did feel like an old dishrag. She could almost envision someone like Gayla on Mark's arm. Someone flashy, a head turner, someone unlike her. She couldn't count the number of times she questioned how she had wound up with someone like Mark Richards.

"It's only a matter of time," Gayla commented, casting her gaze in Mark's direction again. "He deserves better and he'll figure it out before you know it."

"Why can't you just be happy for me?" Angela shouted, looking from one cruel face to the other. "Why? Just once."

"We make our own happiness in this world, Angela," Marlene said. "Ain't up to us to be happy for you. You think you got somethin' in that man, mo' power to ya. I seen his kind come and go."

"His kind? What is that supposed to mean?"

"Oh, grow up, Angela," Gayla chimed in. "Men like him would never stay with a woman like you. It's as simple as that. Take my advice. Cut your losses while you can."

Angela's eyes burned. Her head was pounding so hard she could barely think. Who were these people—her flesh and blood? This was the woman who gave her life but could care less how she lived it. And Gayla, her sister, whom she'd held at night when she had bad dreams, taught how to jump rope, and read to under the blanket with a flashlight, was a total stranger. A vindictive stranger, who seemed to hate her from a place inside her soul that she couldn't name. What in God's name had she done to deserve their scorn?

She made a vow, as they looked at her as if she were last night's leftovers, that once she got into the car and shut the door she was never coming back.

But she had—for her grandmother's funeral, another disaster—and now this.

Angela blinked back the memories and realized that a steady rain had begun to fall and a decided chill was in the air. She shivered, not even sure how long she'd been sitting there. A gust of wind blew, tossing cold rainwater across her body. She shivered again but still didn't get up.

The back door creaked open and to her astonishment Gayla poked her head out.

"What in the world are you doing out here in the rain? You want to catch pneumonia or something?" Gayla tugged her robe around her waist.

"Go back to bed, Gayla," Angela said in a flat monotone.

"Not until you come back inside." She stood there, or rather stooped there, resolute.

"Gayla, as you keep reminding me, you're not well. Go back to bed."

"Not until you come inside," she repeated with more force this time.

"Are we going to argue about this, too?" She looked at her sister from the corners of her eyes, the wounds of the old memories still fresh in her mind.

"You're supposed to be the one with all the sense, and this is what you're going to do. Get up, Angela."

Angela rolled her eyes, refusing to give in even though she was freezing.

"You gonna make me come out in the cold and the rain

after you? Is that the deal? Some bizarre payback for what I said."

"I could never pay you back for the things you've said—today and all the days before."

Gayla shut her eyes a moment. "I . . . don't really mean half the shit I say, Angela. You should know that by now."

"Why would I know?"

"Because . . . you're nothing like the person . . . I say you are. You know that."

Angela turned to look at her sister, hunt for the lie beneath the words, the lure to reel her back into another position of vulnerability. But she found none.

"Then why, Gayla? Do you have any idea of how the things you've said, the things Mom has said to me and about me, have affected me? And not just at the moment, but deep inside to the core of who I am."

Gayla watched the tears mix with the rain and slide down her sister's cheeks. She wished she could say the words, speak from her heart, tell Angela of the thoughts that kept her up at night and sent her into the arms of one man or another, the loneliness and doubts that she felt. She wished she could hug her sister. But it had been so long she didn't know how.

"Fine, stay there. I'm going inside."

Angela listened to the door slam and rolled her eyes just as another shiver ran down her spine and straight to her toes. An angry gust of wind slapped more rain across her face, and that was fine, too.

Gayla shuffled back inside, stopped, and started to go back and get her stubborn sister before she got sick but changed her mind. If there was one thing Gayla knew about her sister, it was that once she made up her mind, no matter how ridiculous it was, there was no moving her. And as much as she was reluctant to admit it, she admired that quality in Angela. Not like her, who waffled back and forth, with no clear direction, no real or even imagined goals.

She eased her way over to the kitchen table and gingerly sat down, certain that at any moment Angela would give up the foolishness and come in out of the cold. Moments passed, still no Angela.

Just like when they were kids, Gayla thought. There was a time she remembered as clear as if it were yesterday. . . .

Her mother had fixed liver and onions, a dish that Angela hated almost as much as Gayla hated math. They were about nine and six at the time.

"Angela Fleming, don't you get up from that table until you eat every drop on your plate," Marlene had warned.

"I can't stand liver," Angela complained, folding her arms defiantly.

"Did I ask you what you could stand?" Marlene pointed a threatening finger. "You eat your food or you can sit there for the rest of the night. Understand?" Marlene left the kitchen.

"Just eat it," Gayla whispered across the table.

"No."

"Why?"

"Because I don't like it and nobody can make me eat it. I'll sit here until I turn blue."

Gayla's eyes widened with alarm. "Aw, come on," Gayla pleaded. "I don't want to go to bed by myself."

"I'm not eating it."

Gayla stared at her older sister in disbelief and awe. She was actually going to challenge their mother—"Defy her," as Marlene would put it—and didn't seem in the least bit afraid.

"Then I'm not eating mine, either," Gayla announced, pushing her plate aside.

"You're gonna get in big trouble, Gay."

Gayla folded her arms like her big sister. "So what. I hate liver, too."

The two girls giggled and they both sat in that same spot until their father came home and told his wife to "let those children go to bed and stop being ridiculous."

They'd slept in the same bed that night, cuddled up against each other whispering in the dark about how they would always be on each other's side and that they would never let anyone or anything come between them.

"Thanks for sitting with me, Gay," Angela had whispered.

Gayla kissed her sister's cheek. "I love you, Angie."

"I love you, too, Gay."

And they fell asleep in each other's arms. . . .

Gayla looked toward the back door. Angela would never come in, she realized, and if Angela didn't, neither would she.

Eleven

Suddenly Angela felt the weight of a coat being draped around her shoulders. She turned to her right.

"I figured you could use some company . . . and a coat." Gayla eased down beside her. "How long you plannin' on sittin' out here anyway?"

Angela shrugged and pulled the trench coat closer around her body. "Thanks for the coat."

"Sure."

They sat in silence for a few moments watching the rain wash over the grass.

"You really shouldn't be out here, Gayla. You're not well."

"You won't be, either, if you stay out here too much longer."

"I'm okay."

"Are you?"

Angela took a deep breath. "I've had to be, you know." She looked away.

"I guess we both have had to be and do a lot of things over the years," Gayla admitted.

Angela looked curiously at her sister. "Like what?"

Gayla pulled her coat tighter around her shoulders. She looked off into the distance. "Remember that time we sat for hours at the kitchen table and refused to eat our liver?"

Angela chuckled. "Yeah, I remember."

"What happened to us, Angie? The good times we used to have?"

Angela slowly shook her head and sneezed. "I don't know."

"Do you ever think about it?"

"To be honest?"

"Yeah."

"I try not to. But . . . since I've been here, with you, a lot of things have been coming back. Some good, mostly bad." She sneezed again.

"Yeah, me, too," she admitted. "I wish things could be different." She paused and pulled a balled-up tissue from her coat pocket and handed it to Angela.

"Thanks." She wiped her nose. "Still keeping old tissues in your pockets, I see."

"And you're still using them."

They chuckled lightly, both remembering how Angela's allergies always kept her with a runny nose and watery eyes, and she would never have a tissue and would have to bum one from her sister every morning on their way to school.

"But you have everything," Angela said, returning them to the conversation. "All you ever wanted you always got. What could you possibly want to be different?"

"Me," Gayla admitted. She stole a glance at her sister.

Angela frowned and sneezed again. "You?"

Gayla shivered as a chill went through her.

"Come on, let's get you inside." Angela put her arm around her sister's waist and helped her to stand. "I should have never let you sit out here." She sneezed again.

"Don't we make a pair?" Gayla groaned, the aches starting to set in from the dampness.

"Can you stand in the shower?"

Gayla nodded.

"Let's get you in some hot water, and I'll fix you some soup."

"Will you . . . have some with me?"

"Do you really want me to?" She sniffed and pushed the door shut behind them.

"Yeah, I really do."

Angela sneezed again.

"I think you may need it more than I do."

"You might be right."

While Gayla showered, Angela prepared two heaping bowls of soup, found a box of crackers and a block of cheddar cheese that she placed on a tray and brought up to Gayla's bedroom.

As much as she just wanted to give in to the sudden camaraderie, Angela was still leery of Gayla's shift in behavior. *The quiet before the storm,* she thought to herself as she placed the tray on the nightstand. She had no idea what was really on Gayla's mind, what her true intentions were. She'd spent so much of her life guarding her feelings that it came as second nature now. Whenever she'd thought that her sister was being halfway human and let her walls down, Gayla would leap right in and hit her with a sucker punch that would leave her reeling.

Why would tonight be any different from the way it had been between them all these years? She sat down on the side of the bed and looked toward the closed bathroom door. She didn't want to wish for it, didn't want to hope. She didn't want to be hurt again.

Gayla let the steamy water slide over her body, vanquish the chill that was attempting to settle in her bones. What had been on her mind going out there like that? Compassion? Not hardly. She might be a lot of things, but compassionate was not one of them. She'd been told that by more men than she cared to count. She'd forgotten how it felt to care for someone else, to give something of herself for another person. The last time she did, she was seventeen years old, and she'd never been the same since. All her high hopes and big talk crumbled right in front of her—in front of the world, in front of Angela.

Stupid, that's what she was. Plain and simple. But she could never admit that to anyone, especially her sister. She didn't want to be diminished in Angela's eyes. But having a baby at seventeen had done just that. She knew it did, even if Angela never said the words. So she'd been on a constant quest to somehow redeem herself, eclipse her hardworking sister in any way that she could—from marrying James, Steven, then Carl, buying a big house that she could barely afford. Anything she could do to shine again.

In the end what did she really have? What had she accomplished? Nothing. It was Angela who had the steady job, the comfortable home, and a wonderful husband who adored her. When would it ever be her turn? When? When?

Gayla turned off the shower and reached for her towel. All she wanted was a little piece of happiness, she thought, passing the towel over her body. She wanted what her sister had, but she didn't know how to get it.

When Gayla stepped out of the master bath, she was filled with mixed emotions when she saw her sister sitting there. On the one hand, she was glad she'd stayed, and on the other hand, she was resentful. Resentful because Angela would do it simply because she was asked, because it seemed like the right thing to do, because she had a conscience.

"You okay?" Angela asked.

"Fine." She shuffled toward the bed.

"Eat this while it's still hot," Angela advised. "I found some crackers and cheese."

"Fine." Gayla crawled into bed.

"Here." Angela placed the tray with the food on Gayla's lap and stared tenderly at her younger sister for several seconds. "You really should try to get some of this down."

"Why are you always so good to me . . . even when I treat you like shit?"

"It's not an act, if that's what you mean. It's who I am. There's nothing wrong with treating people decently or trying to do the right thing. You resent that about me, don't you?"

Gayla looked away from the truth. "Why would I resent you?"

"Why don't you tell me why?" Angela's heart was pounding, as she both wanted and did not want to hear the answer.

Gayla looked at her intently. "Yeah, I do. I hate the martyr routine, putting everybody first, like you're trying to be a saint. Nobody's that perfect, not even you. Everybody hates that about you. "

Angela felt the sting of her words. "Is it really everybody or just you?" Angela asked, narrowing her eyes. "I was talking about you and what you feel. I'm trying to figure out why you feel you have to play the evil witch with me. What is it with you?"

"Who says anything is wrong with me?" Gayla turned on her side, her face partially obscured by her shoulder. "What about you? You act like you have no part in anything. That you're the one being put upon, like it's all about you."

"Me?" Angela asked incredulously. "What about you, Gayla? It was always you first, last, and always."

"I do what's best for me," Gayla replied. "To hell with everybody else. If I don't look out for me, who will? You damn sure won't. You're too busy with your wonderful life."

Angela jumped up in sheer frustration, clawing her fingers through her hair. "Christ, will things ever change between us? Always this tit-for-tat, looking-for-an-opening bull. Aren't you sick of it? I know I am."

She turned pleading eyes on her sister, demanding eyes that wouldn't let Gayla back down, that determined look that she knew she couldn't escape.

"What could I have done differently, Gayla? How could I have changed things between us? For a minute while we were outside and when you asked me to sit here with you I really believed that something was happening between us. Some of the old feelings I used to have started coming to the surface. And yeah, I'm gonna admit it. It scared the hell out of me. You know why?" She tugged in a breath and let the words flow. "Because anytime I think that I can open myself up to you, be a friend to you, a sister to you . . . you try to find a way to hurt me, ridicule me, make me feel so small. And I'm tired of feeling hurt when I don't know what it is I've done to deserve it."

Gayla stared down into her now-cold bowl of soup.

"It's a real lonely place I've been in all these years."

"You? You have Mark, your job, friends . . ."

"Gayla, why haven't you dated anybody since Carl?" she asked gently. "Don't you ever get lonely?"

"What is this? Twenty damn questions or something! Am I on trial here?"

"No. That's not what this is about."

"You don't know anything about me. What makes you think I don't have anyone, that someone doesn't care about me?" With that question, Gayla sat up on the bed, the tray almost capsizing, her face turning crimson.

"My love life is my business and I'm sick of you waving Mr. Right in my face," Gayla snapped defensively. "Mr. Right, your perfect marriage and perfect life."

"All I'm saying, Gayla, is that loneliness is no good," Angela said quietly. "I've seen what loneliness can do to somebody. It twists you up inside, poisons your soul, and hardens the heart." She hesitated a moment. "Look at Mama."

Gayla scooted over to the edge of the bed, her feet inches from the floor. "Leave her out of this. You made this about me and you. She has nothing to do with what we're talking about."

"She does. She has everything to do with what we're talking about," Angela said. "Don't you see that? We're both products of our environment, our upbringing. Look at what loneliness has done to her. It's made her mean, selfish, and small. With each passing year, she gets harder and harder inside. I listened to her the other day and I thought she was never this bad. Everything that came out of her mouth was designed to hurt, punish, or humiliate. I wonder if she even sees what she's become. And you'll wind up the same way."

Gayla leaned forward and stared her in the face. "Who are you to waltz in here and start judging anybody? What makes you so high-and-mighty?"

"Do you honestly think she's a happy person?" Angela persisted.

Gayla looked away from her, then at the tray with the food. She understood what Angela was getting at, the damage done over the years by being alone, almost friendless, isolated, and frightened by the growing prospect that this was all her life would ever be. Alone and terrified that each minute would bring another wrinkle, another pound, but no man to share her life with. She was alone and would remain that way. But she would never admit it. Never out loud.

"Mama's perfectly content with her life," Gayla said bitterly, making certain that she steered the conversation away from herself. "She doesn't need you or anybody telling her how to live."

"You're becoming just like her," Angela said, sadly. "And you don't even see it. Do you?"

"I . . . don't. . . . You don't know what you're talking about," she sputtered, feeling suddenly disturbed—unsettled and she wasn't sure why. "I . . . need to get some rest."

Angela pushed out a frustrated breath. "Fine." She lifted the tray from the bed. "I hope you at least think about some of the things we've talked about. It doesn't have to be this way, Gayla. And it won't if we can find a way to be honest with each other and ourselves."

Gayla watched Angela leave the room and felt a sudden emptiness in her soul. Even though they'd been virtually at each other's throats, at least they had been talking. When she'd invited Angela to share a meal, she'd really wanted her sister's company. She wanted to see what it was like to simply be kind to each other again—be friends. But like always, that dark side of her jumped in and resisted every attempt Angela made to bridge the gap. Why? Why? Why was she so afraid? Where had her need to hurt everyone who got close to her sprung from?

She leaned back against the pillows and closed her eyes, and Angela's words came back to haunt her. She wasn't like her mother. She wasn't.

Twelve

Angela emptied the half-eaten food into the garbage can and washed the bowls.

She wasn't going to back off this time, let Gayla's barbs set her back on her heels, she decided. She had a degree in social work for heavensake. This was what she did for a living, got to the core of what troubled the people whom she worked with. It was finally clear to her that Gayla's bitchiness stemmed from pain, some real or imagined hurt or disappointment that she'd never admitted, maybe didn't even realize. So she turned those feelings out onto the world, turned it on the people close to her, as did her mother. And for whatever reason, they both found Angela an easy outlet for their anger and frustration, as if she were somehow responsible for the state of their lives.

She wiped her nose with a paper towel. But she wasn't. It was just like she told her students: the only person responsible for you and your actions is yourself. She wasn't going to take the weight anymore, bear the burden. The only person she could be responsible for was herself.

Suddenly she looked up from the sudsy water and it hit her. *That's why she had come back*. "That's why." Not so much to take care of her sister, but to somehow absolve herself of the guilt and inadequacy she'd felt by being a part of this family. It was the only way she would be able to move on with her own life—to the fullest, without being crippled by her past, one that she could not change. She didn't come back to be a martyr, the saint, the do-gooder hoping to score points as she'd always done—in the vain hope that maybe her mother and her sister would love her.

She came back to cleanse her soul, rid it of the stain that hampered her growth as a woman, a person, a wife.

Suddenly her spirit felt light, weightless almost, as the simple reality, the thirty-plus-year quest for truth, slowly began to emerge.

"It wasn't my fault," she said aloud. She turned to face the room. "It wasn't my fault." *They chose to be the people they became.*

And she must finally emerge as the complete Angela she was destined to be.

Gayla sat alone in her room, something she'd grown accustomed to over the years. *Lonely and bitter.* Was that how Angela saw her?

She gazed around at her well-furnished room, envisioned the expensive artwork downstairs, the brand-new Lexus in the garage, the array of designer apparel that filled her closets. She had it all, and she had nothing.

How much like her mother had she become over the years? She'd never thought about it until tonight when Angela brought it up. Sure, she knew her mother could be a real piece of work, but she simply took it as Marlene being who she was, never questioning the reasons why. The old saying "the apple never falls far from the tree" ran through her head—*a product of her upbringing and environment.*

Did she have any of her father in her? She vaguely remembered him as a big, dark, smiling man, who always had a kind word, always stuck up for them with their mother. From what she could remember, he was always working. He'd come home tired, beat down at the end of the day, but he always found time for them. She remembered one night asking him why he had to work so hard and so long. . . .

"A man's got to take care of his family," he'd said. "Want to make sure that you and your sister and your mother have what you need."

"We have plenty of stuff," Angela said. "You don't have to work so hard anymore."

"I want some new skates, Daddy," Gayla said.

Glen chuckled. "You know it's way past your bedtime, little bit," he'd said as he tucked her into bed and placed a kiss on her forehead.

She remembered the scent of him, salty and hot, like the beach at the height of the summer. She smiled as the recollection took shape in her head.

"You got to get up for school in the morning," he'd said in his thick southern drawl.

"Can't you read me a story first?" she'd pleaded.

He shifted his big body on the narrow bed and scratched his chin. "Too late for stories," he'd hedged.

"But you never tell us stories, Daddy," Angela had cut in from the opposite side of the room. "Please, just one."

"Y'all go to sleep." Their mother appeared in the doorway, hands firmly planted on her hips. "Your father can't read you no stories, and if you can't get up for school in the morning you won't be able to read, either."

In that flash of an instant she saw a pain, a shame, on her father's face that she'd never seen before, and her young heart ached. The light seemed to have disappeared from behind his big, dark eyes and his mouth suddenly dipped at the corners. The proud rise of the shoulders he often carried her on curved like the back of a man twice his age.

Slowly Glen turned his head toward his wife and something unmentionable, something Gayla couldn't name, sparked from his eyes. For a moment, her mother seemed to flinch as if she'd been struck, but she held her ground, raising her chin in challenge.

"Yo' mama's right," their father conceded. "You girls get to sleep. It's late." Slowly, almost painfully, he rose from the bed, walked out and past his wife.

Marlene turned off the light and shut the door.

Gayla blinked as the images began to fade like the remnants of a dream upon first awakening, but the sensation of the experience lingered as understanding slowly began to settle inside her. And she wondered if Angela knew.

"You sound like you're catching a cold, babe," Mark said into the phone.

Angela curled up a bit tighter on the couch and sniffed. "Yeah, I think so," she said, not wanting to tell him how foolishly stubborn she'd been, but she did anyway.

"Hmm."

She could hear the smile in his voice.

"Was it worth it—sitting out in the rain and the cold?" he asked gently.

"You know, I think it was, Mark." She explained to him what had happened and how Gayla had brought her a coat and refused to go inside until she did.

"It was almost like old times," she said.

Mark heaved a sigh. "Is that what you want, hon, old times, or something new and better? Neither of you will be who you once were to each other."

"I know. But maybe we can be something. We talked. Or at least we tried to talk, which is something we haven't done. And I came to some real conclusions."

"Like what?"

"That all this bull between my sister, me, and my mother is not my fault. It never has been. I've been walking around with that guilt plastered on my forehead for the better part of my life. And it was never my fault. I have to let it go."

"That's the first time I've ever heard you say that, Angie."

"I mean it, too. Whatever their issues are, they are going to have to find a way to work it out—or not. All I can do is my end, let go of the past and stop allowing it to haunt me."

"So where does all of this leave you and your sister?"

She sighed. "I still have a week and some change to be here. Maybe if we keep talking . . ."

"You do that," Mark said. "Because you know that shifting the weight is still only part of it. To be truly free of this burden you've been carrying, at some point you're going to have to get to the heart of what started it all—what sustained it all. And I don't think it's your sister who has all the answers."

"You don't?"

"No. It's your mother. It's always been your mother. And as long as you and Gayla were at odds, at each other's throats, she never had to address her own issues, her own role in the big picture."

"My mother would no more admit to being at fault about anything than the pope declare he wasn't Catholic."

Mark chuckled. "That may well be. But the truth remains . . . with your mother."

Angela thought about her husband's wise counsel as she prepared for bed. And he was right, she realized. It was always easier for her and Gayla to focus their animosity on each other. Never had they challenged their mother on any level. Angela least of all. But what if they did? What if the two of them, no longer divided, confronted Marlene, made her accountable—demanded answers to the myriad of questions? Because as much as Gayla had protested that their mother had nothing to do with anything, she believed that Gayla knew better—as did she.

Thirteen

Angela pulled open her bedroom door and nearly collided with Gayla, who had her hand poised to knock.

"Oh . . ."

"I . . ."

"Are you okay?" Angela finally got out.

"Yes, I, uh . . . did you know that Daddy couldn't read?" she blurted.

Angela released a breath. "Come in and sit down."

". . . I sorta found out by accident," Angela was saying as they sat side by side on her bed. "I guess I was about ten. I'd come in from school and he was there one of the rare times he was home before evening. I'd asked him if he could help me with my English homework, some reading I had to do." She paused, her gaze growing distant as the memories pieced themselves together.

"So what happened?" Gayla prodded.

"I brought my homework down to the living room. He was sitting in his favorite chair, watching TV."

"Yeah, the one Mom used to hate and threaten to throw out," Gayla said, recalling how comfortable it felt and how it always smelled like her dad, warm and cozy.

Angela smiled. "Yeah, that one. Anyway, I was so happy to see him at home I grabbed all my books and spread them out on the table. . . ."

"Could you help me with my homework, Daddy? It's really hard and I don't understand it."

Glen yawned. "Smart as you are, girl? What is it you don't know?" He patted her shoulder.

Angela smiled proudly. Her dad was always complimenting her on how smart she was and how she was going to make her mark on the world with all those brains she had. It would always make her giggle and try even harder to make her dad proud. She would read for hours, anything she could get her hands on, so she could stay as smart as her dad said she was.

"I just need your help with one thing. Could you read me the questions while I write down the answers?" She didn't really need his help; this was something she did nearly every day. It was just the idea that her dad was home and she could spend some time with him, listen to his voice while she worked. She put the book on his lap and opened it to the homework page. "See right here." She pointed to the first question. "Just read it to me and I'll write the answers down, okay?"

Glen stared at the page for a long moment. His throat worked up and down. Suddenly he shut the book. Angela flinched.

"Daddy, I . . ."

"Can't you see I'm tired, girl?" He pushed the book back at her but wouldn't look her in the eye. "Go on now and let me get some rest. I got another shift to work tonight. Go on now." He shut his eyes and shut her out, but not before she saw that expression in his eyes.

". . . That same look he'd given Mama when we asked him to read a story that time."

"You remember that?" Gayla asked with wonder.

Angela nodded. "I remember."

"So how did that make you know he couldn't read? Maybe he was just tired."

"I kind of thought that. I guess I was really hurt. It was so rare that we ever had a chance to spend any time together, and since he was always telling me how proud he was of me and my schoolwork . . ." She shrugged. "I just figured it was something we could share together. The next day when I went to school my teacher noticed how quiet I was and asked me what was wrong. I told her what happened."

"What did she say?"

"She explained that it wasn't that my father didn't love me or didn't want to be with me, but that he was embarrassed because he couldn't read. . . ."

". . . Is my father dumb?"

"No. Of course not, Angela. Your father is a very intelligent man. He has a good job; he takes care of his family. I've met your father; I've listened to him. He's a very smart man."

"If he's so smart, why can't he read?"

"Intelligence has nothing to do with it, Angela. There could be a lot of reasons why your father is unable to read. Probably because of where and how long he went to school. But he learned to be smart in other ways, and I know he's very proud of you."

"I can help him read," she said, her eyes brightening with hope.

Her teacher smiled. "That's something that your dad is going to have to do on his own, because he wants to. The school has classes for adults who want to learn how to read."

Angela frowned in confusion. "Adults go to school to learn to read?"

"Absolutely. There are millions of adults in this country who can't read but are able to go through life just fine. They discover ways to work around reading, like memorizing locations, listening carefully to everyone around them."

"So that means they must be pretty smart."

"Yes, Angela, it does. So don't think any less of your

father because he can't read. Your dad is a wonderful man. . . ."

"You never said anything," Gayla said. "Why?"

Angela shrugged. "I guess I kinda wanted it to be our secret. Me and Dad."

"Hmm, there was always something kind of special between you and Dad," she said in a faraway voice.

"I miss him."

"So do I."

They both looked at each other and smiled. Gayla reached for Angela's hand and took it in hers. Angela looked at her in surprise.

"I . . . I've been doing a lot of thinking since you've been here, Angie. Thinking about stuff that I'd pushed to the back of my mind. I . . . I don't hate you. I've never hated you. I . . . I've been jealous and lonely." She tugged in a breath. "I've been beating my brains out trying to discover what went wrong between us, and I keep coming back to the same place."

"When Dad left," Angela filled in.

Gayla looked at her sister. "Yeah," she said softly.

"Mom came between us, for some reason I still can't figure," Angela said, frowning. "Instead of us all bonding together, she pushed us apart—especially me." She turned to her sister. "And I don't know why. A couple of days ago you said you saw your opportunity and you took it. You could be important. Why did you feel that way?"

"Oh, Angie, you have no idea how special you really are; you never have. And it used to bug me, you always being so good, so humble when you received compliments. Everyone would always tell you how you were really going to make something of yourself and that I would just be pretty." She swallowed. "When Dad left, Mom fed into that, reminded me how beautiful I was and that I could get any man I wanted, a man who would stick around, work hard, and take care of me. I'd never have to worry. She clung to me for some strange reason and pushed you away. And . . . for the first time, I did feel important. Special. I was the light in my mother's eyes. She didn't shower you with compliments; it was me." She looked around the room as if searching for the images in the folds of the curtains, the nap in the rug, the moonlight that streaked in through the window. And then it all became clear, coming together like the pieces of a puzzle. "Don't you remember . . . whenever she would see us playing or talking, she would find something for you to do, some chore, some errand. And she would sit with me and show me the fashion magazines, ask me what kind of dress or skirt I would like. It was almost as if when she saw me with you, she would find a way to punish you by giving you work and more work. And I would see the look in your eyes, the hurt, the confusion, but also the acceptance of the situation. A part of me wanted it to stop. So I stopped being with you and you withdrew into your books. I hoped, I prayed, that you would stand up to her, but not Angie." She smiled, not unkindly. "Not stubborn, determined Angie. You were going to take whatever was dished out. And I resented you for it. I resented that you had that kind of will, and I knew I never would. So I punished you, too, until . . . I guess I forgot all the reasons why it started in the first place and it became a way of life."

Tears drifted down Angela's cheeks. "I was so goddamned lonely." She sniffed, and wiped her eyes with the back of her hand "I just didn't get it. I loved you so much and I could see what she was doing to you, turning you into this shallow, indifferent person and it wasn't the sister I knew. So, you're right, I shut down and shut the two of you out, turned a blind eye, and just prayed for the day I could get away for good."

They were quiet for a moment, caught in the net of their childhood.

"Do you ever wonder why Dad left?" Gayla asked

softly. "Mom never said anything. It was as if he didn't exist after that day," she mused.

Angela slowly shook her head. "I've often wondered. It could have been a lot of things. I'm sure you remember the arguments they had; it always seemed like Mom was fussing about one thing or the other."

Gayla was quiet for a while, debating whether she should say what was on her mind, then decided to take the risk. "I think I've been looking for him most of my life," she confessed, and looked at her sister for some sort of recrimination. There was none. Angela gave a small smile of understanding. "I kept looking for some guy to tell me I was special, pretty, that he would take care of me—like Daddy did." She snorted. "I found some real winners. But never my father. Never him," she ended wistfully.

"I think all little girls look for their dad in the men they choose. You're no different, Gay. I think part of it was the distorted picture that Mom put in your head about who Dad was, who men were in general. I guess I was lucky on that end. She never had too much to say to me."

"Yeah, you were lucky." Gayla was thoughtful for a moment. "Maybe he just got fed up," she offered.

"Maybe. The only person that really knows is Mom." She sighed. "Sometimes our life back then seems all muddy and murky and other times things are as clear as if it happened yesterday."

Gayla smiled. "Yeah, I know what you mean. Maybe it's just that we've chosen to remember what we want, you know. The memories that work for us."

Angela looked at her sister with a newfound respect. "I think so. Like with you and me. We were both in the same place at the same time, going through the same things, but we both took it differently, saw it differently, and lived our lives accordingly."

"I often wondered if Dad's death so shortly after he moved ever had anything to do with us."

"What do you mean?" Angela asked.

"You know how they say that when people dedicate their whole lives to something and suddenly that thing or that person is no longer there, they lose their zest for life. Like people who work at the same job for forty or fifty years and when they finally retire they die a year later. Dad's family, doing for us, was his whole life. When he didn't have it anymore, what did he have to live for? You know."

Angela raised her brows. She remembered taking a course in college that dealt with that very issue and how it was so important for people to move away from the familiar gradually. During her course work she'd done field visits to retirement homes and saw firsthand the devastating effects of loneliness and inactivity, what it did to the mind, body, and spirit. But she'd never, until this moment, made that connection with her father.

She squeezed her sister's hand in admiration. "Who ever told you that you didn't have a lot under the cap?" she teased.

Gayla lowered her head and blushed. "I never really thought people would take me seriously about much of anything. I was the black version of the 'dumb blonde.' " She laughed sadly. "I've had opinions, dreams . . ."

"We've missed so much, Gay. Wasted so much time being envious, vindictive."

Gayla turned intense eyes on her sister, her voice sounding almost urgent. "I . . . I don't want to be like Mom. I'm not like her," she whispered, her voice breaking. "I see things. I know in my heart that what Mom did over the years to you wasn't right. But . . ."

"Hey, it's the past. And if there is one thing I learned these past few days it's that I'm no longer going to let the past rule my future. I've let old hurts seep into every corner of my life, even into my marriage."

"Your marriage? You and Mark have a great marriage. I don't understand."

"Believe me, it's a long story." She smiled sadly.

"Think maybe you'll tell me about it one day?"

Angela took a deep breath and truly exhaled. "You know, I think I will."

Gayla stiffly rose from the bed. "Get some sleep."

Angela yawned loudly.

"That was another one of your habits that bugged me."

Angela frowned. "What? Yawning?"

"Yeah, 'cause I'd know five minutes later you'd be in a dead sleep and I'd be running my mouth like a fool and you wouldn't hear a thing. Boy, that used to piss me off."

Angela yawned again and started easing toward her pillow. "We won't even get into your annoying habits or we'll be up all night," she said sleepily. She slid her feet beneath the light blanket.

Gayla put her hand on her hip. "I don't have bad habits. I have endearing quirks. I . . ."

Angela's eyes were closed and her chest rose and fell in an even flow. Gayla shook her head, stepped out of the door, and closed it quietly behind her.

"Some things never change," she mumbled, crossing the hall to her room. "But maybe they do."

As she settled down to bed, taking in her room, thinking about the extraordinary day and the revelations that had come with it, for the first time in years she didn't feel so lonely anymore. She actually felt kind of good. She looked toward the door, imagining Angela fast asleep. Her sister.

She reached toward the bedside lamp and switched it off. They had only scratched the surface. And if she remembered anything about her sister it was her determination and perseverance. The doors had been opened, the old scabs pulled back, and she knew that Angela would walk through them and find a way to heal the wounds once and for all. But this time, she wouldn't let Angela do it alone. Not this time.

Their mother had a lot of explaining to do.

Fourteen

Angela was surprised to find Gayla in the kitchen the following morning. "Hi," she croaked and tried to swallow.

"You look awful."

She sniffed, followed by a wracking cough. "I'm fine."

"Yeah, right. Sit down; I'll make you some tea."

"No. I'm fine. Just morning sniffles. I'll fix breakfast. That's why I'm . . . *Achoo!* Here."

"Sit, Angie! Damn. And cover your mouth." She shuffled to the cabinet and reached for a box of tea on the top shelf, the action setting her incision on fire. "Owwww." She grabbed her stomach.

"See." Angela ambled over and slipped her arm around her waist. "You sit your tail down before you really hurt yourself, 'cause I swear, I don't have the energy to help you."

The two sisters stumbled over to the table and sat down.

"Ouch," Angela groaned. "Feels like every joint in my body has rusted."

"That's just old age, girl." Gayla tried to stifle her giggles, but it only made the burn in her belly intensify. "What are we gonna do now? You're sick; I'm sick. I can't take care of you and you can't take care of me."

Angela looked at Gayla through watery eyes. "Drag Ma over here and make her take care of us."

"Aw, hell no. I'd rather take castor oil."

Angela busted out into a fit of laughter following by a bout of coughing. Tears ran from her eyes.

Gayla dug in her robe pocket and pulled out a rumpled

tissue. Angela snatched it and rolled her eyes. "Is this clean?"

Gayla sucked her teeth. "Ma was the worst nurse in the world," she continued. "And now that she had that hip replacement, all she does is complain about how she can't get around, can't get up and down the stairs and on and on. She'd wear us out."

"So what are we gonna do? I feel like crap."

"Yeah, you look like it, too."

"And you've had better hair days."

Gayla's hands instinctively went to her head and began patting and smoothing.

"Unless you're expecting Mr. Wonderful to come waltzing through that door, forget it."

Gayla heaved in a breath and sullenly lowered her hands. "Well, we can't just sit here."

"I can." Angela lowered her head onto her folded arms.

"Maybe we could camp out in the living room. We'd be right next to the kitchen and bathroom. We have remotes for the TV and stereo."

Slowly Angela raised her head. "Sounds like a plan. If you help me up, I'll help you."

"Deal. Let's inch over to the linen closet first and get out the sheets and blankets."

What seemed like hours later they were finally settled on the couch, swathed in blankets and cushioned on pillows, and after much debate settled on watching *What's Love Got to Do with It?*

"Laurence Fishburne works this role. So does Lady Angela," Gayla said. "I really like her style, too."

"I just pray every night that I look half as good as Tina when I get her age."

"You and me both." Gayla watched the scene of abuse unfold and flinched. "Tina was really a strong woman, you know. After everything she'd been through she picked herself up and moved on—bigger and better than before."

"Not many women can do that. Especially when they've been led to believe that they have no value without a man."

"Have . . . you ever felt like that?"

Angela craned her stiff neck in her sister's direction. "What?"

Gayla looked away, focused on the wide-screen television. "Nothing."

They went back to watching the movie. But the question kept bugging Angela.

"I didn't say 'what' 'cause I didn't hear you. I was just a little surprised by your question. That's all." She sneezed once, twice.

"Bless you."

"Well?"

"Well, it's not me, if that's what you were thinking," Gayla said quickly.

"Oh." Angela frowned in thought.

"I was just making a comment, that's all."

"Hmmm."

They watched the movie for a few more minutes in silence.

"Actually I did feel that way," Gayla finally confessed. "Like I needed a man to make me feel worthwhile."

"Why?"

"Because it was drummed into my head to get a man, have him take care of me, use my looks. I thought all I had to offer was my body and a pretty face. That the man in my life was what was important, not me."

"Oh, Gayla." Angela shook her head sadly. "You have so much to offer. You're funny, intelligent—"

"You remember when you asked me why I stopped dating after I divorced Carl?" she asked, cutting Angela off.

Angela nodded.

"After five years I was tired of being treated like an ornament, something that looked good on a man's arm."

"That took a lot of courage, Gay."

"Yeah, maybe I have courage, but I crawl into bed by myself every night."

"Is that such a bad thing?"

Gayla cut her eyes in her sister's direction, the old pangs of jealousy stirring inside her. "That's easy for you to say. You have a husband. A marriage. Everything is right in your world," she snapped.

"Is it? Yes, Mark is a wonderful man. But it hasn't been all picture-perfect, Gayla."

"Why, are you going to tell me he's an Ike Turner in disguise?" She twisted her lips and tugged the blanket up to her chin.

"Our marriage is . . . far from perfect. But it's not Mark's fault. It's been mine."

Gayla's eyes narrowed as she focused in on her sister. "What do you mean, your fault? You?"

"Growing up in that house with Mom did things to me, too, Gayla. It left me uncertain about my worth—in a different way than you. I believed that I was so valueless that I had nothing to . . . offer . . . a child of my own."

Gayla sat up. "What? I always thought you didn't have—"

Angela shook her head. "Mark has wanted children for years. And I . . . I wouldn't—"

"But, Angie, you would make a great mother. I can't believe you would feel that way about yourself."

"I do. I have. That's why I got so angry with you when you said that I was lucky not to have children, that they just grow up to be ungrateful and selfish. You're the lucky one. You have Tiffany."

"Oh, Angie, I didn't know."

Angela lowered her eyes, seeing Mark's face, hearing his voice telling her how much he loved her.

"I want us to have a baby, Angie. Build a family. You're finished school; my job is secure; our bills are up-to-date." He took a breath, then gently kissed her lips, his fingers trailing down her bare arm to caress her breast. "I love

you, baby, and any child of ours would be born out of that love."

She looked across at Gayla, who sat mesmerized by her sister's revelation. "How long can you go on like that, Angela? Have you ever told him about . . . everything?"

"Enough for him to get the picture." Angela coughed into her raggedy tissue.

"She really messed us up, didn't she?"

"The thing is, what are we going to do about it, I mean really do about it?"

"I was thinking the same thing myself last night after we talked. Mama has a lot of explaining to do. She owes us."

"Yeah, she does. Will she pay up is the question."

"It seems to me," Gayla said, "that as long as we were divided we could be conquered. But together . . ."

Angela grinned. "I like the sound of that. Together."

"Yeah, me, too."

The credits from the movie began to roll with Tina Turner belting out "*What's Love Got to Do with It.*"

Angela groaned.

"You OK?"

Angela groaned again. "Now I'm hungry."

"Yeah, me, too."

They both looked toward the kitchen and the distance seemed miles away.

"Domino's," they said in unison.

Stuffed on pizza with the works and lulled by the steady rain outside, neither Angela or Gayla realized they'd drifted off to sleep until the ringing phone pierced through their slumber.

Fifteen

Gayla reached for the phone on the end table. "Hello?" she mumbled.

"Mom? Did I wake you?"

Gayla yawned loudly. "No. Not really."

Angela squinted, then closed her eyes.

"How's everything going?"

"Great."

"Huh? Great?"

"Your aunt and I were laying here together on the couch watching a movie."

"Together?"

"Are you going to repeat everything I say?"

"I'm sorry. I guess I'm confused."

"Well, when you get back we'll talk . . . about everything . . . a lot of things."

"I'll be back next Friday."

"I'm looking forward to it."

"Tell Auntie I said hello . . . and thanks. She'll know what I mean."

"I will."

"Have a safe flight. And, Tiff . . ."

"Yes."

"I love you. And I'm very proud of you."

Silence hung between them.

"I love you, too, Ma."

"See you Friday, sweetie." Thoughtfully she hung up the phone. "Tiff said to tell you thanks. What did she mean?"

"Guess you two will have to talk about that when she gets home. Sounds like a mother-daughter thing to me."

"Fine." She pouted for a minute. "We can't stay on the couch all day."

Angela adjusted herself deeper under the blanket. "I thought that was the plan."

"I have a better one."

Angela sneezed. "You really think this was a better idea?"

"We've waited for almost thirty years. You really want to wait some more? I don't."

"And you said *I* was determined . . . and stubborn."

"Picking up some of your nasty habits."

"Very funny. *Achoo!* I just wish we were in better shape to deal with her. My head feels like it's underwater."

"Did you take the cold pills I gave you?"

She sniffed. "Yeah."

"They'll be kicking in momentarily. Come on."

Gayla inched out of the car and came around to Angela's door. "You know I don't have the strength to drag you from the car."

"I'm comin', I'm comin'." She opened the door and stepped out, her bones creaking in protest.

They walked to the front door of their mother's house.

"I'm really glad we decided to do this. No matter how things turn out," Angela said and sniffled.

Gayla squeezed Angela's hand, then handed her a tissue from her pocket. "You're the oldest; you ring the bell."

"Coward. You always were a coward," Angela hissed as she pressed her finger to the buzzer.

When Marlene Fleming opened her front door and saw her two daughters—standing there together—a fear that she'd kept in abeyance rose to the surface and manifested itself with the sharp lash of her tongue.

"What in heaven's name are you two doing here?" She turned hard eyes on Angela. "You come way the hell down here from New York to drag your sister out in the street less than a week after she just had major surgery!" Her voice rose by hair-raising degrees with each declaration of Angela's stupidity. "I should have known better." She shifted her stare onto Gayla. "I told you and that stubborn daughter of yours to get a nurse. Angela don't have no more sense than a fly." She reached out to usher Gayla into the house. Gayla eased back.

"It was *my* idea to come here. I talked her into coming," Gayla said. "And now that we have that cleared up, are you going to let us in or not?"

Marlene's nut-brown eyes snapped from one daughter to the other. Her thin lips tightened as if she were sucking on a lemon. "Of course. I don't know why you're standing there in the first place," she continued to fuss as she stepped aside to let them pass.

Angela hadn't set foot in this house since her grandmother's funeral five years earlier. To this day she still cringed at the spectacle that her mother had put on and the humiliation she'd heaped upon her in front of family and friends.

She'd been home about a week after her fibroid operation, just beginning to feel like herself, although her strength still came and went in spurts, when she got the call from her mother with her sister wailing and moaning in the background.

"Angela," Marlene began without a *"hello, how are you feeling,"* "you need to come home. Right away."

Angela rolled her eyes, sure this was more of her mother's histrionics. "Why?"

"Your grandma passed last night—and I need you here."

"Ma, I can barely get out of bed. I—"

"Arrangements need to be made and your sister is no good at this sort of thing. And I just . . ." She went off into a fit of sobbing.

The old waves of guilt began to resurface; the sensation that she was needed, could be a part of the family, took over, erasing her good sense.

"All right, all right. I'll . . . be there tomorrow."

"Can't you come today—tonight?"

"Ma, that's impossible. I'll be there first thing tomorrow. Okay?"

"If that's the best you can do . . ."

Angela squeezed her eyes shut. "I'll see you tomorrow."

. . . From the instant she arrived, her mother was on her like white on rice, giving orders, criticizing every decision Angela made. And Gayla was about as useful as a burned-out lightbulb. Her role seemed to be that of the inconsolable granddaughter who needed to lean on her then-husband Carl's shoulder just to move from one spot on the couch to the next.

The funeral itself was unforgettable if for no other reason than the theatrics that Marlene and Gayla put on, but the wake was an affair to remember.

The house was packed, because Marlene wanted to be certain that everybody who was anybody received an invitation. There was enough food to feed an army, which Marlene insisted could not be catered but must be home-cooked—by Angela. She'd stayed up her entire first night cutting, chopping, seasoning, baking until her eyes were crossing and her body felt weak. She'd made so many "personal" phone calls on behalf of the Fleming family that her voice was hoarse.

Angela wanted to bring in a cleaning service to clean the house, but Marlene was adamant about having strangers in her home. So Angela did it.

By the time the actual funeral day came and Mark arrived, Angela felt as if *she* needed to be buried. Her body was screaming in agony, her head pounded, and she could barely put one foot in front of the other. And all her mother did was complain, complain to whoever would listen about how she'd left everything in Angela's hands and how awful everything turned out: the wrong flowers were on the casket, the wrong prayer was selected, there was still dust in the corners, the pies weren't done the way she would have done them, and on and on until Angela simply snapped right in the middle of the living room floor.

She whirled toward her mother, who was in the midst of another complaint session with one of her aunts.

"You selfish, self-centered, evil woman!"

The entire room fell into a shocked silence. Marlene's mouth dropped open.

"You don't care anything about Grandma, about anyone! You begged and pleaded with me to get out of my sickbed to come down here and take care of things. For *you,* because you couldn't and my helpless sister is too helpless to even think for herself! I've been up for three days straight on my feet, cooking, cleaning, and taking orders from you, and never once, not once, have you had a kind word to say—a thank-you." She was shaking now, tears streaming down her cheeks, her mascara creating black streaks leading to her lips.

"Angie," Mark said in an urgent voice, putting his arms around her, and cutting Marlene a deadly glare. "Come on, babe, let's go. Come on." He urged her toward the door. "You don't need this or them."

"I hate you Ma! Do you know that? I hate you and everything you've done to me. No wonder Daddy left."

Every vein in Marlene's face and head stood out. "Get out! Get out of my house and don't you ever come back!"

"I won't. Not even over *your* dead body!"

And she hadn't been back since, hadn't spoken more than a few sentences to her mother since. She looked around at the familiar rooms, the immaculate furnishings, the precise orderliness, and, even at this time of day the totally together, unrumpled appearance of her sixty-something mother and she wanted to run.

Sixteen

Marlene basically ignored Angela and set her attentions on Gayla, attempting to usher her to the couch.

"You look so weak and tired." She tossed a nasty look in Angela's direction. "Come and sit down. Angela, get your sister some tea."

"I'm fine, Mom," Gayla snapped, and took a seat next to her sister.

Marlene's entire demeanor stiffened as if she'd been slapped. With a huff she sat in the wing chair. "Well, something must have brought you out of the house in your condition."

"We came to talk," Gayla began.

"We came to get some answers to some old questions, Mom," Angela added.

"We?" Marlene asked incredulously, then laughed. "Well, isn't that something. What kind of foolishness have you put into your sister's head, Angela? I know this must be your doing."

"Why did Daddy really leave, Mom?" Angela fired off.

Marlene rose up from her seat. "I don't have to answer any of your questions. That's none of your business."

"It *is* our business," Gayla said. "We're not children anymore. And we want to know why."

"It's obvious that your illness has gotten the best of you," Marlene stuttered.

"Was it because he never came up to your expectations, Ma?" Angela countered. "Your vision of the perfect husband, like the ones you picked for Gayla."

"You don't know anything. Nothing! You were a child.

How would you know what it took to keep a marriage together, a home and a family? It takes work, hard work. It takes money. It takes being able to rise up the ladder." She was breathing hard now. "Do you have any idea what it's like to grow up poor, to struggle, to do without? No. Because I made sure you two girls never had to go through what I did. Never!"

Marlene turned away from them and began to pace the gleaming wood floor. "Your father never understood. He thought love was enough. Love! What's love got to do with anything? It's about getting ahead."

"And Daddy could never get ahead because he couldn't read, right, Ma?" Angela said. "You resented him for it, didn't you? He was an embarrassment to you and your friends."

Marlene swung toward Angela. "I had hopes for him, dreams. He could never fulfill them."

"He worked so hard to do for us, Mom. He loved us," Gayla said. "Do you have any idea what you did? How much you hurt him over the years, hurt us?"

"I did it for you. For both of you. I wanted you to have the best. Why can't you understand that? Your father could never do that for you."

"But he could give us something you never could, Mom—integrity and a self of worth, real value, not the material kind that you believe is so important," Angela said.

"I spent my life looking for this Mr. Right that you created in my head. What a joke," Gayla said. "You had me believing that I didn't need anything more than looks and a desire to get a well-established man that could provide me with *things*. What about happiness? Where does that fit into the equation?"

Marlene ignored Gayla's comments and turned on Angela. "So I suppose the tragedy of your life is my fault, too."

"Why, Ma? Why did you hate me so, make me feel as if I'd done something so horribly wrong—that nothing I do is good enough? Why did you turn my sister against me and me against her? Was that part of the upwardly mobile plan as well?"

Marlene glanced at Angela with a hard look, mixed with a flash of pain and regret. "You . . . I . . . I loved your father." Her voice broke. "Loved him more than life itself. I wanted so much for him, so much for us." Uncharacteristic tears flowed from her eyes. "But he never understood that. It didn't matter to him. He didn't understand the fears I had that would wake me up in the middle of the night, that the slightest slipup would toss us into the lifestyle I'd spent my whole life running from."

She turned away from the accusing eyes of her children. "The day he left nearly killed me. Said he couldn't take it anymore, the pushing, pushing. When I watched him walk away that afternoon I made a vow to myself that I would never love that way again, that I would never hope that way again. That I had to make a life for my children the best and only way I knew how."

She took a long shuddering breath. "And then I turned and looked at you, Angela, and saw the spitting image of your father: your eyes, your smile, the way you held your hands, the texture of your hair, the way you were always so self-contained. And . . . and my heart seemed to close up and stop beating . . .'cause I knew I could never love like that again. Never."

Marlene turned and slowly walked out of the room and up the stairs. "You wanted answers. You have them. I hope you're happy. Now, I want the both of you to leave," she added when she'd reached the top. Moments later they heard her bedroom door slam shut.

Shaken by the admissions, the vehemence and then remorse with which they were given, the sisters rode back to Gayla's house in silence. Memories of the scene with their mother obscured any immediate comments they could make. Upon arrival they both found excuses to squirrel themselves away in their rooms and the balance of the day and night were spent in relative quiet.

In each bedroom Gayla and Angela flipped through the pages of their lives, the roles that their parents had played in the women that they'd become, and they wondered with a shiver if blood was indeed thicker than water and, if it was, just how much of their mother's ran through their veins.

Seventeen

The balance of Angela's stay was spent with her nursing her cold, Gayla nursing her wounds, and the sisters nursing each other. Not in big ways with long proclamations of love and friendship, but in the little things: a smile, a touch, a shared memory. They didn't talk much about the things their mother had said. There was no need. In their own minds they had to make individual choices to finally let go of the past and move toward the future.

When Tiffany returned she couldn't have been happier to see her mother and aunt laughing and joking with each other, but Angela was closemouthed on the way to the train station about what had transpired. "That's for you and your mom to talk about," was all she said.

Angela hugged her niece tightly against her as her train was being announced. "Thank you for asking me to come. I'm really glad I did." She stepped back and held her niece at arm's length. "Give your mom a chance, sweetie. She's really someone special. Get to know her."

"You're a completely different person since you've gotten home," Mark said as he stroked Angela's cheek.

"I feel like a different person," she said, turning onto her side to look into her husband's eyes. "So much has happened. For the first time in my life I don't feel guilty, I don't feel unworthy, I don't feel as if everything that was wrong with my family was somehow my fault . . ."

Bit by bit Angela explained to Mark the talks that she and Gayla had, the awakenings, and, most important, the revelations of her mother.

"I'm glad I went."

"I'm glad you went, too, babe." He kissed her tenderly.

Angela propped herself up on her elbow. "You know, I was thinking . . . that maybe before we get too old we should . . . try working on that baby."

A smile like sunshine after a storm bloomed across Mark's handsome face. "Are you sure?"

"Positive."

"Then I think we shouldn't waste any more time," he said, tenderly covering her body with his.

THREE MONTHS LATER

"I thought we could do something special to celebrate your birthday, and," Mark added, gently stroking her flat stomach, "our soon-to-be new addition."

Angela reached up and kissed his lips. She wrapped her arms around his neck.

The doorbell rang.

Mark's expression brightened. "I do believe your surprise has arrived," he said, bowing gallantly before heading to the door.

Angela's eyes widened in utter astonishment to see Gayla, Tiffany, *and* her mother standing on the other side of the door.

"What . . . How . . . ," she stuttered.

Gayla stepped in first and wrapped her sister in a warm embrace. "Happy birthday, old lady." She kissed her cheek and whispered in her ear, "Listen to what she has to say."

"Happy birthday, Auntie," Tiffany said, kissing her aunt's cheek.

Marlene stood there facing her daughter, the first time they'd seen each other since the scene at her house. Tentatively she stepped forward, the first time in Angela's recollection that she'd seen her mother unsure.

Marlene took a breath. "Happy birthday, Angie."

"T-hanks, Mom."

"I hope this can be the start of many more that we can . . . share together. If you'll let me."

Angela extended her hand to her mother. Marlene clasped it tightly in hers, tears shimmering in her eyes.

"Nothing would make me happier," Angela whispered, and pulled her mother against her, all the years of hurt slipping away.

Gayla slid her arm around Tiffany's waist and she hugged her mother back.

"Can a brother get some love up in here?" Mark asked, looking from one teary-eyed face to the other.

Amid giggles and tears of joy, a family was united. Mother and daughters found a new path to follow, husband and wife created a new generation, and two sisters secured a bond that could never truly be broken.

Loving Lola

Carmen Green

One

FOUR-FIFTY-EIGHT P.M.

There were days like this, when life rested in the balance of two minutes, when time seemed interminable and freedom just out of reach.

Sandra Fagan sat center square in a tic-tac-toe of beige metal desks on the fifth floor of Stratton Property and Casualty and watched the second hand on the clock seemingly slow down.

Two minutes until fifty-two hours of freedom. Sandra buried a sigh, feeling like a convict with a weekend pass.

Normally she wouldn't care about leaving so close to five, but tonight was special. Today was her thirty-fourth birthday, and she and her nephew had plans.

The black phone on her desk pealed, and several of her peers gave her sympathetic looks, knowing how badly she wanted to leave.

The clock flashed 4:59.

"Don't play," she said in a voice that would make even a mugger think twice. The likeliest practical joker threw up his hands and nodded toward his cradled phone. Ben Everest, top left of her center square, stood and gave her his best smile. Her blood pulsed at a steady rate through her veins. He wasn't the one.

The phone rang again.

"If you let me, I could make your birthday a happy one," Ben said.

Regretfully, Sandra slid her shoulder bag down her arm and reached for the phone. "Have a nice weekend, Ben.

Stratton Property and Casualty, Sandra Fagan, how can I help you?"

"Sandra!" her sister, Lola, exclaimed. "It's me, baby. Surprise!"

Sandra didn't bother to wade into the verbal depths of Lola's effervescent greeting. Her thoughts were elsewhere. Not on the disappointing bend in Ben's retreating back, but on her blistered plans. Any call from Lola involved a to-do list for Sandra. *Not tonight,* she pleaded silently. *Give me this one night.* "What's up, Lola?"

Lola's voice exploded into her ear. "Girl, I've switched with another flight attendant and will have a layover in New York, so guess what? Lola's coming to town!"

"Oh."

"Is that all I get is an 'oh'? Sandra, you can be so dry sometimes. Why not 'Lola, it'll be so good to see you; I'd love to hear what's new in your life. Come on up; I miss you.' 'Oh' just ain't cuttin' it."

She gave Lola what she was asking for. "I *would* love to see you, but I kind of had plans for this evening." Guilt invaded her conscience as she put her sister off. For years they'd been all each other had. But Lola had long ago chosen to live a life filled with parties, fun, and men. A life so different from Sandra's, night and day bore a closer resemblance.

From childhood Sandra had been designated the responsible sister, and five years ago that responsibility had increased to include guardianship of Lola's newborn son, Brian. Sandra knew it was selfish, but tonight she wanted it to just be her and Brian.

"Where are you going on a school night?" Lola said, surprise raising her voice.

"Tomorrow's Saturday. But Brian does have a play date from nine to twelve." *She doesn't even remember it's my birthday.* "By the way, he's fine."

"My little man is always fine. I'll bet he's too cute." Motherly pride softened Lola's voice as if the simple yet complex act of combining sperm and egg were all it took to make the perfect child.

"He's very bright, too. Looks aren't everything."

Lola's laughter tickled the inside of Sandra's ear and danced on her patience nerve.

"You're right, but they go a long way! I'll see you tonight about nine."

"Where are you?"

"Cincinnati. I'll get to New York in about an hour, but I've got to handle some business first."

Irritated over the inevitability of Lola's visit, Sandra stopped a feeling of helplessness from stealing more than a corner of her soul. She and Brian had plans to eat a quick dinner, then head over to see a special performance by the Alvin Ailey Dance Troupe. Sandra had it timed for them to make it back right at eight and for Brian to be tucked in bed a half hour later. To keep him up on the possibility that Lola might make an appearance was a lot to ask.

"Since you're not already here, why don't we do this tomorrow? It'd be much better for *us*."

"No. I have to take care of something tonight and then I want to see Brian."

Sandra drew back. "What's so urgent you can't see him tomorrow?"

"Because I want to today," Lola quipped, sarcastic.

Irritated, Sandra snapped back, "Lola, you haven't been here in two months, and now all of a sudden you need to see your son. You should have thought of that when you disappointed him the last time."

"I've already apologized for that. What else can I say? Okay, I've been irresponsible in the past, but I'm different now. I want to change your mind about who I am and I want to show you and him I'm serious about being a better mother."

Sandra closed her eyes real slow.

Somewhere deep inside she was sure Lola believed what she was saying. But she'd never been responsible for Brian.

From the hospital he'd been with Sandra. Visiting him once every two months did not a parent make.

But what if this was the time Lola would start to shoulder her responsibility and become a fit mother? Did Sandra have a right to deny her?

If Lola made an honest effort, would that heal the canyon-sized rift that separated them?

A part of Sandra wanted to connect with her sister. Wanted to recapture the love from their youth and use it to bond their adult relationship. Along the way they'd separated like the end of a strand of hair, two parts of a whole that didn't seem capable of joining again.

"Sandra, if I didn't have business to take care of, I'd come over straight from JFK. I promise."

Sandra's grip tightened on the phone. "You promised before. No, Lola." Sandra's heart wasn't in the refusal, and she knew Lola knew.

"I'll be there," she promised.

In her usual way, Lola worked beneath Sandra's skin and burrowed close to her heart. She closed her eyes and heard Lola's voice as it cajoled her.

"I really miss you guys, and I don't understand why he can't be a little late for bed. Please, Sandra."

"Are you staying over?"

"I—I've got a noon flight tomorrow." Lola's springboard response was so quick, Sandra almost couldn't believe the words she was hearing. "I know you two have to leave, so I thought I'd stay at the hotel."

"Stop." Spontaneous anger rose in Sandra and bitter words raced to her lips. "Don't disrupt Brian's world just to assuage your guilt over not seeing him. You come, you stay, you take him to his friend's, and you give him every reason to know you love him or don't bother to set one foot on our doorstep."

Seconds of tense silence echoed through the phone lines. "Ok." Surrender echoed in Lola's voice. "I want to be there. I *will* be there."

Sandra glanced at the clock. Five-eleven P.M. She'd just missed the train. What the hell? The weekend was already shot. "Fine."

A quiet moment passed between them. "You make raising Brian look so easy," Lola said.

"Sometimes it is. Most times not." They spoke with the politeness of supermarket strangers.

"You could help me if you wanted to."

A pained smile pulled at Sandra's mouth, the simplicity with which her sister asked for some more of her life galling. A parent wasn't something she was; it was what she'd had to become in order for her nephew to have a good start in life. Lola would never understand that and Sandra couldn't explain it. "Be at the apartment at nine. Don't be late."

Two

Plastic wrap molded to Sandra's fingers as she folded it around the remainder of her birthday cake before placing it in the refrigerator.

As birthdays went, this one wasn't bad. She tried to cheer herself with reminders that she had her health, a steady job that paid the bills, and a happy nephew. But as she flipped off the kitchen light and walked into the small living room, her thoughts gravitated toward what evaded her.

She turned on a CD of Afro-Caribbean music, a birthday present to herself, and let the music seep into her bones. Without thinking, she stretched her arm high, contracted her chest, and spun on the ball of her foot, imitating the Alvin Ailey dancers. The performance came back in full color, and Sandra lost herself, copying the movements from memory.

"Aunt Saaan-dra, I'm ready for my story."

Reality crumpled her arch until she stood with both feet solidly on the floor. Sandra straightened the silky top over her black slacks. "Coming. Just a second."

It took several minutes to reorient herself as enthusiastic beats from the drums filled the room but now seemed out of place.

With a flick, she silenced the stereo and headed down the hall. The clock chimed on the half hour. Lola was thirty minutes late. Good thing she hadn't told Brian about his mother coming. The heartbreak would have been too intense.

Inside the room, the little boy was waist-deep in book choices. Sandra chose one.

"So what's it going to be tonight?"

"A long one. How about this one?" He held up a book they hadn't even started in hopes of delaying his bedtime, but well aware of his tricks, Sandra took the book and placed it on his bedside table.

"Not tonight, bud. In the morning you're going over to Mussa's house, and if you don't fall asleep, tomorrow won't get here."

"Yea!" Brian's enthusiastic response was what she'd hoped for.

"So we skip thc story?"

"No." His brown eyes pleaded. "Just a short one."

Sandra tucked the covers around his body and lovingly stroked the satiny skin on his arms. He was absolutely precious, and she cherished him. "You're the light of my life."

His little hands took her face, and he kissed her on the forehead. "You're a sweet girl, too."

She chuckled and tickled his side. "You can be so mannish sometimes. Where did you get that from?"

"Mussa's father. He says that to the new baby they brought home from the store."

Sandra crossed her legs, her cheek on her fist. "She didn't come from a store. Mrs. Muhammad had her at the hospital."

Brian shook his head emphatically. "Uh-uh. Mussa's father said there were showers and they had to hurry and go to the register. They probably got her from the Arabian store down the street. They have doll babies on aisle five. Mussa said so."

Sandra held her laughter as she made sense out of Brian's story. She didn't have the energy to explain what a baby shower was, nor the concept of registering for gifts.

Sneaking a peek at her watch, she swallowed the sudden lump of disappointment, lifted a book from the stack, and opened the cover. “How about Mufasa and his beautiful daugh—”

The doorbell rang, halting her words.

“Somebody’s here.” Brian threw his legs over the side of the bed and was halfway to the floor before she caught him.

“Put on your slippers and robe.”

“I can get up?”

“You’re already there, aren’t you?”

With a pat on the bottom, Brian sprang down and scurried after Sandra, who was already in the hallway.

“Wait for me.” He grabbed her hand and tugged her forward. “Who is it?” he yelled, excited to have been given the special treat of being up very late.

“Open the door and find out.” Lola’s voice was filled with awe as it pushed through from the other side.

“Mommy?”

Sandra held tight to Brian’s hand and on an impulse knelt, and reached for him. He struggled against her hug.

“Open the door; Mommy’s here!”

Sharp pangs of hurt stabbed through Sandra and she released him instantly. He stumbled into the door, reaching for the knob.

Sandra stood and released the top three locks, leaving the fourth for Brian’s nimble fingers.

“Mommy!” He launched himself at Lola and Sandra could only stand and watch mother and child.

Lola looked great. She’d changed from her flight attendant’s uniform to a chunky sleeveless sweater, and soft cream leather pants that molded her frame. She’d dropped to her knees to hug Brian, packages forgotten at her feet.

To Sandra’s surprise, Lola carried him inside, tears on her cheeks.

Sandra retrieved the packages and leaned them against the counter and gave Lola and Brian some space.

Brian giggled happily when Lola spun him around.

"Gosh, little man, you've gotten so big I can hardly pick you up."

"I eat a lot!"

"I'm so glad to see you," she cooed as she caressed his face. She kissed his forehead and stroked his fine curly hair. "What a big boy you are."

He squirmed under his mother's attention. "You already said that."

Spontaneous laughter bubbled from Lola. "So I did. And you're smart, too. I brought you something special."

"Lola," Sandra interjected, but stopped as Lola talked over her.

"But you can only have it if Auntie Sandra says so. I don't want to break any rules."

Frustration worked into Sandra's bones. Why did she always have to be the bad guy? Brian's room was filled with *special surprises* from Lola's travels, so much so, Sandra recently had spent a full day weeding out the toys he didn't play with anymore and sent them to the Salvation Army. The room was livable again, but now here was more stuff.

"I thought we had an agreement about gifts? Just birthdays and Christmas?"

Lola sashayed over, enveloping Sandra in a big hug. "I didn't think you'd mind. It's just a little something."

"Lola, that's not the point. Don't try to buy his affection." She lowered her voice, not having the heart to curb the zeal with which Brian searched the various bags.

Lola looked at her and Sandra felt as if they'd been transported back fifteen years and she were preaching the virtue of wearing a skirt past her upper thigh.

"What other choice do I have," Lola said matter-of-factly. "I never see him."

"We've lived here for five years and the door still swings open. You've got to do better than that."

For a moment, Lola seemed to reflect on a distant memory. "I needed to get my life together."

From head to foot, Lola was flawless. Her clothes were flyy, her hair half-braided and curled, and her makeup perfect. But with firsthand experience, Sandra knew of the imperfections beneath the finely decorated wrappings, so she wasn't inclined to be impressed with Lola's declaration.

"You could see him more often if you wanted to."

"I do want to. That's why I'm here."

Brian pulled out an action figure and squealed in delight.

"Just look at his face. How can you say no?"

Ecstatic, he threw his arms around Lola's legs. "Thank you, Mommy."

As Sandra stared down into her nephew's eyes, pure adoration radiated. Her throat filled and her eyes smarted with tears. Brian wasn't looking at her.

As if on autopilot, Sandra grabbed the dishcloth and began wiping the already-clean counter. Anything to not have to look into the face of the child she had raised.

"Do you like it, Aunt Sandra?"

She blinked several times before finding her voice. "It's very nice. Let's get you settled in bed and you can play with your toy for five minutes before lights-out."

"Aw. That's not enough time." He stomped his feet and Lola backed away. It was as if she knew what was coming.

Sandra walked over and extended her hand. "Give me the toy."

Brian tried to make eye contact with Lola, but she'd turned to study a crack in the wall. *Figures.*

When he realized he would only be dealing with his aunt, he put the toy in her hand and hung his head.

"Brian, if you don't like the rules, you can lose the toy until tomorrow and go to bed now. Your choice. Five minutes of playtime, or you can try again tomorrow."

Again his eyes strayed to Lola, who looked at Sandra and then back at her son. The air was thick as both waited for her to say something. "Honey, Auntie Sandra's right. I understand you have a play date tomorrow. If you don't get to sleep, you won't be able to share your toy with your friend."

Brian shuffled his feet, then looked up. "Sorry."

On instinct Sandra reached out and stroked his head. "You're forgiven. How about if Mommy tucks you in?"

His face lit up and he stood on the tips of his toes. Sandra bent and hugged him, placing a kiss on his cheek. "Good night, sweetheart."

Lola and Brian walked off hand in hand, and Sandra took the few minutes to gather herself.

She fixed a soothing cup of tea and prepared a cup for Lola. Tension had tightened her shoulders, and she massaged them but stopped when she heard the soft click of Brian's bedroom door closing.

Lola's spike heel tapped the wooden floor as she tipped up the hallway and into the living room. "He's already asleep."

Sandra glanced at the clock. "I'm surprised he didn't beg to stay up for another five minutes."

Lola sat on the couch and crossed her long legs. A gold ring encircled her second toe. "I explained to him that I was staying over and we'd have a chance to spend some time together in the morning."

Drawing back in surprise, Sandra reached for her tea. "Wow. So you're actually going to stay."

"I said I was. Why the funny face?"

She shrugged. "You're not known for following your word to the letter."

"I've changed." Lola sounded mature, causing Sandra to look real hard at her.

"I get the feeling this isn't just a social visit. Why did you drop by?"

Lola placed her teacup on the saucer and positioned her fingertips against her mouth as if she were praying. "I never could keep things from you."

Sitting forward, Sandra regarded her sister. "Spit it out. What's going on?"

"I'm getting married." A bright smile lifted Lola's cheeks and her long curly hair bounced happily. "His name is Randy Bivens and he's the most wonderful man I've ever met in my life. He adores me."

"Is that why he's so wonderful?"

"He *loves* me unconditionally."

The tea turned bitter on Sandra's tongue. She'd made the ultimate sacrifice of love by putting aside her dreams to raise Brian. If that wasn't unconditional love, she didn't know what was.

But marriage?

She'd seen Lola two and a half months ago and she'd made it clear there was no one special in her life. In that rare moment they'd shared wine and listening to Angie Stone, they'd bonded, sharing intimacies and marveling over the strangeness of life.

Lola had just been dumped by her boyfriend of six months and she'd professed then that in the next man she dated she was looking for only two things: a big wallet and a big dick.

Sandra had laughed, mellowed by the wine, a small part of her connecting with Lola's crudity. She, too, had met men whose "hit it and quit it" lifestyle disagreed with her self-contained existence. But she'd still hoped to one day have a man who took care of business not only on his job but in the bedroom as well. "He must be impressive in bed."

"It isn't about sex," Lola said, then laughed. "Well, he does take care of business in that department, but it's more." She caressed the column of her neck, a chunky university ring on the third finger of her left hand. "I sound so corny, I can't explain it."

Rising, Lola's leather pants swished as she walked.

"How long have you known him?"

"Two months."

"And you're getting married?" Sandra didn't try to hide her disbelief. "You're not pregnant, are you?"

"Hell, no!"

"Shush!"

Lola ducked her head and covered her mouth. "I don't want any babies right now. I'm still young."

"I guess you would be since I'm raising your son."

The mood shifted as if a heater had been turned on high. For an instant, Sandra regretted the words. She prided herself on being levelheaded and strong, but her mouth spoke what her heart had held inside for so long.

"How many times do I have to say thank you?" Disgust sharpened Lola's tone, giving insight to the level of selfishness she possessed. "How many ways? I wasn't ready for a baby five years ago and you stepped in and helped me. Damn! What else do you want me to say?"

Sandra couldn't answer her, because she couldn't sum up the extent of what she wanted from her sister.

"What do you want from me, Sandra?"

"I want you to be happy and healthy and I want you to find whatever it is you're looking for. I want you to come to see your son more often and maybe one day share in raising him. Marrying a man you've known for two months is a mistake."

"We know each other so well. It's like every day I've known him has been a year. He's smart and funny and savvy and generous." She meet Sandra's gaze. "It's real."

Sandra shook her head, trying to head off Lola's next colossal failure. "You're being impetuous and at this point in your life, can you afford to be making these types of mistakes?"

"Our love isn't a mistake."

"Then if you won't think of yourself, think of Brian. He doesn't need to see you parading around with another man like the last two you brought over. Do you think he doesn't have questions about his father and why he lives with me instead of you? Fortunately, he's accepted his situation, but don't you think he'll resent you marrying someone and maybe one day having other children that live with you?"

"I've thought of that. Randy and I have spent hours on nothing but what's best for Brian."

A sudden and engulfing fear crawled over Sandra's skin, leaving chills. "What do you mean, 'what's best'? He's with me, happy and healthy. What more is there?"

With each step Lola took toward Sandra, her anxiety grew. Lola had that "I'm about to drop a bombshell" look on her face. Sandra had already seen it once before. The night Lola confessed to being pregnant with Brian.

Lola's hands were warm when they engulfed hers. Sandra pulled away. "You've been wonderful for taking care of my son, being there when I needed you most and helping me through a tough time in my life."

A bark of laughter shot from Sandra. "Was that the first twenty-four or the last five years of your life? I've been taking care of you since you were born."

"I know and God knows I needed it, especially after I had Brian. Caring for him was such a big job for me."

Sandra modified her tone, trying to lessen the sting in her words. "Lola, you never wanted the responsibility of caring for Brian. In just the last year, you've finally taken responsibility for yourself. So why are you in my face acting like you're about to divulge a world secret?"

"I'd hoped this would be easier, but there's just no easy way. Randy and I are getting married over the Fourth of July holiday."

"That's five weeks away."

"Right and . . . and we want Brian to come live with us."

Sandra rose on unsteady legs and backed away from her sister. "What?"

"I'm getting married and I want custody of my son."

Three

Sandra had dreamed this nightmare ten thousand times since she'd assumed guardianship of Brian. She held her chest, shell-shocked, as if the victim of a catastrophic violation. Why hadn't she seen this coming?

Lola had done it again. With a casual twist to her hips, a flip of her mass of curls, she'd upended Sandra's life again.

Instinctively Sandra's muscles bunched, ready to do battle. "You're crazy if you think I'm going to give him up."

Eyes bright, Lola shook her head firmly. "He's my son."

"Your throwaway son," Sandra corrected her. "You couldn't even look at him, or hold him, or kiss him when he was born. He's beautiful, Lola, as you so eloquently announce each time you see him. He looks just like you. Beautiful wavy hair. A warm smile that could melt a heart at a hundred paces. An incredible spirit." She grabbed her sister by the arm and forced Lola to look into her eyes.

"You wanted nothing to do with him until now so you can parade him in front of your new boyfriend like he's a prize trophy." Helpless anger shook Sandra and she steadied her voice. "Why can't you leave him alone and go on with your life as you have been?"

Lola yanked her arm away. "You don't own the market on loving Brian. I've always loved him. Right from the beginning, but you're right about one thing."

"What's that?"

"When I was in the hospital, I was in pain from childbirth, but also from the disappointment that Brian's father didn't want me or him." Her eyes welled. "I just knew he'd come to us. Once he saw Brian, he'd fall in love with him."

"Life isn't a fantasy, Lola. Raising him isn't a temp job you have the option of showing up for. Brian's a person who enjoys a routine and existence here in New York with me. He has friends and a network of people who care for him and have since the day he arrived."

"He can have that with me, too." Defensively Lola turned away and raised her hand. Sandra knew she was rubbing her forehead. Lola hated pressure but never knew how much she inflicted upon others.

"I'm nearly thirty years old and in the last five years I've become a woman. Sandra, I've grown up. I know more now than before. I don't make foolish mistakes."

"What's so different today than in January when we had the hearing before Judge Amos? You said then you weren't ready."

"That was months ago. I've changed." Unable to express herself, Lola flopped on the couch, her hands stabbing the air. "I just know better."

"How could you when you've never really dealt with Brian before? How would you handle a supermarket tantrum? Or a parent-teacher conference with the topic being 'Is Brian well adjusted?' "

Defensive again, Lola jumped up, streetwise energy pounding through her. "What they trying to say? There isn't anything wrong with my son."

Sandra stared at her. "He'd wrapped himself around the leg of a visiting father and asked him if he could be his daddy, too."

Shocked disbelief had Lola making unintelligible noises.

"What would you do?" Sandra let the silence stretch, waiting for an answer.

Before her eyes, Lola deflated. Her hands journeyed through her hair to no definite destination as her eyes reflected insecurity and fear. She tucked her chin and her shoulders jerked.

"If it makes you feel better, I'll admit it. I don't know."

Victory raced through Sandra. This was all going to blow over. She used to think Lola would grow out of her selfish ways after their parents had died eighteen years ago, leaving the girls alone. Instead Lola had become wilder, taking pleasure in doing things that went against the grain of their aunt and uncle's middle-class lifestyle. And although Lola had matured in many ways, some things remained the same. She was still impetuous and unrealistic.

"I want to do this."

Sandra just looked at her. "Becoming an instant mother doesn't work. You've never spent more than a few hours alone with Brian since he was born. You don't know anything about him."

Bitterness flashed in Lola's eyes. "I know I've missed the first mother joys. His first steps, his first fall. His first teeth and his first words. Those memories and the last five years belong to you, Sandra. I don't want to cut you out of his life, but it's time for me to raise my son. Randy and I want Brian."

"How would he know anything about Brian?" Sandra exploded. "The boy isn't a robot: add batteries and you have the perfect toy. What if your son doesn't like your new boyfriend? Then what? Are you going to leave him?"

"Who, Randy?" Lola's head swung. "Never. We love each other."

Sandra raised her eyebrows. "That's the dedication you should feel toward your son."

"I will. I mean, I do," she stumbled. "I'm giving my son something neither of us can be."

"And what's that?"

"A father."

Once again the silence was almost as engulfing as the news. Sandra stared at Lola, wondering if anything she'd said was sinking in. "You met a man two months ago and now, sixty days later, you want him to become the father of your son."

"It sounds unbelievable, but I love him, and he loves

me, and he'll love Brian. We want to be a family."

"How old is this guy? Does he have children?"

"He's thirty-eight and yes, he has a daughter that's eighteen."

"I take it she doesn't live with him."

"She lives with her mother. I've met them and they're happy for us. I don't see why you can't be."

Sandra lifted her forgotten cup of tea and emptied it.

"If it were just your life, I'd wish you well. But Brian has been my responsibility for five years." Sandra didn't want to tear Lola down, but the truth had to be told. "Ever since Mom and Dad died, you chose a path of self-indulgence and self-destruction. I'm afraid this may be another of those moments. I don't want Brian to be a casualty of your life."

Lola leaned forward, her gaze on her hands. "I never met a person who didn't have regrets for mistakes or unkind words or illegal acts or"—she looked her sister in the eye—"having a baby and giving it away. But as Daddy used to say, 'What doesn't kill you will make you strong.' I've learned from my failures. I am who I am because of them."

"Dragging Brian into what could be your biggest failure—"

"Or success."

Sandra conceded with a nod. "I can't let it happen."

"Brian's father agrees with me."

Sandra's stomach dropped and she held onto her cup with a death grip. "You've discussed this with Wendell."

On more solid ground, Lola moved confidently across to her bag and pulled out an envelope. Smug, she lifted her chin. "That's why I couldn't come over directly from the airport. He signed over full custody to me and agreed to let Randy adopt Brian."

"You've got it all worked out, don't you," Sandra said, feeling stripped of power. She searched her soul for more strength to fight for the family she'd worked so hard to save.

"You always said I never think things through." Lola's face was rounded, gloating, proud. "Not this time. I've got a man to love, and he accepts my son. Wendell has agreed to give up custody." She shrugged. "And now there's you."

The legal document Lola had laid on Sandra's lap fluttered to the floor, landing on her toes. She felt the prickle of the paper but didn't want to touch it.

Lola was talking, but Sandra only heard the rush of the ocean in her ears. She focused hard.

"We want you and Brian to come to Martha's Vineyard and spend some time with us. We want the transition to be smooth for him, and if you're there to help ease the way he should be all right."

Two packets of papers were nudged into Sandra's limp hands. "We'd hoped you could come up on Sunday and stay the week."

"What? No. I have a job. I can't make instant decisions where my livelihood is concerned. Besides, Brian has school."

"Sandra, he won't start kindergarten until the fall, so that's not an issue. Don't you have four weeks of vacation?"

"You come in here with the most shocking news of my life, and now you're trying to act as my personal travel agent. What *don't* you do?"

Lola regarded her long and hard. Sandra knew she'd broken the unspoken rules of fighting fair, but dammit, what Lola was doing wasn't fair.

She gathered her bags and moved toward the door, digging inside her purse as she went.

"Where are you going?"

"To a hotel. I've had enough of this crap for one day and I don't want to say something I'll regret. We both need to think about what's happening and how we're going to deal with it." Stepping away from the door, Lola dropped an envelope on the table. Sandra stared at it, too afraid of the bombshell within.

"You promised Brian you'd be here."

"Do you want me here?" Lola demanded.

Sandra avoided speaking the truth. "Don't disappoint your son."

Lola nodded. "I'll be back at eight."

The front door closed and the whirlwind that surrounded Sandra's sister's arrival had transformed into stale, dank air.

Bad news always had that effect.

The white envelope stayed on the table as Sandra stumbled from the couch and into the kitchen. She moved on autopilot, straightening until she realized her actions were a useless waste of energy. Sandra clamped back her shoulder-length hair and wished she could clear her mind.

The impossibility of the action reiterated what she knew she had to do. The white envelope held the secrets to her future. She had to open it.

The night-light cast a shadowy glow over the hallway as sounds from the city shimmered against the darkness. Distant sirens wailed against honks from impatient drivers, the door below slammed, and murmurs of lovers greeting each other bounced off the walls.

Even with the sounds, she still heard the swish of her stocking feet slide against the floor on her way back into the living room. "She won't win. This is going away." Sandra's back cracked when she bent down and reached for the envelope.

Carefully she turned on the lamp, slid her index finger beneath the envelope flap and across, held her breath, and let the contents slide into her hand.

Two round-trip tickets to Martha's Vineyard dated for the following Sunday and a return date of July 5. The day after the wedding.

Four

The distraction of going to work Monday did Sandra good. It kept her mind off Lola's bombshell. In the wee hours of the morning, she finally decided she and Brian weren't going to Martha's Vineyard. Lola's life had been her own for five years, and it would remain that way.

Although bleary-eyed and tired, Sandra listened to claimant Abigail Rogers. Two weeks ago Abigail's house had burned down, and Stratton Property and Casualty was the insurer. The woman called each day sounding depressed, which didn't improve Sandra's blue mood today.

"Ms. Rogers, have you gone to see the counselor I recommended?"

"Too sad to go out of this hotel."

"How do you eat?"

"Red Cross man brings me food before he goes home."

"You've got to stop that," she chastised gently. "You could get him in trouble. Why not try the temporary housing?"

"I don't like the area. I'm too old to fight for my purse. Besides, I'm fat. I could stand to lose a few pounds."

Sandra chuckled, glad the woman's sense of humor had snuck through. "Do you have any family you could stay with for a few weeks?"

"Got a brother in San Francisco. My sister lives an hour away, but we fell out fifteen years ago. Can't even recall what it was about," she remarked with regret. "We don't see each other unless somebody dies."

"You could change that now. Make the first move." The words tripped over Sandra's tongue and she hated feeling like a hypocrite. "Give her a chance. Fifteen years is a long time to hold a grudge."

A long sigh seeped through the phone. "Maybe I'll call. Are you going to call about my check?"

"Right away. I'm also going to look into a nicer place for you to live until your house is rebuilt. Hotel living is too expensive."

"I guess so," Abigail agreed reluctantly. "You will call about the check, right?"

Sandra nodded; the daily phone calls seemed to be the only thing the woman had right now. "I already promised I would. Have a good day, Ms. Rogers, and go outside. It's pretty out today."

"Alrighty. OK. Bye."

Sandra hung up and waited a few seconds, knowing Ms. Rogers would call back. Sandra caught her supervisor's eye and indicated with a flick of her finger that they needed to talk.

The woman held up two, telling Sandra to give her a couple minutes. *Enough time to grab a cup of coffee,* Sandra thought as she started toward the break room, stopping when her phone rang.

Her body shook, tired and in need of the daily caffeine fix. Sandra debated letting voice mail pick up but decided against it. "Sandra Fagan."

"It's me."

Lola's voice came through clear, low, and intense.

Tension filled Sandra as her patience took a nosedive.

Lola probably wanted an answer, and Sandra didn't want to have the discussion while at work. "I really don't have time to deal with you right now."

"I know you're busy, but I wanted to say a couple of things."

A heavy sigh crept past Sandra's lips, and she dropped her chin to her chest. She rubbed at the stiffness in her neck and took slow steps back to her chair. "Talk fast. I've got a conference with my boss in two minutes."

"Happy birthday."

Sharp laughter caught the attention of Sandra's closest desk mate, and she lowered her voice, resting her head on her fist. "What made you think of that?"

"I won't lie. Randy reminded me."

"He doesn't even know me."

"I know, but we put all important dates in the computer and he reminded me over a week ago, but I guess it just slipped my mind. I'm sorry."

Taken aback, Sandra sat silent. "If this is a trick—"

"Why the hell would I do that?"

On familiar ground with Lola's sometimes-abrasive attitude, Sandra prepared to end the conversation. "If you think a lame apology is going to weaken my resolve, think again."

Sniffles filtered through the phone, shocking Sandra, and she stopped moving, focusing on her sister's voice. "I've never begged for anything, but, Sandra, I'm begging now. I want you to come to Martha's Vineyard. Spend some time with us. See how we live so you can know Brian's going to be all right."

"Why are you doing this?" Sandra whispered, close to tears.

"I've said it and I'll say it again. I love him. I want him there, but I want you there, too. Please, Sandra. Please."

"This is ridiculous."

"No, it's not. I'm for real. Randy, too. I promise I'll listen to you, and you can teach me about my son. What do you say, please, Sandra?"

Tears trickled down Sandra's face. Her sister had done three things in the past two minutes she'd never done. She never apologized, she never begged, and she never cried. Lola's attitude Sandra understood, but she felt defenseless against her baby sister's tears. Something inside pushed and Sandra gave in.

"Okay," she whispered, her voice full. "But no guarantees."

"Thank you," Lola cried. "You don't know how much this means to me."

"Yeah, I do." Sandra searched for a tissue. This was the first time the sisters had cried together in what seemed a lifetime. "I've got to go arrange the time off. We'll be there Sunday."

"Thank you."

Sandra couldn't fix her mouth to reciprocate. The receiver slipped from her fingers, clanging into the cradle. Sandra took a minute to compose herself, mopped her face, and went to talk to her boss.

Five

Settling into her seat with Brian next to her, Sandra caught her breath.

Although the flight to Boston was completely booked, she prayed the passenger stuck in the row with them would not arrive. She needed to spread out, space to breathe, and perhaps a moment of privacy if the tears came. They'd deluded her all week, sneaking up at inopportune moments, burdening her spirit with a sadness she hadn't experienced since the deaths of her parents.

She needed her mom and dad today, she realized, wished for her father's steady voice of guidance to give her direction as to what to do. And she yearned for the warmth and comfort of her mother's arms, where solace lived eternal.

Sandra sniffed, the sting behind her eyes stark evidence that before this was over more tears would be shed and her heart would never be the same.

Unaware of her dilemma, Brian jumped on the seat beside her, peering over at the other passengers. "How many people are on this plane?"

"I don't know." She rubbed her nose with a tissue and patted his leg. "You're not at the gym."

"But I can't see if I sit down." He spun around, still standing, eyeing the controls over their heads. "Do you think my legs can touch the floor?"

"No."

"Is there a plane driver like a bus driver?"

Sandra pressed the aching nerve over her eye. "He's called a pilot. Now be quiet and sit down."

Passengers streamed by and filled empty seats around

them. Sandra prayed the occupant of the aisle seat in their row wouldn't show. *Please,* she begged. *I need this.*

A tall man, dressed in neatly creased camel-colored pants and a crisp beige shirt, approached. She held her breath when he stopped, lifted his computer bag, and pushed it into the overhead bin.

He eyed his ticket, then the seat she occupied, then sat one seat behind her.

"Ma'am, may I help you?" The flight attendant looked down on her with distracted eyes.

"No, thank you. I'm fine."

"You pressed your call button. This is the light indicator and this"—she tapped with a "duh" expression on her face—"is for the attendants. All passengers that have boarded should be seated with their seat belts securely locked in place. *All passengers.*" She eyed Brian, who was still standing on the seat, looking at her with an innocent smile on his face.

Flustered, Sandra took his hand firmly in hers and yanked him into his seat. She showed him bared teeth and snapped the belt in place. "Don't move again."

"My arm hurts where you pulled me," he whined just enough to capture the attention of the sympathetic senior crowd.

At home she would have threatened to hurt another part of his anatomy, but on the plane she used another tactic. "Would you like to color?"

"Mm-hmm," he whined, frowning. He earned a fixed stare and he muttered, "Yes, ma'am."

Looking around for the bag of goodies she'd brought, she realized she'd stowed it in the overhead bin. Standing, she didn't reexamine her response to Brian, even in the face of the unfriendly stares she was receiving from an elderly white couple.

Too bad, she thought, her attitude making her stare back until they looked away. *I'm not raising an animal.*

She opened the bin and stared at the large computer

case, reached on the side of it, and tugged on the handle of her cloth bag, but it wouldn't budge.

No one offered to help and the flight attendants stayed busy at the back and front of the plane. "Is this your case?" she asked several people, but they shook their heads or ignored her.

The seat behind her was vacant, so she pulled the case and was startled when it dislodged, hung in air with her hand on the handle, and then jerked her with swift force.

The case hit the ground with a sickening thud just as the man who had been seated behind her strode up the aisle. "What are you doing?"

"Your bag was blocking my bag."

He lifted his computer case and frowned. Deeply. "I hope you didn't break this."

"I hope so, too." Sandra grabbed her bag from the bin. "Would you like me to check?"

He shook it and items rattled and he glared at the crayons and coloring book Brian dug out, then at her. "You've done enough, thanks."

Grateful for the empty seat, she sat on the aisle and left Brian to his coloring by the window.

"Flight attendants, prepare for final boarding. Passengers, please obey the NO SMOKING and seat belt signs."

Sandra had settled back, glad they were almost under way, when the flight attendant escorted a harried couple up the aisle. Sandra peeked at them when they stopped and she opened her eyes fully when the attendant pulled out the manifest.

"Mark Turner?" the attendant eyed the man behind Sandra.

"Yes?"

"I believe you're in the wrong seat. You're in seat thirteen-C not fourteen-C."

When he stood, his height dwarfed the attendant and the eager couple waiting to be seated. Normally Sandra was attracted to tall men because of her five-foot, nine-inch height, but this Mark Turner reeked of intolerance and impatience. She smirked. "Take him to the back" she wanted to say but didn't. She'd already said enough for one day.

"Ms. Fagan," the attendant said, "you're in Mr. Turner's seat. Please take your correct seat and allow Mr. Turner to take his."

"Excuse me," Mark Turner said before Sandra rose. "Do you have anything in first class? I'd be glad to use miles for an upgrade."

"Sorry, sir this flight is already overbooked, and first class is full. Please take your seat so we can prepare to leave."

The couple settled behind them, oblivious to Sandra and Mark.

She glanced at him and he gestured. "After you."

It took her a few minutes to get Brian settled in the middle seat, but she finally stepped over him and sat down. Purposely keeping her eyes averted, Sandra didn't watch Mark sit but heard him.

"Excuse me. You're on my crayons."

"No, I'm not," he said to Brian and smiled.

"Yes, you are. Your butt is sitting on them."

Several people around them snickered and Sandra bit her lip. "Brian, keep your voice down and don't talk to adults that way. Now where did you put them?"

Tearfully he pointed. "On his seat."

Bracing his hand on the armrest, Mark seemed to struggle for patience. "I'll check." He removed the seat belt and stood.

"There they are! But"—Brian let out a long moan of disappointment—"they're broken."

"Is there a problem?" a male flight attendant asked firmly. He looked from the adults to the child with an air of disdain.

"No, we're fine," Mark said crisply.

"Then sit, buckle in, and don't move again."

Sandra's hand flew to her mouth and she caught a dangerous glint darken Mark Turner's coal black eyes.

"I'm taking care of my business, so you can go."

"Fine," the attendant said, each man backing down enough to prove his point had been made.

Mark strapped himself in and closed his eyes.

"Auntie, where do you go to the bathroom?"

Heat crept up Sandra's neck and she felt as if every eye on the plane were on her.

"Do you have to go?"

"No. So where do you go on the plane?"

She breathed a sigh of relief. "There are bathrooms in the back."

"Do we fly over houses?"

She stared out the window, glad when the plane began to taxi away from the gate. "Yes."

He colored contentedly as the lights were extinguished. Sandra closed her eyes, relishing the peace of those stolen few seconds.

Brian tugged her arm. "When you boo-boo and pee-pee on a plane, does it land on people's houses?"

Laughter rang out around them and Brian burst into delayed giggles.

"Okay, buddy," she said, totally embarrassed. "Enough with the questions. Color and keep it down."

"You've got tons on your mind?" Brian asked, borrowing one of her expressions.

"Yes. Shush."

The plane gathered speed as it raced down the runway. Suddenly it lifted into the air and broke through clouds that had rumbled all night but didn't deliver rain.

"I want something else to do."

Brian closed the coloring book and pushed the crayons into Sandra's hand. She did have a surprise waiting but hadn't planned to break it out until they'd been on the island for a couple of days. But today her nerves were stretched thin. She needed quiet time to think. She dug through two bags and came up with a video game.

The seat belt light extinguished, and some travelers pulled out laptops. To the delight of all, Brian was happy. Sandra inserted batteries, gave the game to him, and sat back.

Her eyes drifted closed and just as she entered the dream, she was tapped on her shoulder.

Sandra opened her eyes. "Can he turn the sound off?" Mark asked, bent over the tray table, staring up from the fractured computer screen. "It's very distracting."

She blinked slowly, not realizing she'd fallen asleep so fast. *Too much on my mind.*

The computer toy played musical songs as Brian pressed the buttons with nimble, quick fingers. "Is he really bothering you? I mean, he's being quiet, the questions have stopped, and he's focused. What do you think will happen when I turn the sound down?"

"I like the sound," Brian offered absently.

Mark's pointed look over Brian's head was directed at Sandra. She noticed how he spoke with quiet authority; that riled her. "You should have some consideration for the other passengers."

She leaned in, not wanting him to know how upset she truly was. "I'm doing everything I can to keep him quiet."

Mark had turned back to his computer. "Except turning down the game."

"Fine." Sandra took the game and fiddled with the sound button. It increased but wouldn't go down. Pushing and pressing, she worked with the toy but couldn't get the sound to lower.

Several nearby passengers pressed their signal buttons, and when the flight attendant appeared Sandra wasn't surprised at her annoyed expression.

"I can't get the sound down."

She laid the game in the woman's extended hand and watched her walk away. Sandra grimaced at Mark Turner, her guilt lessening in degrees as he hunched over his broken computer.

She sat back and had latched her seat belt when Brian's sniffles caught her attention. "What's wrong?"

"I don't have anything to do. Can we go home?"

His question brought back the reason for the short flight. They might never share a home again. She took his hand, held it. "We'll be there very soon."

"My ears hurts, Auntie."

Sandra rubbed his leg as he bumped it against the seat. "How about singing quietly to yourself while I find a snack."

"Okay." The bag was closer to Mark's leg, but she refused to ask for his help. Instead, she dragged it by the handles and reached through Brian's feet to dig inside.

At an awkward angle, Sandra noticed Mark looking at her, an odd expression on his face. A feather-light streak of awareness tingled down her spine.

Irritated with herself, she grasped the snacks, sat up, and realized he'd had an unobstructed view of her boobs.

Sandra readjusted, connected her seat belt, more aware of his masculinity than she cared to be. His fingers flew expertly over the keyboard.

"Get a cheap thrill?" she demanded coolly, watching him from the corner of her eye.

He never looked up. "I like my thrills willing and aware. Never cheap."

Brian started to clap and sing aloud and Sandra clamped her hand over his mouth and pierced him with a warning look. She dropped a plastic bag into his lap along with a napkin and a juice. "Eat, please."

The break in singing and conversation gave Sandra a chance to examine Mark. His legs were long, too long for the seat, but he made do and crunched them under the tray while he worked. He had the long, graceful hands of a maestro, she realized, liking them despite how she felt toward the man they belonged to.

Yet there was power in his conservative movements and confidence in the focused expression on his face.

"If I were a painting, what would you see?" he asked, his fingers working.

Sandra blushed, busted. "Not looking at you."

"Not?"

She averted her gaze to the window. "No."

This time, he gave her his complete attention and Sandra felt as if she'd been pushed from the plane and onto the wing. She was lying and he knew it and she knew he knew. He didn't utter a word but turned his attention back to the computer.

The flight attendant pushing the cabin service cart returned Brian's game, earning a loud and delighted yell from the child. "YIPPEE!"

The sound had been readjusted to the initial level and Brian began to play again. "Get it looked at," the attendant ordered, and hurriedly delivered snacks and drinks.

Sandra felt like crawling into a hole and dying. Brian was singing, playing the video game, and making so much noise he was practically a one-man entertainment show. Sandra leaned her head back and tried to ignore both her seat companions.

Brian perched the juice in his right hand, trying to balance it on his knee, and Sandra knew what was going to happen before she heard the yelp.

"He's getting red drink all over my pants!"

Her nephew looked mortified, and for the span of several heartbeats nobody moved. Sandra reacted first.

She took Brian by both his arms, brought him eye-level, and spoke. "Do not move again."

"Yes, ma'am," he croaked.

She grabbed napkins from a plastic bag and dropped them on Mark's lap. "I would swab you, but . . ."

"I should make you," he said, shaking his head. "But never mind."

"Flight attendants, prepare for landing."

She assessed the damage and could tell juice had run down his thigh and pant leg. More than likely the pants were ruined. As well as the computer. Weakened by the stress of the weekend, Sandra felt tears prickle, but as she dug into her purse for a card and a pen, she waited for the feelings of inadequacies and impotence to pass.

"I apologize for my nephew's behavior; this is his first flight. I would like to replace your computer and your pants. Here's the number of my insurance company. I'm sorry."

Sandra hadn't realized how close they were to landing until the wheels touched down and caused her to push back in her seat. Brian had fallen asleep in thc last few minutes, his cracker-filled hand resting on Mark's arm.

Guiltily she removed it and waited for the plane to taxi to the gate.

When Mark stood, her shame grew. Juice had run into the creases, looking like angry veins leading to his groin.

She looked up and straight into his eyes. "Take it." Sandra thrust the card into his hand.

He shook his head, watching as she gathered Brian and her carry-on bag into her arms.

"Being away from you two will be enough. Good-bye," he said and started up the aisle.

Six

Despite the plane ride, Sandra prayed to get to Martha's Vineyard, if only to be there. The bus ride from the airport to the ferry had been taxing with Brian wired, anxious to see his mother and her new home.

When the decision had been made that Sandra and Brian would come to the island, Sandra had struggled with how to tell Brian about his mother's fiancé.

Lola had wanted to tell Brian about his "new father," but Sandra had vetoed that, erring on the side of extreme caution.

Her sister had been known to go through men like water down a drain. If and when it was necessary to tell Brian of the marriage, the two women would find the words.

And when the questions came as to why he wouldn't live with Lola, Sandra knew she would have to find words for that also.

Brian stood by Sandra, straining to see land as the boat headed to Martha's Vineyard. "Are we there yet?"

"Not quite." She checked her watch. "Another twenty minutes."

"I'm hungry, Auntie."

"We're almost there."

"I'm still hungry."

A blond-haired boy about Brian's age, decked out in a pressed sailor suit, burst through the door in front of them.

He bounded up the stairs to their right, one at a time, when he suddenly stopped and turned. "I have permission to get a hot dog," he announced to everyone.

Several people snickered. A ship's officer rounded the corner ready to take the stairs.

He saluted the boy, who restated his earlier announcement. "Wait for your mother, then carry on."

The boy returned the salute, until the officer disappeared through the upper door. Then the boy bounded down the stairs and stopped in front of Brian.

"Are you hungry?"

"Yes!"

"They have hot dogs upstairs."

"I heard about that," Brian said as if amazed.

Sandra could barely contain herself.

Suddenly the female version of the boy walked through the door, her eyes pealed for the youngster. "Carlton Ulysses Hollister McArthur the Third. You are in big trouble."

"I was going to get a hot dog, ma'am," he stated, military-style. "And I found a friend who needs a hot dog, too."

Sandra watched as Brian saluted Carlton's mother, too. The woman's jaw worked; her lips sucked in, her head shaking as she contained her laughter. She was a definite blueblood, with pearls and heels, in expensive capri pants.

Passengers seated on the bench behind Sandra giggled quietly.

Sandra felt it best to take control. "Sandra Fagan and Brian. May we join you for lunch?"

The woman extended her hand and gave a warm, friendly shake. "Cassie McArthur. It would be my pleasure." She turned her attention to the boys. "Carry on, gentlemen."

Sandra grabbed the handle of their suitcase and reached for the other. "I'll get the bags."

Cassie motioned with a hand that wore a five-carat marquis diamond. "You can leave them; they'll be fine. Come up and enjoy the water. I'll hurry and try to find a table."

On deck, wind whipped Sandra's hair, stealing her breath before she could call after Brian, who ran to the railing, his mouth wide in astonishment. The view of the harbor was breathtaking. Boats were docked in slips, and the blue-green water was calm. Seagulls dipped in arcing circles while other birds dove headfirst into the water for breakfast.

Sandra stood at the rail, letting the ocean spray mist her face. *This is wonderful.* She inhaled but couldn't dislodge the knot of trepidation that seemed to have become part of her chest.

They'd been under way for about ten minutes and were surrounded by water, the shore a distant mass of earth and trees. The wind and the splash of the ocean against the boat created their own music, and she began to hum an old classical song. She caressed the rail, stretched into the wind, her eyes closed, and for a moment the heaviness in her chest dissipated.

What would it be like to dance on the shore?

Sandra listened and heard the music. Crashing waves became the percussion; thunder behind the clouds, the drums; singing birds, the strings. The symphony played.

"I don't know why she's smiling," Brian said as he pushed her thigh to look up at her. "Auntie? Come on; we have a table."

Sandra opened her eyes, the music fading. Slightly disoriented, she rubbed her temple. "Come on, guys. Let's get some lunch."

She turned and standing on the other side of the fifty-foot boat in a navy jogging suit was Mark Turner.

Cassie crossed Sandra's line of vision and pointed to an empty table. "We got lucky. I'll take the boys and get them some food. You want anything?"

"No thanks," she said, aware Mark Turner was on his way to her. She fumbled in her purse, pulling out a ten-dollar bill. Cassie waved it away, but Sandra insisted. "Please, take it."

The money disappeared into her hand and Sandra tried to draw in a refreshing breath.

"I guess today isn't my lucky day," he said.

"You could fall overboard."

Mark slid into Cassie's seat. "Is that what you want?"

"You're the one who said you wanted to get away from us."

He laughed, his smile asking for forgiveness. "Your son ruined a good pair of pants, and I had cracker stuck to the hairs on my arm. He can't sing worth a dime and he's not very good at video games."

Sandra couldn't help but smile. "He's my nephew and he's five. Why don't you pick on someone your own size."

"Your nephew." He rubbed his hands together. "I don't normally pick fights with kids. Just their aunts."

She gave him her best look of dismissal. "That's big of you." Sandra turned her attention to the blue water and the clear sky. Brisk wind lifted napkins from the table next to theirs, and one flew over and covered Sandra's mouth.

Mark laughed strong and hearty.

She crumpled the napkin into her fist. "If you think that's funny, you have a bizarre sense of humor."

"Things are funny when they're funny. God was trying to tell you something about that smart mouth of yours."

His reproach stung a little, but she didn't let on.

"Mark, did I invite you over here?"

"So you know my name."

She shrugged, embarrassed. "I heard the flight attendant."

"You have me at a disadvantage. I don't know yours."

"You didn't read my card."

"Your card was thrown away with my pants in the Boston airport."

"I offered to replace them."

He gave her a self-assured grin. "I don't need you to dress me. Just tell me your name."

If she could scrape the smug grin off his face, she wondered what would be left. His smile made him handsome and the confident tip of his head made him irresistible.

She debated the right or wrongness of telling him and couldn't find a reason not to. "Sandra."

"Last name?"

"Why?" she demanded. She'd always believed that by only knowing a person's first name that kept the relationship impersonal. There had to be millions of Marks in the world.

But when someone knew your last name, that was . . . intimate. His was Turner. Mark Turner.

I don't have time for Mark Turner.

"I want to know." His voice reminded her that she'd drifted.

He wanted to know.

As simple as it sounded, somehow she knew Mark Turner got what he wanted. "We don't always get what we want, now, do we?"

He shrugged. "Life is more fun when you do, but that's ok. You'll tell me."

She reached for something less personal. "How is it that we didn't see you on the bus?"

"I met with a client who drove me over to meet the ferry."

"You had your meeting in a car?"

"Who said meetings had to be in the boardroom?"

Sandra shrugged, looking him up and down. "Nobody."

He chuckled. "How long will you be on the Vineyard?"

She shrugged. "A couple weeks, maybe less."

"That's just enough time."

Sandra eyed Brian and Carlton eating hot dogs several tables over. She wished Cassie had returned to their table, so she could give Mark a New York kiss-off, but her head was buried deep in a magazine.

"No comment?" Mark asked.

"What? Oh, just enough time for what?" she hoped he wasn't thinking of asking her out. She didn't need the distraction. This trip held only one purpose, and that was to convince Lola that Brian was better off where he was.

"There's just enough time for you to see the island, get to know some of the people."

The implication wasn't missed; she just hated his approach. If he thought that was a way to ask her out, he needed to go back to the school of fundamentals.

Disappointment soared through her and she knew she had no right, but an attitude worked up her spine. He was just like so many New York men. Wanted something but didn't know how to ask. She wouldn't make it easy. His gaze held hers and she counted slowly to five.

"Been nice talking to you, but I've got to go." Sandra stood, rubbed her hand on her thigh. "See you."

She moved away, trying not to look. "I will see you," he said.

As ferry personnel prepared to dock, Sandra slid into a seat beside Cassie.

"He's cute," the blonde said without looking up. "In that kind of—"

Sandra hoped she wouldn't say "Denzel kind of way." It was as if white women only could relate to Denzel and none of the other black actors on the big screen.

"He reminds me of a beefed-up Jeffrey Sams."

Impressed, Sandra nodded. "Right. I agree."

Announcements were made for passengers with cars to head belowdecks, while everyone headed for the stairs and gangplank.

Locating their luggage, one hand locked with Brian's, Sandra started her descent, her gaze searching for Lola. She told herself she wasn't looking for Mark and almost believed it until Cassie tapped her on the shoulder and pointed to the docks.

"He's over there talking to that pretty lady in the black shorts. Darn, too bad."

"That's my sister."

"Ooh, that's worse," Cassie moaned as Mark rocked Lola in a big hug. "Well, try to enjoy your stay on the Vineyard."

Sandra and Brian took slow steps toward Lola and Mark. She hated how her heart rammed against her ribs, and she hated that she'd majored in dance and not swimming. She had an overpowering urge to swim to freedom with Brian on her back.

Sandra glanced around. Everyone wore smiles. Everyone except her.

Lola spotted them. Waved.

Brian wrested his hand from Sandra's and ran.

Sandra walked over, searching her heart for a flickering light of happiness as Brian climbed his mother's body as if she were a yard fence. Sandra noticed Lola's protective hands on his back as she plastered his face with kisses.

"Sandra! Get over here, girl; you've got to meet my *fine* neighbor. Mark Turner, this is my very eligible sister, Sandra Fagan."

Mark looked at her with confidence in his eyes, his expression pleasant. "Sandra Fagan, is it? The pleasure is mine."

Seven

"Lola, we need to get something straight right now."

Sandra read the defiant sparkle in Lola's eyes and narrowed her own. Where did her sister get off embarrassing her? Like she couldn't get a man without a public-service announcement. She wasn't a charity case, and Lola wasn't going to start treating her like one just because she had a man.

Mark looked between them, opened his mouth, breathed heavily. "You're old enough to settle this." He crossed the street and headed through a park of mowed grass and beautiful trees.

Sandra planted her foot in front of her sister. "If I want someone to know my marital status, I'll tell him. Got it?"

Lola rolled her eyes, Brian's legs still wrapped around her waist, his arms around her neck. "Damn! What's your problem?"

"First of all, don't curse in front of him. Second, you don't need to broadcast my business. *That's* my problem."

They crossed on red, a silent militia, following the paved path toward a row of huge houses. "It's hardly broadcasting when I tell a close friend." She sucked her teeth.

Sandra forced her sister to stop. "Let's be clear about a few things, Lola. We came here only to figure out what to do about our situation." She emphasized Brian with a jerk of her head. "Nothing else."

Aggravation and impatience registered on Lola's face and she rolled her eyes again. "Whatever! Can we go now?"

"As long as we understand each other."

"I said 'whatever.' "

"Fine," Sandra said.

"Fine!"

"Don't fight." Brian's little voice against his mother's shoulder stopped the bickering and their forward progress. Sandra reached for him, realized Lola wasn't giving him up, and dropped her hands.

"We're not fighting," they said in unison.

"Yes, you are."

The sisters shared a look of silent agreement and called a truce.

Sandra shook her head, disgusted with herself. "We won't have any more disagreements in front of you. Deal?"

"Deal," he said, pleased.

He squeezed his arms around Lola's neck and accepted a kiss on the cheek from his aunt.

She turned her attention to her surroundings, trying to calm down. Pale blue ocean water reflected off the overcast sky, but the clouds didn't stop people from flying kites and heading to the beach to swim.

They walked through a park heading toward a semicircle of houses, larger than any she'd ever seen in Bensonhurst or South Jersey.

Mark had stopped outside a massive white-and-green house, talking to an older couple. By the architecture Sandra could tell the homes had been built more than a century ago, the structures boasting of history.

Normally Sandra enjoyed hearing a good story, but her mind was full of too many questions, the first being which house was Lola's?

Lola walked on through the neatly kept park, Brian still in her arms, and Sandra squelched a desire to tell her to let him walk. That would start another unwanted argument, and her desire to fight was now gone.

"Where are we going?" she finally asked, surprised there hadn't been a car waiting for them. If anything, Lola traveled in style.

"Brian," Lola said in a hushed tone. "Do you see where Mark is standing? That's where I live now."

"Wow!" He scrambled down and raced across the remaining ten yards, up the stairs, and inside the screen door.

Lola paused at Mark's side long enough to get a reassuring squeeze on the arm; then she hurried into the house after Brian.

Sandra stood alone with Mark for the first time. She pushed down the handle on the suitcase, for lack of something better to do, and took a deep breath. "I, uh, have something to say."

He turned, studied her for a moment. "Go ahead."

The tips of her black shoes were suddenly interesting. Words rushed to her tongue as emotions she'd never shared with another soul floated around like particles of dust.

Mark looked her in the eye. He waited, without speaking, his eyes an instrument of patience. They cut into her, opening the wound, and with every ounce of strength she possessed she dammed it closed.

Those same eyes would turn. First disgust, then anger. Other men hadn't understood her raising her sister's child, had been her judge and jury. She told herself to spit out the words and leave. "I want to apologize."

He remained quiet for a moment. "For?"

"I've always felt ashamed of women who get loud in the streets. Always felt bad about the finger-pointing, neck-rolling low-class behavior. I didn't mean to drag you into that."

Mark pulled a gold dollar out of his pocket and began to work it through his fingers like a magician. "Is that it?" Caring surrounded the words. He gave her an opportunity to speak, but she couldn't. He would not become her confidant.

"That's it."

He raised empty hands. A strange tingle raced up her spine when he tipped up her chin.

She shook to move him and he reached behind her ear,

pulled out the gold coin, placed it in her palm.

"A tip. Never apologize for demanding to be treated the way you want to be treated." He looked toward a green-shuttered gray house. "I live right here. Whenever you need a friend, I'm next door."

"I'm not staying long." The words came from nowhere and she wished she could bite them back.

This time he seemed to consider his words carefully. "I hope to see you before you leave." The screen door smacked closed behind him.

Salty ocean air misted her skin, her New York clothes inappropriate for the casual climate.

Sandra yanked on the handles of the suitcases, carried one up the stairs, and was coming down for the other when a man walked up.

"You must be Sandra. I'm Randy Bivens, Lola's fiancé."

Her breath caught. Randy Bivens was as fine as French cuisine. The color of honey, he had a warm smile that reflected in his eyes. Normally she would have smiled back, his warmth was so inviting, but Sandra knew what he wanted and a smile wasn't going to get it. She reluctantly extended her hand. "Sandra Fagan."

"Well, Sandra Fagan," he said slowly, as he released her hand. "It seems there might be something I can do to help you."

She cocked her head. Was he boasting that he could take Brian from her? Convince Lola he was sincere in wanting to raise her son? What did he hope to accomplish by turning her nephew's life upside down?

"I don't think you can do anything for me. In fact, I know you can't. I'm here at Lola's request so we can come to some agreement as far as Brian is concerned. I don't want to get off on the wrong foot with you, but don't press—"

"I'm glad to hear you say that. I was worried you'd come here with predisposed ideas about me and why I love your sister and will come to love her son. Getting off on the wrong foot is definitely not what I want to do." He made a smacking sound in his cheek. "I'm glad we think alike when it comes to that. Let me help you along here."

He stepped up one stair, and Sandra stepped forward. She wasn't going to back down from him, ever. They faced each other at eye-level. Oh yes, he was a smooth talker, but she wasn't letting a man run a game on her or her sister.

"I managed to make it here all the way from New York. I think I can navigate the last few steps. Excuse me."

The suitcase seemed to have gotten heavier, but Sandra showed no discomfort as she pulled the bag up the stairs and through the door Randy held open.

"Sandra," he said, his bass voice smooth as buttermilk. "I know you just got here and probably want to get settled, but I wanted to get your advice on something before it's too late."

She turned, wondered why he was speaking in a hushed tone all of a sudden. "What do you want to know?"

He headed over, glancing up the stairs as he came.

"Lola's birthday is in two weeks and she told me she's never had a birthday party."

Startled, Sandra looked at him. Eager amber-colored eyes stared back, awaiting an answer.

"So?"

He smiled bright. "So I want us to give her a surprise party."

"Us?"

"Yes, you, her only sister, and me, her happy-to-be-in-love-with-her fiancé. I want *us* to give her a party."

He registered the look on her face that said, *Brotha, please, let's keep it real.* Sandra prayed for patience. She was going to need it to endure the next month. "I took off four weeks from work to settle the issue of what's best for Brian, not throw Lola a birthday party. Did you know the day she decided to drop her bombshell on me was *my* birthday?"

Randy drew up in surprise. "I'm sorry."

"I am, too. I'm sorry we're in this situation and I'm sorry my sister and I couldn't make more permanent decisions concerning Brian a long time ago. I'm here only to settle this."

She pulled the suitcases to the base of the stairs. "Throw her a party; she'll enjoy it. But don't expect me to help."

He lifted his hands, shrugged. "That's fair. You feel like you're losing something. I can see why you wouldn't want to be involved."

His gall grated her. "Don't analyze me. You don't know me from a man on the street."

"I know you raised my fiancée's son when she couldn't, and I know you love them both very much."

"You need to also know I won't give up Brian without a fight."

"Neither will we."

As far as Sandra was concerned, the lines had been drawn in the sand. "Which room—"

"The sunroom, top right. I would give you a hand—"

The words died on his lips when she lifted her hand. "I've got it."

"Figured you did. Nice talking to you, Sandra."

She didn't know if he was being sarcastic, and she didn't turn around to find out.

Eight

The sounds of waves lapping at the shore awoke Sandra before dawn on her fifth day on the Vineyard. Normally she'd wake about seven, get toast and tea, and take a long walk on the beach or along the road heading to Edgartown.

As had been the case for the week, Lola would rise and take Brian and be gone by the time Sandra rose, but she'd see Brian in the afternoon or at dinner.

To her surprise, he loved the island. His eyes would light up as he recounted his adventures with his mother. Brian's and Lola's skin had turned a warm bronze and they looked more and more alike.

Sandra tried not to let their growing closeness disturb her, but she couldn't help feeling a certain amount of loss.

Neither she nor Lola had spoken a word about Brian, and for the time being that was fine with Sandra. Four weeks was a long time, but she was vaguely aware that a week had already passed.

Turning over on the pillow-topped bed, peering out the sunroom window, she saw the sky was still charcoal black, hues of blue, red, and purple creeping in to wake up the island.

Isolated yet not alone, Sandra listened to the sounds of the waking day: birds whistling, a toilet flushing, a child coughing.

She sat straight up, grabbed the duffel bag, her feet hitting the floor in a dead run. Sandra made it to Brian's door just in time to run into Lola's back as she exited, cough syrup in hand.

"What's going on?"

"He had a little cough and I gave him some of the medicine from his bag. That was ok, wasn't it?"

Sandra glanced at the bottle of medicine and mentally calculated how much Brian should have. "How much did you give him?"

"A half-teaspoon. He fought the whole time. I got about half of that in him. The other half is on his nightshirt and the sheets."

As Lola spoke, Sandra took the bottle from her hand and eased open Brian's door. The child lay on top of the covers, his cobalt blue Pokemon pajamas contrasting sharply with the white blankets. "How much is he supposed to have?" Lola asked from over Sandra's shoulder.

"You have to go according to a child's weight and not age. Brian weighs more than the dosage stipulates. He needs a full teaspoon from a medicine spoon." Sandra dug deep in the duffel bag designated for Brian's medicine and pulled out a Baggie. Inside were clear medicine cups and spoons.

"I didn't know he had that." Sounding defensive, Lola stopped just inside the door, acting more like a visitor rather than the lady of the house.

Sandra gave her a reassuring glance. "He'll be fine." She rubbed her nephew's arm and waited until he stirred. "Hey, Angel face, you having a hard time?"

He took her hand and laid it on his cheek, his eyes half-open. Sandra stroked the tender skin lovingly.

"I got a cough."

"I heard. You know what we have to do, don't you?"

"Get rid of it," he said, waking more to play the familiar game. "I don't like medicine," he reminded her.

She made a sad sound, shaking her head. "I know. So I'm afraid we're going to have to do surgery." Exaggerating, Sandra dug into the pockets of her robe. "I've got a throat knife in here somewhere."

He smiled, coughed a little. "I *need* my throat, Auntie."

"You do?" she exclaimed and he nodded. "Then what

should we do about that bad cough? We only have two options. The throat knife. Or . . ." She paused for effect. "Cough medicine."

Neither of the options seemed to please him. He sat up, a broad smile on his face. "I'll take the throat knife."

Sandra burst out laughing. He'd never chosen that before. "Not on your life, buddy."

"You'd miss me if I were dead?"

"Of course I would."

"Mommy, too?"

"She'd cry buckets."

"I sure would," Lola said from the dimly lit corner by the door. She walked in some, her eyes captivated, a small smile on her face. "So you've got to take your medicine; otherwise I'll cry and cry until I shrivel into a tiny raisin."

Brian grinned at the idea. "Oookay."

Sandra had prepared the medicine cup and held it out to Brian. "Drink up."

He swallowed the medicine in one gulp, then shook like a wet animal. "Are all medicines yucky?"

"No." Sandra pulled back the covers and urged his legs beneath.

"He didn't want covers."

Sandra nodded. "He needs them."

"He's going to get too hot. This room gets very warm." Lola spoke with know-it-all authority that Sandra recognized as useful but misplaced. Going against her wasn't aiding in the decision to rescind guardianship of Brian. If anything, Lola's resistance further demonstrated the depth of her maternal immaturity.

Instead of responding, Sandra maintained eye contact with Brian and with deft hands snuggled him beneath the covers.

"It's hot, Auntie." Sandra smoothed the sheet, mentally taking a step back to assess the situation. The room was cool, the window elevated about an inch, a steady breeze blowing in. She'd promised Brian she wouldn't argue with his mother, yet Lola seemed intent on challenging her. Sooner or later, she'd have to be dealt with, but not now. The day had hardly begun.

Sandra leaned down and kissed Brian's forehead. She licked her finger and stuck it in the air. "It's just warm enough for pajamas and one cover. I'll pull down the blanket if you promise to stay under the sheet."

He yawned, snuggled down. "Promise. Can I have a story?"

"Not now. It's nearly morning."

"Looks like night. It's still dark outside."

"Just like winter in Brooklyn. If you go to sleep soon, I'll have a special surprise for you later." She rubbed his back, in gentle strokes, pleased when his eyes drifted closed.

He smiled, yawned. "Yea."

She waited a little while before heading for the door.

"Mommy?" Sandra and Lola turned, looked at each other, then Brian. Sandra felt as if she were in a standoff. With Brian's back to them, she wondered if the question had been meant for her sister. He'd called Sandra Mommy for a time, influenced by the children in day care, but she had to honestly admit it had been about a year since he'd uttered the word to her.

"How come all the good stuff always happens later?"

Five seconds, ten passed when she realized Lola wasn't going to answer. Her face was blank, sadness hanging over her shoulders. Lola didn't have an answer.

"Adults know how important rest is for children. So they always plan things for after rest time. Good night, Angel face."

"Night, Auntie. Night, Mommy."

Lola was waiting for Sandra in the hallway.

"I didn't know you're supposed to go according to a child's weight. Why doesn't the medicine bottle say that?" Defensive, hands on her hips, Lola confronted her as if she had purposely kept the information from her. Sandra had learned to care for Brian by asking professionals and using instinct, and trial and error. She didn't know how to explain that without sounding uppity.

Though she understood Lola's perplexed look, Sandra couldn't help her. "I don't know."

"I mean, you could give them too much or too little and that could hurt somebody," she complained angrily.

"Stop worrying; he's fine."

Tension radiated off Lola in waves. Dressed in cutoff shorts, she wore a crisply pressed long-sleeve T-shirt. Her braids were loose, streaming down her shoulders, her face void of makeup.

This was the first time in years Sandra had seen her sister look like a natural woman. Lola had their mother's brown sugar coloring and eyes that slanted up. Age had made her more beautiful.

Sandra looked away, realizing she was staring. "Weren't you in bed?"

Her sister swept her hands over her shorts. "We sleep naked. This was the first thing I grabbed when I heard him coughing."

"I see. You might want to dress in case Brian ever comes in your room in the middle of the night." Sandra had tried to sound casual but knew she failed when Lola rolled her eyes.

"The body is natural. We're not ashamed of it."

"That's true and fine for people who haven't had a child around, but you might traumatize your son. Surely you can understand how seeing you and your fiancé naked might be uncomfortable for him."

"Okay," Lola said, still unsure. "Well, yeah. We can change that."

Silence fell between them and Sandra started for her room.

"Will he get a cold?"

Sandra turned, shaking her head. "He'll be fine. His body has to adjust to the change in climate. Good night."

"Sandra?"

"Yes?"

"You're so good with him."

The compliment seemed to have been made with a built-in caveat. She wondered when the "but" would come. "Thank you. What are you getting at?"

"It's just we went around and around about the medicine and he wouldn't take it. I felt good just giving him what he got. But then you walk in, play a game, and he swallows the medicine like it's candy. How do you do that?"

"It's a ritual, Lola. I know he hates taking medicine and he knows he has to take it. We have to compromise. So I play a game. He takes the medicine and each of us gets what we want."

Her sister nodded, seeming to understand, yet unwilling to let her go. "Where did you come up with the throat knife?"

"Sounds gory, but one day we talked about the worst thing that could happen to him, and Brian decided it was to have a part of his body cut off."

"Yikes. He thinks like that?"

"He's a boy, Lola." She chuckled. "Boys are rough. Anyway, the way he sees it, anything, including medicine, is better than having something cut off."

Lola's hand restlessly slid across the banister. "That's really smart thinking for such a young person."

"I've learned to never underestimate children; otherwise you're imposing barriers on them."

"I think I'll just sit with Brian for a while until he falls asleep."

"He's probably already halfway there."

"Yeah, but I'd like to. Just this once."

Sandra felt her brows knit together but couldn't find a reason to stop her sister from watching over her son.

Lola hesitated. "Let's talk in the morning. No need to delay what has to be said."

"I agree."

They used to share a hug before bedtime, but that was a lifetime ago. Air brushed their shoulders as they walked past each other.

Back in bed, Sandra watched the sun peek over the horizon, reflecting off the expanse of ocean water. The sunrise wasn't something she ever managed to see from her apartment in Brooklyn, so it captured her full attention. She sat up in bed, hugging her knees, feeling honored that she was the recipient of God's magic.

She looked out the east window at Mark's house and wondered where in the vast mansion was his room? Could he see the sunrise? For a moment she imagined him beside her, his gaze as captivated as hers as the fiery ball made its ascent. He'd put his arm around her shoulder and lean her back for a kiss that would be as drugging as wine.

Sandra berated herself. She and Lola had made public spectacles of themselves. Why would a man like that want anything to do with a person who didn't know how to conduct herself? She'd made such a stink about his knowing her marital status. Why?

The sun slipped past the water and heated the clouds. *Didn't want him to think of me as hard and unattractive, that I couldn't get a man if I wanted one.*

Her eyes grew heavy, and she slipped down under the covers. Lola's announcement to the first man that had warranted a second glance took away Sandra's option of explaining her situation, just like she was trying to take Brian away.

The sun took its place in the sky and Sandra blinked slowly, turning onto her side, thinking somebody ought to put the sunrise to music so everybody could dance.

Just before sleep claimed her, a movement on Mark's porch made her open both eyes. Beautiful and bronze in the morning light, Mark stood, bare-chested, thin pants covering his lower body, a cup of steaming brew in his hand.

He inhaled deeply, his chest rising to the sun as if to acknowledge its brilliance, then turned and faced her.

For a moment they were frozen, gazes locked, and Sandra wondered if he knew she was watching him. He lifted his cup in salute, and she reluctantly wiggled her fingers. Then he walked back into the house.

Sandra slept soundly.

Nine

At noon, Sandra sat across the dining room table from Lola, the breakfast dishes washed, the lace tablecloth the only thing between them.

Randy had been outside with Brian since Sandra had awakened, winning the boy over with a kite. All morning she could hear her nephew's whoops of pleasure any time the kite caught the wind.

At first she'd thought Randy was merely trying to impress her, but after the fiftieth command from Brian for Randy to run with the kite, she knew the pleasure was mutual.

About an hour ago Randy had asked Sandra if he could take Brian fishing, and she'd consented. Even if Brian was to remain in New York with her, he'd still have to know his stepfather.

The screen door banged shut and the two walked in, sweaty and smiling. "Have fun?" she asked.

"Randy was running with the kite. He looked funny," Brian said, giggling.

"I looked funny, huh? We'll see what funny looks like when you catch your first fish."

The boy's mouth dropped open. "We're going fishing?"

Lola went to the kitchen, returning with a big bag and a small backpack. "Not only are you going fishing, but you're going to have a complete guys' day."

Brian's nose crinkled. "What's that?"

Sandra watched the exchange silently. Lola's son had no idea what it was to bond with a man. Lola looked shamed as she held the bag in front of her. She spoke quietly to her son. "You're going to go fishing, and it's only for men and boys. Ladies are not allowed."

"I don't think it's a good idea if I get these gym shoes wet," he said with much authority. "Auntie says if you can't swim, you can't get in the water."

They looked at her, surprised. "Brian, those are your old shoes. It's okay to get them wet, but," she added for Randy's and Lola's sake, "he doesn't know how to swim."

Randy headed for a closed door. "I think we can make Auntie feel better if you're protected." He dug around inside as he spoke. "We have a life preserver that will probably be fine until you get your own."

He shook dust off the orange vest and looked to Sandra for approval.

Before she could consent, Lola spoke up. "I think it's perfect. Every boy needs to be well protected."

"Wow," Brian said in a hushed tone. "Can I wear it now?"

Randy laughed. "Sure. We've got a ways to walk. Are you sure you want to put it on before we get to the water?"

"Yes!"

Sandra watched Brian's face light up like a pinball machine as he was latched into the vest.

Lola handed Randy his vest, two poles, and a tackle box.

"We'll be back by dinner. Have the grease heatin', woman; the men are bringing home the bacon."

"Aww. I thought we were going fishing."

"We are, bud. Let me say good-bye to your mother and we're outta here."

Brian fell in step behind Randy, who gave Lola a heart-stopping kiss. "Play nice," he whispered and winked at Sandra.

She looked away, the intimate act too provocative for witnesses. He certainly acted like he loved her sister. Or was he *just* acting?

Brian and Randy set out and as the chatter from the pair faded, Sandra focused her attention on Lola. She watched the door, looking forlorn and lost without Randy to run interference for their discomfort.

"It's time we talked," Sandra said, wanting to get it over with.

Lola sat across from her. "They look good together." When Sandra didn't comment, Lola snapped, "Don't you have anything to say? The man I love and my son look good together." She scrubbed her hands on her face.

"They do. But looks aren't everything."

Lola shook her head. "No, they aren't. But they count for something. You get a feeling from a look. You can interpret emotions from watching others. I've been watching Brian and Randy for days now and they can love each other. I know it in my heart."

"What about *your* heart?" Sandra demanded. "What can you offer Brian that he doesn't already have?"

"Me. Full-time."

"You're quitting your job?"

"I'm taking a leave of absence for a while. Flying has lost its appeal."

Sandra swallowed, wondering if her sister realized what she was doing. "How does Randy feel about that?"

She looked away. "He doesn't know yet, but he feels I may be trying to change too much too quickly."

Sandra hated to agree but did. "He has a point. What if you get bored? What happens to Brian when you decide you like flying better than being a stay-at-home mom?"

"There's day care, Sandra. Besides, with the summer approaching, there'll be lots of kids to play with."

"He's in day care now. It isn't fair to uproot him and take him away from everything he knows."

"I want him, Sandra. Why can't you understand that?"

Tears clogged her throat and she rose, walking to the stereo. Randy's collection of music was extensive and eclectic. She picked up an Al Jarreau CD and held it in her hand. "I do understand."

"You do? Then why are you fighting me?"

A tear slipped down Sandra's cheek, and she wiped it away. The curtain billowed around her bare legs and she fought for control of her emotions.

Lola rose, tears marring her face, her voice emotional. "You've always accused me of being selfish, when you've got that locked down. He's my son. Mine! And I want him. I won't wait forever for you to decide. There are other ways, Sandra. Legal ways to get what I want."

The chair scraped the floor and her sister's deck shoes made thudding sounds as she escaped the room.

Sandra laid down the CD and hurried for the back door.

She ran down the path, tears streaming from her eyes. With one hand she swiped them and with the other pushed aside tree branches. Just as she pushed back a thicket of thin branches, one flicked back and smacked her in the forehead.

A sob tore through her and Sandra let it come. She held her head, her other hand covering her mouth as she made her way to a swinging bench. She sat down and tried to calm herself.

This whole thing was too much. She should just let Lola have Brian. Give him back to his mother and pray for his life. But she knew she couldn't and there was one reason.

She wanted Brian, too.

The realization hit her and a fresh set of tears flooded her eyes. She put her feet up and the swing swayed.

Sandra wiped her face on her sleeve, tilted her head, and rested her chin on her arm.

The breeze dried her face, but a steady trail of tears ran from her eyes. She closed them, going inside herself, wishing desperately for someone who saw things as she did.

"Pretty day to cry in the garden."

Mark.

She knew he stood just feet from her but didn't want to open her eyes and face him. She cleared her throat but didn't speak.

"Funny thing about the island. Not too many places to run and hide here."

"Not hiding."

"No reason to." He sat on the swing and she drew her feet up, crossing her arms over her knees to block her face from him. He tugged on her ankle until she peeked out and watched as he lowered her feet to the cement floor. She braced her hands beside her legs, her face down.

Sliding close, he put his arm around her shoulder. "Looks like you could use a friend."

The weight of his arm settled into her body, and all she wanted to do was lean into him. The tears came faster, dripping off her nose as she fought giving in.

Her hands gripped the bench and she could feel herself shaking as her control slipped a little at a time.

"You have nice shoulders."

The useless compliment made her laugh and she accepted Kleenex, wiped her face, and scooted back. His hand guided her until her head rested on his shoulder.

"You knew I was here." Sandra felt him nod.

"Big houses, thin walls."

"I don't believe you. These houses are built to withstand mighty storms."

"Our windows were both open," Mark finally admitted.

She sniffed, catching her breath. "Remind me to do something about that the next time I fight with Lola."

He looked into her eyes. "I will, or you could stop fighting with her."

Sandra tried to rise, but his strong hand kept her head against his shoulder. "Hold on there. You don't take constructive criticism well, do you?"

"Not from people I don't know."

He rubbed her arm in reassuring strokes. "Don't start that again. You've already ruined a pair of my pants, offered to swab me. Broke an expensive computer and followed me home. Where I grew up, that makes us practically family."

Sandra laughed and it felt good.

"Want to talk about it?" he asked.

She hesitated, then shook her head. "Not yet. I don't feel like crying anymore. Let's talk about something else. Anything. Tell me where you grew up."

"I grew up in the SWATs."

"Southwest—," she filled in.

"Atlanta. I have a three brothers, two sisters, parents dead five years."

"I'm sorry. Together?" she asked, thinking of the car crash that had claimed her parents.

"Cancer. Five months apart. I've lived here for four years. Came here on vacation one summer and the next summer never left."

"Do you mind if I ask what you do?"

"I buy and sell property."

Her heart started to pound. "Like on the infomercials on TV late at night."

"Kind of."

"So you're rich."

He smiled. She could feel it. "I'm comfortable," he said with a lightness she knew made it true. She also recognized another fact. She was comfortable, too.

"Wow."

"What's that mean?" he said, holding her away from him.

Sandra suddenly had a mental picture of herself. Her eyes puffy from crying, her nose bright red from being rubbed too hard, and her cheeks flushed from exertion. Embarrassment slid through her hot like whiskey.

Not only because she probably looked like the bottom of somebody's foot but also because Mark had also passed the five-question test and hadn't hesitated or evaded a single answer once.

She looked down at her hands, then at the lush garden she'd wandered into. "I wish talking to Lola was as easy as talking to you."

"It can be."

"You know we're having a custody issue over Brian?"

He nodded slowly. "I know."

"She wants him here with her and I believe he needs to stay in New York with me where he's grown up and has a stable life."

"You aren't sure he'll have the same quality of life here?"

"My sister is a good person, Mark. She's had a past—"

"Who hasn't?"

Wouldas, couldas, and shouldas traipsed through her mind with the casualness of Sunday strollers. "Everyone does. It's just that she's never been one to settle down for any period of time and my biggest concern is dragging Brian into a lifestyle that isn't good for him."

"How long have you cared for him?"

"Every day of his life."

"Lots of responsibility. Oldest?"

She nodded.

"Then you'll do what's best for him." He sounded so sure, she looked at him.

"But how do I know I'm not making the biggest mistake of his life? I love that boy as if he were my own."

He didn't say anything and she looked away. "I'm not being selfish, dammit. I'm doing what I'm supposed to do."

"Who are you trying to convince, me or you?"

"Neither." She huffed, wishing she could breathe through her nose.

Gently he scratched her back and Sandra realized she'd arched to his touch. "I'm here because of Brian."

"And?"

She cocked her head. "Lola."

"And," Mark said gently.

Sandra didn't want to make the final admission. "You're as bad as an armchair psychologist. I'm here for me, too. I want to know everything about them. Have to be sure I make the right decision."

"Ever been wrong before?"

"I try very hard not to make mistakes where Brian is concerned."

"It's good to know you're not Joan of Arc. If you listen to the words you've said, you'll make the right decision."

He stood, bringing her with him. Taking her elbow, he guided her up the path that separated his house from Lola's.

He held the brush for her, reminders of the snapping twigs evidenced by her pounding forehead. The space between the monstrous houses was large enough for a footpath, the one between Mark's and Lola's slimmer because of spider bushes. Sandra had been wondering whom to ask and hadn't wanted to share her thoughts with Lola or Randy. "Mark?"

He turned, his stride lessening. "Yes?"

"Is there a dance studio around here?"

"Like Arthur Murray?"

"Uh, no. Modern dance."

"There's one in Oak Bluffs not too far from here. They're a talented group. Thinking of taking a class?"

"I just wanted to check out the studio. Get a little exercise."

"Let's stop at my house for a minute and I'll get the information."

"I can look it up. I just wondered."

"Sandra, it's not a problem. I'll have you at your door in five minutes." He headed toward the back door of his house and she had no choice but to follow.

Built similar to Randy and Lola's, Mark's house had been modernized with wallpaper and bold paintings. They walked through a slender hallway off the kitchen and he headed for what she knew would be the den. To her surprise, he had no dining or living room furniture. She didn't want to inquire if he'd recently lost his fortune, but she couldn't help but wonder where the furniture had gone.

He passed her as she stood in the doorway. "I just had

the floors cleaned. The furniture is being refinished," he whispered.

"I didn't say a word."

"Your eyes speak for you. Sit down a minute."

Sandra sank into the most lush black leather sofa she'd ever sat on.

Mark dialed a number from memory and regarded her as he talked. "Akira? . . . Mark Turner. A friend of mine would like to take a class or two at your studio . . . I don't know if she's had experience." He looked to Sandra.

"I have a doctorate in dance education from NYU."

He whistled and his eyes roamed her body. "She's got a doctorate, NYU. . . . Come by after two? Thanks."

He cradled the phone, staring at her. "She said she won't leave until she meets you." The boxy push-button phone rested on his thigh, his big hand palming it as if it were a ball. "A doctorate?"

She nodded.

"So you've got skills. You rich?" he asked, looking at her from the corner of his eye.

She grinned, her face protesting after all the crying. "I'm comfortable," she admitted.

"Do you still dance?"

Sandra stared right at him. "No."

"Because?"

"I need to pay bills."

"Starving artist not working out for you?"

"For me, but not Brian."

He nodded, accepting her answer. He grabbed a pad and pen, wrote quickly, and handed her the sheet. "Directions to the studio. Ready for me to walk you home?"

She wanted to say no, that talking to him and being in his company had been the best part of her week on the island. But she didn't. Instead she rose from the sofa. "Ready."

They walked up the back steps of the quiet house. Suddenly she felt shy. "Thank you. I appreciate everything you—"

He quieted her with a finger to her lips and pointed past her. Sandra followed the direction of his finger. "That's my house. You're welcome there anytime. The furniture won't be back for another week, so if you want some privacy or want to practice"—he shoved his hands deep in his pockets—"whether I'm there or not, come over. Understand?"

He must be single and uninvolved, because he had no fear about her being in his house without him.

The first time he'd made the offer, she thought it nothing more than a subtle booty call, but today it felt different. Like he really meant her to take him up on his offer.

Sandra had never met a man like him. Ever. And she didn't know what to make of him. But something in her wanted to find out. "Got it," she said softly.

"I'll be away for a few days, but I'd like to pick you up Tuesday morning."

"For what?"

"A date."

Her heart skipped a beat, this offer so much better than the first. Why not? She hadn't had a date in a long time. "Sure." Sandra wondered if he would kiss her. She wanted him to but wouldn't ask. Another day, under different circumstances, but not now.

Mark did her one better. He gathered her into a hug, the expensive cotton T-shirt concealing a body she'd pay money to see nude. Sandra didn't tip up, didn't want to express too much need, but for as long as he wanted to hold her, she allowed it. Mark's heartbeat accelerated, the ocean a melodic backdrop. There was nothing more beautiful.

He pulled away, his hands lingering with hers. "See you Tuesday. Dress warm."

Sandra went inside, her body ripe, her senses piqued. She felt overexposed, like a crustacean without a shell.

In the bathroom she applied a cool cloth to her face, the

swelling in her eyes a reminder of the tumultuous day.

Exercise would be good right now, the thought of being in a dance studio again filling a need she'd long ignored. Gathering clothes in a bag, she wrote a brief note and hurried to the dance studio.

Ten

The sun had begun to set when Sandra finished folding laundry and journeyed downstairs to find her sister. Sandra's body protested moving too quickly, the dance class taxing but wonderful as well.

Lola sat in the living room, leafing through her list Sandra knew regarded the wedding. Her sister barely gave her a second glance, and Sandra was determined to end the standoff now. After all, she was here to decide what was best for Brian, and not talking wasn't helping the situation any. "What time are the guys coming back?"

Lola closed the book and stood. "In about an hour." She moved past Sandra and headed toward the kitchen.

"Lola, I want to say something." They met face-to-face in the center of the kitchen floor. "This isn't easy. It's one of the biggest decisions I've had to make in my life."

"Do you think it's easy for me? How do you think I feel having you as my judge and jury?" Lola answered her own question. "It's hard. I know you love me, but you also resent me."

Sandra shook her head in disbelief. "Where did that come from?"

"Do you think I don't see what you've become?"

Unspoken insults flew at Sandra and she evaded, "I think I've heard enough."

Lola walked around the kitchen, pulling ingredients from the spice rack and pantry. "You used to laugh when you talked to Mother. I'd hear you in the kitchen with her and you two would be cracking up like crazy. I'd be in my bed, laid up with asthma, and I'd hear you."

"I used to like to help her cook, and while we were cooking we'd be talking and laughing. So?"

"You don't laugh anymore."

This wasn't what Sandra expected. Lola had never seemed to see her as a person but only as a big sister. Someone to badger and later defy. For Lola to speak of her in personal terms shook Sandra. "I laugh," she said, unable to recall the last time.

"Lately you look as if you've seen a horrible death. Your mouth is always tight, like Daddy's."

The sisters regarded each other for a long moment until Lola deposited cornmeal, seasoning salt, and pepper on the counter. She dug an egg out of the refrigerator, cracked it into a shallow bowl, and whipped it.

Sandra came to their father's defense. "Your asthma worried him. He couldn't help his little girl and that broke his heart. He stopped smiling the day we found out Mother had a lump in her breast."

The whipping stopped as Lola's mouth fell open. "Oh my God. She did?"

"Yes. Daddy didn't stop smiling because of you."

Lola braced her hands on the counter and shook her head. "How come I didn't know? It's like you three had a secret club and I wasn't allowed admittance."

"You're so good at that."

"What?"

"Turning every situation to be about you."

Lola pointed, her eyes flashing angrily. "How come I didn't know *my mother* had a lump in her breast? I had a right to know!"

Sandra swallowed her own anger at her sister's outburst. "You'd had an asthma attack, and Mama thought it prudent for your health to wait until you were better. You never really got better."

The furious expression on Lola's face turned contrite. "I wasn't that—" She stopped herself, apparently startled at the words about to tumble out of her mouth. "You knew. Didn't you?"

"Yes." As a child Sandra had an idea her sister wasn't as sick as she put on, but it only took one backhand slap in the mouth to cure her of making accusations. According to their parents, Lola was weaker; therefore, she needed the attention and care of the entire family.

Lola's guilty eyes met Sandra's. "You'd look at me sometimes, and I would wonder what you were thinking. I guess I've known you knew for a long time. Don't get me wrong, I was sick, but not as much as I put on. You know why?"

The casual admission shocked Sandra. Her sister was speaking as if faking an illness were an everyday occurrence. All the days and nights, weeks, and years she'd had to wait on Lola hand and foot seemed to crash like a dilapidated house in a storm. Their mother had instilled in Sandra that it was the responsibility of family to care for family. She'd followed the words to the letter, and now her efforts were being thrown in her face. Suddenly the reason for Lola's deception became all she could focus on without sinking into the floor like a boneless rag doll. "Why?"

"They loved you more than they loved me."

The simply stated words made Sandra's heart thunder and adrenaline-fueled blood rushed through her veins. "You're crazy! Mama and Daddy *worshiped* you. Waited on you. How could you think that?"

"There was always laughter when you were around." Words like "selfish" and "manipulative" came to mind, but Sandra didn't speak them aloud. Didn't want to go there again on Lola. But knowing wasn't enough. Sandra had never encountered this side of her sister, and as much as it infuriated her, she wanted to make sense out of Lola's logic.

Lola pulled fish from the refrigerator, rinsed off the fillets, and began to season them. She laughed at Sandra's expression. "Don't act like you didn't know. You were the apple of their eyes. I just wanted an occasional blink."

Not knowing what else to say, Sandra defended their parents. "They cherished you."

"No! They felt sorry for me," Lola spat. "Big difference. Did you notice by middle school the asthma came and went? By high school it was nearly gone?"

"You grew out of it." Even as Sandra spoke the words, she added "naive" to adjectives she'd use to describe herself.

Lola poured Crisco into the deep-frying pan and turned on the burner. "True, but I would use it when I had to."

"You conniving bitch."

Instead of hating her sister, Sandra felt heaps of resentment and anger fade, then disappear. For years she'd tried to turn Lola into a version of herself, and she now realized her efforts were futile. Lola was living the life she was supposed to and she was paying for that life, too.

She'd missed the joys of having their parents around, and somewhere deep inside that had to hurt.

Lola broke into the silence. "I was a bitch.

"Sandra, sometimes I wish I could have one more day with them. I wish I'd gotten the chance to spoil them and show them what their girl grew up to be. I can't even say I'm sorry." Lola blew out a breath, adjusting the fire. "I've suffered for my selfishness. You got straight A's and I didn't give a damn about school."

She executed a perfect pirouette and Sandra watched in amazement. "You were the dancer and I was a man chaser." She grinned at Sandra. "Do you ever think about what you could have been?"

"Doesn't everybody?"

"Sure, but I've a lot of my dreams. I was flaky in school and I finally got a degree. I was wild and now—" She laughed. "I'm not so wild. What would you do, Sandra, if you could control your destiny?"

Dance. "I'd take more vacations. Redecorate my apartment."

Lifting a plastic bag of cornmeal, Lola battered the fish and put it into the bubbling oil. "That's so boring. Really, what would you do?"

Memories of the Alvin Ailey dancers exploding in a burst of movement captured Sandra's fantasies with her in the center of the group. "I'd dance."

Lola clapped and hugged her. "I knew it. Your body is still good. A little soft in places, but nothing you can't work on."

She removed Lola's hands from her waist. "Thanks, I think."

"You were always so smart. We used to lay in my bed and talk for hours about our dreams and what we'd do when we grew up."

Sandra hated strolling down memory lane. Her brain always seemed to get stuck on their parents' deaths. "Dreams are for children."

"Honey, I'm living my dream!" Lola switched over to the stove and stabbed fish with her fork, moving it around the pan. "I might not have it all figured out, but some of the best parts have already happened. I've got you, my son, and Randy is the love of my life."

"Did I hear my name?"

Through the back screen door, Randy pressed himself against the house, a sleeping Brian over one shoulder, tackle box and bag in the other hand.

"Hey, good-lookin'," Lola said, the flirt still in her.

Randy raised interested eyes and wiggled his eyebrows at her. "You want to help me out or just admire my chiseled physique?"

Lola and Sandra moved at once. Lola got the door as Sandra reached for Brian. They both stank of fish and sweat, and mud had dried on Brian to his waist.

Alarm must have registered on her face, because Randy tried to brush off Brian's sleeping form.

"Just a little mud. We had to go to a couple fishing holes. He's a master with a rod and don't worry about the minnows in his pockets. They were already dead long before he put them in there."

Despite herself, Sandra smiled. "Dead fish in his pockets?"

"He wanted to carry them home." Randy glanced at the bubbling pot and turned to Lola. "I told you we were bringing home the bacon."

"I know, sweetheart, and everything is ready. I was just fixing this fish so it wouldn't go bad. Waste not—"

"Want not. You say that all the time."

Sandra kept surprise to herself as she removed Brian's mud-crusted sneakers and deposited them in the laundry room.

"Baby girl," Randy crooned. "We wanted to bring you something tonight."

Sandra was at the door leading to the hallway but couldn't help but look back at the couple.

She'd wanted to hate them, but all she had was a better understanding of them.

Lola sidled up to Randy and, oblivious of his scent, kissed him fully on the mouth. "We're not eating that fish tonight. We're eating what my man brought home."

He wrapped his arms around Lola. "That's my girl. I need a shower."

Lola tipped up for another kiss. "Not until you go outside and clean that fish."

Randy backed her up to the sink. "Clean it? Woman, in the old days all the man had to do was catch the meal."

Sandra took that opportunity to head upstairs, even as she listened.

"Lucky for you we don't live back in the Stone Age. Get busy so we can eat something besides potatoes and peas."

"Aww, you know I hate peas."

Sandra held onto the railing as she carried her nephew up. She heard Lola commiserate, "I know; I know. They'll make you grow big and strong."

She heard a tiny yelp before closing the bathroom door. "I like peas," Randy said, and then there was silence from the kitchen.

Sandra had Brian nearly in the tub before she realized she was smiling.

Eleven

Sandra walked from the studio more exhilarated than she'd felt in years. Dancing each morning for hours left her rejuvenated and exhausted all at once.

Sister Akira had tested her knowledge the first three days, forcing her to dig deep in her repertoire, but when Akira got winded the third day, Sandra had earned her respect.

For the next week Sandra danced with the company as a guest, but she was asked to contribute today and that made her day.

Each day she tried to understand Lola better as she watched her interact with Brian. Lola's admission made Sandra question everything she'd ever done for her. And although a part of Sandra wanted to hate her, she couldn't. But she was honest with herself.

Sandra didn't know if she could ever love Lola the same.

Walking home that evening, Sandra saw Brian and Randy from a distance with Randy explaining the finer points of bike riding. She couldn't help but smile as the big man pretended to ride the small two-wheeler, with training wheels.

She missed Brian, but having free time was like having a succulent treat after dinner. Sandra waved at the pair when Brian took off and ran to her.

"Auntie, where have you been?"

"Sightseeing, you nosy little boy. What are you up to?"

"Randy's teaching me to ride my bike." His happy gaze roamed her. "I missed you today."

Sandra bent and hugged the little boy she loved so much.

"I've missed you, too. Let's play tomorrow, okay?"

"Deal."

"Where's your mommy?"

"Resting on the couch. She ran out of gas."

"Did not, you tattler," Lola said affectionately from the house. "Come in, Sandra. Let Randy have his turn wearing him out. I'm pooped."

Sandra deposited her dance gear on the stairs and sat across from her sister in the living room.

"Where've you been?" Lola asked.

Sandra drew back, smiling. "Out. Why?"

"You got here two weeks ago and I never see you anymore. Where do you go, Sandra, when you sneak out early in the morning with your secret bag?"

Sandra laughed. "None of your business."

Lola's mouth fell open. "Have you met someone?"

"No."

"Good, 'cause you need to be getting with Mark. I don't know what your problem is, but in case you can't see, he's fine."

"Thank you, Lola, for the rundown on Mark Turner. However"—she blinked and was intentionally evasive—"he's out of town, so I can't see him."

"Then what are you doing at his house every day?"

"Are you spying on me?" Sandra relaxed, enjoying this different relationship with her sister.

"No, I just saw you coming out one day and I wondered. So—" She waited expectantly. "What are you doing over there?"

Sandra stood. "Watering his plants. I need a shower. Be down soon."

Lola scratched on a list. "Take your time. All I know is that Mark doesn't have any plants, but that's our little secret. I swear," Lola mumbled to herself. "It's hard being the responsible one."

Sandra snickered, her legs protesting as she climbed the stairs.

"Lola, get out here and help me teach this boy to ride," Randy called.

"Coming!"

Sandra walked into the bathroom and laughed out loud.

A persistent tapping dragged Sandra from sleep and she woke to complete darkness. A voice from behind her said, "Get up. You're late."

Her head whipped around and Sandra looked into Mark's face brightened by a nearby streetlight. It had been almost a week since she'd seen him, six days without her eyes feasting on chocolate dessert à la Mark. And she'd missed him.

Her eyes grew wide, her skin warm, but the voice of reason said, *Stay on the bed. Straddling him while he's standing is so Diana Ross.*

"What are you doing here? In here?"

"Lola let me in."

In his smile she could see his pleasure in seeing her again. She needed a moment to wake fully before she followed the instincts of man and mated with this guy.

Sandra realized her legs were the object of his gaze and tried to cover them. "What time is it?"

"It's four-thirty in the morning. We've got to get going."

She quit fighting with the covers, concern evaporating over his seeing her in her two-piece cotton pajamas. Instead, she grabbed her pillow, her eyes sinking shut. "No way."

"Come on; you're making us late," he said like he didn't hear her. Typical.

"Honey, if it's four-thirty in the morning, I'm not late for a darned thing but a good night's sleep. See you later." She was glad to see him, but he was trippin' if he thought she was going anywhere with him in the dark.

"Then I'll stay with you." Mark promptly sat on her bed and put his feet up.

Sandra turned over and looked at him. "Are you crazy or do you want to get hurt?"

Suddenly he was beside her, their bodies meeting in one long line. "You're a roughneck and a ballerina? Sexy combination."

"Good heavens you're hard." She meant his body but couldn't take the words back. They were stuck in her throat.

The hall light clicked on and the soles of Lola's deck shoes hit the stairs. "I hope you boys and girls are playing nice up there. Minors are in the house."

Embarrassed at being chastised by her wild sister, Sandra scrambled on the bed, arousing herself with every twist against Mark's body.

"Your sister is the one misbehaving," Mark called, his hand over her mouth. "She won't let me off this bed."

Lola giggled. " 'Bout time. At least *try* to keep it down. Good night." The hall light went off and the door to Lola and Randy's room closed.

"Alone at last," Mark sighed. He traced her cheek with his thumb, tickling the fine hairs at her temple. He took his hand off her mouth and traced her lips.

"You got my sister thinking I'm a skank."

"What kind of talk is that?"

"It's true! She didn't come up here to rescue me. She left me up here with you. You could be a rapist or something."

He opened his eyes wide, acting incredulous. "That isn't me. Or you. Right?"

There he was again, taking it to a new level with the flip of a few words. But he spoke the truth. "Right."

The tension in the room eased as he slid his forefinger down the bridge of her nose. "Besides, today is Tuesday."

Sandra pushed playfully at his shoulder, a small part of her hoping he'd get up, the majority wanting full and complete coverage. "I assumed you meant later, like daylight."

His thumb tickled her collarbone, sending thrills straight to the center of her body. "You know what they say about assuming." Sandra did punch his arm this time.

"Ow. I didn't say *I* said it." His voice got softer and he nipped at her jaw. "Come on, Sandra. I have a lot of plans for us. Or . . ." he said, drifting off, leaving her in anticipation.

She felt a breeze where he'd lifted her pajama top and stole underneath. His fingers hovered over her skin, creating heat. "We can stay here and . . . talk."

She groaned involuntarily. "It's so early. Don't you want to pick me up when it's light—"

In response, he pressed his mouth to hers. The kiss was tender and sweet and very sexy. Suddenly no objections lingered in her mind. If they didn't get off the bed, the sun wasn't going to be the first thing to rise.

Mark didn't give her a chance to accept. Taking her hands in his, he stretched the length of her body, and Sandra felt the only part of him that could grow, grow.

"Are you ready to go now?" he asked, breathless.

She nodded, mute.

"Good." He let her up and she sat on the side of the bed. Mark lay where she'd lain and she had a sudden urge to return to Brooklyn.

With Mark.

And be alone.

"Hurry up," he prodded.

Sandra pressed her desire-ridden body into action and was in the hallway when he said, "And brush your teeth."

No, he didn't invade my bedroom and then go there.

She tiptoed back, retrieved the pillow from the floor, and hit him in his very defined six-pack.

Outside the house, Mark took Sandra's hand and led her through the park and headed toward the marina. It was odd being up this early, most every house dark. Sandra wished she were one of them but then wondered how many of the single sisters she'd been in dance class with all week would trade places with her? Every single one of them.

She wanted to tell Mark of her week but decided to wait until later. Right now getting wherever he was taking her was the priority.

They rounded a corner and headed toward docked boats, their sneakered feet thunking against the wooden planks with exact precision. Up a hill, they walked a few hundred feet; then Mark grabbed her hand, leading her toward a boat with several couples already aboard.

An old man with skin weathered by the sea slapped his hands together. "Thought you weren't going to make it. We're all ready to cast off. Come aboard."

Sandra boarded first, followed closely by Mark, who assisted her with her life preserver, then fastened his own.

"I'm Captain Bob and this is the *Lucky Lady.* My wife Anna is belowdecks. Thank you for joining us for your sunrise/breakfast cruise. We need to get under way, but in about fifteen minutes Anna will be serving champagne or mimosas or juice, if you like. Choose a private viewing area or stay up here with me, I don't care, but enjoy yourselves. Have any questions, feel free to ask. If not, we'll cast off."

Mark took Sandra's hand and led her to a cushioned seat as the ropes were released and the yacht led from the deck.

"Surprised?" Mark said.

"And beyond. I'm speechless."

They sat in silence, Sandra's head resting on Mark's shoulder, a wool blanket capturing their warmth. She closed her eyes, enjoying the gentle ride and good company.

They had traveled for about twenty minutes when Captain Bob slowed the boat and announced they were stopping.

Sandra accepted a mimosa from Anna, as did Mark.

"Let's get a good spot," Mark said, and Sandra gave him her hand. They settled on an oversize cushioned chair made for two, and when he indicated for her to sit between his legs, her back to his chest, she only hesitated for a moment.

Touching Mark made her want to be with him. But Sandra couldn't reject the proffered hand because of her inability to control her desire. So she sat and waited.

"Look; here it comes."

The birth of the sun started as a dot on the horizon. Faint shades of orange and red colored the midnight sky purple and brown. Rays struck the water, expanding and doubling, scampering away the night.

Sandra had never seen anything so beautiful.

Mark's hands caressed her arms and his breath dusted her neck. Sandra closed her arms over his and held the sinewy muscles as if they were gold. It had been too long since a man had held her, too long since she'd felt this much fulfillment.

She turned her head and his lips grazed her cheek. "Mark?"

"Mmm?"

She twisted until their lips hovered. "Kiss you."

"Do it," he said.

Sandra raised her head and met his mouth. She tasted him with her tongue, savoring the feel of him against her. She'd turned in his arms and his hands spanned her waist through her jogging suit, but she felt the pressure and wished they were someplace where restraint was unnecessary.

Drawing back, their lips met again in rhythm, signaling the end. Sandra let her eyes slide open and looked into Mark's.

His eyes drooped and his mouth looked swollen. This was power. His breath fanned her face and his hands had ventured toward the small of her back, his fingers approaching one of her most sensitive spots.

Sandra slid down his chest, turning to sit against him again. "Damn, that was good," Mark whispered. "Promise me there'll be more."

The sky lit in degrees. Sandra felt as afire as the ocean water that had burst into flames from the rising sun. It all felt good. The ocean. The relaxation. Mark. "I promise."

Twelve

Seven o'clock that evening Mark walked Sandra home. They stood between the two houses, hands intertwined, neither seeming ready to part. He pulled her to him and showed her what kissing was all about.

His lips expressed the hunger and passion and desire that had been her constant companion all day. The day had been perfect and Sandra was glad to have spent it with him.

After the breakfast cruise, they'd walked along a private beach, speaking of their lives and families, and had even tackled tough topics like politics and religion and sex. It was no surprise to her that Mark was a pro-sex man.

His honest opinions took some getting used to. The few men she'd dated had never expected answers to questions, just amenable agreement. Perhaps that's why the relationships had never developed into more than mere acquaintanceships.

It had taken Sandra a while to get used to Mark challenging her opinions with facts and wisdom, challenges she realized she enjoyed. But there were times when he'd shocked her into silence, making her reevaluate her thoughts. And when she'd battled a certain point, he'd concede she was right or they'd agree to disagree.

During the walk home, they'd talked about Lola and Brian and what had transpired between them.

"What have you decided?"

"I haven't decided anything yet."

"Why?"

"I've been too busy getting my head together. My sister revealed things to me that are taking time to digest." Sandra hesitated, then pushed on. "All that said, I'm wondering why I'm resisting what on the surface seems to be a fine atmosphere for Brian. Lola's made mistakes," Sandra admitted. "But so have I."

"Then what is it? Why can't you let go?"

She took a few minutes, gathering her thoughts. "I've dedicated five years of my life to raising Brian. It's only been two weeks."

"Lola's been his mother for five years, even though she didn't handle the day-to-day responsibility. Doesn't that account for something?"

"If a person were to suddenly leave a five-year relationship and profess to love another person after only two weeks, wouldn't you question their judgment?"

Mark nodded. "I would question the strength of the relationship prior to the profession of love. I would examine the previous circumstances, but most of all, I'd listen to the reasoning of those involved and base my decisions on fact, instinct, and trust. Do you know Brian will be taken care of? Do you believe what your eyes are seeing? Despite all that's been said, can you trust Lola and Randy to raise the boy in a good family? Those are the questions I'd ask."

His reasoning was on point. Mark had managed to sum up her concerns in less than a minute.

"You're smart."

When he started to grin with pride, Sandra shook her head. "Don't go getting a big head."

"Hell, yeah, I'm going to let my head swell. Those are two words you don't hear every day. I'm smart."

Sandra chuckled, enjoying the feel of his fingers wrapped in his.

Mark had pulled her between the houses, where he clasped her around her waist and slow-danced. "The day isn't over."

Every bit of her wanted him, but Sandra held back. "My family is going to think you've kidnapped me."

"I don't think so. They've got wedding plans to finalize,

and Lola's birthday party is Friday. I don't think they'll miss you for a few more hours."

The reminders of all she'd refused to be part of left Sandra with guilty feelings. The merit in Mark's words made her realize where she could improve on her relationship with her sister and her future husband.

"I need to help more," she told Mark. "Randy seems to have everything under control, but I could at least offer."

"A regular old buttinsky."

Sandra dropped his hand. She hadn't asked to be here, and as she examined the pieces of their fragmented lives, she was becoming an outsider to Lola's suddenly perfect existence. Frankly, it was wearing on her. "I don't butt in. Randy asked for my suggestions."

"Okay."

Sandra started for the front of the house and then stopped, her mood dampened. "Thanks for everything. I had a great day." She pivoted and started up the path.

"Psst, pretty lady, can I get your phone number?" Mark mimicked one of the hoods from the subway.

She smiled, knowing he was working his way back into her system. "I don't give out my phone number to just anybody. "Who are you?"

Their chests met and he tipped her head. "The man who's been dying to end his evening like this." Mark kissed her like there was no tomorrow.

Sandra approached Randy's office and knocked on the door. She'd never ventured into his territory, never once really had more than two-question, two-answer conversations with him. She knocked again, hoping either he'd answer or she'd escape, but hanging around outside the door made her nervous.

"Come in."

Opening the door, she stuck her head inside. "You busy?"

Randy seemed wary and relief flooded her. He hadn't

taken it for granted that she would fall all over him for his money or charm. She stepped inside and closed the door behind her.

"Hi."

"Hi," he said back.

"I wanted to know if you needed any help with anything."

"Excuse me?"

Nervous, Sandra started to gesture. "A couple of weeks ago you asked for my help with Lola's birthday party, and I said I wouldn't help you."

"Yes, you did."

Sandra swallowed. "Well, I've had a chance to think about things and I don't mind helping if you need something done."

Randy closed the folder he'd been working on and pushed back from his desk. Sandra had no idea where he was going or what he was about to do, so she reached for the door.

"Sit down, Sandra. Let's talk."

"I'd prefer to stand."

"Fine." He perched on the corner of his expensive black desk. "You are a difficult woman. You should be proud of yourself."

"Why?"

"You hold the future of my family in your hands, and I swear I've practiced law for fourteen years and I can't say one way or the other what you'll decide."

"That's between me and Lola. If you didn't need my help you could have said so." Sandra jerked open the door.

"My family, too," he said, and she stopped. "Please, sit down. Lola and Brian won't be back from the beach for another half hour. We should break the ice because no matter what, we're going to be family."

Sandra ventured inside and sat at one of the leather chairs that faced the desk. Randy took the other.

"I fell in love with Lola on a flight from New York to California. Did she tell you that?"

"No." Sandra couldn't admit she'd never given her sister a chance to explain her and Randy's relationship. "She never mentioned it."

"I was in first class and she was my attendant. But Lola wouldn't give me the time of day. I did everything to get her to talk to me, but she wasn't having it. She'd sworn off men and didn't feel compelled to change just because I was in her section."

"Lola swore off men?" Sandra couldn't believe it.

"Yeah, which made it extra hard for me to get with her. When I finally got her attention, I asked her if I could take her to this club in Hollywood. I thought I'd impress her with my famous celebrity clients and throw a few bills around and she'd be mine."

"She didn't want that?"

Randy started to laugh and touched Sandra's arm. "In front of all of first class she told me if I wanted to take her anywhere I had to have put an engagement ring on her finger. She was through dating men who were only out for sex."

"That didn't shut you up?"

"Oh, hell yeah, it did. First class was quiet the rest of the night."

Sandra had to laugh. Interest piqued, she turned toward Randy. "Then what happened?"

"Three days later I finished my business and boarded a plane to go home and there was Lola. She didn't give me the time of day. Took my drink order, served me food, cleared my tray. I'd tucked a little something beneath the cloth napkin."

Curious, Sandra hurried him. "Was it a ring?"

"Let me finish. Lola was called to handle a problem in coach and didn't return for thirty minutes. I was sweating bullets. Suddenly she was at my side, dropped a piece of paper in my lap that had a box with an *'X'* checked that said: "Don't fuck around on me. I'm going to be your wife. Love, Lola Fagan.' "

Sandra and Randy laughed together.

"Sounds just like her. So had you given her a ring?"

Randy nodded. "A three-carat diamond." Sandra gasped, her mouth open. "She'd taped it to the bottom of the note, giving it back. She leaned down, took my college alumni ring, put it on her third finger, and said she would exchange one for the other the day we get married."

"Wow." Sandra saw her sister in a whole new light. The Lola she used to know would have taken the ring, shown it off, and told outrageous stories about how she'd talked a man into giving her a ring in exchange for a date.

"Do you think she's settling just to settle down?"

Randy shrugged and threw up his hands. "I hope not. I love her. And her son. And she loves me."

"She says you have a daughter. What does she think?"

"Cara thinks a lot about herself, as most teenagers do, but she wants her old man to be happy."

The front screen door slammed and they both heard Lola calling.

Sandra noticed how Randy's eyes lit with excitement and how eager he seemed to go greet his wife-to-be.

"You asked what you could do to help with Lola's birthday."

"Is there anything I can do to help?"

"Just being here."

"Randy? Sandra? Where is everybody?" Lola yelled from the hallway.

"In here," Randy called and got the door.

"Hey, baby." They kissed noisily until Randy pulled her away. "I haven't had enough yet," she said.

"We have company. Where's Brian?"

"Asleep on the couch. Who's in here?"

Lola looked fabulous in a bright yellow two-piece bathing suit, a sheer wrap knotted at her waist. She walked around Randy and stared at Sandra in surprise. "Hey," she said, her eyes wide with questions. "What's going on?"

"We were just talking about the wedding. Sandra wanted to make sure wearing aqua blue wasn't going to clash with the wedding party."

Lola looked at him in total disbelief. "You're a terrible liar. You can just say it's none of my business."

"Okay," Randy said. "It's none of your business."

She laughed at Randy and so did Sandra. Lola looked at her sister. "We don't have a wedding party. It's just Randy and me and Brian."

"Oh." They were the perfect family without her.

Lola stood in the circle of Randy's arms. "When we planned this little to-do, I didn't know if you were going to stay or . . ."

Sandra backed toward the door. "I'm staying."

Lola launched herself at her sister and tears wet Sandra's neck. "Thank you."

She hugged her back. "You're welcome."

Thirteen

Sandra fell into a routine of sharing the sunrise with Mark, dancing all morning, and playing with Brian during the afternoon so his mother could finalize wedding plans.

It was unusual for her to be at the studio on Friday afternoon, but Sister Akira had requested a special performance and Sandra was honored to oblige.

Sister Akira, the owner of the studio, had danced with the Joffrey Ballet in the late seventies and now taught only modern and African dance. Today she stood in the studio watching Sandra, who performed the routine she'd spent a week choreographing.

Sinking into the music, Sandra forgot Akira's presence and let the rhythm touch her feet, arms, and hair. She used the floor as an instrument to aid her expression, and when the music peaked she felt her body practically float through the movements.

Sandra became the dance and she lost perspective as her body followed instructions from her soul. She poured everything into it, and when the music faded and Sandra came back to reality, she heard clapping.

Slowly she focused and for the first time saw Lola, Randy, Mark, and a man she'd never seen before.

Her already-racing heart sped up. What were they doing here? Dancing had been her private diversion. Sandra hadn't mentioned it to them because she didn't want anyone to make light of something she held so dear.

Sister Akira put her hands to her lips, nodding her head. "Remarkable. Bravo!"

Sandra slowly pulled her body in, her limbs shaking

from the exertion. She rose, not wanting to go near them but needing her towel. She walked over, adrenaline pumping, grabbed her towel, and saw tears shimmering in Lola's and Randy's eyes.

Panic set in. "What's wrong? Where's Brian?"

Her sister tried to regain control of herself and Sandra grabbed her arms. "Where's the baby?"

"He's fine," Randy said. "She's just moved beyond belief."

"Oh my God," Lola said, around a sob. "You're amazing."

Sandra swallowed the lump in her throat. "Me?" She covered her eyes with her fingers, then looked at the five adults smiling at her. "What is everybody so happy about?"

"It's my birthday."

"Yeah," Sandra replied, still embarrassed. "I was there for the first twenty-nine, remember?"

"This is my present from Sister Akira."

"Sister Sandra, I knew you would never consent to allowing your sister to see the magnitude of your skills, so being the great visionary that I am, I took the liberty of inviting them and my friend Dr. Frank Zimbash from NYU for a private performance. He, by the way, would like to speak with you later. Everyone is here at my invitation. Be angry with me, if you must."

Sandra had too much respect for the older woman to be anything but grateful. She felt a suspicious burning behind her eyes. "I could never be angry with you. As for you three, and you, sir, I . . . I hoped you enjoyed the show."

Randy reached her first, hugging her hard. "You're the next Judith Jamison."

"That's stretching it, but thanks," she said sincerely.

Lola just hugged her and Sandra hugged her back. "I can't wait for you to get married so you'll cut off these waterworks."

They all laughed and Frank Zimbash took her hands into his warm ones. "You are gifted with amazing talent. When you return to New York, I'd like to speak to you about a position I have available to teach dance at an academic level. The salary is outstanding and the benefits incomparable. You would be in charge, reporting directly to me."

Lola gasped and Sandra felt her mouth drop open. "Are you for real?"

The older gentleman smiled and handed her his card. "Always. Nice to meet all of you." He took Akira's hand and he looked at Sandra. "I expect to hear from you early next week."

Her eyes fluttered, blinking back tears. "You can count on it."

The others stepped outside the studio and Mark took her hands. "You're the best dancer I've ever seen."

Leave it to honest, wise Mark to make her cry.

Sandra melted in his arms and before she knew it, she'd done a Diana Ross and wrapped her legs around his waist. "Thank you."

He held her away, awe reflecting from his eyes, and Sandra couldn't help but feel honored. "Do you know how incredible you are?" he asked. "I've never seen anything like it in my life."

"Don't keep saying that."

His gaze turned serious. "Sandra, don't be like that. You've got skills and you're cheating yourself if you don't acknowledge them. Dr. Zimbash wouldn't lie and neither would any of us. I don't know how you can be so cool."

Joy erupted inside her and she giggled. Mark's eyes lit up. "There it is."

He lowered her to her feet and Sandra squeezed his hands, knowing as soon as she finished this laughing jag, she'd be in tears. "I really do feel special. I feel great!"

Sandra laughed aloud and Mark laughed with her.

A tear slipped down her cheek, and Lola, who'd come back into the studio, started to cry again. "Oh no, here we go." Randy and Mark wore silly grins and Sandra sank to the floor, trying to cover her face.

Mark folded his large frame beside her and gently took her hands. "You are special."

Her heart flowered and even as she tried to stem her tears and laughter at the same time, she couldn't. "I feel as if I don't have a care in the world. Like when Mother and Daddy were alive."

Mark pursed his lips and Sandra just wanted to kiss him, but she didn't. She went into his arms and accepted his strength. Took a minute to absorb all of him. Minutes later, she regained control.

When she could focus, she realized they were alone.

"Where's my sister?"

"I think Randy took her outside. She's happy for you."

Sandra swallowed a lump in her throat. "I know. Loving Lola wasn't always easy, but I understand her much better. I really do love her."

"She loves you, too."

"I'm not going to fight them over Brian. I believe he's going to be just fine."

"You're smart *and* beautiful. I'm glad you decided to do what you feel is best. When are you going to tell them?"

"Tonight."

Mark helped her into her lightweight hooded jacket and she pulled on dance pants and sandals.

Sandra was nearly at the door when Mark drew his hand down her shoulder. She turned and met him halfway in a kiss that defined love in its simplest form.

"Baby," she murmured.

"Mmm." He held her cheeks between strong hands and Sandra felt as if they were alone in the world.

"After the party . . ." Their need filled in the blank space.

His thumb grazed her cheek. "Definitely."

A half hour before the party, Sandra ran into her sister in the kitchen. Neighbors had come over with food and gifts for the wedding, so the birthday party had turned into a bridal shower as well.

Lola looked sexy in lightweight leather pants and a sleeveless shirt, while Sandra had settled on shorts and a sleeveless tank. They both wore their hair long and loose and more than once had received double takes.

"Can I talk to you for a minute?" Sandra asked her sister.

Lola finished her dill pickle and wiped her hands on a napkin. "Sure. Come outside. It's a freaking furnace in here."

They stepped onto the back porch and Lola leaned against the rail. "What's up?"

Sandra looked at her only sister. She remembered her arrival home from the hospital, her first bike ride, and her first day of school. Sandra also remembered the birth of Lola's child and how special she felt for being asked to raise the boy. It was now time to bestow that gift back on her sister.

"I came here prepared to hate you and Randy and find a reason to keep Brian with me. But I don't hate you. Or Randy. In fact, I feel like I've finally got a brother."

Lola's eyes welled.

"Don't start or I'll never be able to get through this." Sandra wiped her wet eyes. "You taught me a lot while I've been here."

"Me?" Lola squeaked in disbelief. "What?"

"How to forgive. And how to say 'I'm sorry' and how to grow up. I love Brian, Lola. Giving him up is almost harder than losing Mother and Daddy. But your son belongs with you. You *are* his mother."

Lola grabbed Sandra, crying against her sister's shoulder in great gulping sobs. "Thank you," Lola moaned. "I won't let you down."

"I know you won't."

"I love you, Sandra. Even when we were kids. I loved you."

"I know. Me, too."

They held each other as they had so many times as children. Pain that had been locked away was freed into a Martha's Vineyard wind and replaced with love. "You were fantastic dancing today. What are you going to do with those skills?"

Sandra shrugged. "It seems Akira knows everything in my heart. I'm going to take the job at NYU providing the deal is right."

Lola patted her back. "Forget a great deal. Go where your heart is leading you and you'll be fine."

Sandra nodded against her sister's shoulder. "Okay, that's what I'll do."

Randy stuck his head out the door. "What's up?" he said softly.

Lola reached for him and he engulfed her. "Our family is complete."

Wide-eyed, he stared at her. "Yeah?"

Laughing, Lola nodded. "Yeah."

He gave a loud whoop and Sandra edged past, prepared to give them their privacy.

"Oh, no, you don't. Come here."

Randy pulled Sandra into a three-way hug and gave her a big kiss on the cheek. "Thank you."

"You're welcome," she said and meant it.

Sandra hadn't had so much fun at a party in a long time. Lots of island friends Sandra had not met stopped by and helped fill the large house with noise and laughter. Brian had gone to Carlton's house, having reconnected with the boy and his mother on the beach. When the guests were ready, they had the Soul Train line, played spades, drank wine, and talked junk until the wee hours.

Around 2:00 A.M., Sandra sought relief from losing at spades against Lola, who sat on Randy's lap with a cigar between her teeth. Sandra headed out the back door and collapsed on the steps. Cold wind floated over her warm skin and she shuddered.

"Psst, hey, baby, can I get your phone number?"

A smile worked her lips as she stood. The backyard was

dark, but she didn't need light to see her suitor. "Who are you and why would I want to give you my phone number?"

Mark stepped from the shadows of his back porch, two bottles of wine in his hands. He took slow steps up the stairs. " 'Cause I want to make love to you."

Sandra put her hands on her hips, laughing low and sexy. Leave it to Mark to get right to the point.

His mouth grazed her right breast and she shook from the sudden burst of inner heat and the cool outdoor temperature. "I've got the wine and me," he said. "What are you bringing to the party?"

"Me." She met his gaze. "Where's your party?"

"My house, right now."

Sandra looked over her shoulder to see her sister looking straight at her. Lola waved good-bye and lowered her mouth to Randy's.

"I just got permission. Lead the way."

Instead of stepping down, Mark stepped up and kissed her full on the lips. Sandra knew she'd have followed him to the ocean just to be in his arms. As it was, she ended up in his bedroom a minute after she stepped off her sister's porch.

Alone, with the muted sounds of the party going on next door and the shadows cast from the streetlights, Sandra experienced the power of Mark's touch as he caressed her from the tips of her hair to the soles of her feet.

She let her fingertips wreak havoc on his back, legs, and every space in between until his groans became soft curses.

When he took her, Sandra was sure this slice of heaven could never be duplicated, never repeated, and even as she crested seconds before him, she vowed to make this moment last forever.

Fourteen

Sandra awoke the morning before the wedding to a five o'clock shadow grazing her cheek. She knew Mark's chin and smiled, her eyes still closed.

He'd been coming to her room for sunrise every morning since Lola's birthday party. Sandra had worried the morning she'd tried to sneak from his house if he'd have regrets, but he'd squashed those thoughts when five minutes after her arrival in her room he was there reminding her of his power.

She turned over and kissed him. Sandra recorded his features in her mind. She only had two days left on the island and then she'd be returning to her new life and job in New York.

The thought of leaving them didn't make her feel great, but she'd tried to keep everything in perspective. She'd done what she was supposed to do. And had gotten so much in return.

"Why are you looking at me like that?" he asked.

"No reason. Sleep good?"

"I did until you left."

She turned her back and fit into the spoon of his body. "You're spoiled."

"Look at me."

Mark sounded serious and Sandra slid to her back. "What?"

"I don't want you to go back to Brooklyn alone. Let me go with you. I'll stay for a few days and then come home."

Sandra closed her eyes. He wasn't asking her to stay, but he wanted to go with her. He loved Martha's Vineyard, and she knew how he hated being off the island. For Mark to volunteer to stay in the city was enough to make her heart swell.

"You'd really do that, wouldn't you?"

"I would and I will."

She smiled sadly. "I can't let you." Sandra thought of the empty apartment and the fact that she'd have to face it alone one day. It was better to do it now.

"Why not? I don't mind," Mark said easily.

"I'm a big girl."

His hand strayed down her stomach. "I know, but you don't have to go home alone. Have you told Brian yet?"

"Later today," she sighed, loving the feel of his touch.

"You could stay with me and not go back," he offered.

Sandra wiggled against his searching fingers. "I can't. I've got a potential new job and an apartment and friends and mmm . . ."

"Like that?"

"You've got me sprung. Stop; I can't think when you touch me like that."

Being honest with Mark was so easy. Sandra didn't fear he'd use her emotions against her.

He stilled his hands, and she focused.

"You're going to come next month with Randy and Lola to pick up Brian's things."

He looked at her with questioning eyes. "Tell me what I mean to you."

Sandra breathed hard and his eyebrows shot up. "I know what you mean to me, but I want to hear you say the words," he said.

The predawn sky was overcast and hazy. In the dark with Mark beside her, she took a step out on a limb she'd never ventured onto before. "I like being with you. Talking, debating, even arguing with your smart-ass self."

"I've been called worse. Keep going." His hands roamed her thighs.

"I like listening to you. Making love to you. Listening

to you laugh. The way you look at me makes me feel good."

He nestled his face in her neck and moved above her. "What else? Do you love me?"

She accepted his smooth thrust with pleasure. On a sigh she said, "Yes, I do."

They rode together, his gaze shuttered, his face stretched into a concentrated mask. "Let me come with you."

Even as Sandra muttered, "No," he took her to a new height. Sandra knew if he came home with her, she wouldn't be able to let him go. With her arms around his back, her legs around his waist, Sandra shook with release, her heart never wanting to let him go.

After dinner, Sandra, Lola, and Randy along with Brian, settled in the living room with ice cream. They'd planned to tell Brian at the end of the day when they were all home and could answer questions.

"Brian," Lola said. "You know tomorrow Randy and I are getting married."

The boy nodded enthusiastically.

"Well, Randy and I thought it would be fun for you to stay with us," she stumbled and put down her bowl of ice cream. "For a while." Sandra knew surprise lifted her eyes as Lola struggled. "Forever."

Brian stared between the three, his lips hanging open, ice cream dripping off. "I'm going back home with Auntie, Mommy."

Shock rippled the silence. "Brian, you're going to stay with us."

He shook his head, his bowl forgotten. Sandra's stomach sank. "No, I live in Brooklyn with Auntie Sandra. You can come visit like always."

"What about if Auntie comes to visit you here? Then you'll hardly miss her."

Brian's chin started to quiver and Sandra's eyes smarted.

"Brian, your mother wants you to live with her and Randy now."

"You don't want me at our house anymore?"

Sandra swallowed her tears. "Of course I do. That'll always be your home. But Mommy—"

Panicked, he dropped his bowl. "No, I'm going with you! Where will Mussa visit me? I want to go home now." He started crying in earnest and Sandra crossed the room and gathered him in her arms. "Okay. We'll talk about this later. Shh. You're okay."

"Can I go home, back to our house with you?"

Sandra met his teary gaze. "Yes."

Lola covered her face with her hands and wcpt softly. She looked at Sandra over Brian's head, then walked from the room.

Randy stood, too. "You could have supported her more."

Sandra held her nephew in her arms, knowing the words derived from hurt rather than anger. "Go see about her. She needs you right now."

Taking Brian to bed, Sandra sat with him until he was asleep and then even longer because he wouldn't release her hand. Lola came in around midnight.

"How's he doing?"

"Worried."

They both looked at the sleeping child. "Lola, I never thought he'd react this way. I guess we're not so smart."

A strangled cry cam from her sister. "Guess not. Let's talk about it tomorrow. I've got a big day ahead of me."

Sandra hugged her sister and they walked from Brian's room together.

The wedding took place at six o'clock the following evening, bathed in candlelight. Sandra and Mark sat beside each other, his hand intertwined with hers.

Lola looked stunning in a cream gown and gold accessories. Sandra couldn't believe her sister was actually getting married until the pastor pronounced them man and wife.

Brian was antsy, happy, but eager to get out of his suit so he could play.

The reception was intimate, just friends and neighbors, with a larger one planned when Randy and Lola returned from the ten-day honeymoon, which was supposed to include Brian. Now those plans were up in the air.

At the reception, Brian barely left Sandra's side, whining when he didn't get his way. Sandra understood his behavior but hadn't anticipated Lola's sad reaction. She was subdued and she tracked Brian's every movement with her eyes.

Mark sat beside Sandra. "How's Brian?"

She looked for her nephew and found him by the wedding cake, licking his finger. "Unchanged. He's insisting on going home with me. I don't know what to do. What do you think?"

Mark smoothed Sandra's V-neck bodice. "You know him best. Will he be okay in a few days or will he need longer to adjust to all of this?"

"He needs time. But what about Lola?"

"She'll have to understand."

"What if she doesn't?"

"Then maybe she isn't ready to be Brian's mother." He tugged her to her feet. "Dance with me. I want to be close to you."

Floating, Sandra melted into Mark's arms, wishing this night would never end. They danced together slowly, savoring time as the moments ticked away.

Soon the reception ended and Mark and Sandra, along with a sleeping Brian, returned to Lola's empty house.

Sandra tucked in the tired child and cherished watching him sleep. This was her last opportunity for a while, she supposed.

In the morning, Brian, his mom, and Randy would board a plane and go to Hawaii.

This was it. Sandra's last opportunity to be alone with

the little boy she'd raised. She caressed his smooth skin, remembering his first tooth and his first step. Her eyes welled as she recalled his first haircut and his first fall.

The tears spilled when she thought of his first day of day care and his first best friend.

She lay beside him, tears slipping down her cheeks when the door opened.

Gently she was carried to her room and laid on the bed. She turned in to Mark and let her heart break. When she was spent, she slept in the arms of the man she loved.

Fifteen

The bags were packed and stowed in the waiting cab. Sandra sat next to Brian on the last seat in the van while Lola and Randy sat in the row ahead of them.

We're sure a sad group, Sandra thought as the driver slammed the door and shifted into drive.

A tap on the back window caused him to brake suddenly. They all turned.

Mark was outside.

Unable to believe her eyes after their emotional goodbye this morning, Sandra watched as he settled into the front seat.

"How's everybody?" he asked as if he didn't notice the heavy silence.

They all replied in unison, "Fine."

Brian gripped Sandra's fingers and whenever she shifted to get comfortable, he'd cast her a worried look. This parting wasn't going to be easy, so when she closed her eyes, she fingered the gold dollar Mark had given her her first day on the island and asked God for a special blessing.

Finally they were inside the Boston airport and Sandra stood next to Mark with Brian wrapped around her leg. "Have a meeting in the area?"

"Yes." He nodded, offering no additional information. His closed expression scared her. He wasn't angry, but he looked determined.

"Angel face, I can't walk."

"Are we almost home?" Brian whined.

Sandra's gaze shot to Lola, who was whispering in Randy's ear.

"Yes, sweetie. Just a couple more hours."

Randy signaled Mark and the two walked off.

"What's going on?" she asked Lola.

"I just wanted to talk to Brian." He stiffened and she waved him over to a row of chairs. "Come sit and talk to me. Sandra, would you join us?"

Lola looked at her son after he sat down. "I'm so happy to have spent this past month with you. I never realized what a joy you are."

"Thank you," he said solemnly.

"You're welcome. I was afraid Auntie would be the saddest of us all when I thought of you coming to live with us. And she was. What I didn't consider was how sad you'd be."

"I like your house, Mommy."

"I'm so glad to hear you say that."

Over the loudspeaker their flight was announced and passengers were asked to start boarding.

Lola took her son's hand. "I'd like to prove to you you'll love living with me—"

"No," he moaned.

"But," she said, "not so fast."

Sandra's heart raced. *Where was Lola going with this?*

Randy and Mark rushed up, tickets in hand. Lola accepted them with a big smile. "Brian, how about if Randy and I come stay with you for a while?"

His eyes widened and his mouth dropped open. "For real?"

"For real."

"Yea! You can sleep in my room."

Lola looked at Sandra. "Is this okay with you?"

Typical, Sandra thought. *Asking me after the fact.* But this time she didn't mind. "I think it's a great idea."

Lola held her son's hand for the first time since announcing his new living arrangements and walked behind Sandra. "I think your sweetheart has something to say," she said and got in line to board.

Nervous, Sandra pushed back strands of her long hair and looked at the man she'd fallen in love with. She didn't want to say good-bye but knew there wasn't time for anything else. "Baby," she murmured.

He took her hands. "Mmm." Mark engulfed her.

"I'm going to miss you."

"Sandra, this doesn't have to be good-bye. Say the word and I'm there."

Sandra kissed his neck, knowing he liked it. "Just like that?"

"Yeah."

Her heart thundered. "Come see me," she whispered.

Mark held her face between his hands. "Done."

Euphoria swept through her. "When?"

Final boarding was announced and he backed toward the gate, bringing her with him. Mark handed Brian's bag to Randy, who then boarded.

Love blossomed in her heart until she was overwhelmed.

Mark kissed her tears. "Right now. First class. We're going home."

A delighted scream tore from her, and for the first time in her adult life, Sandra felt completely loved.

Best Left Unsaid

Janice Sims

A book is always a collaborative effort. My thanks go out to Margaret Johnson-Hodge, who had faith in me when I didn't have faith in myself. To Editor Glenda Howard who dreamed up the project and offered me a part in it. And to Editor Monique Patterson who bravely came in in the middle of the game and ran with the ball! Thanks, ladies.

One

Leon instantly recognized her, on a fine April afternoon, as she stepped into the elevator of the Hotel Montalembert. He followed her inside and tried not to stare.

She wore a minimal amount of makeup and her thick, wavy, shoulder-length jet-black hair in a ponytail. Black jeans, a plain white shirt, and a black leather jacket adorned the famous body he'd seen nearly nude in the latest *Sports Illustrated* swimsuit issue.

Supermodel LuAnne Copeland. She held her leather shoulder bag close to her chest and planted boot-clad feet apart before requesting, "Lobby, please."

Leon couldn't help noticing the catch in her voice.

Since he was nearest to the control panel, he pressed the button.

With a defiant expression in her dark, glistening eyes she retreated to her corner. Silent tears fell as she stalwartly stood there looking straight ahead.

"Are you all right?" Leon ventured.

"Do I know you?" she asked belligerently, eyes zeroing in on him, itching for a fight. Troy hadn't been inclined to give her one, the coward. She wanted to lash out at someone. Anyone. She sized him up. He would do nicely.

"No, but—"

"Then don't bother me."

Silence, as the car descended.

One floor later the doors slid open, but no passengers were waiting to board.

She was disappointed. He was a talker. She sensed it.

He was barely restraining himself and would start in again the moment those doors closed.

As they closed, she dug in her purse for tissues, pointedly turning her back on him. If that didn't send him a "not available" signal, she didn't know what would.

The elevator began to move again and, sure enough, he cleared his throat and said, "What happened? Your dog died?"

He sounded like a Brooklyn tough guy. She'd lived in New York City for seven years before making Paris her home. Turning, she slowly perused him as she dabbed her face with a tissue. He certainly had the build: well over six feet, solid, broad shoulders, slim hips, a muscular neck any linebacker would be envious of. Big hands, big feet. Skin the color of California plums: purple-black. And he was bald as an egg. He looked like a jock.

At that moment, she hated jocks. Troy played for the San Francisco 49ers.

"Back that thing up, bruh. I am not in the mood to play word games with the opposite sex this afternoon, thank you. Now you stay in your corner, and I'll stay in mine, and nobody will get hurt."

"That bad?" he asked sympathetically. Worry lines creased his brow. "You know, they say talking to a perfect stranger can be worth hours on a psychiatrist's couch."

Fed up, she was about to throw down on him when the elevator violently bucked and came to an abrupt stop. The jolt made her lose her balance. He caught her in his steady embrace. Glaring up at him, she wrenched free of his hold. "What the hell was that!"

"Let's hope it wasn't a cable snapping."

"Oh my God!" she cried, clamping onto the handrail with both hands. Slowly she pried her hands loose and turned to look up at him. "Can't you *do* something?"

"Calm down, Miss Copeland," Leon said, coming to grasp her by the shoulders. "It's probably some minor malfunction. They'll have us out of here in no time."

Her whiskey-colored eyes mirrored her terror as she continued to stare at him. Placing a hand on her flat stomach, she drew a deep breath and said, "You obviously aren't familiar with these old buildings. We could be stranded for hours."

Leon laughed at her assertion. "We'll be out of here in a matter of minutes."

He released her to go over to the control panel. There was no phone box concealed in it. There was, however, a red "emergency" button. He pushed it, and a shrill alarm blared. "See?" he said with satisfaction. "You have nothing to worry about."

LuAnne only grimaced and continued to hold her stomach as if her life depended on it. She began to nervously tap her foot on the elevator floor.

Leon's gaze went from her worry-creased face to her midsection, then back again. "You've just found out you're expecting?"

LuAnne's eyes grew wide with shock. "How did you—"

"Your body language," he said with a gentle smile. "Let's get comfortable." He shrugged off his leather jacket, folded it, and placed it on the floor for her to sit on. LuAnne noted that chivalry wasn't dead after all, then sat down with her legs tucked underneath her.

"Is that why you're here?" he asked quietly, dark brown eyes questioning.

"Are you sure you're not a tabloid reporter?" LuAnne asked, eyes narrowing.

"Cross my heart and hope to live forever."

"That's not how the saying goes."

"I don't hope to die. Too many things left to do." He offered her his hand. "Hello, I'm Leon Jackson of—"

"Brooklyn, New York," LuAnne completed for him.

He gave a deep chuckle. "And where did that sexy southern accent come from?"

"Richmond, Virginia."

Suddenly the alarm was silenced and anxious French

voices could be heard on the other side of the elevator doors. LuAnne listened carefully. Her French was pretty fair after living in Paris for three years, but she got lost if the speaker spoke too swiftly.

"They want us to confirm that we're all right, and they say the wait shouldn't be long. The repairman is on the way," she translated for Leon.

"Tres bien," she called to the people in the hallway. *"Merci, merci!"*

Getting comfortable, she turned toward Leon. "So, what are you doing in Paris, Leon Jackson?"

"I'm licking my wounds and trying to find my literary soul in one fell swoop," he said, a slightly embarrassed look crossing his features. "I always wanted to go to the places Richard Wright and James Baldwin frequented while here. In the past week, I've been to quite a few of them."

"Another writer trying to find his muse?"

"A writer, not really. But definitely a bibliophile."

"Why did you qualify your reply with 'not really'? Makes me think you're actually a writer. You just don't want to admit it."

"We're getting way off the subject here," Leon countered. "You were going to tell me what you're doing here. And while you're at it, I'd like to know why you were so sad. Is the guy married or something?"

"You're pretty nosy," LuAnne accused lightly. "Let's be fair about this exchange of information. You obviously know what I do for a living. What about you?"

"I was a professional football player until a hip injury benched me. After the operation, the doc said I could play another season or two, but why would I want to do that? I don't want to be in a wheelchair by the time I'm sixty-five. So, I quit," he said easily.

"No wife, family?"

"Had a wife. I lost her because I was a fool."

"Pussy hound, huh?"

"Of the first order," he admitted, looking her straight in

the eye. "They were offering it at every turn and I was too stupid to say no. Cheryl forgave me once, twice, but drew the line at three times. And I don't blame her. I let it all go to my head."

"So, you've got your head on straight now?"

"I've been celibate for nearly a year."

"Get outta here!"

"I figured if I couldn't take control of the problem, there was no hope for a lasting relationship in my future. It was a question of willpower."

"Or won't power," LuAnne quipped, smiling at him.

Leon returned her smile with a megawatt one of his own. "Okay, Lulu, spill."

"I hate that nickname!" LuAnne protested, frowning.

"That's what they dubbed you, Lulu the Lovely. A Barbie doll dipped in chocolate."

"Is that supposed to be some kind of a compliment?" she asked archly, her nose in the air. "That's an insult! Are black women more attractive if they look like a white beauty ideal? I don't think so!"

"If Barbie had back like you, Ken would never let her out of the playhouse," Leon said. He smiled roguishly as he awaited her reaction.

LuAnne laughed. "You're slightly twisted, aren't you, Leon?"

"A little."

LuAnne leaned her head back against the wall and sighed. She was silent for a moment. "How do I describe Troy? First of all, I was cold to you because you reminded me of him."

"Then I take it he's a brother?"

"Yeah."

"Good."

"Good?"

"You weren't dating a white guy."

"Oh, that matters?"

A frown drew thick, luxuriant brows together. "Damn

right it matters. It does something to us every time we see a sister on the arm of a white dude."

"Well, it wasn't his color but his build that I was referring to. You're both athletes."

"Troy . . . not Troy Granger!"

"Unfortunately," she said in a small, sad voice.

"I guess you don't follow football," Leon said gently. "Because if you did, you would have known Troy's reputation with the ladies is even worse than mine was."

"My mistake. I'm a single-minded gal. Work, work, work. It's something my mother drummed into me at an early age." She laughed softly to herself. "I should have listened."

Needing a sugar fix, she rummaged in her purse and withdrew a box of jelly beans.

After she'd popped a few in her mouth, she offered him the box. "Have some."

Leon looked skeptically at the box. "I don't eat candy." He took the box, however. "And you shouldn't, either."

LuAnne's eyes narrowed menacingly when she realized he was taking her jelly beans hostage. Getting up on her knees, she lunged at him. Shaking him by the collar, she demanded, "Give them back, you big jerk. It's the one vice I have, and I've had a lousy day! Do I have to get physical with you?"

"When we get out of here, I'll take you to Sunday dinner at Haynes' Bar," Leon said reasonably, holding the box out of her reach. "You can have sweet potato pie for dessert. It's better for you than these things. Do you want your baby eating candy? Remember, whatever you consume, he consumes."

Pouting, LuAnne sat back down, her arms folded across her chest. She refused to look at Leon. "I can't believe this day I'm having."

"So, you were returning from doing the deed just now? Telling him he's gonna be a daddy? That's why you were crying?"

LuAnne sniffed. "I think I feel another one coming on."

Leon relinquished the jelly beans. "Oh, hell, take them if they'll make you feel better."

LuAnne's hand closed around the box, but she didn't hasten to eat the treats. "You really think they're bad for the baby?"

"You be the judge," Leon said. "My mother ate cornstarch like it was going out of style when she was carrying me, and I ain't crazy." He smiled. "Well, not too crazy."

LuAnne slipped the box of jelly beans back in her purse. Then she smiled at him and leaned against the wall again. "You're a man."

"That's the general consensus."

Her smile faded as she studied him. "Why do you think Troy told me to get rid of his child? It really floored me when he told me to get an abortion. I would never have thought that of him. That he wouldn't want his child, let alone take responsibility for creating it. Him, I mean." She closed her eyes. "I've gotta stop calling this child 'it.' He's a human being, and I want him." She placed her hand gently on her stomach.

"Why?" Leon asked softly.

She looked askance at him. "Because I'm not getting any younger and this may be my last chance to have a child. I'm thirty-two—"

Leon pursed his lips. "Nowadays, women are having children well into their forties."

"Besides, I've never been caught before."

His brows shot up in surprise. "And you've been sexually active for how long?"

"Since I was sixteen."

"I was the same age my first time."

LuAnne stretched her long legs out before her and flexed her feet. "How old are you now? Late twenties?"

"Three years older than you are."

"Well, you look good."

"So do you."

"Good enough to make you break your vow of celibacy?"

His face broke into a wide grin. "I'd break it in a New York minute!"

LuAnne issued a throaty laugh. "You're good for my ego." Her smile vanished. "Which has been damned near smashed to smithereens."

"Oh, you'll recover, Lulu."

LuAnne sat watching him. She didn't seem to mind when he called her that anymore.

"Because he's scared," Leon said after a long pause.

LuAnne had to think a moment. "You think he's afraid of becoming a father?"

"Becoming a father, being responsible for someone other than himself. And, really, Lulu, is he responsible for himself right now? I was a pro ballplayer for nearly fifteen years and I was well taken care of. All I had to do was play ball and stay in relatively good shape. My accountant took care of my money, which was a mistake, but I won't get into that right now. My agent took care of my career. The housekeeper cleaned up after me. The coach told me how to play ball. The doctor took care of my health. All I had to concentrate on was keeping myself fit to play ball.

"Troy is probably no different. Responsibility? It scares him shitless. Believe me. But, on the flip side, most men come to their senses after a reasonable length of time and realize being a father might not be all that bad a proposition. Give him time. Give yourself time. You're both in shock."

The elevator bell sounded, and the doors opened, revealing a hallway full of relieved-looking hotel personnel.

Leon helped LuAnne to her feet, retrieved his jacket, and slipped it on.

They were immediately set upon by the apologetic staff.

LuAnne assured them that they were both perfectly fine and would be taking the stairs down to the lobby.

Leon followed her toward the exit, admiring her hip action in those jeans, then chided himself for lusting after a pregnant woman. *Bad Leon!*

Once out front, he hailed a taxi, and they climbed into the backseat.

"Trois rue Clauzel," LuAnne told the driver.

"All right," Leon said, grinning. "Collard greens and corn bread! I'm famished."

"I hope you've got plenty of money on you," LuAnne said seriously; then a wicked smile curled her full lips. "Because I plan to break the Leon bank this afternoon."

"Yeah, right!" Leon returned, taking up the challenge. "You models eat like birds."

"I eat my words," Leon conceded an hour or so later as LuAnne polished off a large slice of pecan pie. He'd ordered the sweet potato pie and she'd had half of that, too. "You definitely know your way around a fork. Where do you put it all?"

LuAnne daintily wiped the corner of her mouth with a linen napkin and a low burp escaped. She laughed shortly. "Excuse me."

Leon smiled at her. "In some cultures that's a sign you enjoyed your meal."

"Oh, I did." She reached over to trail a finger along his clean-shaven jaw. "Thank you, Leon." Brightening, she pushed her plate away and said, "I don't usually have such big meals, but I needed comfort food today. I come here whenever I'm homesick."

LuAnne looked around the large dining room. Their fellow diners were from diverse cultural backgrounds, all of them enjoying themselves. Haynes' Bar was founded in 1949 by Leroy Haynes, a black ex-GI and artist who stayed behind after WW II. Haynes passed away a few years ago, but the popular spot was still family-owned and-operated.

"What was home like?"

"A study in contrasts, really. My sister, Rhonda, and I were close, very close, growing up. It was Ronnie and I against 'Nessa. That's what we called our mother, Vanessa, behind her back. Ronnie's a photographer living and working in New York now."

"How many years separate you and Rhonda?"

"She's a year and a half older, and she never lets me forget it," LuAnne said fondly. She loved her sister. Although it had become increasingly difficult to nurture their friendship over the years with her living in Paris and Rhonda living in Manhattan. Lately even the phone calls had become less frequent, less warm, less personal.

"Mother hen?"

"Sometimes." She raised her gaze to his. "I don't know how she's going to react when I tell her I'm pregnant. She'll probably want to organize an ass-kicking party with Troy as the guest of honor."

"Sounds like a warrior-woman."

"Oh, you don't want to cross her," LuAnne said with a laugh.

Beep.

"I had a dream about you last night. In it we were in the Caribbean and making love on the beach. I can still feel your lush body against mine—"

Hurrying into her kitchen this morning, attired only in a sleeveless T-shirt, boxers, and socks, Rhonda snatched up the receiver before Maceo could continue.

"How many times have I told you to stop leaving erotic messages on my machine?" she asked, trying to keep the amusement out of her voice. "When I'm pressed for time Bobbie gets my messages. I don't want her to have to listen to your wet dreams."

"Go out with me and I can stop dreaming," Maceo said, his deep baritone sexy in spite of the early hour. The kid had potential. He could give Tyson Beckford a run for his money. But Maceo was five years younger than she was, and his career as a model was skyrocketing. In a minute, his head would be so blown up he'd forget she ever existed.

He'd been pestering her to go out with him ever since their first shoot together nearly a year ago. They'd had six subsequent shoots and he'd flirted outrageously with her every time. Her best friend, Heaven O'Riley, thought she should take him up on his offer.

"Rhonda?"

"Sorry, daydreaming," she said, laughing softly.

"About me, I hope. What are you wearing?" he asked, husky-voiced.

Laughing, Rhonda said, "I'm not encouraging your hedonistic tendencies, young man."

"You sound like my second-grade teacher. Did I ever tell you I had a huge crush on her?"

"I see you've had a long history of being attracted to older women."

"Why are you hung up on five years? Women live longer than men anyway. Thirty years from now it won't matter. By then our children will have children and no one will be the wiser."

"You've given me my sexual thrill for the day. Now hang up like a good little boy and let me go shower. I've got an important appointment this morning."

"You saw my photos in the 2001 Alaye calendar. You know I'm not a little boy by any means," Maceo returned teasingly. "Let's make a wager, Miss Copeland: I'll take you to dinner tonight and kiss you good-bye at the door. If you're unmoved, I'll stop leaving messages on your machine. Deal?"

"Promise?" Why not? Someone had to put the young pup in his place.

"You have my word as a gentleman."

"Judging by your past messages, you're no gentleman, Maceo Duncan."

"You're saving them, aren't you?" he guessed, sounding rather pleased with himself.

"Damn straight," Rhonda wasn't ashamed to say.

Maceo chuckled. "Then I must be doing something right.

Okay, I'll say good-bye. Under the Stairs, tonight at eight?"

"All right," Rhonda said, sighing. "If it's the only way to get rid of you."

"That or go ahead and make love to me. I'd probably die of ecstasy, and you'd be free of me. You have to promise to come to my funeral in a red dress and make a scene."

"Damn, boy, you're making me hot. Good-bye!" Rhonda hung up and trudged to the bathroom, a silly grin on her face.

Half an hour later she was running down the steps of her Amsterdam Avenue building, yelling hello to Rudy, the doorman, and almost colliding with Jo, the theatrical agent who lived upstairs. An ash-blond baby boomer, Jo was returning from walking her dog, Butch, a sweet-natured Cairn terrier. Rhonda thought it an inappropriate name, but Jo was a walking misnomer herself. In a field dominated by men, anyone would have expected her to be aggressive in business. However, Jo preferred to win people over with charm and finesse. She flashed large white teeth at Rhonda now, her blue eyes sparkling. "Slow down, darling; you're gonna pull something."

"Hopefully nothing important," Rhonda said, still moving down the sidewalk. "You have a good one, Jo!"

"Honey, it's all important when you get to be my age," Jo shouted back. She peered down at Butch. "Shall we go have our first cup of coffee of the day?"

The neighborhood was buzzing with life. Kids going off to school, the worker bees heading to their offices. Rhonda loved living on the Upper West Side.

Possibly because of its central location, her building was a magnet for creative types: actors, painters, dancers, singers, musicians. She'd lived there nearly ten years, ever since graduating from Spelman College. As a photographer, she fit right in and had always felt as if she belonged there.

Practically every morning found her walking up 96th Street to get the #2 or the #3 express train uptown. Occasionally, if she got a really late start, she'd take a cab, but if you weren't savvy, cabdrivers would play you, pretending they didn't speak English. Therefore, the subway was her most frequently used mode of transportation.

A panhandler, his clothes threadbare but moderately clean, waylaid her. "Can you spare some change, sister?"

He had too much dignity to offer her his outstretched palm. Not until she appeared willing to oblige him. Rhonda went into her jacket pocket and came out with a few dollars. She pressed them in his hand. "Have some breakfast."

"God bless you, sister," the man said, and ambled down the street in the opposite direction. Rhonda picked up her pace. She didn't want to miss her train.

Rhonda had a hard and fast rule about panhandlers: If they smelled of booze, she kept walking. But if they appeared just down-and-out, she freely gave. Her friends often ridiculed this practice, calling her a soft touch. But Rhonda didn't care how others perceived her, just how she saw herself.

A couple of bucks were a pittance to her, but to someone like the man she'd just encountered it could mean not having to go a day without food.

The subway platform was congested at eight in the morning. Several commuters were close enough for her to smell their breakfast on them. She firmly held onto her shoulder bag and portfolio, realizing that kids took the opportunity to snatch your bag and flee, the press of the crowd preventing you from giving chase. Which Rhonda would not do anyway. Let them have the bag. She kept her wallet with her money and ID in it strapped to her left leg underneath her jeans. A habit she'd begun shortly after being mugged seven years ago.

She was headed to Fifth Avenue. She had a meeting with an editor, Barbara Lewis of Beacon Publishing. Rhonda was going to pitch a book of photographs and musings with the city's homeless as subjects. The proceeds would go to area shelters.

Rhonda's mainstay was fashion photography. It paid the

rent. But her first love was finding beauty in the ordinary faces of ordinary people. In the past two years she'd spent every spare moment on the street talking to and photographing the homeless, but she only photographed those who gave her permission to do so. Their dignity was important to her. She had rarely been refused when she explained her purpose behind her invasion of their privacy.

On the train, after standing a few minutes, she was lucky to find a seat between an elderly black woman and a teenage Latino with a rolled-up magazine clutched in one hand. He gave her the once-over as she sat down. Rhonda turned her eyes toward the front of the car. She could almost hear his mind clicking away. And when he laughed suddenly, she knew he'd mistaken her for her sister. It had been happening ever since LuAnne had graced the cover of *Sports Illustrated*'s swimsuit issue.

"Oh my God!" he cried, quickly getting to his feet and looking down at Rhonda with the joy of discovery in his light brown eyes. "I can't believe you're riding the subway!"

Rhonda had long ago learned that trying to deny she was LuAnne Copeland was a losing battle. If she denied it, the accuser sometimes became defensive. Thinking LuAnne was denying who she was simply because she was too good to spend a measly couple of minutes with the common man.

"Listen, keep your voice down, will you?" Rhonda pleaded, giving him a warm smile as the train picked up speed. "Please, sit." Enough attention had been directed her way.

He glanced nervously at the subway doors as he reclaimed his seat. "You cut your hair," he said in awe, his eyes caressing her face. "My boys'll never believe this."

The open adoration in his eyes made Rhonda uneasy. The whole idea of her sister's face being recognized the world over took some getting used to. That she and LuAnne so closely resembled each other was something she'd lived with all her life.

They shared the same shade of golden-brown skin, heart-shaped faces, large, wide-set light brown eyes, small noses above full mouths, and dimples in both cheeks. In grade school the similarity had been cute, and their mother had dressed them in matching outfits. And in high school there had been certain advantages to being a dead ringer for your sister: if you didn't want to attend an event, she could go in your place. Of course, their tricks never worked on their parents or anyone else who knew them well enough to tell them apart. It had been fun while it lasted, though.

These days, in Rhonda's opinion, it was easier to tell them apart. Rhonda wore her sooty black hair short, whereas LuAnne's trademark was her long, thick, wavy head of hair. Plus, Rhonda outweighed her sister by at least twenty pounds.

He thrust the dog-eared magazine at her and pleaded, "Would you please sign this for me? My stop's coming up real soon."

Now she knew the reason behind his anxious behavior.

Rhonda took the magazine, grabbed a felt-tip pen from her bag, and hastily scribbled: *"LuAnne Copeland"* across the photo of her scantily clad sibling.

She finished just in time for him to dash out the door, with a grateful grin and a wave in her direction.

Two

LuAnne fingered a ripe plum at Alimentation Gabrielle, her favorite open-air produce market. It was located in the Eighteenth Arrondissement, or district, a section of Paris that many people of African descent called home. She came down here every Saturday morning to buy fresh fruit from the produce market and also to shop in Afro-centric shops. Nowhere else in Paris could she find black hair care products. Today, she had Leon in tow.

They had been nearly inseparable the last twelve weeks. Because Leon had concentrated on literary venues before their meeting, LuAnne insisted on showing him the seedier side of Paris. She dragged him to some of the funkiest clubs on the West Bank. She even went as far as introducing him to a couple of exquisite models.

To her utter delight, Leon preferred her company to that of a roomful of hedonists.

Soon they were in a comfort zone that belied her distrust of jocks in particular and men in general.

Against her better judgment, Leon had stolen her heart.

Tomorrow they would celebrate their third-month anniversary with Sunday dinner at Haynes' Bar. Sunday dinner there had become a tradition with them.

Leon bit into one of the succulent plums. The juice dribbled down the side of his mouth. LuAnne quickly reached into her purse for a tissue and tenderly wiped the juice away. "You're like a child, Leon Jackson. You'll get that beautiful shirt all stained. I swear, I can't take you anywhere." Her small hand momentarily rested on his chest.

Leon flashed white teeth. "You just like playing

momma." He took the tissue and finished wiping his mouth. "I'm surprised you didn't spit on it first."

LuAnne laughed gaily and went to pay for her purchases. She had her eye on a *boulangerie* next door. Fresh croissants would make a great on-the-run lunch for her and Leon. It gave her great pleasure to spoil him with small things.

"Have you ever had croissants fresh from the oven?" she asked when they stepped back onto the street. She went into the bag and handed Leon another plum, then chose one for herself. She wiped it on her cotton dress before biting into it.

"Is that something like eating Krispy Kremes right out the oven? Now *that's* a heavenly experience." His brown eyes looked dreamy, remembering.

LuAnne smiled. She and Rhonda used to sneak down to the local Krispy Kreme doughnut shop in Richmond when they were teens, *"sneak"* being the operative word. If 'Nessa had caught them ruining their diets, she would have done them both bodily harm. She was intent on her daughters' winning every beauty contest she entered them in. They did win more often than not. However, deprivation in the name of beauty left both LuAnne and Rhonda feeling as if they had missed out on their childhoods.

"I have to agree with you on that," LuAnne said to Leon now, her smile fading. "Those things'll make you hurt yourself." She began walking swiftly toward the *boulangerie.*

"What were you thinking just then?" Leon asked, stepping in front of her.

LuAnne painted on a smile. She was used to portraying emotions she really didn't feel. "Oh, it was nothing," she lied, moving around him.

Leon held the door of the bakery open for her. "It looked like it was something," he said, close to her ear, as she slipped past him.

LuAnne lost herself in the array of baked goods. But

even though she would have liked to have tried some of the gooey confections, she limited herself to croissants only.

Back on the street, Leon pressed the subject. "Am I supposed to be impressed with your inscrutable nature?"

"I don't know what you're getting at," LuAnne returned, picking up her pace. She placed her right hand over her growing belly as she was wont to do out of habit lately. In her loose, flowing summer dress of bronze and with her hair braided, she looked like a black Madonna to Leon. He cautioned himself against falling too hard for this woman. He knew where it would lead. To a broken heart, more than likely. His broken heart. He couldn't bring himself to walk away, though. She had affected him that much.

Leon easily kept up with her. "You looked sad back there, Lulu. Why? Have you heard from Troy?" All the while, he selfishly prayed that she had *not.*

LuAnne paused in her steps and peered up at him. The August sunlight made her dark eyes appear to be the color of toasted almonds. "No, I haven't heard a thing from Troy. But I have heard from various girlfriends who thought it their sacred duty to keep me informed about his love life. Apparently he's dating a certain actress and they're very happy together."

"Son of a bitch," Leon muttered.

"Well, that just blows your theory right out of the water, doesn't it?"

He frowned. "What theory?"

"That he'd come to his senses."

"He may very well change his mind, but first he has to act the fool."

They continued their trek along the colorful streets of the Eighteenth Arrondissement, the different African dialects blending into a pleasing mélange of rich sounds. Mouthwatering aromas came through open windows and doors of homes and restaurants. In shop windows were clothes, housewares, objects of art, all strategically displayed to remind passersby of home and lure them into the shops.

Leon reached out and touched LuAnne's arm.

She turned to face him.

The look he gave her was so tender, LuAnne felt her heartbeat accelerate and a lump form in her throat. "Lulu, you can't depend on Troy to support you when you need him most. You've got to go home. You don't have anyone here." He quickly scanned their surroundings. "Paris is wonderful. It's everything I thought it would be, and then some. The last three months here have been dreamlike. Largely because of your company, no doubt." He paused. "What I'm trying to say is, when you have your baby, you need people around you who love you. Family, not casual friends, or acquaintances."

It wasn't the first time Leon had tried to convince her to go home. And she knew it wouldn't be the last. "My relationship with my family is complex, Leon. I've burned some bridges. You wouldn't understand. It's nothing like your family. You're still on speaking terms with your *ex,* for God's sake. You left your kid brother in your brownstone while you toured Europe. My family and I don't share that kind of closeness, or trust."

"I wouldn't understand?" Leon cried, hurt. "I know how family can be. They can drive you nuts at times. But when you need them, they're there for you. You told me you and Rhonda were close. How did she react when you told her you're expecting?"

"I haven't told her yet," LuAnne said, her voice so low Leon barely heard a word.

"Why not?" Leon asked, puzzled.

They stood on the street, gazing intently into each other's eyes, as other pedestrians glided past them. Leon, hoping to wrest from her one drop of trust in the form of openness. LuAnne, fearful of the consequences. Her eyes grew misty. She'd known him only ninety days, but she didn't want to lose him.

After a few intense minutes, Leon gently took her hand. "Let's get you home."

"Edith, Dara, I want you two back-to-back," Rhonda instructed. She moved farther away in order to get a better view of them. Stepping across several electrical cables that lay crisscross on the studio floor, she nodded her approval. "That's good."

Edith was from Britain and had a peaches-and-cream complexion. Dara hailed from Somalia, and her skin was a smooth, rich dark brown. Together they made a startling, eye-catching contrast, which was the image Jumanji wished to project. Their line of hip yet timeless clothes was targeted to Generation Xers, male and female, who had plenty of disposable income.

Surrounding Edith and Dara were four male models of various shades but all prime examples of male beauty. Jumanji appealed more to young women, and the company was intent on giving their desired consumers exactly what they wanted.

"Bobbie, would you get me the digital?"

Rhonda's assistant was never far away. The petite Puerto Rican woman went to the heavy black case that held Rhonda's camera equipment and chose the Nikon D1.

"Thanks," Rhonda said, accepting the camera. She quickly removed the lens cap, lined up a shot, adjusted the setting, then clicked off several shots. Moving around the staged tableau, she took photos from all angles.

This spread would appear in magazines across the nation to kick off Jumanji's fall season. Therefore, the models were in bold fall colors, with the ever-present chic black. Because they were wearing heavy clothing while outside the temperature was more moderate, every now and then the makeup artist had to dab at perspiration on a model's brow before Rhonda could continue.

This was the sixth wardrobe change for the models, and they'd been at it since eleven o'clock this morning. It was now close to five. Rhonda had allowed them lunch and a break between then and now.

Though Bobbie often accused Rhonda of forgetting everyone and everything except the work when she was taking photographs, it wasn't entirely true. She knew a happy subject was much more cooperative than a disgruntled one. It was just that, sometimes, when she was in the zone, it was best not to interrupt the creative flow. So far, today, she hadn't *felt* this shoot. She wondered if it was because her mind was elsewhere and not entirely on the task at hand. So much was riding on the publication of the book, and Stuart Mitchum's office had called wanting to know if she could meet the publisher for dinner tonight. "Loosen up, guys! Derrick, remove the headphones. Tad, take off the shades. I want to see your eyes. That's great." She took several photos in quick succession. "Bobbie, a little more volume on Macy, please."

Macy Gray's unique voice filled the studio. Rhonda got into the rhythm of the music, the camera clicking along with the beat of the music.

At one point, Rhonda felt so in sync with the music, the camera, and the moment she achieved that level of sublime elation that always accompanied a great shoot. She knew she'd been able to capture on film the very essence of her subjects.

She was finally in the zone. And, having achieved it, she knew the shoot was over.

"Okay, we're done," she announced, her eyes on the last digital image on the tiny color screen of the Nikon D1. She liked the D1 because with it she didn't have to wait until the pictures were developed to see the results of her work. She could look at every photograph she'd taken, right now, and choose the ones she liked best.

"Good working with you, Ronnie," Dara called, heading to the back of the room to change. Her long, graceful limbs gave her an elegant swagger.

"Liar," Edith accused lightly as she playfully elbowed

her friend. "You know she's a slave driver."

"Yeah, but she's damn good, and that's what counts in this business," Dara said, her smile showing perfect short white teeth.

"Good working with you, Ronnie," Edith echoed Dara's sentiments. A model's career could be made on her association with a good photographer. No use behaving like a diva when she wasn't one yet.

Rhonda was engrossed in the digital images. "Great working with you, too, girls."

Bobbie was already taking down the tripods and strobe light stands, folding them, and placing them in the padded forest green zippered bags they stored them in.

She wondered if Rhonda's dedication to her craft could ultimately be detrimental. Oftentimes the models made friendly overtures after a shoot. They would invite her and Rhonda along for a drink or a meal. She accepted, on occasion. But Rhonda invariably made the excuse of having to work.

Bobbie worried that Rhonda would never get back to being the ebullient person she'd been before her fiancé Raj's death. A news correspondent for a major network, he'd been killed while on assignment in Botswana. A random bullet had hit him when soldiers shot in the air to celebrate their victory in a minor skirmish.

After Raj's death Rhonda became a workaholic. Assignments she normally might pass on she happily accepted. Anything to keep her mind preoccupied so she wouldn't have to think of Raj. Bobbie knew Rhonda's work on the book about the homeless was a tribute to Raj. Day after day, she'd watched with curiosity as Rhonda combed the streets of New York, talking to people most New Yorkers were afraid to approach. Determined to do some good with the life left to her. A life without Raj.

As she observed Rhonda's pain, Bobbie's resentment of her sister, LuAnne, grew. Where was she when Rhonda was in mourning for the only man she'd ever loved? LuAnne didn't even put in an appearance at the funeral. Rhonda's parents came, as did her maternal grandmother. But no LuAnne. Bobbie supposed she had a show to do in Paris that day. She'd like to get LuAnne alone in a room for just five minutes!

She'd never forgive her own sister, Jennie, for some crap like that. But, of course, Jennie would never do anything so cruel.

"What are you doing tonight?" Bobbie asked. She was nearly finished packing the camera equipment and other paraphernalia. The models had hightailed it for greener pastures. Rhonda was still studying the digital images on the D1.

"I have a meeting with Stuart Mitchum at Tavern on the Green."

"A meeting?" Bobbie said, with an expectant note to her voice. "A meeting about the book, at a posh restaurant? What time?"

"Eight."

"Eight o'clock on a Friday night? Doesn't the man have a life? Doesn't he suspect you have one? Wait a minute. Describe this Stuart Mitchum."

Rhonda looked up. What was Bobbie getting at? A frown brought out the lines in her forehead. "He's just a man."

Bobbie humphed. "Leave it to you not to even notice!"

Rhonda rolled her eyes and walked over to the cart to gingerly put the Nikon D1 in its carrying case. Straightening up, she smiled at Bobbie. "Don't go into matchmaking mode, Barbara Jean." She was ready to leave this rented space, get across town to her apartment, where she could remove the film from the cameras and store it in the fridge until tomorrow, when she could spend some quality time in her darkroom.

They finished loading the cart in companionable silence. But as they were rolling it through the door, Bobbie said, "Just tell me this: does he invite all his prospective authors to dinner meetings at Tavern on the Green?"

"He very well might!" Rhonda said. What did she know about Stuart Mitchum except he had a sterling reputation and was respected in his field? Her agent had recommended Beacon Publishing to her as a company that made an effort to publish books of substance. She wanted to go with a company that cared about her subject matter.

"I suppose he's attractive," she said to appease Bobbie, as they walked down the hallway toward the elevator.

Bobbie smirked. "Define 'attractive.' "

"He won't make you lose your lunch."

Bobby laughed. "So, he could be the Creature from the Black Lagoon for all you know?"

"Okay. He puts you in mind of Billy Zane, only a few years older."

"Does he belong to a known ethnic group, or did God *recently* form him from clay?"

"I'm not a hundred percent sure, but I think he's Jewish."

"Mmm, we can work with that."

"We are not working with anything, Bobbie. This is strictly business."

They had reached the elevator. Bobbie pressed the down button, then drew herself to her full five feet, two inches before saying, "I know you'd rather not think about this, Rhonda, but we live in a city of eight million and at any given time I'd wager half of them are getting it on. You may have been masquerading as a nun for some time now, but the rest of us are not interested in how much penance we can do before we kick the bucket. We'd like to live before we die. I bet your Mr. Mitchum is one of the many, and he's mistaken you for one, too."

The elevator arrived and they pushed the cart inside.

As the doors closed, Rhonda sighed. "I wish all my well-meaning friends would just leave me the hell alone."

Bobbie uttered an expletive in Spanish. "Your friends

are not going to leave you the hell alone, because we love you!" she said vehemently.

Rhonda met Bobbie's eyes, her expression contrite. "I know you and Heaven, since you're my two best friends in the world, think you're doing right by me. But between the two of you, I'm getting a constant barrage of 'get on with your life' rhetoric. I'm just not ready to put myself out there and give my heart, my soul, to anyone else. It hurts too much when they're taken away."

"Don't you think I know that?" Bobbie said, softly.

"You know it here," Rhonda said, as she gently touched Bobbie's temple. "But you don't know it here." She placed her hand over her own heart. "You've got Fred to go home to every night. You've got two beautiful children to rock to sleep. You're in a privileged, blessed place, Bobbie."

Bobbie closed the space between them and fiercely hugged her friend. "I'm sorry; I'm sorry. I didn't mean to make you sad. I just know that if anyone on this earth deserves to be blissfully happy, it's you."

Rhonda's cell phone rang in the middle of their embrace. "Guess I should answer that."

They stepped apart and Rhonda reached inside her shoulder bag for her phone.

"Hi, Rhonda here," she answered, sniffing.

"Ronnie! It's me. I'm coming home. Would you meet me at the Mark tomorrow night, at around nine? Pack a bag; we can talk all night. Say you'll come, Ronnie. I've really missed you! I have a surprise for you. And there's someone I want you to meet."

"LuAnne?" she asked, incredulous.

"Yeah," LuAnne said, laughing. "Have you forgotten your only sister's voice?"

"Just about. It *has* been a long time since I actually heard it. Where have you been? Siberia?"

LuAnne sighed wearily. "I know I've been a bitch. Oops, do you still detest that word?"

"With a passion."

"All right. Sorry. But the thing is, Ronnie, I want to make it up to you. Come on; let's make a night of it, like we used to do. We'll eat spicy crabs till they're coming out of our ears. We'll catch up on each other's lives and gossip about everybody we know. We'll watch old movies and talk back to the screen. Laugh until we cry."

"You know this wouldn't be necessary if you would've just spoken to me more than a couple minutes whenever I phoned you," Rhonda said, still pouting.

"So are you going to get back at me by not showing up tomorrow night?"

"Hell no, I want to see you. I've miss you, you little brat!" Rhonda said, laughing.

LuAnne giggled girlishly, reminding Rhonda of all the times they used to sit up at night talking about the future and how much better their lives would be once they were out from under 'Nessa's thumb. "I miss you, too, Ronnie. I'd better finish packing. There's still a lot to do. So I'll see you tomorrow night."

"Wait, LuAnne," Rhonda said, her tone serious now. "What do you mean you're coming home? Permanently? You're moving back to the States?"

"I'll tell all once we're face-to-face, Ronnie. Wait until you see me; I've gotten fat!"

"Now I know you've lost your mind," Rhonda said, laughing again.

"I did for a while there," LuAnne said seriously. "But I'm on my way back."

The doors of the elevator opened, and in the hallway were four or five people waiting to board once Rhonda and Bobbie, along with the luggage cart, vacated the conveyance.

"Gotta run, LuAnne. Can't wait to see you! Have a safe flight," Rhonda said regretfully. "Love you!"

"Love you, too," LuAnne intoned, a note of sadness in her voice.

Bobbie and Rhonda quickly rolled the cart into the hallway, smiling their apologies to those who were waiting to get on.

"That was LuAnne. She'll be in the city tomorrow night."

"Oh?" Bobbie's eyes stretched in surprise. "Does she have a gig here?"

Picking up on Bobbie's sarcasm, Rhonda said in her sister's defense, "She's sorry for the past and wants to make amends. She sounded very excited. But wouldn't tell me why."

"It's none of my business," Bobbie said, looking straight ahead.

Rhonda knew Bobbie only used that phrase when curiosity was eating her up. "I'm giving her the benefit of the doubt, Bobbie."

"She's your sister."

"That she is."

From Rhonda's tone, Bobbie knew it was wise to drop the subject. She was a fervent defender of her sister, Jennie, and knew Rhonda would do the same when it came to LuAnne. Even if she didn't deserve it. That's just the way Rhonda was.

"Back to Stuart Mitchum," Bobbie began as they rolled the cart through the double glass doors of the building and onto the street.

Rhonda groaned.

Rhonda had been to Tavern on the Green on one other occasion: the night Raj had proposed to her. They'd been seated in the Crystal Room. Above them were sparkling chandeliers, and windows on all three sides afforded a spectacular view of Central Park.

As she climbed out of the cab tonight, an ache began to dig a deep well in her heart. Memories of that night came rushing back. It had been the most magical night of her life. The next day Raj had left for Botswana, and then he had been gone forever.

She was on the mezzanine level, where she'd been told Stuart would meet her. She was nervous. To her left, she could see one of the gardens. She couldn't recall whether it was Chestnut Garden or Rafters Garden. But they'd strung Japanese lanterns between the trees' branches and the effect was very romantic. She almost wished she *had* come here to meet a date.

Bobbie had been right: this environment wasn't conducive to business. Not on a Friday night, when couples were making an evening out of dining and dancing under the stars.

She suddenly felt like running after the cab, shouting, "Wait! I've changed my mind!"

Stuart Mitchum had been strolling in the garden adjacent to the restaurant's entrance when he spotted her. His breath caught in his throat. Just as it had the first day she'd walked into his office. He hadn't remembered exactly how lovely she was.

The sky blue summer dress she was wearing had delicate spaghetti straps and clung to her curves. Its hem fell two inches above well-shaped knees, displaying a beautiful pair of legs. On her feet were strappy sandals the same ice blue shade. Stuart thought her pixie cut gave her a gamine appearance. But she wasn't a girl, and he knew it. She did have a somewhat ephemeral quality, though. He was afraid she might disappear into thin air at any moment. Like any fairy-tale creature might.

Or maybe that was just his heart talking.

"Good evening, Rhonda."

Rhonda turned at the sound of Stuart's voice and smiled slowly. At their introduction three months ago, she must have missed how tall he was. She was five-eight. He was at least four inches taller. Nor had she noticed how strong his hands were. Nice.

She liked the crinkles that appeared at the corners of his deep brown eyes when he smiled, not to mention that sensual mouth of his! Had she been blind three months ago?

"Hello, Stuart. Have you been waiting long?"

He came, took her by the elbow, and directed her toward the entrance. "No, I arrived only a few minutes before your cab pulled up."

Her cologne, Truth, by Calvin Klein, assailed his nostrils. It had never smelled that exquisite on other women.

They were immediately shown to an intimate corner table for two in the Crystal Room. Stuart held Rhonda's chair for her, then sat down across from her.

The waiter presented them with menus. "Would you like a few moments?"

"Please," Stuart said.

In the waiter's absence, Stuart took the opportunity to observe Rhonda. She'd applied her makeup so expertly, he was hard pressed to tell where nature ended and artifice took over. She wore no jewelry, but then she didn't need any to enhance her beauty.

After a few moments under his scrutiny, Rhonda grew self-conscious. She lowered her eyes. "You were going to tell me what your editors thought of my work."

Stuart smiled ruefully. He hadn't meant to make her uneasy. "Not a dissenting voice among them," he happily reported. "The book's a go, Rhonda."

Rhonda's full lips split in a wide grin. Her eyes lit up. In her excitement, she reached across the table and clasped one of Stuart's hands in hers. "Oh, Stuart. You don't know what I've been through to make this happen. I'm so relieved, I could cry!"

Tears shone in her eyes.

Stuart gently squeezed her hand. "Tell me what inspired you to do the book. You've told me how you did it, but not what sparked your interest in doing it."

She paused a long while and he thought he'd overstepped his bounds. "If you don't feel comfortable enough telling me, I'll understand."

"It's all right," Rhonda hastily assured him.

She glanced around the room before beginning. "More

than two years ago, I was proposed to in this room."

Stuart glanced down at her left hand. He knew he hadn't seen any rings there when they'd met. There were none there now, either.

"Three days later, Raj was killed by a stray bullet. He was a journalist assigned to cover a coup in Botswana."

"I'm so sorry," Stuart said, shocked. "That must have been hard on you."

"Have you ever lost anyone, Stuart?" She was unable to mask the pain in her voice.

"My dad died three years ago. I was thirty-six and thought by then I should be prepared for the inevitable, you know? You always expect your parents to die before you. It's the correct order, right? But I took it hard, realizing I'd never see the old man again. We'd been very close. My dad wasn't ordinary by any means. He was affectionate, whereas other dads were embarrassed to hug their sons. He loved Mom and was always faithful to her."

"I'm sorry for your loss," Rhonda said, meeting his gaze.

"What was he like, your fiancé?" he inquired softly, his eyes raking over her face.

Rhonda smiled at the thought of Raj. "He was bold and brash, and full of piss and vinegar. He was also sweet and thoughtful, gentle and kind. We met, believe it or not, at a bar on amateur night. He did this really horrible stand-up comedy routine. I heckled him from the audience. Well, my loudmouth girlfriends and I. He told me, 'Get up here if you think you can do better!' "

"And you did," Stuart supplied, enjoying her story.

"I sang and won the grand prize, two hundred dollars, that night. Because I felt bad for jeering him while he was onstage, I paid his tab. When the waiter informed him that I'd done that, he came over to my table and asked me for a dance."

"Were you instantly smitten?"

"I've always been charmed by a man who has the nerve to get up in front of a roomful of people and make a fool of himself. Yes, I was lost from the first moment he bombed."

"Raj is the reason why you began photographing homeless people?"

Rhonda nodded in the affirmative. "Raj and I had talked about doing a book like this. He'd do the writing, and I'd take the photographs. Following Raj's death, it seemed the only thing that could soothe me was walking. On these walks I invariably encountered the homeless. It was then that I remembered our promise to do the book.

"What sparked it, though, was an incident that happened not too far from here as a matter of fact, when I saw a young mother with a child who couldn't have been more than eighteen months old. It was cold that day. And she didn't even have on a coat. Her child was wrapped in a tattered blanket. This child was vibrant, so energetic. He was wriggling to be released from the confines of the blanket, and when he succeeded, I saw the reason why the mother was trying to keep the blanket around him. He only had on a thin pair of pants and a T-shirt. A pair of dirty sneakers, with no socks."

"What was her story?" Stuart asked, riveted.

"The father of her baby sent for her. She came from Boise, Idaho, with only the address he'd given her and three hundred dollars in her pocket. Turns out he hadn't lived at that address for months and hadn't left a forwarding address. She went to the police and was told they didn't track down people. She'd have to hire a private detective for that. Okay, she knew that if she hired a detective her three hundred dollars would be gone in no time flat. She didn't think she could go back home. She'd had a falling-out with her parents over following the guy to New York. She was too proud to beg them to take her back. When I met her, all her possessions had been stolen and she had been sleeping in the park for nearly two weeks.

"I bought her a ticket back home, gave her some food money, and personally put her on the bus," Rhonda concluded, laughing. "This story had a happy ending. Many others don't. I got a letter from her the following week. Her parents were so relieved she was back, they didn't give her any flak. She attended the local community college and got a license to practice nursing. She's an LPN. She and her son are doing just fine."

Stuart shook his head in amazement. "Why didn't you include that story in the book?"

"It just never occurred to me to include it."

"You should include it as a counterpoint to the sad stories."

"All right, I will," Rhonda said, delighted with his suggestion.

The waiter, a handsome young man who was probably an actor waiting for his big break on Broadway, stopped back by their table. "Are you ready to order now, sir, madam?"

Stuart looked to Rhonda.

"Sure," Rhonda replied. "I'll have the shrimp cocktail to start. Then the bibb lettuce and watercress salad. For my main course, brook trout meunière with parsley, new potatoes, and *haricots verts.*"

"Very good," the waiter said, turning to Stuart. "And you, sir?"

"I'll have the vichyssoise, the caesar salad, filet mignon with sauce béarnaise, and a baked potato."

Alone again, Stuart regarded Rhonda with keen eyes. "Rhonda, I have a confession to make. I don't often do this sort of thing, so please take that into consideration after you hear what I have to say."

Rhonda leaned forward. She was having such a wonderful time with this fascinating man. He was a good conversationalist, a good listener, too. She hadn't enjoyed herself this much in a man's company since Raj died.

"Go ahead," she coaxed softly.

Stuart cleared his throat and bit his bottom lip before continuing. "I've been a little dishonest with you. I could have told you over the phone that we'd decided to publish the book. I didn't do that because I wanted to see you again."

Rhonda eased back a bit on her chair and sat up straighter. "Oh." It was more an exhalation of pent-up air than a word.

Their eyes met and held.

He ran a hand over his chestnut hair, leaving a tuft sticking up. His tanned skin went a shade darker on his cheeks. Smiling, he said, "I'm a little out of practice. I feel like I've never told a woman I'm interested in dating her before."

He frowned suddenly and quickly added, "And I don't even know if you're already involved with someone. If you're—"

"I'm not," Rhonda said, shyly smiling at him. "I haven't been since Raj was killed."

"Over two years ago." He leaned closer to her.

"Yes." She moistened her lips. God! She was actually flirting!

"If you don't find me attractive, I'll understand. It's just that I haven't been able to get you off my mind since the day you came into my office." His eyes possessively swept over her face. "To think that if Barbara hadn't called in sick that morning, we might never have met."

"I think you're very attractive, Stuart," Rhonda cautiously began. Her heartbeat was visible at her throat. "I'm simply not sure of the rules here. You're my publisher."

Stuart's mellow brown eyes held an amused glint in them. He smiled, revealing a boyish dimple in his left cheek. "Rhonda, our deal is solid whether you go out with me or not. Barbara will be working with you on the project. So everything will be perfectly ethical." He paused. "As for you and me, my divorce left me wary. Lately, it's been nothing but work. But, really, work's a poor substitute. I'm rambling, I know. What I'm saying is, I think you're wonderful and I'd like to get to know you better."

Rhonda crossed and uncrossed her legs. She didn't know how to proceed or what to say. In the past, she'd dated only brothers. Brothers with rich brown skin, dark brothers. They were her preference. She was attracted to brothers with skin so black, her own golden-brown was a perfect complement to it.

She was appalled by her superficiality.

Her ingrained racial prejudice.

Sure, there were some white males she found attractive: actors like Billy Zane and David Boreanaz. Unattainable ideals. However, it had never crossed her mind to pursue a relationship with either of them.

She'd told Bobbie that Stuart reminded her of Billy Zane. The truth was, Stuart was more appealing to her than Billy Zane ever would be. Stuart's face was utterly masculine. He had a scar over his right eye, a slash through the brow. It was faint but noticeable, and it lent character to his overall look.

"Rhonda?"

She'd been ruminating far too long. The tips of her ears were hot from embarrassment.

She smiled at him. "I'm sorry, Stuart. I'm out of practice, too."

"I should have waited until the end of the evening," Stuart said regretfully. "Then, at least, we would've had pleasant memories to take away. Now, I've ruined what will probably be our only night out together because I couldn't wait to tell you how I feel about you." His squint told her he was finding this process as painful as she was.

"You didn't do anything wrong, Stuart. It's me. You know that saying about how you can never know how you'll react to any given situation until you're faced with it? Well, here I am, a woman of the twenty-first century, warring with my prejudices."

Stuart frowned, confused. But, to his credit, instead of tossing questions her way, he sat quietly and sought her gaze, allowing her to explain in her own time.

"I've never dated anyone outside of my own cultural background," Rhonda said at last. She smiled warmly at him. "I liked you from the beginning, too, Stuart. On an elemental level. I hadn't entertained the notion of dating you."

"Just working with me."

"Yes."

"Which is safer," he concluded, smiling.

"Undoubtedly." She sighed inaudibly. Relieved that was over with.

Stuart laughed shortly. His eyes did that sexy perusal of her face again. "I've never dated a black woman, Rhonda. I think black women are among the most beautiful women in the world, but I've been hesitant about asking one to go to dinner with me."

Rhonda leaned slightly forward. This was getting plenty interesting.

"Why?"

"Afraid of being shot down, I guess."

"I'm not shooting you down," she told him, and reached for his hand.

Stuart grasped her hand. "We'll last until dessert, huh?"

"Oh, I think we'll last longer than that," Rhonda said with a smile that made his heart pound. He felt like a teen on his first date.

The waiter arrived with their appetizers, served them with a flourish, and then offered them freshly ground black pepper from a pepper mill, which they both declined.

"I thought he'd never leave," Stuart joked. "I want to hear all about you. I can tell by your accent you're not a native New Yorker."

"No," Rhonda said. "No matter how long I remain in the city, I can't seem to lose my Virginia twang."

"Please don't," Stuart said. He truly couldn't take his eyes off her. Nor could he believe he hadn't chased her away with his ineptness. "It's lovely."

Rhonda had a heady feeling, what with all the compliments being laid at her feet. And why did she believe Stuart, when Maceo's approach had left her totally unconvinced of his sincerity? Maybe it was because Maceo had come on to her like gangbusters from the get-go. With him, she had no doubt his attraction to her was based solely on her physical attributes. It felt different with Stuart. Perhaps because he'd seen, and appreciated, her work, which was a bit like having a glimpse into her soul.

All her life, she'd been told how beautiful she was. From infancy, it seemed, her mother had coached her and LuAnne on how best to use their attractiveness as a means to an end. By the time she was ten and LuAnne was eight, they were old pros on the beauty pageant circuit in and around Richmond. Why had they been put through it all? 'Nessa hadn't done it for the money or the fame. Rhonda had figured that much out over the years. She didn't know exactly what had fired their mother's compulsion. One of these days, when she got good and pissed with 'Nessa, she was going to get some answers to the question of why she'd put her daughters through such shallow, degrading rituals. What kind of satisfaction had their mother derived from it?

The end result, for Rhonda, was that she now looked upon beauty as not an asset but a liability. Some people didn't take you seriously if you had a pretty face. She worked twice as hard as male photographers just to prove she was capable of doing the job, and doing it well. She *still* sometimes got rejected based on her appearance. The fashion industry might have women as the main focus in front of the cameras, but behind them beings with penises controlled the purse strings.

"I'm glad you think so," Rhonda said of Stuart's comment about her accent. She speared a shrimp with her fork. "My friends jokingly call me Ellie Mae."

Stuart laughed. "Don't tell anyone, but that inane sitcom cracks me up."

"Oh, you like fish-out-of-water stories?"

"I've often felt like one myself. I grew up on Flatbush

Avenue in Brooklyn. My dad was a butcher. He was Italian. His real name was Guido Mastrantonio. He changed it to Mitchum after Robert Mitchum, the actor. The Guido he changed to Will. Will Mitchum married Ruth Cohen, a Jew. They had three children. Two boys and a girl. I'm the youngest. We never had much, except love. Had plenty of that."

"Sounds wonderful," Rhonda said with longing. Because in spite of the fact that she and LuAnne had grown up in an upper-middle-class neighborhood in a Richmond suburb, they'd never really felt as if they were loved. Their father rarely had time for them. Andrew was one of the few black attorneys in Richmond and a pillar of the community. He came from a well-to-do family. The Copelands had owned and operated three black mortuaries in and around Richmond for nearly a century. They all thought Andrew had taken leave of his senses when he announced he was going to become a lawyer and not follow in his father's exalted footsteps and take over the family business.

Virginia and Andrew Sr. had threatened to disinherit him when he married Vanessa Boyd, a girl from the wrong side of the tracks. Not only was she poor, but she'd never known her father. He'd run off soon after finding out her mother, Ruby, was pregnant with his child. Ruby never married even though there were many suitors who would have gladly claimed the beautiful, gregarious woman. Once burned, twice shy.

Vanessa inherited her mother's looks but not her stalwart attitude. Vanessa didn't want to scrape for a living. Andrew Copeland was one of the most eligible bachelors in Richmond, and she set her cap for him. Andrew didn't know what hit him.

Vanessa gave him two pretty little girls.

Andrew gave her a house in the country, a maid, and a hefty bank account.

A perfectly equitable exchange.

"I got a scholarship to Princeton," Stuart was saying. "And then I got kidnapped by aliens and traveled among the stars with them a few decades. After that, I came back and was elected president."

Rhonda snapped out of her reverie and stared at Stuart. "What?"

"I know the look of a person whose mind is elsewhere," Stuart said, smiling. "I've seen that look on the faces of my staff whenever I talk about budget concerns."

Rhonda looked him in the eye. "It's just that when you started talking about your family, I was reminded of my own."

"Miss them?"

"Yes, I suppose I do." She missed what could have been. It was sad, but she'd never established a rapport with either of her parents. They'd treated her as if they'd learned the art of parenting by rote. Three meals a day. School. A bath before bed. Brush your teeth. Stand up straight. But how many times had she gotten a warm hug or a kiss to the forehead? How many times had she been tucked in at night?

Stop it, Rhonda! As 'Nessa would say, "You're a grown-ass woman; stop moaning for what might have been!"

She'd grown into a perfectly fine woman. No visible quirks. A little resentment of her mother, perhaps. But who didn't resent their mothers at one time or another? That was normal. It was healthy. You didn't need to see a therapist for mother resentment. They'd laugh you out of the office. Besides, black people didn't go to shrinks. And if they did, they never told anybody about it. That was a secret you took to the grave.

Stuart sat there, smiling at her.

Rhonda reached up and smoothed that tuft of hair Stuart had earlier mussed up.

"You went to Princeton?" she asked softly.

"Yeah, I went to Princeton. On scholarship. After that, I went to Oxford for a couple of years. It was there that I decided I wanted to go into publishing. I had a slight detour by Wall Street, however. I was fortunate, extremely lucky, in market forecasting. I invested in Beacon Publishing with a sudden windfall when I was twenty-seven. We fought to find our niche. But for the past decade, we've been going strong."

Rhonda suddenly had an impulse to shout, in her best Don King imitation, "Only in America!" Stuart's story was, indeed, a rags-to-riches tale. He was a self-made man.

What she said, though, was, "You're so young to have achieved so much."

"That depends," Stuart said with an enigmatic grin. "Look at the techno geeks who're making millions on the Web, Jeff Bezos of Amazon.com, all young. Compared to some of them, I'm dragging my feet." He paused to sample his vichyssoise. "Mmm, that's good." Raising his eyes to hers again, he continued, "There are drawbacks to being as driven as I am. My marriage didn't survive because I didn't devote the time to Sharon that I should have. I want children, but that hasn't happened for me yet, either."

"I feel you," Rhonda said with a soft sigh. "I wanted to have children with Raj."

"How many?"

"Two or three."

"Me, too."

"There's still time for you, you know."

"I want a solid marriage before the kids come along," Stuart said.

"So do I."

"You and I would have beautiful children together," he murmured, his voice seductive. He awaited her response, amusement glittering in his dark eyes.

"This is true," Rhonda replied, surprising him. "Let's go out again first, though."

Three

Just in case, Rhonda thought as she applied the fingertip toothbrush to her right index finger and began brushing her teeth in the ladies' room. LuAnne had turned her on to the brushes that were about the size of a dime and adhered to your finger. They were indispensable when you were away from home and needed to freshen your breath. With fish as a main course tonight, she needed all the help she could get.

Finished, she gargled and rinsed. Not a pretty sight. She was glad she was alone in the room. This done, she dried her mouth and reapplied her lipstick. Gazing into the mirror, she wondered what she was getting herself into. Was she really thinking of dating a white man? 'Nessa would have a stone-cold fit!

She grinned at her reflection, checking out her teeth. No signs of anything in there that should not be there. Blowing into cupped hands, she checked her breath. Minty fresh. Did men go through all this when they went to the rest room? Or was it pee, zip up, wash hands (she hoped!), and back out to their dates?

"You're losing it, girlfriend," she said aloud, snapped her purse closed, and headed for the exit. Stuart was probably wondering what was keeping her.

In the men's room, on the opposite side of the wall, Stuart was assessing his appearance in the mirror. He bared his teeth; good, there was nothing stuck in them. Reaching into his inside coat pocket, he retrieved a packet of Certs and popped one in his mouth.

He was as ready as he'd ever be. The prospect of kissing

Rhonda good night began to simmer in the back of his mind. She probably didn't kiss on the first date. If you could call this a date. He should have been up front with her from the very beginning. The tactics he'd used to get her here made him look desperate. Well, needy anyway. He was lucky Rhonda was such a good sport. One day, he'd make it up to her.

He spotted her standing near the entrance, waiting for him. She'd draped the matching shawl around her shoulders. A tall, broad-shouldered black guy walked up to her and pulled her into his arms for a hug. Jealousy gripped Stuart.

When he got closer, he recognized the guy: actor Marques Washington.

"Damn, girl, you look like new money," he heard Marques say. "Fine, as always."

Rhonda pried herself from Marques's clutches, her smile never wavering. "Good to see you, too, Marques. Let me introduce you to my date, publisher Stuart Mitchum."

Stuart graciously offered his hand to Marques, who pumped it a little too long and hard. His eyes swept over Stuart's dark summer suit, casual crew-neck shirt underneath, and Italian loafers. His style bespoke wealth and quiet elegance. Too bad.

"You're a lucky man," he told Stuart. "Ronnie wouldn't go out with me."

Stuart came to stand close to Rhonda, his right hand on her lower back. She almost sighed with satisfaction when a wanton fluid fire suffused her. She liked his touch.

"I don't date my subjects," she said, explaining Marques's comment. "I did a spread on Marques for *In Style Magazine*. Right after he won his first Emmy."

"Congratulations," Stuart said, smiling.

"Thank you," Marques returned, although his eyes were on Rhonda. He drew his gaze away from her to regard Stuart. "What do you publish, Stuart?"

"Books," Stuart said simply. "Fiction and nonfiction."

"Wonderful," Marques said, his voice devoid of interest. "If you don't mind my asking . . ." He looked from Rhonda to Stuart. ". . . Are you two seriously dating?"

Rhonda watched the momentary indecision on Stuart's face as he recovered from the boldness of the question and came up with a response.

She would have gladly dealt with Marques's impertinence, but if Stuart was serious about dating a black woman, he should get used to the subtle, and not so subtle, remarks that were bound to come their way.

"I don't see how that's any business of yours," Stuart said with a cool smile.

"Marques, there you are!" a tall, leggy blonde cried, hurrying toward them.

She possessively hooked her arm through Marques's and gave Rhonda a quick, cutting appraisal, with knowing eyes. Rhonda supposed that with a man like Marques, she was used to having to guard her territory against encroaching females.

Rhonda was thankful for the interruption. She didn't wish to hang around for forced introductions, either. The blonde didn't want to know her name any more than she wanted to know hers.

She felt Stuart's hand reaching for hers, and she gratefully grasped it.

"We'll be going now," Stuart announced. He smiled at the blonde, sympathy for her plight evident in his eyes. "Enjoy your evening."

"Yes, you, too," Marques said to their backs as he disengaged himself from the blonde's viselike hold. He hated clinging women.

"Is that what we have to look forward to?" Stuart asked as he drove the Chevy Tahoe up West 67th Street on the way to Amsterdam Avenue. "Perfect strangers thinking they have the right to comment on our being together? Showing no respect whatsoever?"

"As you probably noted, Marques dates anyone under

the sun. Therefore, his behavior was hypocritical. He reacted from the gut, though. Black men don't like to see black women with white men. On a more personal note, I wouldn't go out with him when he asked me. It was only a few months after Raj got killed, and I just wasn't interested in romance. I'll be frank with you, Stuart: I don't have the patience for men whose only goal is to have me on their fast-dial list in case they get horny in the middle of the night. Marques is that kind of guy."

"You haven't dated *anyone* since you lost Raj?"

"Three months ago, I went out with someone I've known for more than a year. He's a nice guy, but he's just not for me."

"Why not?"

"For one thing, he's five years younger than I am. I like older men. He's also in the fashion industry. He's already got groupies following him everywhere. Call me selfish, but I like to think I'm not going to be yesterday's news before things even get going. But the main reason I'm not dating him is the chemistry. I just wasn't feeling it."

The chemistry was definitely there with Stuart. Her pleasure points were at full alert. She was afraid of those stirrings. There was no telling what kind of trouble they'd get her into. She blamed Bobbie for filling her head with talk of half the people in New York getting it on at any given moment. Suddenly she was entertaining thoughts of joining their ranks. There must be something in the air tonight.

Stuart glanced briefly at her. "This has been a most enlightening evening."

"Still want to date me?"

He laughed softly. "You know how you can read a good book, and even though you might not be able to quote passages from it, the essence of the book lingers on?"

"Mmm-huh."

"Well, that's the feeling I got from your photographs and from reading what you wrote about your subjects. I knew I wanted to get to know the person behind such passionate, resonating work."

The sound of his voice, in the close, silent confines of the moving car, was turning Rhonda on even more. Once again, she tried to rein in her emotions. She was long overdue. No doubt about that. LuAnne, in her place, would throw caution to the wind and take Stuart Mitchum. Why couldn't she, for once in her life, be the impulsive sister?

The man had her breathless and he hadn't even kissed her. Now this was crazy. Totally insane. He wasn't even her type, for God's sake!

"To say I'm flattered would be an understatement," she said, her voice husky.

"Flattery isn't my intention. Truth is. Let's make a pact, here and now, Rhonda. I will not lie to you, and you won't lie to me, or yourself."

"I'm a truthful person, Stuart."

"I know we think of ourselves as truthful people. But the fact is we lie for all sorts of reasons. Not to hurt someone's feelings, for example. I don't want you to lie to me in order to spare my feelings. I'm a big boy and I can take the unadulterated truth."

Stuart stopped the Tahoe at a red light.

Rhonda undid her seat belt.

Stuart turned to say something, but before he had scarcely opened his mouth, Rhonda had taken his face between her hands and kissed him on the mouth. What he was about to say was no longer important. He was too busy unbuckling his own seat belt and fully pulling Rhonda into his arms.

She didn't know exactly why she'd done it. Some quality in his voice incited her to action. Made it impossible not to touch him. Perhaps it was curiosity. Then again, maybe it was her fear that made her test the waters of desire. She'd never been able to resist a challenge, and Stuart Mitchum was definitely a challenge.

Their breath mingled. He tasted clean and sweet. His

lips were firm yet nicely mobile. She breathed in his after-shave, sandalwood. She liked sandalwood. There was another scent, too, something utterly masculine. Just his own skin.

She sighed against his mouth. "The truth is, I've been wanting to kiss you all night."

"What took you so long?"

He bent his head to meet her mouth again.

This time they didn't come up for air until the sound of honking car horns pierced the hypnotic cocoon of mutual need that surrounded them.

Rhonda drew away, her question answered. Yes, Stuart was a damn good kisser.

Stuart didn't want to let her go. But he couldn't very well seduce her in the middle of 67th Street. He reluctantly drove through the intersection.

"Thanks for being so honest with me," he murmured, his voice thick.

LuAnne tried to sleep on the flight from Paris, but she couldn't. Her mind was a jumble. Leon, next to her, was having no such trouble. He slept like a baby. He slept like someone who had no skeletons in his closet. They were all out in the open now. What she loved most about Leon was the fact that he seemed to have gotten his life on the right track again after it was derailed by his womanizing and the injury that had made him rethink his career.

He was even on speaking terms with his ex-wife, Cheryl.

He'd told LuAnne all this. There was nothing they couldn't talk about.

Or so he thought. LuAnne hadn't been as forthcoming.

There were things about her she was afraid to tell him. Things that would make him see her in a whole different light. She hoped Leon would appreciate the surprise she had in store for him at the Mark. Most of all, she hoped the "surprise" would appreciate *him*.

She reached over and gently touched his clean-shaven cheek. He slept on.

"I don't want to hurt you, Leon," she whispered.

Stuart phoned Saturday morning, just after eleven.

Rhonda was in the darkroom developing the Jumanji photos. In the middle of immersing a photo in developing fluid, she let the machine get the call. When she heard Stuart's voice, she quickly washed her hands and snatched up the receiver just as he was about to hang up. "Stuart, I'm here. Would you please hold on a moment? I'm working in the darkroom. I just need to quickly hang up a few photos to dry, and then I want to change extensions."

She didn't like remaining in the darkroom, with the fumes from the developing fluid permeating the air, any longer than necessary.

"Sure," Stuart immediately agreed.

She'd closed the door to the darkroom, which was adjacent to the kitchen, and grabbed the cordless handset from the counter. "I'm glad you called," she said, smiling. "Gives me another chance to tell you how much I enjoyed myself last night."

"Me, too." She could hear the warmth in his tone. It made her smile grow even wider.

It was the first time they'd spoken over the phone. His secretary had phoned to set up the Tavern on the Green meeting. He definitely had a sexy phone voice.

She stood in the small kitchen, barefoot, wearing only a pair of loose-fitting jeans and a white crop top. The tile floor felt cool beneath her feet.

Stuart was pacing the hardwood floor of his apartment with the cordless phone to his ear. He paused at the picture window that looked out over Central Park and beyond. The park was beginning to fill up. Parents and nannies pushed baby strollers. A group of college-age men were engaged in a pickup game of touch football. Earlier, he'd gone jogging. He was still wearing athletic pants and shoes. No shirt. He was just getting ready to get in the shower when a compulsion to surprise Rhonda struck him.

"I know your sister's going to be in town tonight," he began. "I'm sure you have lots to catch up on. Therefore, I was wondering what you're doing *next* weekend?"

Rhonda placed her hand on her bare midriff, thinking. He hadn't mentioned a specific day. Could he mean the entire weekend? "What day?"

"I'm going to my house in Connecticut for the weekend. I need to get out of the city. We could leave Friday night. It's only about a two-hour drive, if traffic's good."

Rhonda wriggled her toes on the floor. She did that whenever she was barefoot and nervous. "The whole weekend?" she finally asked, uncertain.

Stuart laughed softly. "You would have your own bedroom, of course. It's a big place. We could be there all weekend and never see each other."

Rhonda laughed, too. "That wouldn't be good."

"My sentiments exactly."

"It's a little early to be going away for the weekend." She still wasn't sure.

"Technically, we've known each other more than three months," he pointed out.

"I usually need more time than that."

"All right," he demurred, sounding perfectly happy to give her all the time she wanted. "Call me when you've made up your mind. In fact, call me anytime you get the urge. You have the sexiest voice I've ever heard over the phone."

"Funny, I was just thinking the same thing about you."

"You're joking, right?"

"Not hardly. I don't think you realize how attractive you are."

Stuart switched the phone to the other ear. "You find nerds attractive?"

"Whoever called you a nerd needs to have their eyes

examined. Besides, there's nothing wrong with being a nerd. Intelligence is very sexy."

"You're an unusual woman, Rhonda Copeland."

"Ready for a bit more truth?"

"If it's as delectable as your truth was last night, yes. Although I don't know how you'll manage it with me on Central Park West and you on Amsterdam Avenue."

"What I did last night . . . that was an aberration," Rhonda admitted. "I really don't know what came over me." Her sensuous tone denoted there were no regrets, however.

Stuart gave a deep, happy sigh. "Let's just say I hope that spirit hits you often whenever we're together."

"Oh, I think you can count on that," she said, and meant it.

Her doorbell chimed.

"Stuart, that's my doorbell. Can I call you back?"

"I think I know who that is," he said cryptically. "I'll wait until you get it."

"Okay . . . ," Rhonda returned skeptically, wondering how he could possibly know who was at her door. She put the receiver on the countertop and went to answer the door.

"Yes? Who's there?"

"Flowers for Ms. Rhonda Copeland," came a masculine voice.

Rhonda cautiously peered through the peephole before unlocking the door and swinging it open. A young African-American man held two dozen long-stemmed cellophane-wrapped red roses toward her. "Miss Copeland?"

Rhonda was so delighted, she burst into laughter. "Oh my God!"

The man smiled and gently placed them in her outstretched arms. "Enjoy." Then he turned and walked away without waiting for a tip.

She hurried back to pick up the receiver. "You?"

"Mmm-huh," Stuart said. "I hope you like roses."

"I like the man who sent them even more."

* * *

The Mark, the hotel LuAnne had chosen, was located at Madison Avenue and East 77th Street. Rhonda had been there once: when she was a cub reporter with a local paper and trying to get an interview with a foreign statesman. He'd agreed to give her the interview only if she would meet him in his suite at the Mark.

She wound up being chased all over the suite by the randy Nigerian. Little wonder she'd come to the conclusion that being a reporter wasn't for her and begun focusing on photography. She still used her journalism degree. Being a competent writer came in handy for her travel articles. She took the photos *and* wrote the copy.

The Mark was among Manhattan's elite hotels. It had a European flavor. Old-world style. Rhonda realized, as she crossed the lobby, that LuAnne would feel right at home here. LuAnne was always saying how living in Paris had made her appreciate and revere history and age. Europeans were seasoned, refined, whereas Americans were brash and immature. Unable to discern the finer things in life.

Rhonda thought that was a bunch of hooey. Just LuAnne putting on airs.

She paused outside LuAnne's suite door. Peering down at the tips of her boots, she took a deep, cleansing breath and released it. Why did this feel like a chore? She should be excited about seeing LuAnne again after more than two years. Two years? Had it really been two years? They'd never gone that long without visiting. What had happened to make LuAnne stay away? Of course, that worked both ways. She could have gotten on a plane to Paris. But the phone conversations she'd had with LuAnne didn't make her feel welcome, and LuAnne had never issued an invitation.

Shoving her hurt aside, she went ahead and knocked before she changed her mind about the whole damn thing.

Leon was awakened out of a sound sleep when the knock came. He groaned and rose. LuAnne had obviously forgotten her key. Why she couldn't postpone meeting her agent until tomorrow was beyond him, anyway. Their long flight had worn him out.

All he wanted to do was get a little rest; then he was out of here. He was going back to his brownstone in Brooklyn, hoping, all the while, that his brother, James, hadn't partied too hardy in his absence. He'd left his baby in his younger brother's hands.

"I'm coming!" he said gruffly. LuAnne Copeland would be the death of him yet.

He swung the door open and immediately turned away, eyes still half-closed, grumbling, "Finished your important business deal?"

"Don't tell me you're her latest boy toy," a feminine voice said with a hint of humor. She strode past him into the suite, set down her bag, then peered up at him expectantly.

Leon's eyes focused on her. Or tried to. He thought he must be seeing things. She looked like LuAnne, but her hair was shorter, she was around fifteen pounds heavier, and LuAnne would probably have to pay a plastic surgeon for breasts like that.

Suddenly, his fuzzy brain had a rational thought. Rhonda.

He grinned, showing teeth and gums. "Rhonda?"

She was looking him up and down, hands at a saucy angle on her hips. And what hips.

"I admit, you're a sight better than that Troy Granger. I never did like his hincty ass."

Leon was delighted by the turn of events. He would have liked it if LuAnne had seen fit to mention that her sister was going to drop by, though. It had all obviously been planned. Why else would Rhonda have an overnight bag with her?

"You're just like Lulu described you," Leon told her with a welcoming smile.

"She never mentioned you!" Rhonda exclaimed, backing up to get a good look at him.

"I think she might have wanted it to be a surprise," he told her as he eyed her with just as much boldness. The resemblance was uncanny.

The word "surprise" clicked in Rhonda's mind. LuAnne had said she had a surprise for her and there was someone she wanted her to meet. "She did say she had a surprise for me." She smiled at him. "Nice surprise."

Leon stood there blushing like a big fool as Rhonda circled him. She glanced around them. "Where is the diva?"

"Her agent phoned not five minutes after we arrived and told her to get down to the Motown Cafe. She had a client there who wanted to discuss LuAnne's endorsing some hair care product or other."

Rhonda sighed and pursed her lips. Returning her gaze to Leon's, she said, "Well, aren't you going to introduce yourself?"

Leon held out his hand. "Leon Jackson."

Rhonda took it and gave it a firm shake. "Nice to meet you, Leon."

She stood in front of him with her arms akimbo. Her brows arched in curiosity.

Leon had been staring at her. "I'm sorry. It's just that you two look so much alike, it takes some getting used to."

"Don't worry about it, sugar. We've gotten that all our lives." She bent to retrieve her bag. "It does get a little old, though."

Leon liked her manner already. Excusing his observation but letting him know it irritated her nonetheless was honest and real. "Why don't you make yourself at home," he said. "Lulu should be back soon."

"She hates being called Lulu, you know."

"That's what she tells me," he replied, as if he knew something she didn't.

Rhonda smiled. She could get used to Leon Jackson with a quickness.

She went over to the window. They were on the sixteenth floor. The hotel sat smack-dab in the middle of the Upper East Side historic district. The Guggenheim, the Metropolitan Museum of Art, and Central Park were close by. She suddenly turned back around and found Leon's eyes on her. "Let me guess; you're an athlete, right?"

"I suppose my size gave me away."

"Nah, you could have been anything. It's the way you move."

With a grace born of sheer endurance. She would never have spoken those words out loud, though. She didn't know Leon well enough.

She strode over to one of the two sofas and set her bag in the corner of it. Then she sat on the chair opposite the sofa. "How long have you known LuAnne?"

Leon came to sit on the sofa across from her. "Going on four months now. We met when the elevator at my hotel broke down, with just the two of us inside."

Rhonda laughed shortly. "LuAnne probably freaked, right?"

"In the beginning, yes," Leon said, smiling at the memory. "But she soon calmed down. We spent the next few minutes getting acquainted. After the elevator was repaired, we went to dinner at Haynes' Bar."

"I love that place. LuAnne took me there about three years ago. Does Delicious Thompson still sing there Friday and Saturday nights?"

"I must have missed her," Leon said easily. He stretched his long legs out before him. "I went for the Sunday dinners."

"They do have great food." Then, "What team do you play for?"

"I was a linebacker for the Jets."

"Leon Jackson. You're not that Leon Jackson!" She came off her chair, went, and playfully punched him on the arm. "Man, you were bad! You used to power your way through the line like a bulldozer. Damn! I was wondering what happened to you."

Leon rose and put up his hands as if fending off her punches. "Whoa! You mean you're a football fan?"

Rhonda regarded him with a smirk. "Just because I'm a girl doesn't mean I don't know my football. Sorry, I didn't recognize you right off, but let's face it: you guys look like hell when you take those helmets off on the sidelines."

Leon chuckled. "I suppose we do."

Rhonda reached up and smoothly ran her hand over his bald pate. "And you've shaved your noggin since I saw you last. What's up with that? You had a nice fade."

He shrugged. "New life, new look."

"How's the hip?"

"The hip's good. All healed."

"But you retired anyway."

"It was time. There's more to life than football."

Rhonda sat back down, and Leon followed suit.

She spoke quietly now. "Did you find it in Paris?"

"What?"

"That thing that's more important than football."

He didn't get the chance to answer her question because, at that instant, LuAnne came into the room like a whirlwind.

"Leon! Leon, baby, wake up! I just signed the biggest contract of my career!"

Rhonda and Leon had risen when they heard her coming into the suite. Rhonda stood beside Leon, but from the angle LuAnne was approaching them, Rhonda was hidden behind Leon's large frame.

Rhonda moved around Leon, and LuAnne froze in her tracks when she saw her sister.

"Ronnie!"

Rhonda had expected to feel all the hurt come down on her once she was looking into LuAnne's face again. Instead, tears of relief sprang to her eyes. Finally, to see a part of herself standing there in the flesh. She no longer cared about the abbreviated phone calls or the missed holidays. She even forgave LuAnne for missing Raj's memorial service.

"Welcome home, sweetie!"

As the sisters ran to embrace each other, Rhonda noticed LuAnne's distended belly for the first time. Her stomach muscles constricted painfully.

When LuAnne went to hug her, Rhonda refused to return her embrace. Instead, she held her at arm's length and angrily shook her. "You couldn't pick up a phone to tell me you're pregnant?" Those tears of joy were suddenly bitter, she was so mad.

"There's so much we need to talk about, Ronnie," LuAnne pleaded with her. "Please, let's not start out with anger between us." She glanced back at Leon, who Rhonda had momentarily forgotten was in the room.

Rhonda took a deep breath to calm herself and met LuAnne's eyes. "Is Leon . . . ?"

"No!" Leon and LuAnne immediately cried in unison.

LuAnne grinned. "No. The baby belongs to Troy."

Rhonda grimaced. "He's supporting you in this?"

LuAnne shook her head in the negative. " 'Fraid not."

"I'll kick his ass!"

LuAnne and Leon looked at each other and burst out laughing.

Rhonda frowned at the both of them. "What's so funny?"

Leon supplied the answer: "That's exactly what Lulu *said* you'd want to do after you found out."

Rhonda went and hugged her sister. "Well, I can't personally kick his ass. But I know some fellas who'd do it as a favor to me."

"So do I," Leon said. "But we won't get into that right now." He went over to the sofa and picked up his leather jacket. He'd left his large suitcase and carry-on bag near the door in anticipation of this moment. Putting on his jacket, he looked back at Rhonda and LuAnne. "I'm going to let you two catch up. Nice meeting you, Rhonda."

LuAnne and Rhonda stood with their arms about each other's waists, smiling at Leon.

"Thanks for making the trip with me, Leon. I'll call you," LuAnne promised.

"You'd better."

"Thanks for escorting my sister back home," Rhonda said sincerely.

"It was my pleasure," Leon replied, blushing again.

He knew there had to have been a terrible rift in their relationship to keep them apart for so long. Just seeing the emotion in their faces when they set eyes on each other again was enough to convince him they truly loved each other. Whether they could heal the pain or not was entirely up to them. He wished them luck.

With one last gorgeous smile directed at them, he departed.

When she heard the door click shut behind Leon, Rhonda said, "Nice man!"

"Very."

"Fine, too."

"Just your type, isn't he? Dark, rich black skin. Tall, hard-bodied." LuAnne watched her sister's face for any indication she was interested in Leon. She hoped so. "At any rate, I brought him here for you."

Rhonda laughed. "You must be joking. That man has eyes only for you. Did you lose your perception when you got pregnant?"

LuAnne smiled at her sister's assertion, but there was a sad aspect to her eyes. "Just think about it, all right? Leon is the nicest guy I've met in a very long time. He's been divorced about a year, and he's not involved with anyone." She went and picked up Rhonda's overnight bag. "Come on; I'll show you to your room. You can get into something comfortable while I do the same; then we'll have a nice, long chat. Have you had dinner yet? I'm starved. Lately, I'm always hungry."

"No, I haven't eaten yet," Rhonda answered, right behind LuAnne. "Leon's in love with you!"

LuAnne paused in her steps to look back at Rhonda. "What makes you think that?"

"The way he looked at you when you burst into the room a few minutes ago. It was all over his puppy-dog face."

LuAnne laughed. "Oh, he's just infatuated with me. Most men are in my presence."

"You don't say?" Rhonda returned. "Your ego is monstrous!"

LuAnne continued to Rhonda's bedroom. "I'm not being egotistical. It's just the effect this business I'm in has on the average male. Most of it's image. You know that. Leon just hasn't woken up yet. He will soon enough. Then, he'll be looking for someone more down-to-earth. That's where you come in."

"Trying to keep him in the family?"

LuAnne pushed open the door of the large bedroom that had been set aside for Rhonda. They walked inside. The room was decorated in antique furnishings. On the floor was plush carpeting in tan. The girls felt as if they sank an inch when they stepped on it.

Rhonda went and sat on the queen-size bed, looking up at her sister. "Okay, time to get down to business." Her gaze lowered to LuAnne's protruding belly. "We've got to find you a competent ob/gyn first thing Monday morning."

"That's all taken care of," LuAnne assured her. "My doctor in Paris faxed all my records to a colleague of his here in the city. I have an appointment to see him next week."

Rhonda was impressed. "I'm glad to hear that. Because I want my niece—I'm putting my order in for a girl right now—to have the very best of care from the start."

LuAnne massaged her belly with both hands. Her eyes sparkled with genuine joy. "I'm going to be a mom!" She met Rhonda's eyes. "Can you believe it?"

Rhonda's reply to that was to come and hug LuAnne

once more. "I'm so excited! I was beginning to think neither of us would ever get knocked up! I know my chances of having a child died with Raj. So, this is wonderful news. I'll get to be an aunt."

LuAnne suddenly turned serious and held Rhonda at arm's length, giving her a stern look. "I don't want to ever hear you say that again. Your chances of being a mom didn't die with Raj. You're only thirty-three! You have plenty of time to have a baby." She shook her for good measure before letting her go. Turning, she said, "Honestly, I figured you would have met someone by now and moved on." She paused. "Raj was a nice guy, but he wasn't a paragon of virtue. Not like you're making him out to be. There is life after Raj Davidson."

Rhonda wasn't about to let her disparage Raj's memory. "Did you love Troy?"

"He was a good lay."

"Is that all he was to you, a good lay?"

"Apparently, that's all I was to him, too."

"That's your bitterness talking."

"That's my common sense talking."

"Okay, maybe you've got to be hard in order to survive what you're going through right now. My situation was different, though. Raj and I were in love, and we were devoted to each other. It's going to be next to impossible for me to find someone else who makes me feel that way."

LuAnne adeptly changed the subject. "Well, I'm home now and I'm going to make it my business to hook you up." She grinned at Rhonda. "Girl, you know you look like 'Nessa more and more!"

Rhonda wasn't going to take that insult lying down. She quickly pulled the covers back on the bed, selected a pillow, and threw it at LuAnne.

Laughing, LuAnne easily avoided the pillow. "Now, don't get all upset because the older you get, the more you look like 'Nessa."

"Don't be surprised if that baby comes here looking exactly like her," Rhonda returned.

LuAnne's face fell.

Rhonda was immediately regretful.

"Gotcha!" LuAnne exclaimed. She quickly closed the door.

Smiling, Rhonda went to get her pajamas out of her overnight bag. She hadn't felt this spiritually complete in months. It was wonderful having her sister back.

"I'm so proud of you," LuAnne told Rhonda as she selected another soft-shelled crab from the pile sitting atop newspaper in the center of the table. "I always hear about your work from other models, photographers, everybody in the business. You're going to be right up there with Annie Leibovitz before long."

Rhonda was busy chewing a bit of the succulent crabmeat. "I'd rather be compared to Jeanne Moutoussamy-Ashe. She's done some astounding work over the years."

"She's talented," LuAnne conceded. "But I was referring to a photographer who stays within the parameters of your chosen subject matter, which happens to be celebrities and fashion models."

"I'm branching out a little," Rhonda said with a secret smile. She was thinking of Stuart. She told LuAnne about the book she'd proposed to Beacon Publishing. Then she told her about Stuart.

LuAnne sat with her mouth open in amazement. "My conservative sister is dating a white man?"

Rhonda laughed shortly. "What does being conservative have to do with it?"

"Oh, it's just that you never step out of the role you're supposed to play as today's black woman, that's all. Now, me? I'm expected to be experimental."

"You've had white lovers? You never told *me*."

"Girl, please. Black, brown, white, yellow. Been there,

done that! I draw the line at girl-girl. But when it comes to men, I've had my share."

Rhonda wasn't a bit surprised. She tried to feign the emotion for her sister's benefit, though. She knew how LuAnne liked to shock her. "Then what's your verdict? Who're better in bed? Black men or white men?"

"They're all the same in the dark," was LuAnne's considered opinion. "I've had great white lovers. Paul, a Frenchman, was the best of those. He never failed to please. He was extremely acrobatic and had a huge schlong. I cried for days when we broke up." Rhonda nearly choked on her crabmeat. She coughed. "And who was the best of the black guys? Troy? Marques Washington?"

"Troy was good. Marques cared only for his own fulfillment. Very selfish in bed."

Just as Rhonda suspected. "He tried me, too."

"That canine!" LuAnne cried, laughing. "Believe me, he isn't worth it."

"Oh, I believe you."

"Okay," LuAnne said, cocking her head to the side. "Your turn. Who was the best lover you ever had? And I hope you have a long list to choose from."

Rhonda pursed her lips before replying. "Without a doubt, it was Raj."

LuAnne rolled her eyes. "I knew you were going to say that."

"Well, he was!"

"Haven't you had anyone since Raj died?"

"No."

LuAnne's jaw fell in surprise. "You've got to be kidding me!"

Rhonda placed the crab leg she was about to crack open down on the table. "Listen, I don't think it's unusual to want to wait until you're in love with someone before screwing him."

"Don't tell me you're still hung up on that romantic crap. You'd better screw a few good men before you get too old to want to. That's my motto. Love?" She placed her hand on top of her stomach. "This is where love got me."

"Then you did love Troy!" Rhonda said with a note of triumph in her voice.

"As much as I can love any man," LuAnne allowed. "But you know what 'Nessa always said about a man: never totally give yourself to him because when he leaves he'll take your heart and your soul with him. Troy might have made off with my heart, but damned if he got my soul."

"Don't you think it's time we cut 'Nessa some slack?" Rhonda asked seriously. She wiped her hands on a cloth napkin. She'd had her fill of the spicy crabs. " 'Nessa wasn't a perfect mother, but she can't be blamed for every bad thing that happens in our lives."

"Oh, you can talk," LuAnne said, cutting her eyes at Rhonda. "You got out at eighteen. I've never forgiven you for abandoning me."

"You were sixteen. What was I going to do, take you to college with me?" Rhonda asked, hackles rising. "I wish you'd stop throwing that in my face after all this time!"

"Don't you remember our promise to each other? We were both coming to New York City to pursue modeling careers once I turned eighteen. You were supposed to wait for me. Instead you decided to go to college," LuAnne vehemently cried.

"I can't believe you actually feel this way," Rhonda said, hurt. "I explained to you that I couldn't stand to be objectified one minute longer. I hated those pageants. I hated everything about them. Especially when we got to be teens. 'Nessa was stuffing our bras to make us look more developed—"

"She didn't have to stuff yours!" LuAnne accused.

"Are you going to grouse about that, too?"

"You abandoned me!" LuAnne petulantly yelled, pushing her chair back from the table and rising.

Rhonda got up, too. "You could have left when you

turned eighteen. Daddy gave both of us that option. Go to college or get a job. You chose to go to New York."

LuAnne paced the room. Looking like a big yellow bird in her pj's. "With 'Nessa right there managing my career, I couldn't do anything without her permission."

She turned and looked directly into Rhonda's eyes. "The only thing that made her go back home was Daddy giving her an ultimatum. It was either my so-called career or their marriage. 'Nessa chose the marriage."

"I never knew that," Rhonda said, nonplussed.

"You never knew a lot of things," LuAnne said, seemingly taking pleasure in Rhonda's ignorance. "Did you know that my period stopped for a few months when I was seventeen and 'Nessa took me to the doctor for a *pregnancy* test? She kept it a secret from Daddy because if I was pregnant, she planned on getting rid of the kid before he found out. Luckily, I wasn't pregnant. The doctor said I was exercising too much. 'Nessa had me on one tough workout regimen."

Rhonda sighed, remembering those five-mile jogs every Saturday and Sunday morning. Early enough to make it back home to get ready for Sunday school on time. She had to give it to 'Nessa, though. She ran right alongside her and LuAnne.

"All I know," Rhonda said, walking around the table to face LuAnne, "is until we let it go 'Nessa will still have an influence over us. She wasn't the most loving mother. She was demanding and obsessed with turning us into perfect examples of female beauty. Who knows why she did it? I just want to get on with my life."

"Is that what you're doing, getting on with your life?" LuAnne asked with a disbelieving expression on her face. "We've been talking for three hours now, and for the life of me I haven't been able to detect a great deal of happiness in what you've told me so far." She began to count off Rhonda's deficiencies on one hand with the other. "You don't have a man in your life. You just met Stuart, so he doesn't count. There are no kiddies because your hopes for them died with Raj. I would say the only things you have going for you are your career and your looks."

"I have my friends," Rhonda said, sounding pitiful even to her own ears.

"That's more than I have," LuAnne admitted and ran sobbing to embrace Rhonda.

Rhonda held her as LuAnne wept. Rhonda was past that. She'd assessed her life and found it lacking long before her sister arrived from Paris to lay it all out for her.

After a few moments, LuAnne drew away and wiped her face on her pajama top sleeve.

"Must be the hormones. I've been crying at the drop of a hat."

"Feel better?" Rhonda asked with a smile. "Because I have an idea."

LuAnne brightened. "Yeah?"

"Let's phone 'Nessa and tell her about the baby."

"And your white boy," LuAnne suggested. "That'll kill her."

Rhonda grinned. "I'll go phone her from the extension in my room. I'll yell for you to pick up in here."

She trotted back to her bedroom.

As she sat on the bed, she glanced at the read-out on the clock radio. One-fifteen A.M. 'Nessa would be sound asleep. She dialed anyway.

"Hello," her father's muffled voice answered.

Rhonda fleetingly thought of hanging up. That was cowardly, though, so she spoke up. "Dad, it's me, Rhonda."

"Rhonda, baby, is something wrong? You been in an accident?"

"No, no," she hastily responded. "LuAnne is here and we just wanted to call you to hear your voice."

"LuAnne's in New York with you?" he asked excitedly.

Rhonda felt a twinge of jealousy. Why hadn't he sounded as excited to hear *her* voice?

"Yeah, hold on a sec, Daddy."

She yelled for LuAnne to pick up her extension.

Then, she listened.

"Hi, Daddy. It's good to hear your voice."

"LuAnne. Child, do you know how long it's been since we heard from you?"

"Too long," LuAnne admitted, ready to take her punishment.

Rhonda could tell some of the fight had gone out of them both. They wouldn't be able to confront 'Nessa tonight. You needed conviction to wrestle with Vanessa Copeland.

'Nessa got on an extension. "You two monkeys"—that's what she'd called them when they were small children—"couldn't wait until daylight to phone? This had better be good." Then the girls could hear her speaking in low tones to their father. "Go on back to sleep, Andrew. I'll fill you in in the morning."

To them she said, "I'm on the cordless. I'm going to get up and go downstairs. Let your daddy sleep. He hasn't been feeling his best."

"What's wrong with Daddy?" Rhonda asked, concerned.

"If you'd phone more often, I would've told you he's been having some problems with his heart."

"Oh, no!" LuAnne cried.

"How serious is it?" Rhonda wanted to know.

In their Colonial-style home on the outskirts of Richmond, Vanessa Copeland was slowly descending the winding stairs that led upstairs. A petite woman of fifty-five, she was attired in a long sleeveless cotton nightgown in peach. Her café au lait complexion was unmarred. Except for spiderwebs around her eyes, her age didn't show on her face. Because she exercised regularly, she still wore a size 6.

Vanessa was a woman who believed in making wise choices. She'd chosen well when she married Andrew Copeland thirty-five years ago. She had a high school education and saw nothing on her horizon that was half as enticing as Andrew. It didn't matter that she wasn't in love with him then. Love had come later on.

She paused a long time before she answered Rhonda's question.

Those girls deserved to be punished for their neglect. Didn't they realize that their parents were getting older, their bodies were wearing out? They showed no awareness whatsoever. She'd broken her back to give them everything they needed when they were children. Ingrates, both of them.

Rhonda visited only on major holidays and phoned infrequently. She phoned her grandmother, Ruby, more than she phoned her own mother. And LuAnne. Don't let her get started on that piece of work! She hadn't been home for Christmas two years in a row, always claiming she had to work. Vanessa could hear the lie in her tone of voice whenever she phoned with the excuse.

Nah, these girls had to be set straight, and now.

"If either of you had taken time out of your busy schedules to phone more often, you might have learned that your father was diagnosed with a murmur. He's on medication. He's had to change his diet, too, and start exercising. Nothing strenuous. We take a walk around the neighborhood every afternoon."

Rhonda shifted uncomfortably on the bed in her bedroom. Why hadn't she been more cognizant of her parents' needs? She supposed she'd thought they'd remain young and vital forever. 'Nessa was such a strong woman. And Rhonda couldn't recall her father being sick a day in his life. Now this.

"Then he won't require an operation?" LuAnne asked.

Rhonda thought she sounded like another crying jag had taken possession of her. LuAnne always had a soft spot for their father. Even though she heartily complained about Vanessa, in her eyes Andrew Copeland bore no blame. He was just an unwitting participant. Vanessa was the one who ruled the roost. Andrew was the handsome prince the two imprisoned princesses wished would someday storm the castle and rescue them out of the clutches of the evil queen.

"For now, medication and a proper diet seem to be working," Vanessa said. Her voice had lost its edge. "All right, out with it. Why did you phone? I know it wasn't just to chat. And although I'm surprised you're back in the States, LuAnne, I know you didn't phone to tell me that, either. What's happened? And don't lie to me. I can hear it in your voice when you lie to me."

"I'm going to have a baby," LuAnne said quickly.

Vanessa screamed with delight. In the kitchen of the Colonial now, she clamped a hand over her mouth. Perhaps Andrew hadn't heard her. She'd pulled the door to the bedroom shut behind her, and he was a sound sleeper. "A baby! How far along are you? Who's the father? Troy Granger? Or did you break up with him? You never tell me anything about your personal life anymore. I have to read about you in the tabloids."

"Slow down, Ma," Rhonda cut in. "Let LuAnne speak. Go ahead, LuAnne."

"Troy's the father," LuAnne said. "I'm around five months. Now I know I should have phoned before now, but I had some things to work through. Troy doesn't want the baby, Mom. I'm doing this alone."

"Like hell, you are," Vanessa contradicted her. "You've got me and your father, and your sister. You're never alone, LuAnne."

"That's what I've been telling her," Rhonda agreed.

"Listen to your sister," Vanessa advised her younger daughter.

"You're not disappointed in me, Ma?" LuAnne asked cautiously.

"Come on, child. This isn't the Dark Ages. There isn't as much of a stigma attached to having children out of wedlock nowadays. Not like when I got pregnant with Rhonda. Back then, a woman was looked down on—"

"Slow your roll, 'Nessa Copeland," Rhonda said, her voice brooking no disobedience. "Did you just say I'm a bastard?"

"Your father and I got married when I was three months pregnant," Vanessa said as though the information were old news. "You're thirty-three, Ronnie. This shouldn't come as too much of a shock to you." She actually laughed. "This is a night for revelations. It felt good to get that off my chest."

"Anything else you want to get off your chest?" Rhonda asked. "Because there are a few things I'd like to get off my chest, if you're finished."

"No, that's it," Vanessa said. "What do you have to tell me, dear?"

Dear, Rhonda thought. *Who is this woman, and what has she done with my mother?* She was still pissed off by the way 'Nessa had carelessly revealed her state of birth, though; and now was as good a time as any to lay into her about the way she'd raised her and LuAnne.

"Okay, I'd like to know what you were thinking when you entered me and LuAnne in all those crazy-ass beauty pageants—"

Rhonda didn't finish because LuAnne appeared out of nowhere and wrenched the receiver out of her hand. "Ma, gotta run. Love you!" She hung up the phone.

Rhonda glared at her. "Why'd you do that?"

"She's an old woman. Our father has a heart ailment. Let her slide. Isn't that what you suggested only a few minutes ago?"

"Yeah, but—"

"You just wanted to get back at her for telling you you were conceived out of wedlock in such a nonchalant manner. Now, tell me I'm not right."

Rhonda momentarily closed her eyes and deeply breathed in and out, trying to quell the burning anger she felt toward 'Nessa at that moment. 'Nessa was so selfish, it didn't occur to her that information of that magnitude should be imparted in person and not through something as impersonal as a telephone.

LuAnne went and placed her arm about Rhonda's shoulders. "You know, your niece is going to be born out of wedlock. And she'll be as wonderful as her aunt."

Four

Rhonda watched as Leon and LuAnne, their heads together, spoke in whispers at the dinner table. She smiled to herself. It was plain to her that Leon was in love with LuAnne. She didn't know why LuAnne refused to acknowledge it.

Leon suddenly threw his head back and laughed, his Adam's apple moving up and down in his throat, white teeth showing. Rhonda liked the sound of his laughter. She especially liked the fact that LuAnne had elicited such delight. They were good together.

"Ronnie, is it true that you streaked across the stage buck-naked once?"

Ronnie. He called her Ronnie now. Everything about Leon Jackson was warm and easy. She grew fonder of him each time she saw him.

"Did she tell you I was five years old at the time?" She shot LuAnne a wicked glance.

LuAnne giggled.

They were all sitting around Rhonda's dining room table after Sunday dinner. She'd cooked. LuAnne had offered to help, but LuAnne and kitchens didn't mix. Patience wasn't her forte, and it took patience to prepare an edible meal.

"Go ahead; have your fun," Rhonda said. She regarded Leon. "I bet she didn't tell you about the time we were at the lake for summer vacation and she got into ants. By the time we all ran over to see what she was yelling about, she'd stripped to her birthday suit and jumped into the lake."

LuAnne laughed even harder. "Those ants were tearing my ass up!"

"She was fourteen," Rhonda put in. "After that, every boy at the lake followed her around like little lost puppies the rest of the summer."

"It was the only way I could get their attention," LuAnne defended herself. "You had them eating out of your hands."

"I didn't even notice them," Rhonda said truthfully. She rose and began collecting the plates. "That was the summer I decided I wanted to be a poet. I was too busy trying to pull emotions from all the teenage angst I'd built up over sixteen years."

"Yeah, she wore black every day of our vacation. Even a black maillot swimsuit. She was very Audrey Hepburn–ish," LuAnne told Leon. "Back then, Ronnie's hair was longer than mine is now."

"Horse hair, Grandma Ruby calls our hair," Rhonda picked up the story.

"Because it's so thick and strong," said LuAnne. "Naturally wavy, you know? All you have to do is wash it and put a little hair dressing on it and you're set to go."

"Which was fortunate," Rhonda injected. "Because 'Nessa couldn't braid hair to save her life. She wound up taking us to the beauty parlor once a week. Miss Rose did our hair up until we both graduated from high school." She peered at LuAnne. "Whatever happened to Miss Rose, anyway?"

"Retired, according to Tamara Baker."

"You've spoken with Tamara recently?" Hands full, she turned to go to the kitchen.

"Girl, since I've been home, I've been calling everybody in my old address book. You would be surprised by the number of folks still hanging around home. Some of the kids we grew up with have even moved back into their parents' houses. But in Tammy's case, her mom gave me her number. She still lives in Richmond. She's married, and they have three kids."

Leon leaned back in his chair, enjoying the give-and-take between the sisters. He was convinced that talking

LuAnne into coming home was the right thing to do. He looked at her now. Her golden-brown skin had an inner glow. She'd gained a few more pounds over the six weeks they'd been back in the city. Her belly was nice and round. She'd taken to folding her hands atop it. Occasionally he noticed her jumping abruptly. The baby was becoming more and more active.

Rhonda's two-bedroom apartment wasn't large, but she had a flair for decorating, and the spare furnishings, all good pieces, and muted tones on the walls and floors all worked to give the illusion of space. The hardwood floors gleamed. She'd recently had the kitchen refurbished. Now, the dark cabinets had been replaced with light-colored cabinets that had glass doors. She loved to cook, so her kitchen was equipped with copper pots, which hung from the high ceiling on a rack that was operated by remote control. She pressed a button, and the rack lowered or rose at her discretion.

While at home, Leon noticed, Rhonda rarely wore shoes. She was barefoot now as she reentered the dining room carrying a chocolate cake on a pedestal-style cake server.

She placed it in the center of the table. "Be right back with plates and the coffee. Decaf for you, LuAnne."

"Wasn't Stuart supposed to join us for dinner tonight?" LuAnne called after her.

"Yeah, but something came up. He said he'd phone later," Rhonda said from the kitchen. Stuart usually made them a foursome for Sunday dinner. She missed him.

"You don't think he's seeing someone else, do you?" LuAnne whispered to Leon.

"No," Leon immediately replied. "He doesn't strike me as the type."

Rhonda frowned. "Yeah, well, I hope he doesn't hurt her."

Leon had mixed emotions about the manner in which LuAnne regarded him. She used him as a sounding board. A girlfriend. A confidant. Nothing was taboo between them.

All good. But what he wanted her to do was let down her guard.

Just long enough to admit she wanted him. She called this doing the noble thing, denying she was attracted to him. He wasn't blind, though. He saw the longing in the looks she gave him when she thought his attention was elsewhere. It was the same way Stuart Mitchum looked at Rhonda. Made the brother in him uneasy until he'd gotten to know Stuart better. Then he was okay with it. Stuart was good people, as his mother would say. No, LuAnne didn't have to worry that Stuart had eyes for some other woman.

"I hope everything's all right," Rhonda said when she entered the room again, carrying a tray laden with dessert plates, silverware, a carafe of coffee, and mugs. She set the tray on the table. "He didn't sound like himself."

Rhonda rolled over in bed and checked the luminous dial of the bedside clock.

A quarter past midnight.

Why hadn't Stuart phoned? He'd never promised her he'd phone and not done it.

She was worried about him. What if he'd been in an accident and *couldn't* phone?

She picked up the phone from the nightstand and sat up in bed. There was only one thing to do. She quickly dialed his number before she could talk herself out of it.

A sleepy feminine voice answered. "Yeah?"

Taken aback, Rhonda said, "I'm sorry. I must have dialed the wrong number." She went to hang up.

"Wait! Who were you calling?"

"Stuart—"

"Is this Rhonda?"

"Yes," Rhonda replied, surprised. "And you are?"

The other woman laughed. "Eileen, Stuart's sister. Bet you're awash with relief about now."

Rhonda laughed right along with her. "I sure am!"

"Stuart's at Lenox Hill Hospital. Our mother had a scare

with her heart tonight. She's stable, but it was touch and go for a while there."

"I'm so sorry," Rhonda said sympathetically.

Eileen gave a deep sigh. "You know, we lost our dad about three years ago. And to imagine losing Mom is devastating. Especially on Stuey, because he's always been the one who doted on her. Not that we don't all love Mom, but when Dad died, Stuey sort of stepped in and made sure Mom was being taken care of. Joe and I both have families, and Stuey just naturally assumed it was his job. Plus Joe and I both live out-of-state, and we can't seem to blast Mom out of her Manhattan apartment. I think she believes until Stuey finds a wife, it's her responsibility to look after him."

"Sort of a reciprocal relationship," Rhonda said when she could get a word in.

"Yeah," Eileen said. She grunted a little. Rhonda envisioned her shifting in bed. "Excuse me. Had to get the rug rat from right under me. She's two, and unless her elbow is pressing in my back she just can't get comfortable."

Then, "Stuart forgot to phone you, didn't he? I love my brother, but he can be absentminded. And he refuses to carry a cell phone. I don't understand the man. He's old-fashioned in a lot of ways. But I guess you know that."

Rhonda was beginning to wonder how much Stuart had told his family about her.

"I like that about him," she told Eileen.

"Don't get me wrong," Eileen said. "My girlfriends swear Stuey's a hottie. I changed his diapers, so I guess I just can't see it. I know I'm running on at the mouth, but this whole thing with Mom has me so keyed up, and I can't sleep anyway. Hey, Stuey should be home pretty soon. I'll tell him you phoned," she ended with a questioning tone to her voice, as if she was giving Rhonda an out if she wanted it.

"I'm wide awake now, too," Rhonda answered. "Tell me about yourself."

"There isn't much to tell," Eileen said with a note of laughter. "My one claim to fame is, I'm very fertile. Martin and I have five children. I don't know if Stuey told you, but Joe and I are a lot of years older than he is. We call him 'the afterthought.' I'm ten years older and Joe's twelve years older. We have two grown kids, two in college, and Martin and I have an afterthought of our own, Miss Kelli, who thinks she's going to be the one to take the old lady out, but I've got news for her!"

Rhonda was laughing so hard, she missed the sound of the downstairs buzzer.

She heard it the second time someone leaned on it.

"Eileen, I've got to go, somebody's buzzing me," she regretfully said into the receiver.

"Okay, Rhonda. Hope to meet you soon."

"Me, too, Eileen. Take care."

They rang off. Rhonda climbed out of bed and ran to the kitchen to deal with the irritating buzzer. She held down the button on the wall unit and spoke into it. "Yeah, yeah. This had better be good!" She caught herself. She sounded just like 'Nessa.

"Rhonda—"

"Stuart!" She quickly buzzed him in. Then she tore back into her bedroom to grab her bathrobe. Stuart had never seen her in one of the diaphanous nightgowns she preferred. And she didn't have time to jump into more suitable clothing.

Their weekend in Connecticut had been repeatedly postponed due to cold feet, on her part. She was sure she was capable of making love to Stuart. Her body told her that whenever she was in the same room with him. However, the mere thought of making love to a man who wasn't Raj terrified her. It was juvenile, bordering on the asinine. That's how she felt, though. But, oh, Stuart had a way of getting under her skin!

She returned to the living room, wearing a short purple silk kimono-style robe over her lavender nightgown. Running a hand through disheveled hair, she ended with a puff of air blown into her hands. She'd brushed before bed and hadn't been asleep long enough to get morning breath.

Before Stuart had knocked twice, she'd swung the door open.

Her breath caught when she saw him. A weary smile crossed his lips as he stood in the doorway, his brown suede jacket hanging open to reveal the denim shirt tucked neatly into a pair of Levi's. That dimple winked at her. Rhonda peered downward. He was wearing his black motorcycle boots.

She took him by the arm and yanked him inside. "You're riding the Harley? Exhausted as you are?"

Stuart leaned in and kissed her. The stubble on his cheek scratched her, and his skin tasted salty. Forgetting what she was about to say, she threw her arms around his neck. Hard chest pressed against soft breasts. She moaned as the kiss deepened.

Turning her head to disconnect their mouths, she breathlessly asked, "Your mom?"

"She's going to be fine. How . . . ?"

"Eileen."

"You phoned the house? I bet Eileen talked your ear off." He sounded pleased. Those dark eyes of his, though tired, were terribly sexy.

"I was worried about you." She gently caressed his lower lip with her thumb.

"I'm sorry I didn't phone. I won't do it again."He kissed her thumb.

"It's all right," she said, her voice so low he had to strain to hear.

"It's not all right," he said, tilting her chin up so that she was looking him in the eye. "I want you to be a part of my life, Rhonda. I want to include you in all aspects of it. I should have told you what was going on."

"Is your mom really going to be okay?"

"Yes, her doctor says she can probably go home by Tuesday."

"That's wonderful news."

He had his arms wrapped around her waist. Rhonda placed her hands against his chest.

"Did I wake you?" Stuart asked. He breathed in her essence. "You're still warm from bed." He could hold her like this all night. Wished he could. But he didn't want to rush what he knew could be his greatest love affair ever. He burned for her. Images of her sweet face continually invaded his thoughts. How it would be when they finally made love. He hadn't forgotten to phone her tonight. He just hadn't wanted her to hear the need in his voice. Not when he feared his mother might be dying. Rhonda wasn't ready for that kind of intimacy. Though he would've liked for her to have been there beside him, she should to be the first one to make a move toward that level of togetherness.

"I was on the phone with Eileen when you buzzed me. Have you eaten?" He was touched by the concern in her warm brown eyes. There was something else there, too. Could it be . . . ? "Are you hungry?" she asked, her voice husky.

His heart thumped in his chest. His groin grew tight. "Not for food."

Rhonda's hands were moving over his chest, pushing the jacket downward. Stuart wriggled his shoulders and the jacket fell to the floor. She felt the corded muscles on his arms and an instant thrill shot through her like a bottle rocket, spreading a delicious sensation the entire length of her body.

The fire down below blazed hot, and this time she didn't want to turn back.

She grabbed him by his shirt lapels and pulled him down to meet her mouth.

Stuart didn't have to be coaxed. Her eagerness fed his desire. His was not to question why, only to reap the benefits of her largess.

Rhonda was moving backward, toward the bedroom, pulling him with her. Stuart broke off the kiss. He held her about the waist with one hand while he slapped the palm of the other against his forehead. He'd just thought of something. "Baby, I don't have any condoms with me."

"I bought a package the other day, just in case," Rhonda told him. She gazed up at him with dreamy eyes. "Unless you'd rather not—"

"Oh, no, hell no," Stuart assured her, determined. "I want you."

Rhonda stepped back a little and glanced down at the bulge in his jeans and smiled, her full lips so luscious, Stuart couldn't resist tasting them again.

She untied the sash at her waist and doffed the bathrobe. The gown was completely see-through. All she had on under it was a pair of bikini briefs. "I hope you like what you see." She advanced, going to place her hand on his belt buckle and loosen it. "I have a little quirk you should know about, Stuart. I like to be on top."

Stuart hadn't yet gotten over the initial punch of seeing her nearly unclothed body. His hands cupped her heavy breasts, moving downward to outline her hourglass figure and, finally, to rest on a bottom only God could have created on His best day.

His erection pushed against the jeans. Rhonda ran her hand across it, feeling the throbbing member pulsate beneath her touch. She languidly turned away. "I'll be waiting. It's the door on the right."

Then, she sprinted down the hallway.

Stuart couldn't get out of his clothes fast enough. He hopped on one foot, then the other, as he struggled out of the boots. Three buttons flew from his shirt. He didn't give a damn. Not wanting to hurt himself, he had to be more careful coming out of the zipped jeans. He took time to remove his socks before calmly, with as much restraint as he could muster, following Rhonda to her bedroom.

The queen-size bed, decked in white from comforter to sheets to pillow shams, sat high off the floor upon a large multicolored braided rug. The rug sat on a hardwood floor.

Stuart's eyes took a few seconds to adjust to the lack of

light. Rhonda had dimmed the settings on the two bedside lamps sitting on nightstands on opposite sides of the bed.

"Welcome," she said as she came up behind him and wrapped her arms around his waist, then over his flat, rippled belly upward to his chest. She tweaked both nipples between her thumbs and forefingers. While she did this, she was raining kisses down the hollow of his back. The feel of her mouth on his body made him weak.

What had she been afraid of? This was so natural, so right. She gave herself to the moment.

Stuart could feel her warm, naked breasts on his back. The tips were hard and he wanted, more than anything, to turn and touch her. Mold her with his hands. Taste those ripe buds on his tongue. Desiring to see where her ministrations would lead, he did none of those things.

After a few more tense moments, Rhonda walked around to stand before him.

"Damn!" Stuart uttered. Rhonda wore nothing but a smile. In her left hand was a latex condom she'd already removed from its wrapping. Still smiling that mysterious smile, she pulled down the waistband of his briefs and rolled the condom onto his engorged penis. Stuart sighed. Rhonda rubbed her body against his. Stuart's big hands grabbed her bottom and gently squeezed. Then he lowered his head and kissed her.

"Rhonda . . ." Her name was a mantra between kisses. Said over and over again.

Rhonda's body tingled with expectation. Her center felt as though an ember had been lit and Stuart's kisses were the kindling feeding the flames. It had been so long. So long since a man touched her like this. Since a man wanted her this much. As much as she wanted him.

She held her breath as Stuart took her in his strong arms and carried her to the bed. He lifted her 140 pounds as though it were nothing. Under those conservative publisher's suits was a very fit body that was all male. The knowledge only turned her on more.

On her back now, she watched him as he knelt on the bed. She scooted back on the bed, a playful expression on her face. *Catch me, if you can.* Stuart's full lips curved in a knowing smile. He was game.

He approached her on his hands and knees. Rhonda had backed up against the headboard. Stuart went and gently pried her legs apart. Rhonda feigned resistance, but when he licked the inside of her right thigh, she gave up the pretense and freely spread her legs for him.

Stuart went for the prize. His tongue teased her soft inner thigh, as he worked his way upward. Rhonda slid down until she was reclining with her head on the pillows. Stuart pulled her closer, and then his tongue dipped into her warm, hot center until she ended up squirming with the need to climax. He withdrew just as he felt her body tense.

"Not yet," he said.

Up on his knees, he reached for her hand and placed it around his sheathed manhood. Rhonda felt him grow hard again in the palm of her hand. She directed him inside of her.

Raising her hips, she felt him, hard and sure, going deep, deep. Holding onto the backs of his arms, she gave as readily as she received. Muscles that hadn't come into play in aeons, it seemed, now flexed and found an age-old rhythm. Yes, yes, this was what she'd been denying herself.

The bed creaked. The headboard banged against the wall, but neither of them seemed to notice. Stuart looked down into her face. Her lips were parted and she was actually softly panting, her eyes closed, with a look of rapture that made him grow even more inside her. Filling her up.

He could have had an orgasm when she stood before him, buck to the bone, a few minutes ago. His desire for her was that intense. But tonight was for her pleasure. He wanted her to remember this night for as long as she lived.

"Ah!" she cried out. "Oh God!"

Stuart smiled to himself. Before they were done, they'd both be calling on God.

Pushing deeper, moving in and out slowly, with her

moans in his ears increasing in frequency and volume, Stuart reveled in her. How her beautiful brown skin glistened, dewy with perspiration. How her breasts, full and the tips pointing north, shook with each thrust, just as breasts should. He closed his eyes; he was getting too turned on.

Deep inside her, he gathered her against his chest, and, in tandem, they rolled over in bed. She was now straddling him. "You said you liked to be on top," he reminded her with a wicked grin.

Rhonda leaned down and gently kissed his lips. Then she threw her head back, arched her back, as he cupped her breasts, and rode him home.

She came before him. Stripped of all inhibitions, she moaned loudly as she bucked harder. Stuart slammed into her with more ferocity as he joined her. Rhonda locked hands with him, fingers entwined. They held on as they both drifted down, down until a peace suffused them. On their bed of white, they looked like lovers engaged in carnal bliss, while suspended upon a billowing cloud.

Back to the physical, damp skin touched damp skin and frantic breathing slowed to a more balanced pace. Rhonda lay on top of Stuart. After a moment she went to get up, but he held her there. "Don't move," he said. "I want to hold you a little longer."

Her curly lashes tickled his cheek. "Why did it take me so long to come to this?"

Stuart ran his hand through her hair. "You had to trust me first."

Rhonda smiled and gently kissed the side of his neck. "I do trust you."

"Enough to move in with me?"

"Why the hell not?" Heaven O'Riley asked, wrinkling her nose at Rhonda.

It was Friday night. They'd just gotten out of Heaven's Jeep Cherokee and were hurrying up the walk to LuAnne's new digs, a loft in Soho.

Wrapped in coats, the two women were about the same height, but Heaven was a full-figured sister with abundant dreads spilling down her back. They were arriving early because they'd agreed to help set up the get-together designed to introduce LuAnne to some of Rhonda's friends.

On the way over in the car, Rhonda had told Heaven she'd decided not to move in with Stuart. Now, Heaven stood on the street with her hands on her ample hips and cried, "Let me get this straight; you're turning down a card-carrying millionaire who's a dead ringer for Billy Zane, rides a Harley, and *eats* you!"

"Heaven, keep your damn voice down," Rhonda hissed, pulling on her best friend's sleeve. "Will you come on? It's cold out here."

The November wind whistled in their ears. It had a sharp bite, too.

Heaven started walking again. "I can't understand you, Ronnie." And she was an economics professor at NYU. Heavy. Not many things got past her. "Shit, if you don't want him, I'll take him."

"I don't think black women are interchangeable to Stuart, Heaven," Rhonda said as she pulled the door of LuAnne's building open and allowed Heaven to precede her. "I never said I didn't want Stuart. I'm not ready to move in with him, that's all."

"What are you afraid of?" Heaven asked, lowering her voice once they stepped into the building, because voices tended to be amplified.

"I'm afraid of hurting him," Rhonda honestly replied.

"Or are you afraid of getting hurt?" Heaven intuitively hit on.

"That, too."

They fell silent as they took the stairs to the fourth floor. By the second-floor landing, Heaven could no longer stay quiet. "It's Raj, isn't it? You're still in love with him."

"I think I'll always love him."

Heaven sadly shook her head. "Okay, but do you have

to let that get in the way of your happiness?" She paused on the third-floor landing. Rhonda kept walking. "Look at me, Rhonda Copeland." Rhonda turned to face her. "Raj isn't coming back for you. His body is rotting in Woodlawn Cemetery, and his spirit is wherever spirits go. Now, you. You are still here. Living, breathing, lately copulating. Thank God. It's your life. You can waste it if you want to. But, I swear, I'll personally whip your ass if you ruin what you have with Stuart over some misplaced loyalty to a dead man!"

"Are you finished?" Rhonda asked patiently.

"Knowing you," Heaven said, once again climbing stairs, "probably not."

At eight months pregnant, LuAnne was wobbling rather than walking. Rhonda smiled when she saw her sister crossing the room carrying a tray of crisply fried shrimp, a bowl of shrimp sauce in the center. LuAnne had had the meal catered. All she had to do was set the table and allow the guests to serve themselves.

LuAnne's loft took up the entire floor. She was surprised by the cost of lofts in Soho nowadays. Seven years ago, the prices were not nearly as high. Today, the area south of Houston Street was in the middle of a major overhaul and lofts like hers went for a million-plus dollars.

It was a good thing she'd recently signed that Revlon endorsement contract. So far she'd shot three commercials for the company's new line of black hair care products. Head shots, only. They were talking about casting her as a young mother along with a child four or five years old. The national spots would feature her in all her expectant glory. She liked the thought of that.

Rhonda went and took the platter out of LuAnne's hands. "I want you to get off your feet."

"Yes, mother," LuAnne said with a slow smile, her love for her sister shining in her eyes. With her hand on her lower back, she walked over to one of the large leather couches and sat down beside Bobbie who was there with her sister, Jennie.

Over the months, Bobbie had grudgingly accepted the fact that LuAnne was sincere about becoming closer to her sister. She'd come at Rhonda's insistence.

Besides Bobbie and Jennie, Heaven and Rhonda were the only other guests.

The five women's private and professional lives were largely dissimilar. Bobbie and Rhonda had photography in common. However, Heaven was part of the academic world. Jennie was the executive assistant to a television producer. She was going to night school to earn a degree in Mass Communications in hopes of moving up someday.

Bobbie and Jennie were Puerto Rican, of African descent; Heaven's people came from Haiti, and Rhonda and LuAnne were African American. Only one of them was married, Bobbie. Jennie, at twenty-eight, had never married. Heaven was divorced. Rhonda had come close. LuAnne avoided it like the plague.

LuAnne had a Joe CD on the CD player.

Rhonda was pleasantly surprised by how easily LuAnne blended in with her group.

The other women genuinely seemed to like her.

The evening was winding down. Then, Heaven flashed a mischievous look at Rhonda.

"Who's up for a game of Truth or Dare?"

Rhonda narrowed her eyes at her erstwhile friend. Or she would be, if she kept this up! "It's getting late, and that game tends to go on and on," she said, against the idea.

LuAnne had noticed the irritated look her sister had given Heaven. She wanted to find out what was up. "Sounds like fun," she said with a dazzling smile.

So, to please their hostess, the other women agreed to play.

Heaven took the lead. "Okay, I'll be 'it.' " She started

out slowly by calling on Bobbie. "Bobbie, truth or dare?"

"Truth," Bobbie chose, thinking it was safer than dare.

"Were you and Fred intimate before marriage?"

"Hell, yeah," Bobbie easily replied. "Intensely and frequently. Often accompanied by lots of noise. We couldn't keep our hands off each other, still can't."

"Ask a question we all don't already know the answer to," Jennie joked, playfully mussing her sister's hair.

"My turn," Bobbie said, pursing her lips and cutting her eyes at Jennie. "Jennie, truth or dare?" She flipped her long locks back into place with a toss of her head.

"Truth," Jennie said bravely, meeting her sister's eyes.

"When was the last time you made love? And with whom?" Bobbie challenged.

Jennie smirked and said, "Last Saturday night. You don't want to know who he was."

Bobbie looked to Heaven as the game moderator. "She can't do that, can she? She has to answer the question, or she's out of the game."

Heaven wanted to know the mystery man's identity, too. "She's right, Jennie."

Jennie rolled her eyes. "It was Frank!"

"But you broke up with him," Bobbie whined, sounding like Rosie Perez on helium. "I can't believe this. He's no good for you! Why do you lower yourself to be with him?"

Gesticulating wildly, Jennie rose. " 'Cuz he's in my blood, okay! Here we go again; Saint Bobbie is going to tell me how I'm *screwing* up my life!"

"Nah," Bobbie said, getting to her feet and getting in her sister's face. "Bobbie is staying the hell out of it. I wash my hands of you two. He can't keep a job, and you'd rather take care of him than go without a man between your legs long enough to actually meet someone who wouldn't treat you like shit!"

Heaven, outweighing each of the sisters by at least fifty pounds, stepped between them. "This is not how the game is supposed to go, ladies. Would you please hold off on this conversation until you can discuss it in private?"

Bobbie's chest heaved with pent-up anger. Jennie's eyes met her older sister's dead-on. She was tired of Bobbie interfering in her personal life. She wasn't going to back down this time. Just because she'd practically raised her after their mother died didn't make Bobbie her mother.

Bobbie suddenly stomped her foot in frustration. "No, Heaven, we need to discuss this right now!" She turned to LuAnne, her face softening somewhat. "I'm sorry for breaking up your get-together like this, LuAnne." She walked over to LuAnne and gave her a quick hug. "Welcome back to the city."

LuAnne grasped Bobbie's hand. "Work it out," she said.

Straightening up, Bobbie pointed at Jennie. "You want a ride home, or are you walking?"

Jennie sighed loudly, threw up her hands, went and hugged both LuAnne and Rhonda, whispering, "Sorry," to LuAnne, then followed her sister over to the coat tree by the door, where they collected their coats. LuAnne insisted on seeing them out and padded over to the door while the sisters got into their coats, then thanked them for coming as they left. "We'll do it again sometime," she promised.

"Hold that door," Heaven said. She hurried into her own coat. "Wanna make sure they don't kill each other before they get to the car."

She and LuAnne embraced at the door. Rhonda was right behind Heaven. "You go on, Heaven; I'll stay and help LuAnne clean up."

Heaven sucked air between her teeth. "That's right; you came with me!"

Rhonda placed a kiss high on Heaven's cheek. "Don't worry about me; I'll get a cab."

After LuAnne closed the door behind Heaven, she stood with her back against it for a moment or two. Pushing away, she smiled at Rhonda. "You never know what's simmering below the surface, do you?" Her smile faded.

Rhonda's practical side took over as she surveyed the

large, airy room. She could have this mess cleaned up in twenty minutes flat, get a cab across town, and be at Stuart's place by ten. There *was* an upside to a party ending early. She and Stuart had planned on her coming over around midnight. She was to spend the night there.

LuAnne seemed to sense her sister's mood. "You've got sex on the brain."

Rhonda was smiling to herself as she picked up dirty glasses from the coffee table.

LuAnne moved closer, the soft silk material of the designer maternity dress settling over her huge stomach. "Admit it: you're in love with that man."

Rhonda wore a contemplative expression. She frowned. "I'm not about to fall in love with anyone," she said as she turned to go into the kitchen.

LuAnne picked up a couple of food trays and followed Rhonda.

As Rhonda began separating the glasses, plates, and cutlery from the disposables at the sink, LuAnne sidled up to her and asked with a hopeful note to her voice, "What you meant was, you're not yet certain about you and Stuart, right?"

Rhonda turned to go finish clearing the coffee table. "No, I meant what I said," she tossed over her shoulder. "Once was enough for me."

LuAnne's back hurt. She was tired. She hadn't been sleeping well. The baby had started doing laps in her stomach while she was trying to sleep. Or it felt like it. Therefore, her nerves weren't what they should be.

She didn't follow Rhonda back out to the living room. Leaning against the refrigerator, her face pressed to the cool surface, she was at war with her conscience. Momentarily closing her eyes, she gathered her strength about her and waited for Rhonda's return.

Rhonda came into the room humming. She put the last of the glasses and dishes in the sink and began running water over them, rinsing them, getting them ready to put in the dishwasher.

"You don't have to rinse them before putting them in the dishwasher," LuAnne said, her voice tense.

"Force of habit," Rhonda said, continuing to rinse the dishes.

LuAnne went and snatched a plate from Rhonda's hand and threw it in the sink. The delicate bone china plate cleanly broke in half.

Startled, Rhonda stepped back from the sink, looking at LuAnne as if she'd lost what was left of her mind. "What's wrong with you?"

"I've got to sit down," LuAnne announced and waddled over to the kitchen table, pulled out a chair, and sat. Rhonda cautiously approached the table and stood looking down at LuAnne.

"Are you feeling all right? You're not in any pain, are you?" she asked, concerned.

"Not the kind you're referring to," LuAnne replied, sounding exhausted.

Rhonda sat down across from her and reached for her hand.

LuAnne eagerly clasped Rhonda's hand, brought it up, and rubbed it against her cheek.

When she raised her eyes again, tears sat in them. "You know why I came home?"

She placed Rhonda's hand on the tabletop, gently patted it, and removed her own. She folded her hands over her stomach as she awaited Rhonda's reply.

"You wanted to have the baby here, where you'd be around people who care about you?" Rhonda guessed.

"That's part of it," LuAnne allowed. She looked Rhonda straight in the eye. "The main reason I came home was to make it up to you."

"Make what up to me?" Rhonda asked, a puzzled expression creasing her brow.

"I thought Leon would make a difference. He's so special. I just knew you two would hit it off. But you'd already met Stuart. I was happy for you. Really happy. When you opened up to Stuart and made love to him, you can't imagine what that did to dispel some of the guilt eating away at my insides. I even thought of never telling you. I mean what good would it do? They say confession is good for the soul. But some things are best left unsaid," LuAnne said sadly.

Rhonda's stomach muscles constricted painfully. Dread reached out its icy fingers and clutched her heart in a death grip. Some part of her slowly began to die.

"Are you going to tell me what's up, or not?" she asked with a nervous laugh.

"I didn't like him from the moment I set eyes on him. I thought I had radar for guys who were habitual cheaters. God knows I've known enough of them. How he'd duped you, I couldn't understand. You'd always been savvy where men were concerned. Not with him. You were a sap, Ronnie. I couldn't let my sister go out like that."

LuAnne pressed her lips together and gazed far off as if she were looking through a window to the past. "It was right after Christmas. We'd returned from Richmond the day before you flew off on another assignment. I was to stay at your place until you returned; then we'd spend a few more days together before I left for Paris."

"I remember," Rhonda said. "The last Christmas we spent together in Richmond."

"Yeah," LuAnne confirmed listlessly.

"You were gone when I got back," Rhonda said, remembering the hurt of finding a hastily scribbled note stuck on her refrigerator with a piece of Scotch tape.

"I couldn't face you," LuAnne told her in a low voice. "My plans backfired on me. I was going to come on to him, and when he tried anything, I was going to go running to you with the news of his true nature. You'd thank me for saving you from a life with a pig like him, and that would be the end of it." She couldn't meet her sister's eyes.

The realization of what LuAnne was trying to tell her hit Rhonda with the force of a hurricane. She tried to draw a breath, realized she'd been holding her breath for some time now. Inhaling, she abruptly got up out of her chair, nearly toppling it as she did so. "You're lying!" she accused, unable to wrap her mind around something as inconceivable as this intentional lie. "This is something you and Heaven cooked up between you to shock me out of grieving for Raj."

With effort, LuAnne rose and reached for Rhonda. Rhonda backed away from her.

"I wish it was, Ronnie." Her big brown eyes, so much like her sister's, pleaded for mercy, understanding. "I'd been drinking. I know that's no excuse. I have no excuse. All I have is a heart full of pain that I've been carrying around for nearly three years. I love you!" Tears spilled down her cheeks into her mouth. "I never stopped loving you. You've got to believe that. I know you'll think I did it out of spite, or jealousy, but that isn't true. I was too cocky, thinking I could manipulate him. He had me figured out from the beginning, and went in for the kill. Afterward, he told me I'd better not say anything to you. He'd deny it, and it would cause a rift between you and me."

Rhonda felt sick. Her legs were weak. She didn't know if she'd be able to walk out of there. But she had to. Before she struck a pregnant woman.

She had been staring at LuAnne. The words she wanted to shout at her were frozen in her throat. If someone shot her at that point, she wouldn't feel it. Too numb. Her nerve endings had quit functioning. Her mind was as sharp as ever, though. How facetious. If only that part of her would shut down. Then images of LuAnne and Raj, their naked bodies writhing together as sinuously as two entangled snakes, wouldn't be running around in it.

She grasped at one last hope.

"Prove it!" she croaked, her voice thick with emotion.

LuAnne was openly sobbing as she stood, dejected, her ignored hand, now, at her side.

Five

The passage of time seemed to have acquired a snail's pace.

Rhonda stood with her feet slightly apart, hands at her sides balled into fists. Her nails dug into the flesh of her palms. The pain kept her from totally losing control.

If LuAnne didn't start talking soon, she was going to fly over there, jump down her throat, and *pull* the words out of her.

"Answer me!" she screamed.

LuAnne fell back against the sink as though she'd been dealt a physical blow.

"Why do you need to hear the details? I told you I did it. Why would I lie about something like that?" LuAnne choked out.

Rhonda began pacing the kitchen floor, her sharp gaze never leaving LuAnne's face. "If you screwed Raj, then you know whether or not he was circumcised."

"Rhonda, please!"

"Answer the question!"

"No," LuAnne said, defeated. "He wasn't."

Though that bit of information made Rhonda want to throw up, she was led by some masochistic compulsion to hear more. "Did he immediately respond to you when you came on to him, or did it take some coaxing?"

"What good will it do for you to know that, Ronnie?" LuAnne asked in a low, anguished voice.

"The least you can do is humor me now that you've destroyed any illusions I might have had about Raj loving me," Rhonda returned, giving no quarter. "And of my own sister having any respect for me, whatsoever!"

That got a rise out of LuAnne. She stood a bit taller, her belly not allowing her to straighten gracefully, and walked over to the table. She sat back down. With narrowed; angry eyes, she said, "You want to know everything that happened? All right, I'll tell you everything." She waved her hand in the direction of the chair across from hers. "Sit!"

"I'd rather stand."

"Suit yourself."

"I will from now on."

LuAnne sighed wearily and began: "I phoned him and asked him to meet me at that Chinese place around the corner. We'd have a meal together. We needed to get to know each other better since he was soon to become my brother-in-law. He said no. He'd pick up the Chinese on the way over, and we could talk at your place.

"When he got there, we ate and talked about you, mostly. He asked me how it had been growing up with you. Specifically, if you and I had ever dated the same guy. I told him you and I had an 'I Saw Him First' agreement. Whichever of us met the guy first was the one who got to date him and the other kept her hands off. He wondered who got left in the cold with that deal more often than not. I admitted that I did, because you were older and more filled-out and the boys liked you best. Then, he looked at me and asked, 'Wouldn't you like to even the score?' "

Her words rang true to Rhonda. Raj could be very provocative, even cruel, when he wanted to be. "What did you say?" she asked LuAnne. She held her breath.

"I shot up, knocking over my plate. We both grabbed napkins and bent to clean up the mess. Our heads bumped and then, before I knew it, he'd grabbed me and kissed me. I tried to push him away, but that only made him more determined. He totally caught me off guard. My head was spinning."

"Are you saying he raped you?" Rhonda asked, her voice rising.

"No, I'm saying I weakened; and because I'd had a few glasses of wine, I had a momentary lapse of judgment." LuAnne closed her eyes as fresh tears began to fall.

"Of course you didn't come to your senses until it was over," Rhonda said sarcastically.

LuAnne didn't respond to that comment but continued: "Ronnie, please believe me, I was devastated by what I'd done and told him to leave. He smugly told me that he'd chosen the right sister to marry because you were much better in the sack than I was. That was when he issued the threat that he'd make sure I looked like the instigator if it ever got out."

"Isn't it convenient that Raj isn't here to defend himself? You could tell me anything!"

"It's the truth, Ronnie. I swear it is. He was cold, and ruthless. He treated me like shit after I told him to get out. It was as if he expected me to thank him, or something. I don't believe he felt any remorse about what he'd just done."

"Liar! You screwed him because you resented me. You said it so well when you came back home in August. You've resented me ever since I decided to go to college instead of waiting for you so that we could go to the Big Apple together and pursue modeling careers."

"That happened when we were kids, Ronnie. I got over it years ago!"

"Did you?" Rhonda asked skeptically. She couldn't stop pacing. She felt another walking spell coming on. Soon, she'd be walking the streets of New York, just as she'd done when Raj had gotten killed. This time not out of grief but rage.

"I've always been proud of your accomplishments, Ronnie. Maybe I was a little jealous when you got a college degree and I didn't go any further than high school. But I was still proud of you!" LuAnne said in her defense.

Rhonda shook her head, unconvinced. "No. You had to hate me to do what you did, LuAnne. I can't accept the excuse of booze being behind your behavior. I've never seen you so high that you didn't know what you were doing."

"That's because I hid it. Just like a drug addict hides his habit from his loved ones as long as he can, I hid my drinking. Oh, I was one of the good girls. No *drugs!* I thought I could handle the booze. I was wrong. After the incident with Raj, I knew I had to get help. I wound up spending more than three months in a French sanitarium."

Rhonda did recall a period in LuAnne's career when she wasn't working much. It had lasted over a year. Could that have been the time she'd been trying to overcome a problem with alcohol? Her rational mind said, *Yes.*

The anger overrode rationality.

"Why now? Why didn't you tell me soon after it happened, or after Raj died?"

"I didn't tell you because I didn't want you to hate me, Ronnie. I knew how flimsy the alcohol excuse was going to sound to you. Trying to look like LuAnne the Wonder Girl, I hadn't let my family know what I was going through. I didn't want you all to lose faith in me. That I was a success meant that I was competently living my life. Hell, I was sending ten-thousand-dollar checks to my parents as Christmas gifts. I was doing all right! But I wasn't, Ronnie. I was literally running myself into the ground. Partying like a fool. Living large. Denying myself no indulgence, whether it was a new bauble or a new man. Everything looked better through intoxicated eyes. I could forget how miserable I was."

A dam broke inside Rhonda. In spite of what had transpired between them, she hurt for her baby sister. If what LuAnne said was true, she'd gone through pure hell. Why hadn't she turned to her?

The fact that LuAnne *hadn't* angered her even more than the Raj incident!

"To hell with Raj!" she cried. "He was just a man. But you! You are my sister. He's dead. I hold you accountable for everything that happened. For the events that led up to your romp on my couch with my fiancé, *and* for the aftermath. You've always been secretive about your private life, LuAnne. Your excuse for not telling the family about your drinking is laughable. You didn't tell us because you knew you'd get a lecture. I would've told you about your ass. You didn't want to hear it."

"That's probably true," LuAnne admitted in a low voice.

"What?" Rhonda asked roughly.

"I said you're right. I didn't want to be judged. It's an awful feeling."

"No!" Rhonda shouted. "Being told by your sister that she had your man is an awful feeling!"

LuAnne went to rise again.

Rhonda shot her a look that froze her. "You stay right there. I'm leaving."

LuAnne rose anyway. "But you asked why I chose this time to tell you—"

Turning her back on LuAnne, Rhonda said, "It doesn't matter."

LuAnne followed, but Rhonda was too quick for her. By the time LuAnne got to the living room, Rhonda had collected her shoulder bag from LuAnne's bedroom and was putting on her coat.

LuAnne watched helplessly as Rhonda reached for the doorknob. "*Please* give me a chance to explain why I had to confess what I'd done, Ronnie!"

"I don't want to hear it," Rhonda said with finality.

LuAnne tried a different tack. "Okay, but you can't go out there like that. Let me drive you home." Her SUV was downstairs in the parking garage.

"I'd rather walk," Rhonda said as she went out the door.

LuAnne hurried after her. "Let me call you a cab!"

"Don't do me any favors."

Tears clouded her eyes and her bottom lip trembled as LuAnne watched Rhonda hurry toward the stairs, too far away now for her to ever catch up.

Lumbering back into the loft, she tried to compose herself enough to phone Leon. He'd know what to do. She closed and locked the door behind her. As she leaned against the door, she felt like sliding down and sitting on the floor right there and never getting back up. Rhonda hated her. The only person who'd ever loved her with her whole heart. Without reservations. Unconditionally. Asking for nothing except that she love her, too.

She was alone.

Rhonda aimlessly wandered the streets of Soho for more than an hour, not seeing the Friday night crowd she passed on the sidewalks, nor the trendy shops, bars, and restaurants.

It was only when she walked past a bookstore, its display window replete with the latest best-sellers, that she remembered she hadn't phoned Stuart.

She ducked inside the next lit-up place of business she neared.

The bar was a neighborhood watering hole. The patrons were mostly male. Decorated in early "fern." The leafy plants were everywhere. She figured she'd stumbled into a gay bar. That theory was disproved when several males checked her progress across the room. The phones *would* be in the back, near the rest rooms. Why hadn't she remembered to put her cellular phone in her bag before leaving her apartment tonight?

She checked her watch before picking up the public phone's receiver. It wasn't yet midnight. Funny how earth-shattering news only took minutes to deliver. Then, you had the rest of your life to live with the effects.

"Hello?"

"Stuart—"

"Rhonda, where are you?" he anxiously asked.

Shouldn't he think she was still at LuAnne's? Unless . . . "LuAnne phoned, huh?"

"No. It was Leon."

Good old Leon. Too bad he's in love with a woman who is incapable of loving anyone other than herself, Rhonda thought cattily.

"Oh," was all she said to Stuart.

"What are you wearing?"

"Stuart, not now—"

Stuart laughed shortly. "That comes later. I was thinking of bringing the bike. Are you appropriately dressed?"

Rhonda laughed, too. It felt good after the evening she'd had. "Jeans and boots. Long coat, though."

"No problem. I'll bring you one of my jackets and we can put your coat in the storage compartment in the back."

"All right. The place is a bar called the Triad. It's on Houston Street."

"I see you took quite a stroll."

Last month, she and Stuart had had dinner at LuAnne's new place, so he knew the area.

"I felt like walking."

"Obviously," he said with a note of laughter. "But now I want you to stay put. Order a drink, and I'll be there before you finish it."

Leon had finally gotten LuAnne quieted down. She'd bawled through the confession, bawled through his phone call to Stuart. Now, they were huddled on one of the leather couches with the lights dimmed. LuAnne's head was on his shoulder, his arms around hers. Every now and then, he heard her sniff. Otherwise, they'd not said a word in more than half an hour. She seemed to be talked out, her energy reserves exhausted.

Her hair was in disarray, her eyes were swollen from crying, and mascara had left streaks down her face. But it was the forlorn, totally dejected expression she wore that worried Leon. She sat up suddenly and reached for the box of Kleenex sitting on the coffee table. Leon bent forward and retrieved them for her.

LuAnne blew her nose. "I shouldn't have said anything,"

she suddenly spoke up. "I should have kept my damned mouth shut!" Sighing, she added, "I'll die if she can't forgive me. I'll still be living, trying to raise my child as best I can, but I'll be dead inside."

Leon pulled her into his arms. "You did the right thing, Lulu."

Her mouth open in shock, she just stared at him a moment. "The right thing? How can you say that? Nothing will ever be the same again."

"Are you the same person you were back then?"

She looked confused.

"Are you still boozing? Still changing men as often as you change your clothes?"

"I stopped doing both nearly two years ago. That's why I stayed with Troy so long. I was trying to make it work. I refused to cheat on him, even if I wasn't happy being just a trophy on his arm."

"Why do you suppose you made such drastic changes to your behavior?"

LuAnne thought for a long while. Leon imagined the machinery turning in her mind. Then, she smiled as the fully realized epiphany presented itself to her. "I've grown."

"When you weren't even looking," Leon said in that lazy way he had. Dark brown bedroom eyes swept over her face and lingered on her full lips. "Your evolution sneaked up on you. And know what else you've been totally clueless about?"

"What?" LuAnne asked, leaning in.

"This." Leon bent his head and pressed his mouth firmly against hers.

Leon didn't pull her into his arms. From this angle, her belly prevented that. His hands didn't come into play. LuAnne was perfectly free to stop the kiss at any time.

Instead, she fell into his strength, his compassion, his wisdom. She was no longer denying she wanted and needed this big, alive, passionate man that was Leon Jackson.

The kiss deepened, as Leon's hands now confidently cupped her lush bottom.

LuAnne moaned and reluctantly turned her head to the side for an air break. "Leon," she breathed, her eyes dreamy with pent-up sexual longing, "you're making me hot."

"Talk is cheap," Leon said, kissing her again.

When they parted, LuAnne patted her belly and said, "I'm afraid that's all we can do."

Leon's eyebrows arched. "Are you saying what I *think* you're saying?"

Nodding, LuAnne cried, "I know it's crazy. Here I am eight months pregnant and I'm so horny, I could scream."

That's all Leon needed to hear. He rose and swept her up into his powerful arms, as if she weighed next to nothing, and began walking toward her bedroom.

"Leon, I can't have intercourse!" LuAnne halfheartedly protested.

"Baby, there are all kinds of ways to pleasure you besides having intercourse."

Stuart's bike was a 2001 Road King Classic from Harley-Davidson. A touring bike, it easily accommodated two riders. Rhonda was comfortable with her arms wrapped around Stuart's waist as they sped through the streets of Manhattan.

She wondered what LuAnne had told Leon. The truth? Not hardly. It had taken her more than two years to tell *her.* LuAnne wouldn't risk losing Leon's friendship by telling him what she'd done. She'd be too ashamed.

As well she should be, Rhonda thought hatefully. *Personally, Leon could do a lot better. LuAnne will eat the poor man alive.*

"Mmm," Leon moaned.

Up on his elbows, he watched as LuAnne flicked her tongue slowly up and down the length of his penis, tasting him, delighting in the reaction she was getting. She flashed pearly white teeth. "I never knew pregnancy could be such fun."

She lowered her head again and this time didn't raise it until Leon sighed with release.

His seed spilled onto the sheets.

LuAnne lay in his arms, her nude body golden-brown, plump, and ever so satisfied.

Leon's right hand was lovingly massaging her belly. He paused when he felt the baby kick. "Little Miss Lulu is awake."

"I've come up with a name for her," LuAnne said. "Ruby Diane."

"I know Ruby's your grandma's name. But where did Diane come from?"

"It's Rhonda's middle name."

In the basement garage of his building, Stuart helped Rhonda off the bike. As she stood to the side removing her helmet, he secured the bike and switched on the alarm. This done, he took off his helmet and reached for her hand.

Rhonda placed her hand in his and he drew her to him. She felt some of the tension sliding off her. Though her heart was breaking, she found she was capable of deriving pleasure from having his arms around her.

Stuart placed a kiss on the side of her neck. "I've missed you so much."

Their careers had kept them too busy during the week even for a meal together.

"But first," he said, peering into her upturned face. "If you want to talk about what happened between you and LuAnne, I'm more than willing to listen."

They began walking across the garage toward the elevator. "You really don't want a recap of our catfight, believe me. Just something between sisters." Rhonda couldn't believe her ears. Lying to Stuart. Knowing how much he valued the truth. She felt like a fraud.

Stuart seemed deep in thought as they traversed the garage and stepped onto the elevator. He studied her face. Even in this harsh lighting, she was beautiful to him. He was hesitant to voice his thoughts, though. Rhonda was still a closed book to him. The more he tried to read her, the more she drew herself into a ball, leaving him on the outside. If he touched her the wrong way with his words or his deeds, she would react by shutting herself off from him. He felt it every time he brought up a subject she wasn't comfortable with. Like now. More than words ever could, her body language told him she didn't want to discuss her argument with LuAnne.

Okay, he'd let it drop. But damned if he was going to allow her to stay in a funk all night. "I've got a surprise for you."

He could tell she was feigning the look of astonishment that crossed her face.

His heart fell. Could it be him? Could Rhonda have come here tonight to tell him it was over? Because if that was it, he wouldn't let her give up on them.

She'd told him how relieved LuAnne had been to learn she was finally dating again. If she'd told LuAnne of her plans to break up with him, that would have probably precipitated a fight.

Left to his own devices, he was liable to cook up all kinds of scenarios to explain her emotional detachment.

Feeling remorse for having lied to him, Rhonda used physical contact to allay her own fears. Sidling up him, she pressed her body to his. "Let's not talk about anything negative tonight. I just want to enjoy you." She dropped her bag to the floor. Off went her jacket. Then she boldly grabbed two hands full of his bottom. "C'mere."

Stuart cocked an eyebrow. They hadn't done it in an elevator yet. His office, her kitchen, his sunken tub. Nah . . . He nixed that thought. He would never dream of making love to Rhonda in such a public place; she'd be mortified if they got caught.

Her hand was doing crazy things to his crotch now.

Maybe she . . . That thought was cut off when Rhonda pulled him down for a long, slow, wet kiss.

By the time the elevator doors opened on the twelfth floor, he'd stopped wondering whether or not this was their last night together.

"I had some Chinese delivered," he said as they hung their coats in the foyer closet.

A slight frown momentarily marred Rhonda's rosy, well-kissed face. He saw her mentally shift gears and paint on a smile. "Great. I'm famished."

Stuart gamely went about trying to cheer her up. "Now, for your surprise."

He playfully pulled her along to the living room. Outside the picture window, the Manhattan skyline looked golden with promise. Rhonda glanced longingly at it in hope of being imbued with that spirit. It didn't work. All she could think of was LuAnne and Raj, on her couch.

She suddenly had the urge to turn to Stuart and tell him she was going home, she wouldn't be very good company tonight.

But before she could form the words, he'd plopped her down on the sofa in front of the coffee table. Spread atop the coffee table were the page proofs of her book. She had to do a double take before she recognized them for what they were.

Then, she gazed up at Stuart with something akin to horror mirrored in her dark depths.

Now, Stuart was so confused he did the very thing he swore he'd never do with her: he forced the issue. There was something wrong, and he would find out what it was or die trying.

Rhonda had managed to bury her initial reaction to the page proofs and paint on a reasonably convincing smile. She even picked up a page, sat down, and began to study it. Too late for the act, though, because Stuart had already been infected by her poisonous mood. "What was that look for?" he asked evenly.

Rhonda dropped the page in her hand and rose. "I can't look at those right now."

She tried to walk past him, but he grabbed her by the arm and spun her around to face him. "I thought you'd be pleased. The staff was really fired up about this project. They worked overtime. I put a rush on it, hoping to get the book out for the Christmas buying season. That was no easy feat."

When she looked up at him, her eyes were bright with tears, and a panicked expression sat in them. Her breath had become ragged with the effort to hold the tears at bay. He held her arm even tighter. "You're going to tell me why you're so upset, and you're going to tell me now!"

Rhonda jumped at the force of his anger.

He was immediately regretful. Letting go of her arm and allowing his own to fall to his side, he said in calmer tones, "I'm sorry." Sighing, he went to stand in front of the picture window and gazed at Central Park below. "This is just so frustrating. All I want to do is make you happy, and you're so emotionally repressed, I can't get close enough to you to make you see that."

Rhonda hadn't moved. Her back was to him. Inside, she was dying because she didn't want to alienate Stuart. She saw no alternative but to tell him everything. He'd said he could take the unadulterated truth. But would this be *too* much?

She walked over to him and placed her hand on his forearm.

He peered down into her face, waiting.

"I apologize, Stuart. But when I saw the culmination of all the work that I, you, and your staff have put into that book, I couldn't help feeling horrified because of who inspired it in the first place." The tears began to fall in earnest. She went on in spite of them. "LuAnne told me, tonight, that Raj cheated on me, with her!" She buried her face in his chest, sobbing, "She managed to destroy everything I held dear."

Stuart rocked her. "I don't know what to say to console you after something like that happens . . ." He repeatedly kissed her forehead. "But you'll survive this."

"I feel like a damned fool!" She raised her eyes. "I made love to that creep two days after he'd been with my sister. He must have been mentally comparing the two of us." She fell silent. Then she looked up at Stuart with determination. "Well, he won't win!"

She turned out of his arms and walked over to the coffee table. Bending to pick up one of the page proofs, she scanned the photo and the copy. This page was devoted to Essie Mae Campbell, a forty-something woman who'd formerly been a teacher in the NYC school system. She'd been laid off, couldn't find another job. Within six months of losing her job, she'd been unable to pay her rent. We are all only a few paychecks from the streets. That was her lesson learned. Her life lesson suffered through.

"She's no longer homeless," Rhonda said with a genuine smile. "She's living in Savannah, Georgia, now, running a seaside stand, selling souvenirs to tourists. She says she's happy."

She perused another page, and another.

Stuart left the room to go find a box of tissues. When he returned, her tears had dried up, and she was engrossed in the pages. Looking at him, she said, "You were right. They're excellent. So much better than I ever imagined."

Stuart's heart beat faster at the look of joy on her face. "You're really pleased?"

Rhonda went to him and planted a moist kiss on his unshaven jaw. "Very much so."

"Good," he said, taking her by the hand. "You can look at the rest of them tomorrow. Tonight, it's my job to feed you, bathe you, and then put you to bed. You've had a rough day and you could use a little tender loving care."

Rhonda liked the sound of that. Her curiosity was piqued, however, when he led her right past the kitchen and the dining room, back to his bedroom.

Stuart was a minimalist. His apartment was decorated with ultramodern furnishings that boasted clean lines. He prized space. Therefore, his bedroom only had the basic pieces in it, bed, bureau, nightstands, and a cabinet that housed an entertainment center. Tonight, though, he'd brought in a folding table and sat it near the fireplace. A white linen cloth covered it, and he'd set the table with fine china, crystal, and flatware. Sitting in the center of it, though, were cartons of Chinese food. He couldn't cook to save his life.

"Cutting down on the steps to the bed, huh?" Rhonda joked.

"You've got it," Stuart wasn't ashamed to admit.

He held out her chair. Rhonda sat down. Stuart knelt before her and began unzipping her black leather boots. "Your feet are probably sore from all that walking."

She didn't miss the mischievous gleam in his eyes.

"Are you going to rib me because I've been hit by the walking bug again?"

"I can't help myself," he said as he sat back on his haunches and continued pulling the boots off. "Your eyes spark fire, and your chest heaves. I get aroused every time you tell me to kiss your ass."

"Kiss my ass, Stuart!"

He pushed up her right pant leg and kissed her from her toes to her knee instead.

Now, who was arousing whom?

She fairly squirmed in her chair, it felt so good.

He removed her left boot and kissed her left leg as he had her right.

Rhonda slid off the chair, into his arms. They rolled onto the carpeted floor. She wound up on top. "I thought you were going to feed me first," she said with a sensual twist to her lips. "A girl could starve around here."

Stuart ran the palms of his hands across her nipples. Their imprints were immediately evident beneath the soft cotton denim shirt. "I plan to fill you up, believe me."

She felt his erection pressing against her crotch. "A bath first. I feel grungy."

She quickly rose and ran toward the adjacent bathroom.

Stuart was right behind her.

Rhonda was unbuttoning her shirt when he entered the spacious bath. He was pleased when he saw her heading for the shower instead of the tub. A soak in the tub was fun, but a shower was much more expedient. He was hungry for her.

He got an eyeful as Rhonda stripped. Her body was a study in sensuality: golden-brown all over, except for her panty and bra tan lines. That skin was paler in color. Her breasts' areolas were dark brown, as were her nipples. A flat stomach with an inny belly button. Well-shaped thighs and legs (obviously from all that walking).

He smiled. She was so unselfconscious. He'd known women who were ashamed of their bodies. They starved themselves out of some need to conform to society's distorted view of them. Not Rhonda. She loved her body. And not one bone was sticking out.

She was struggling with the clasps on her bra. He moved forward. "Allow me."

Once the bra was off, he stepped back to watch again.

Rhonda smiled at him. "You're a voyeur, Stuart Mitchum!"

"I could look at you twenty-four hours a day."

Rhonda's eyes traveled over his still-clothed body. "Get busy, boy. I'd like a bit of eye candy, too."

In the shower, Stuart used long, indolent strokes with the sponge to soap Rhonda's body. They'd adjusted the water temperature to tepid since it was already too hot in there. After she was sufficiently soaped-up, she took the sponge and returned the favor.

Water ran over their heads, plastering Stuart's wavy hair to his head. Rhonda's natural hair was more resilient. Water droplets sparkled in her dark mane.

Stuart was already semierect, but when Rhonda ran the

sponge over him, he grew hard. She couldn't resist taking him in her hand. When she did that, Stuart groaned and pulled her to him with one arm for a kiss, while pressing her back against the shower wall. The tub was slip-resistant; otherwise that movement would've made them both go crashing through the stall door.

An hour or so later, they were clothed in bathrobes, sitting at the table ravenously chowing down on the Chinese food.

Stuart had put singer-songwriter Brenda Russell's CD, *Paris Rain,* on the player.

Brenda's lovely voice filled the room. And when she launched into "She's in Love," Rhonda realized she was, too. In love with this man who shouldn't be a part of her life but was. The implications frightened her. Would she love yet another man who didn't return her feelings? Stuart hadn't mentioned love. He expressed it in so many ways. Just not in words.

Maybe because of his failed marriage, he was now holding his cards close to his chest.

"Why do you think LuAnne chose now to tell you about her and Raj?" Stuart suddenly asked. His eyes met hers across the table.

It felt like a million years since her encounter with LuAnne. Rhonda was in a mellow place now. A safe place where pain couldn't touch her. She wanted to stay there awhile.

Stuart's hang-up with the cleansing power of truth!

She would go there with him, though.

"I know the reason why she'll *say* she chose this time."

"I'm listening. . . ."

"We were joking about you and me. She said she thought I was in love with you, and I shrugged it off and said I wasn't going to fall in love with anyone. At that point, she asked me if I was serious about that. I said yes, once was enough for me."

She hadn't noticed how still Stuart had gone. Nor that

his nostrils were flaring and his eyes had narrowed ever so slightly. No, she blithely went on: "She has this crazy notion that she has to save me from myself."

She went to take a sip of the Chardonnay; her eyes glanced at Stuart over the rim of the glass and she swallowed hard. He regarded her with eyes grown cold.

Rising, he said with a decided chill to his voice, "So, it's okay to screw me, but not to fall in love with me?"

"That's not what I meant," Rhonda cried, rising, too. "It was all bravado, Stuart. Like whistling in the dark when you're frightened. I was afraid to admit how I felt about you. If LuAnne had waited, I would've explained that to her. But I think the guilt had been building up in her a long time, and tonight was when she got brave enough to go ahead and tell me."

She went and grabbed him by the shoulders, peering into his eyes, an intensely warm expression in her own. "I've never been able to rationalize my feelings for you, Stuart. They're just there. I'm happy when I'm with you, and I miss you when I'm not."

"But you still felt the need to deny it."

He was hurt because of her callous comments to LuAnne. Rhonda understood that. She would be devastated if she'd overheard him speaking to one of his friends about her: *"She's not bad in bed, but love? I could never fall in love with her."*

He suddenly shrugged her hands off him and reversed the hold. His big hands firmly grasped her upper arms. "Your problem is, you don't dream big enough. I told you what I wanted from you the first night we were together. I haven't changed my mind."

"But I never thought . . ." She faltered.

"Oh, you thought I was only interested in you as a lover, but not as a candidate for marriage? Well, think again."

Think.

That's all Rhonda did for the next few weeks.

One Saturday morning, a few days before Thanksgiving, her phone rang.

She was sitting at the kitchen nook enjoying a bagel and a glass of orange juice. Swallowing, she picked up the phone from its base on the counter. "Hello?"

"I thought about that thing, and I thought about that thing—" 'Nessa's voice said without preamble.

"Good morning, Ma. What thing is that?" Rhonda asked, a bit impatient. She hadn't failed to phone her parents each Sunday since she and LuAnne had awakened them in the middle of the night with the news of LuAnne's pregnancy. Whenever Vanessa Copeland answered the phone, she'd been distant with Rhonda, telling her father to pick up the extension, *his* daughter wanted to speak with him.

"That snide remark you made about my entering you and LuAnne in pageants!"

"Forget about it, Ma. I was just angry at the way you'd just told me you and Daddy weren't married when you conceived me. It's no biggie." Rhonda wasn't in the mood for an argument with 'Nessa. She had film to get to in the darkroom shortly after breakfast.

Besides, LuAnne's revelation had made that bit of news pale in comparison!

That was life, always making you put things in perspective.

'Nessa sighed heavily on her end. "Your daddy says I should have told you that in private. Not blabbed it out like I did. He says I should apologize."

Rhonda smiled on her end. The prince had finally defended her against the evil queen.

"It was the wrong way to do it, and I'm sorry," 'Nessa said, but quickly added, "I don't think it's anything to be ashamed of, Ronnie. Your daddy and I rectified the situation as soon as we found out I was pregnant."

Rhonda found her attitude toward her mother softening. "Apology accepted."

"Good! Now maybe your daddy will stop giving me evil looks." By the tone of her mother's voice, Rhonda imagined her father was standing nearby nailing 'Nessa with his gaze at that very moment.

"When I married your daddy, I brought nothing to the table except my looks," 'Nessa began. Rhonda prepared for a long monologue. "The first few years I sat at home, raising you, and then LuAnne. You were both my prizes. My little dolls. When I saw the advertisement in the paper calling all mothers with adorable children to enter them in a citywide beauty contest, I jumped at the opportunity. In the beginning, I did it just to get out of the house. Back then, we were the only black family in the area. Your daddy bought this big ole house and put me in it, and I was lonely out here! But when you and LuAnne started winning time and time again, suddenly I was somebody! Your pictures were in the papers. My mother-in-law finally saw me as worthy of your daddy. I don't like to speak ill of the dead, but that witch hated my guts the moment she laid eyes on me and let me know it every chance she got."

Rhonda knew, then, that her father wasn't in the vicinity.

"Anyway," 'Nessa continued with a drawn-out sigh. "After a while, I realized that the dynamics of my relationship with Andrew's mother, and with Andrew, had changed. I was no longer a kept pet, but someone who had a skill."

"Which was putting your daughters on display—"

"No, it wasn't just that, Ronnie. I knew how to teach you how to win! It just came naturally to me. I taught you how to stand, how to move on the stage, how to keep your physical body in shape and working beautifully. Now admit it, you still use some of the skills I taught you!"

Rhonda gave herself a manicure and a pedicure every Saturday night like clockwork. When she walked, she made sure she checked her posture. A solution for crusty heels? Rub Vaseline into them and sleep in white sweat socks. Don't eat the skin off of the chicken. Condition your hair only once a month. Too much conditioning made it limp and lifeless. God! She'd been programmed like one of the Stepford Wives!

Laughing, she said, "Okay, I'll give you that. I still use your advice."

'Nessa was on a roll. "And have either you or LuAnne had to marry for security?" She didn't wait for Rhonda's reply. "No! You're both independent, self-assured women who will only marry for love when the time comes. That's what I gave you and LuAnne, Rhonda, a sense of self. I've been thinking about this since you made that comment. I don't regret doing what I did. But I do regret how I did it. I should have listened to you and LuAnne more. I should have hugged you more."

There was a long stretch of silence; then Rhonda said, "Thank you, Ma." Tears rolled down her cheeks. Lately she'd been a veritable waterworks.

"No, thank *you,* baby," 'Nessa said with a catch in her voice. "Listen, are you coming home for Thanksgiving? We'd love to have you and . . . your friend."

"Stuart."

"Bear with me, Ronnie. I'll get over the fact that you're involved with a white man before long; just watch me," 'Nessa joked.

"I know you will, Ma," Rhonda confidently said.

"Then you'll come?"

"Not this year, Ma."

"LuAnne and Leon will be here," 'Nessa coaxed, thinking that would entice Rhonda to say yes.

"We've already made plans to spend the day with Stuart's family," Rhonda explained.

'Nessa tried to keep the disappointment out of her voice. "Well, put us down for Christmas. I haven't seen you in a long time—"

"You're always welcome to come here for a visit, Ma. You and Daddy haven't been to the city in ages," Rhonda suggested.

"Yeah?" 'Nessa said, sounding surprised and delighted at the same time. "We just might turn up on your doorstep."

* * *

Two weeks before Christmas, *Walking the Streets of New York* debuted at #25 on the *New York Times* best-seller list. Rhonda was booked on all the major morning talk shows. Awakening and being driven down to Avenue of the Americas was becoming old hat to her. America had embraced the concept of the homeless being more than the detritus of society. The coffee table book garnered praise from critics and readers alike. All the hoopla made Rhonda introspective.

The only critics she was concerned about, the subjects of the book, got their chance to voice their opinions tonight. Her first book signing was to be held at a shelter in Hell's Kitchen on 42d Street. Some of the people she'd interviewed for the book were certain to be there.

She and Stuart took a cab downtown.

The cab pulled up to the curb and Rhonda's heart seemed to fall to the pit of her stomach when she saw the hordes of reporters, photographers, and cameramen waiting on the shelter's front walk.

Stuart reassuringly squeezed her hand. "This is what comes with success, sweetheart. Try not to growl at them."

"They're going to chase off the people I came here to see," Rhonda groused.

Stuart got out first and reached back for her hand.

Trying not to squint and frown in the glare of the camera's lights, knowing that that photo of her would undoubtedly be the one chosen for print in the *Daily News* tomorrow, Rhonda followed Stuart as he cut a swath through the rabid journalists.

Once inside, things were quieter. Two hundred or so people from the neighborhood had shown up to greet her and get their books signed. The director of the shelter, Arianna Jones, an African-American woman in her late fifties, came forward and warmly clasped Rhonda's hand. She was a petite woman with a short salt-and-pepper 'fro and a ready smile. "I put out the complimentary copies as you requested, and, I tell you, the book has generated a lot of debate around here for the past two weeks."

Rhonda smiled. She liked Arianna and had chosen to have the signing here because Arianna provided not only a warm meal and shelter to those venturing in but also solid counseling, educational opportunities, and job placement. As the saying goes, she didn't just give a man a fish; she taught him *how* to fish. Which changed lives.

"I'm so glad to hear it," Rhonda said as Arianna led her over to the table that had been set up for her. A microphone had been placed in front of the chair she'd be sitting in.

Rows of folding chairs borrowed from area church basements were lined up in front of the table. Folks began taking their seats. Stuart went to the back of the room to lean against the wall and watch.

Arianna approached the mike with Rhonda's hand still in hers.

"Good evening. You're all here to speak with Miss Copeland, so I won't keep you from her for long. I'd just like to say a few words. We all know the money we get from our government to run this place is never enough to do what we need to do in the neighborhood. Many of you are volunteers. You know what I'm talking about." She turned to Rhonda. "For Miss Copeland to see a need and desire to do something about it is commendable. But for her to give those who're often denied a voice a forum . . . Well, that's spectacular! I give you . . . Rhonda Copeland."

Rhonda was so engrossed in a conversation with one of the subjects featured in *Walking the Streets of New York,* she didn't notice Stuart at her side until he held his newly acquired cellular phone under her nose and said, "Leon wants to talk to you."

Knowing Stuart wouldn't interrupt if the call weren't important, Rhonda hastily offered an apology to the woman for having to cut their conversation short and excused herself.

Stuart had taken her by the elbow and was subtly leading her toward the exit as she put the phone to her ear and anxiously said, "Leon! What's up?"

"LuAnne made me swear I wouldn't bother you, but she's been in labor for the last six hours and the baby's not moving down. She's not dilating. She's in a lot of pain. The doctor's talking about a C-section if things don't improve, fast."

Rhonda didn't have to think twice. "What hospital?"

"Lenox Hill—"

"I assume Dr. Usmani is with her?"

"Yes, yes, he's been in and out. He's with her now. But, Ronnie, it's you she needs."

"We're on the way."

They were outside on the walk now. The media had all deserted the venue once they'd gotten their photos and had their questions answered.

Stuart, New York City boy that he was, let out a shrill whistle that rang in Rhonda's ears. A Yellow Cab pulled up next to them. Stuart handed Rhonda in and slid onto the seat next to her. "Lenox Hill Hospital," he told the cabbie.

Rhonda gave Stuart a knowing look. Apparently he and Leon had had a little chat before he'd given her the phone. The cab pulled away from the curb.

"Okay, tell me everything Leon told you, and don't leave anything out," she said, turning to him so that she could see his eyes while he spoke.

"For the last hour, LuAnne hasn't let anyone come near her. Not since Dr. Usmani told her that she may need a cesarean. She won't even allow Leon too close to her, which is why he went against her wishes and called you," Stuart filled her in.

What is that girl thinking? Rhonda worried. *Please, God, let her be all right.*

Leon wore a pained expression. Rhonda thought he looked green behind the gills, too. The big man loped up to her in the waiting room and gave her a grateful bear hug. "Ronnie, I'm so glad you're here. LuAnne's not herself. I'm worried to death."

Rhonda forced a smile for his benefit. "Don't worry; LuAnne's a lot tougher than she looks. Southern girls don't fold easily."

She then pushed out of his embrace and, after a glance in Stuart's direction, resolutely went through the door of LuAnne's room.

The head of the bed was raised. LuAnne was sitting with her hands on either side of her belly. Her long hair was matted. She looked exhausted, lips white from dehydration, eyes droopy and bloodshot. Her perfect skin was now ashy and blotchy.

A white-coated Pakistani physician stood next to the bed, a chart in his hand.

"We have no alternative, Miss Copeland. The baby's heartbeat is dangerously slow. Please, sign the form so that we can go in and deliver your child . . ." he was saying.

Rhonda came into LuAnne's line of sight.

LuAnne struggled to raise up on her elbows. "Ronnie!" she cried in a scared little-girl voice. "You came!" Tears freely flowed down her cheeks as she reached for Rhonda.

Rhonda moved swiftly past the doctor, who stepped aside but didn't leave the room, and went to hug LuAnne. "I'm here; don't cry. Everything's going to be all right." She stroked LuAnne's damp hair, kissed her forehead.

Rhonda glanced at the doctor. "What's the problem?"

Sensing an ally, he said, "I assume you're a close relative?"

Most people saw the resemblance in a heartbeat, but Rhonda supposed, in her present state, LuAnne didn't look like herself. "We're sisters," she said quietly.

Looking relieved, he eagerly supplied the information: "Miss Copeland isn't dilating. Unless we deliver the child by cesarean section, the child, Miss Copeland, or both could be in serious jeopardy. Miss Copeland won't sign the release forms so that we can operate. But seeing as how Miss Copeland is under a great deal of stress and is, perhaps, not thinking clearly right now—"

"I'm scared, Ronnie," LuAnne cried, hugging her sister tighter.

"—as her closest relative, you can sign the papers and we can proceed," Dr. Rhahid Usmani, his hospital-issue ID badge read—continued.

Rhonda placed a kiss on LuAnne's cheek. "Shhh . . . Let me speak with Dr. Usmani for a moment." She pried herself loose from LuAnne's firm grip and crossed the room to stand eye-to-eye with the middle-aged physician. "Listen, Doctor, how much time do we have to work with here?"

His large brown eyes were red-rimmed and held a worried expression in them. "I can only give you five minutes. No more."

Rhonda reached for the clipboard in his hand. He handed it to her with a relieved sigh. "Is it possible for me to go into the operating room with her?" she asked hopefully. "I believe it would go a long way towards allaying some of her fears."

Dr. Usmani smiled briefly. "I don't see why not."

Rhonda returned his smile. "Wonderful. Now, if you would get things rolling on your end, I'll see about getting this form signed."

"I'll send a nurse for it in five minutes," Dr. Usmani said before taking his leave.

Rhonda went back to LuAnne. "Move over."

LuAnne lumbered over in the bed with a groan and then lay her head on her sister's shoulder. "You don't hate me anymore, Ronnie?"

"I never hated you, LuAnne," Rhonda softly replied. She exhaled. "I've done a lot of thinking since that night, and I've come to realize that I wasn't as angry with you about sleeping with Raj as I was about the fact that you waited so long to tell me."

LuAnne gazed up at her sister. "I was ashamed. I was also a coward. I didn't want to hurt you."

"You hurt me by withdrawing from me, LuAnne," Rhonda told her. "I knew Raj had serious flaws. But, like a lot of women, I chose to ignore the signs: he flirted too much, he'd break dates without plausible explanations."

"That doesn't excuse my behavior," LuAnne said sadly.

"No, it doesn't," Rhonda agreed. She met LuAnne's eyes. "Neither of us is perfect. You were weak. Being human, we have human frailties. I'm not going to spend the rest of my life holding this against you."

LuAnne was crying anew. She squeezed Rhonda's shoulders. "Thank you, Ronnie."

"And besides," Rhonda said, not finished, "if you hadn't confessed, I might have done something truly stupid and stopped seeing Stuart. I was at that point, you know. I had nearly convinced myself that in order to keep from being hurt, I should drop him."

LuAnne's eyes stretched in surprise. "You mean you and Stuart . . ."

"Love each other," Rhonda said with a warm smile. "That's right, your big sister has a man in her life."

"And her bed, I hope," LuAnne said, managing a saucy grin. Then, "Owww . . ."

Rhonda leaped from the bed, looking down at LuAnne. "Another contraction?"

"Yeah," LuAnne moaned with a pained expression in her huge eyes.

The nurse Dr. Usmani had promised to send came through the door at that moment.

Seeing LuAnne in obvious distress, she went straight to her and placed her palms on either side of LuAnne's stomach. Her brown face screwed up in a frown, she said, "Your little one isn't going to wait any longer, young lady."

Rhonda held the clipboard while LuAnne quickly scribbled her name on the dotted line. Rhonda kissed LuAnne's sweaty brow to seal the bargain. "Let's go have a baby!"

A Family Reunion

AWARD-WINNING AUTHOR

BRENDA JACKSON

It's been fifteen years since the Bennetts were all in one place at one time, and now at a total blowout of a reunion, three generations will gather to remember old memories and reestablish deep roots. But for four special cousins, hidden desires and long-kept secrets will challenge their bond, test their courage, and change their hearts forever . . .

"Brenda Jackson has crafted a family tale that sings with emotion . . . Jackson's full bodied voice will linger long after the melody of *A Family Reunion* ends."

—Donna Hill, author of *Rhythms*

AVAILABLE WHEREVER BOOKS ARE SOLD
FROM ST. MARTIN'S PAPERBACKS